A note on the author

Denzil Meyrick was born in Glasgow and brought up in
Campbeltown. After studying politics, he pursued a varied
career including time spent as a police officer, freelance
journalist and director of several companies in the leisure,
engineering and marketing sectors. Previous novels in the
bestselling DCI Daley thriller series are *Whisky from Small
Glasses* (Waterstones Scottish Book of the Year, 2015), *The Last
Witness, Dark Suits and Sad Songs, The Rat Stone Serenade,
Well of the Winds* and *One Last Dram Before Midnight*.
Denzil lives on Loch Lomond side with his wife, Fiona.

THE
RELENTLESS
TIDE

A D.C.I. DALEY THRILLER

Denzil Meyrick

First published in Great Britain in 2018 by Polygon, an imprint of Birlinn Ltd.

Birlinn Ltd
West Newington House
10 Newington Road
Edinburgh
EH9 1QS

www.polygonbooks.co.uk

1

ISBN 978 1 84697 412 0
eBook ISBN 978 1 78885 003 2

British Library Cataloguing-in-Publication Data
A catalogue record for this book is available on request from the British Library.

Typeset by 3btype.com
Printed and bound in Great Britain by Clays Ltd, Elcograf S.p.A.

In memory of Allister Stewart – one of the first people
I ever knew

'The past is never dead. It's not even past.'
—William Faulkner

PROLOGUE

Greenock, 1994

Count the waves, she told him. Keep counting; every seventh wave is the biggest.

He watched the sea carefully, counting as each sweep of the ocean hissed up the sand on to the pebbles.

Yes, she was right. One wave foamed its way further up the beach, its crest white and broiling, the sound it made louder than the waves that had gone before. It was as though it was shouting, *Look at me – look at me!*

He giggled as he counted again. Sure enough, the seventh wave returned; this time it came closer to the tartan rug on which they were sitting, making him squeal with delight.

As the wave receded, drawing back the way it had come, rasping on the sand against the cries of the gulls, the sky darkened. He looked up; the sun was now hidden behind a cloud, leaching the colour and warmth from the day. Fear gripped his heart as another wave crashed on to the shore.

Where would the next big wave stop? Would he and his mother be caught in its embrace and dragged back out to the sea? He couldn't swim, and nor could she – he knew that because she had always wanted to be able to teach him, but couldn't. That meant that she wouldn't be able to save him when the seventh wave caught them. She hadn't been watching – how could she know?

He stood up, grabbing his mother's arm, tugging with all his might.

'What is it – what's wrong?' she said, puzzled by the little boy's sudden change of mood.

'Come on!' he shouted, desperately trying to pull her off the rug and away from danger. 'The big wave – it'll get us!'

She hugged him, holding him close. 'Darling, the waves won't get us – we're safe. The sea won't come this far up the beach, honest.' She smiled at the little boy as he took this in. She almost anticipated the next question.

'Are you sure?'

'Yes, I'm sure,' she replied, smiling at his earnest face, hugging him, their cheeks touching under the warmth of the sun.

It was the warmth of that day he remembered as he watched the body flailing about in the surf. He knew it was her: he could see the bright red scarf she always wore when she was painted – make-up she called it, but it looked like paint to him – and smelled of perfume, still tied around her neck.

He remembered that she'd been wearing it when she left with her friend, kissing him goodbye, leaving a smear of lipstick on his cheek. Her friend had hugged him too, but he hadn't liked that. She had no right to hug him – that was his mother's job, not hers. His mother was beautiful, slim and bright-eyed. This woman was big and ugly, as far as he was concerned, and her perfume was horrid.

As he heard them clatter down the stone steps of the close outside the flat where he lived, he sniffed at the air, but the light, distinctive scent his mother always wore was undetectable under the heavy sweetness of the other.

He sighed, and ran to the window. They were arm in arm, walking down the grey street, against which their bright clothes were a shock of colour. Like a picture from one of the books his mother read to him. He felt the fat tear as it slipped down his cheek.

Though he held his hand against the cold windowpane, ready to wave goodbye, she didn't look back. She never looked back when she was going out.

He held his cold hand to his cheek, remembering the warmth of her embrace, as he cuddled the doll – he hated teddy bears and toy soldiers – she had given him to his chest.

That had been three sleeps ago.

Now he was standing on the pier. His granny had said a wee walk there would take his mind off his mum.

Looking down at the body being tossed about in the waves, he counted. He knew the seventh wave would wash her on to the beach.

He heard his grandmother scream.

The seventh wave crashed the body on to the shingle below, then hissed its way back out to sea, leaving the corpse of the young woman lying pale and bloated on the sand.

1

Kinloch, the present

She winced at the sound that was dragging her from a deep sleep. Reaching out, she pulled the smartphone from the table, almost dropping it, at the same time attempting to mash some moisture back into her mouth and forcing her eyelids apart.

The pool of light coming from the phone illuminated her face as she stared down at the screen, trying desperately to focus.

Time to get up. Dad x.

For a second or two her mind failed to register why this most familiar text, the innocuous few characters blinking at her in the darkness, were wrong. Then, as her brain began to drag itself from the arms of Morpheus, she threw the device to the floor as if it were a hot coal and sat bolt upright in bed, the breath catching in her throat as she gulped for air.

She'd just been woken by a dead man.

Detective Sergeant Brian Scott moaned as he trudged across the muddy field in the half-light. He swore as he tripped on a large rock, yet to be cleared from the site by the construction company. At least they'd managed to dig an impromptu track along which he'd been able to bring the police SUV, rather than having to scale the hill on foot, but now that track was at an end.

Be thankful for small mercies.

The young DC at his side coughed and spat unceremoniously.

'What was that, Potts?' asked Scott, his face drawn into an expression of disgust.

'Sorry, Sergeant, can't shake this cold. I always get one when the summer's on its way. Pain in the arse,' his companion replied.

'Aye, well, just keep it tae yourself. My wife's on her way here tae see if she'll be able tae make the move tae Kinloch mair permanent. The last thing we need is me snottering all o'er the place when she arrives, son.'

'Sorry, Sergeant.'

'And forby that, you're representing Police Scotland. We've had enough PR disasters without you bounding aboot displaying the content o' your nose tae all and sundry. Try and have some . . .'

'Decorum?'

'Aye, that's the word. Try an' get some o' that aboot you.'

Through the mist, a figure was slowly making its way towards them, the fluorescent yellow of the hi-vis jacket looking almost disembodied until the young woman who was wearing it was a few feet away.

'DS Scott?' she asked brightly.

'Aye, that's me,' he replied tetchily. 'Where's this Professor Francombe? I'm needing tae get oot o' this mist and get a decent cup of tea doon me.' He smiled at the young woman. 'Any chance o' a cuppa, dear? Once we find this professor bloke, that is.'

'I'm Professor Francombe,' she said frostily. 'The only tea I make is green Chinese, not the kind of beverage a discerning gentleman like your good self would be happy with, I imagine.' She stared at him levelly, almost the same height as the detective, a jutting, determined chin reinforcing her confident manner.

Scott hesitated. 'Aye, right. Sorry aboot that. I can see you've got a badge on. This mist – I wisnae seeing you just right, if you know what I mean.'

Francombe rolled her eyes and asked them to follow her.

'Glad you gave me that tip about decorum, Sergeant. Could have made a fool of myself there,' whispered Potts.

Scott stared balefully at the constable and muttered something indistinct under his breath as the two men started after Francombe, already making better progress up the hill than the members of the constabulary, who toiled even more as the mud thickened and sucked at their wellington boots.

As they reached the top of a small rise the mist began to thin, and the bright ball of the early summer sun became visible, albeit diffused.

'Here we are,' said Francombe, bringing their trudge to an end.

A few feet away, three holes in the ground had been delineated from the sea of mud by yellow tape, marking them out as roughly rectangular.

'We've done our best to shore things up. The weather is set to improve today and over the weekend, so we can tidy the scene up further. I'm sure your forensic teams will want to get into the graves and look properly. As soon as we realised what we were dealing with we abandoned this area. I can't be sure that there's been no corruption of potential evidence, though.

For that, you have my apologies. Finding something like this is not an everyday occurrence – in my line of work, at any rate.'

Scott nodded, rubbing the short stubble on his chin thoughtfully. 'I wouldnae worry. Everyone who's been on site will have to provide DNA samples for the purposes of illumination.'

'Elimination, do you mean?'

'Aye, that's what I said.' Scott coughed irritably. 'So, you came upon these last night, Professor Francombe?' He gestured to DC Potts, who quickly produced his notebook and pen and began taking notes.

'Yes, we made the discovery just as we were packing up. One of our young graduates found them. At first we were thrilled – excited, you know, at the prospect of finding something of significance. Something to stop them putting these bloody windmills here.' She spat out the last few words.

'No' a fan o' wind turbines, then?'

'Well, since you ask – no. Especially not on a site as potentially important as this one.'

'Meaning?'

'Surely you've read the papers, Sergeant? This hill could well have been the domicile of a notable figure from Scotland's past. There's enough evidence – for me at least – to indicate that perhaps even Somerled himself called this home.'

'Summer who?'

'Somerled, Sergeant,' interjected Potts. 'Lord of the Isles. Part Viking part Scot, I think I'm right in saying, ma'am?'

'Very impressive, Constable. Maybe you should be asking the questions while your colleague here takes notes?'

'Eh … well, I don't know that much. Just something I picked up at uni.'

8

'Aye, there you are. A university degree's no' much use when you're knee-deep in fitba fans that want tae take your heid off. Aye, and no' when the nightclubs are coming oot all along Sauchiehall Street, and the place is going like a fair,' said Scott waspishly, glaring at the younger policeman. 'So, I take it you thought the bodies you found were ancient, aye?'

'No, not ancient, that's the wrong period. But we certainly hoped that they could be early medieval, or around the time your constable seems to be familiar with. Also, body is not the term I would use. That would suggest something more recent. Apart from some rotting cloth and jewellery, we're definitely looking at bones in all three cases, Sergeant Scott. Sadly, not of the ancient or even historical variety.'

'How did you spot that something was wrong?'

'It's my job, Sergeant. I qualified as an osteo-archaeologist.'

'Right. You'd better spell that for Einstein here. What does that mean, if you don't mind me asking?'

'I'm sure your constable can spell it perfectly well. Am I right, Constable?' She smiled as Potts nodded slightly, pointedly not looking at his superior, but shuffling uncomfortably in his muddy wellingtons.

'So you knew what age they were – just by looking, I mean?' Scott's tone was sarcastic.

'Yes, Sergeant. If I wasn't able to differentiate between historical and modern remains *just by looking*, I wouldn't last long in my job. Must be the same in your line of work, I'm sure.' She was deploying an equal amount of sarcasm, making Potts stifle a snigger. 'I'd take you closer, but I'm sure that wouldn't be appreciated by the Crime Scene Manager.'

'No, it widnae,' said Scott. 'For someone who doesnae deal with the police very often, you seem tae know plenty aboot it.

I'm only just gettin' tae grips wae Crime Scene Managers myself.'

'I said it was unusual to find modern remains in the course of our work, but it does happen. I was involved with the case last year in Yorkshire where the murderer had buried his victim in a graveyard full of sixteenth-century monks. Do you remember it?'

'I've enough tae dae working on a' the problems we have here without concerning myself wae Yorkshire monks. We'll wait until SOCO arrives. Should be here within the hour, so I'm told.'

'Very well. In the meantime, I'll take you to our canteen for some tea. Don't get carried away, it's just a glorified tent.'

'As long as it's got a kettle, I'm no' bothered how glorified it is. You stay here, and think aboot thon Somerled fellow,' said Scott, nodding to Potts. 'You never know, he might come oot o' the mists wae his sword and show you just how much use a university degree is in oor line o' work.'

He smiled to himself as Francombe led him back down the hill. He might not be a graduate, but he was the one about to have a cup of tea and a seat in a warm tent.

2

Detective Chief Inspector Jim Daley sat in the office reception at Kinloch Hospital. The senior staff nurse had bustled off to find community nurse Helen McNeil. From what he could glean, McNeil had been the victim of some kind of hoax, and though she wasn't anxious to report it to the police her colleagues had felt it serious enough to make the call. Concluding that this interview might prove upsetting for the woman, Daley had decided to attend the hospital in person rather than send a junior detective.

He heard the telltale squeak of the trainers that seemed to be the preferred footwear of nurses when in their working environment, and got to his feet just as the door swung open.

Before him stood the staff nurse alongside another woman in a dark blue uniform. The newcomer was quite tall, slightly overweight, and looked to be in early middle age, her short, straight hair, once dark, now turning grey. Daley noted large black rings around her bloodshot eyes.

'Now, Helen, just tell DCI Daley what you told me. You know you can't let something like this go. A prank's a prank, but this is just sick.'

The woman was looking down, seemingly unwilling to meet the policeman's eye.

'Here, please take a seat, Nurse McNeil,' he said, pulling a chair nearer his side. 'Staff Nurse Cox has explained that you've experienced something upsetting. I hope I can help.'

Reluctantly, Nurse McNeil sat down beside him. 'I didn't want to bother the police, Inspector. I'm sure you have much better things to do than waste your time on the idiot who did this to me. It was nothing, honestly.'

'Please, just tell me what happened, Helen – may I call you Helen?'

'Yes, please do.'

'Good. I'm Jim, by the way. Now, just describe to me what the problem is and I'll see if we can help. You've got an important job to do, so we don't want you to be upset in any way. I'm sure Staff Nurse Cox will agree.'

'I certainly do. Our job is hard enough, DCI Daley, without idiots like this causing distress.'

Helen McNeil looked up at him, sniffing back a tear.

'I lost my father about two years ago. Oh, he was old and ill – ready to die, they said – but I wasn't ready to lose him.'

Daley nodded his head slowly, knowing exactly what she meant. He said nothing.

'I work on a two-shift system – early and late. I'm sure you're no stranger to the concept, Jim.' She smiled for the first time at the use of his Christian name.

'No, indeed I'm not.'

'I'm a heavy sleeper. My dad always told me I slept the sleep of the dead. But his family were originally from the Isle of Skye and loved dramatic sayings like that.'

Daley smiled, encouraging her to go on.

'He was always worried that I'd be late for work. He always phoned to wake me up – if I was on the early shift, that is.

Latterly, when he was in hospital, he managed to master the use of text on his mobile. He never missed a morning, no matter how early it was, or how ill he was. He'd send a text . . . well, until near the end, that is.' She held her head in her hands and began to sob.

'I'm so sorry. I know what it's like to lose someone close.' Daley swallowed hard, banishing the growing lump in his throat. 'Can you tell me more?'

She fished in the pocket of her uniform and brought out a mobile phone.

'I received this text earlier this morning.' She touched the screen a few times, then handed it to the detective.

Daley looked at it, peering, not wearing his reading glasses. But the text was clear enough: *Time to get up. Dad x.*

'I can see why you would find this upsetting,' he said. 'We have ways of finding out where this message was sent from, and perhaps who sent it. Would you like me to do that, Helen?'

'That's just it,' she replied, suddenly convulsed by sobs. 'I know where it came from – the number, I mean.'

'Whose is it?'

'The number that sent the text – it's my father's.'

As Staff Nurse Cox embraced her stricken colleague, Daley made a note of the number on the screen.

'Helen, can I take this with me? Just for a short time. I'll have our tech team look at it. I'm sure there's a rational explanation as to how this could happen. And I promise, we'll do our very best to catch the person who sent this text. It's beyond cruel; you did the right thing deciding to bring it to our attention.'

'I have another mobile – for work. I can use that, but I'd like mine back, if that's okay?'

'I promise, we'll keep it for as short a time as possible. Give me your other number and I'll call you to let you know how we're getting on.' He wrote the digits in his notebook, then got to his feet. 'Before I go, can I ask you, did anyone else know about the texts your father used to send? You know, friends, other family members, and so on?'

'No. I'm an only child. My mother left when I was young. There was just my father and me – that was it. And I'm quite a private person, I suppose. It's not the type of thing I would tell people.' Her tears had stopped, but she still looked distraught.

Daley thanked her, took his leave of Staff Nurse Cox, left the hospital and embarked on the short walk to Kinloch Police Office.

He thought about how much cruelty he'd uncovered in the time he'd been a policeman. What had happened to Helen McNeil might appear trivial to some, but to her it was devastating. He resolved to find out just who had sent her the bogus message and make sure they saw the error of their ways.

3

Brian Scott was fast asleep, stretched out on a canvas chair in the large tent the archaeological team used as a canteen. He was snoring lightly as DC Potts peered into the gloom and called his name.

'What, eh – where's the bloody fire?' he shouted, words slurred by sleep.

'That's SOCO just about set up for us to have a look, Sergeant,' said Potts.

'Honestly? They're quick off the mark, are they no'?'

'Been here for over an hour.'

'What?' Scott looked at his watch, noting with some dismay that he'd been asleep for over two hours. 'Why did you no' wake me up, you clown?'

'I was guarding the scene – like you told me to do, Sergeant.'

Scott got to his feet, stretched and yawned, and rubbed the small of his back, now aching after sleeping awkwardly in the chair.

'Right, let's get back doon there.'

As the detectives opened the flap of the tent, Scott screwed up his eyes against a bright early morning sun.

'When did we get the plane tae the Bahamas?' he said, pausing to look at the sweeping vista in front of him.

They were on a hillside about three miles out of Kinloch, on the east side of the Kintyre peninsula overlooking the mirror-calm waters of the Kilbrannon Sound. Above a blue sea arched a marginally lighter shade of blue sky in which seabirds tumbled and wheeled, their cries echoing along the rocky coastline. Far below them, the tide lapped gently on a stretch of white sand. The smell of sea and land in concert in the early summer heat made for a heady mix, a invigorating scent that, in partnership with the echoing cries of birds, the gentle whispering return of the ocean and the beautiful view, assaulted all the senses.

To their left, the Isle of Arran sat indomitable, its peaks bathed in the golden sunlight, while further out in the sound, Scott could see the bread-shaped mound of Ailsa Craig, the island also known as Paddy's Milestone. A thin ribbon of land, already shimmering in the rising heat, was the distant Ayrshire coast.

Scott breathed deeply, filling his lungs, then bent over, coughing spectacularly. 'Bonnie, eh?' he said through the paroxysms of his smoker's rattle. 'You never know with this place. One minute it's grey an' cold, the next it looks like a brochure for your next dream holiday, eh, son?'

'Aye. I've got to say, after the first half hour I was quite happy standing by those graves,' replied the young constable.

'No' dried this shit oot yet,' remarked Scott, as he began the trudge through the cloying mud underfoot.

He could now see a small number of white-clad figures bustling about on stainless steel duckboards around the three graves, now fenced off by police tape. Despite the brightness of the day, three large arc lights, angled into the holes in the ground, were being attended to by a technician. From one grave a white-hooded figure emerged, face obscured by a mask covering nose and mouth.

As they squelched their way nearer to the scene, another SOCO officer, also hooded and masked, walked towards them, raising a hand by way of a cursory greeting.

'Brian Scott, as I live an' breathe,' said the man, his voice muffled by the mask.

'Aye, an' who are you, Darth Vader's fat white brother? Take that mask off so I can get a look at you.'

The SOCO officer did as he was asked, removing his mask and pulling down the hood to reveal a shock of grey, almost white hair.

'Duncan? It cannae be. Duncan Chisholm, is that you?'

'It sure is, compadre,' Chisholm replied. 'I can't remember the last time I saw you – twenty years ago, anyway.'

'I thought you'd left the polis.'

'Nah, swapped forces tae Lothian and Borders.'

'Is that no' the same thing?'

Chisholm chuckled. 'Good to see you've lost none of your charm, Brian. I married a lassie from Selkirk. It was the sensible thing to do. She wasn't keen on moving to Glasgow.'

'Well, I can see the logic in that.'

'Anyway, we're all one happy family now. Police Scotland has brought us all back together.'

'An' you get tae be a real cop again. Magic stuff, Duncan,' said Scott with a wink.

'Chief Inspector Chisholm, can I have a word?' The now familiar figure of Professor Francombe was making her way towards the three police officers.

'Chief Inspector? When I knew you in Stewart Street you couldnae spell inspector, never mind chief. Promotion's rapid wae that Edinburgh mob, right enough.'

'You should have come with me, Brian. I tell you something

for nothing, there was none of that good ol' boys shite we had to deal with back in Glasgow, if you know what I mean. Best move I ever made. Chances for promotion were a hundred per cent better for the likes of you and me.'

'They'd have needed tae be a thousand per cent better for me tae sniff a pip or two. You know how it is, Duncan.'

'You still rocking the boat, Brian Scott? After all these years, too.' He smiled, giving his old colleague a companionable pat on the shoulder. 'Aye, it's good to see you, Bri.'

'When we've quite done with all our yesterdays, can I say something, please?' said Francombe, clearly anxious to move the conversation along.

'Sorry, Professor,' replied Chisholm. 'We're all ears.'

'Well, I've done what you asked and examined the remains – just a cursory glance. They'll need to be analysed properly, as I'm sure you know.'

'Yes, of course. What did you find?'

'All three skeletons are female, relatively young, from what I can judge – not teenagers, by any means, but in the twenty-five to forty-year-old bracket when they died. As a guess, of course.'

'And how long ago would that be?' asked Scott.

'Roughly? Oh, I'd say about twenty-five years ago or so. Not more than thirty. I can't be absolutely certain, but I think it's a pretty good educated guess.'

Chisholm looked at Scott with a grimace. 'Take you back, eh, Brian?'

'Can I ask,' said Scott, 'if there's any sign of foul play? I mean, have you any idea how these women died?'

'The wrist of one of the deceased is broken. I can see that quite plainly. There is no sign of any kind of injury on the second, but the third has a piece of material wrapped round her neck. Too tight for comfort, I would say, but that's just a guess.'

'So she's been strangled?' asked Chisholm.

'Chief Inspector, I cannot be more precise. She may have just had a thin neck – the material could have shrunk over the years. With what is remaining, it's impossible to make that kind of judgement. All three could have died of some kind of soft tissue trauma, for all I know. I'm not really willing to speculate any further. It's not my job, remember.'

'So, Brian, are you thinking what I'm thinking?' Chisholm turned to his colleague.

'Grab a Granny?'

'I beg your pardon?' said Francombe, a shocked look on her face.

'The Midweek Murders, they were officially known as, Professor,' replied Chisholm. 'Eight women from the Glasgow area disappeared in similar circumstances over a relatively short period of time. All aged in their late twenties to mid-thirties. Before your time, I would hazard a guess. Back in ninety-four.'

'Hardly before my time – I was young, but there is something familiar about what you're saying.'

'We found five bodies in various places. Barely hidden at all – one washed up on a beach in Greenock,' said Scott. 'The other three, well . . .' He looked down at the scene, still being pored over by the forensic team. 'Then, as quickly as it started, it stopped. Whoever killed the women just went away, or got fed up.'

'Or died, Brian?' Chisholm suggested.

'Ach, any number o' theories. Still, we never found the last three bodies.' He looked back into the rough graves.

There was silence for a few heartbeats, broken only when Francombe spoke.

'I have to get on. But I take it that this means the site is closed down – for the time being at least?'

'It does indeed,' said Chisholm. 'I'll let you know towards the end of the day how we're getting on, but absolutely no activity in this vicinity until further notice. We'll have to check for more graves. Could take a while.'

'We might be held up, but so are those awful windmill people,' said Francombe, nodding at a large tipper truck that had just appeared in a flurry of blue diesel smoke at the top of the rise. 'It will give me great pleasure to go and tell them.'

'Leave that tae me, please, ma'am,' said Scott. 'This is police business now.'

'As you please. I'll go and inform my team. If you want us for anything we'll probably be in the Douglas Arms in Kinloch. Nothing better to do.'

'I can think o' a whole lot o' better things tae dae than hang aboot the Douglas Arms,' remarked Scott as he watched her squelch her way back down the hill, the sun bright on her white forensic suit. 'That's a right pit o' despair.'

'You use another watering hole, Brian? Don't tell me you've signed the pledge.' Chisholm laughed.

'That's exactly what I've done, Duncan. Och, it's a long story,' he said in response to the bemused look on Chisholm's face. 'Better get back an' tell oor Jimmy what the score is here. He'll no' be chuffed, neither.'

'You don't mean young Jimmy Daley, surely?'

'The very man. He's a DCI, too. Man, yous are just ten a penny these days.'

'Did he not get himself into some hot water over this case – the Midweek Murders, I mean?'

'If that's what this is, aye, he did. But I'm surprised at a man o' your exalted position jumping to conclusions.'

'Jimmy Daley. Big lanky lad the last time I saw him. Had a cracker of a wife, if I recall.'

'Aye, an' your hair used tae be red, Dunky. Times change, my friend. Listen, I'd better make tracks, get things organised up here and let Jim know what the score is. We'll get some uniforms oot here tae take the strain. You'll be here for a while, I guess.'

'Oh yes. We'll be here for quite a while – days, I shouldn't wonder.'

As Scott made his way back to his car, DC Potts in tow, his mind drifted back to the time of the Midweek Murders, or the Grab a Granny case as it had irreverently become known in the job. All of the victims disappeared in the middle of the week, having attended club events known throughout Glasgow as Grab a Granny nights because of the high proportion of older women who chose not to go out on the town at the weekend, either because they disliked the bustle or because they had to babysit on Saturday nights. Many were just prolonging a trip to the bingo, adding to the 'Granny' sobriquet. Grannies in some parts of the city could often be in their mid-thirties. The name had stuck, and now applied to most midweek dancing nights in Glasgow.

'Aye, Jimmy won't like this,' said Scott under his breath, as he watched Potts show his warrant card to the tipper truck driver and send him on his way after a short explanation. 'He won't like it at all.'

4

Glasgow, 1994

Daley stood in Detective Inspector John Donald's office, gazing deliberately over the head of the man seated behind the large, neat desk.

'Why won't you answer the question, DC Daley? Did you or did you not have a drink with Mr O'Leary when you should have been questioning him officially about a rather serious crime?'

'I've told you, sir. I'm not in the habit of drinking on duty. I have too many things to attend to every day, without doing so in a fug of booze. I'll leave that to others,' he continued, shifting his stare to Donald.

'What does that mean, eh?' Donald rushed to his feet, face almost crimson with rage. He balled his fists, but just as Daley prepared for the verbal onslaught he'd become accustomed to over the years from this man, his superior took a deep breath, visibly took hold of himself and sat back down.

'Feeling dizzy, sir?' said Daley.

'You won't goad me, Daley. Just because you're off to the Serious Crime Squad, don't think you've stolen some kind of a march on me.' Donald's voice was slow, low and precise, the rage of only a heartbeat ago apparently gone, but more likely well hidden. 'Remember, I'm the one with rank here, not you. Join any squad you like, but to make true progress in this job you have to be promoted. You don't appear very good at that.' He smiled sickeningly.

'What are you implying?' It was Daley's turn to feel his blood boil.

'Oh, just that wherever you are, the Squad, Fraud – the Court Branch, even – when it comes to your promotion I'll hear about it. I pride myself on having assembled a pretty decent little group of contacts at the top of the tree, so to speak. A few words in a few ears . . . well, it makes a big difference.'

'And everyone listens to what you have to say without question, I suppose?'

'In one way or the other, you've been in my charge for the larger part of your pitiful career. Who better qualified to pass an opinion on your suitability for advancement than me? Grow up, Jim. This is the real fucking world, not the neat little meritocracy you imagine.' Without further comment, Donald opened a file and began to pore over it.

'Can I go?'

Donald didn't look up. 'You can fuck right off.'

Daley slammed the door and stormed back down the corridor to the general CID office.

He only had three weeks more of Donald's pointless jibes before he took up a posting to the Serious Crime Squad. Despite the way his current superior chose to brush it off, the move was a real feather in his cap. For Daley, life wasn't about promotion, but rather experience. Freed from the likes of Donald and Sanderson, whose dead hand guided A Division

CID, he hoped he could learn from proper detectives – men like his original mentor Ian Burns.

He rattled some change into the clanking coffee machine and waited as the muddy brew poured itself into a cardboard cup.

'DC Daley!' shouted a disembodied voice from the corridor outside.

Daley stuck his head round the corner. 'That's me.'

'Oh, right,' said a young probationary officer, clearly flustered by being sent into the realm of the CID from the uniformed section. 'I'm to tell you they've found a body washed up on the shore in Greenock. They reckon it's part of the Grab a Granny case.'

'Thank you. Who told you this?'

'Sergeant Meacher, the gaffer of Three Shift. You've to phone Greenock CID. He said to pass it on.' The young lad smiled, not sure if he'd managed to communicate the message to the best of his ability.

'Right, cheers. First, you can tell your sergeant that the case is called the Midweek Murder investigation. We've had enough hassle from the press as it is over this Grab a Granny nonsense – but that's not your fault. Second, find me DC Scott, would you? I have an appointment I've got to keep.'

'DC Scott is off out there now with DS Sturrock. You were with the DI at the time. He says he'll let you know what's happening.'

Daley nodded and walked to his desk, sipping the hot coffee. As he watched the young cop hurry off, he picked up the phone and dialled two, the internal number of the head of Divisional CID, DCI Sanderson. He could have called DI Donald, but what would have been the point?

Kinloch, the present

Brian Scott walked through the corridors of Kinloch Police Office, yawning loudly. He'd been called out early, and he hated that. Despite what many thought of him, he was a creature of habit and order – of a kind – and any interruption to this well-trodden path resulted in irritability and a feeling, likely to last for the rest of the day, that all was not right with the world.

Certainly, this was how he felt as he sought out his superior. Brian Scott knew that for Jim Daley the ghosts of the past had meaning, haunting him still, no matter how many times he tried to banish the dead faces he'd seen in the course of his career. One such ghost – or in this case, ghosts – was about to raise its head once more. Scott was sure of it.

He chapped on the door of Daley's glass box and opened it. His old friend and colleague was sitting behind his messy desk trying to manipulate something between the fingers of his big hands.

'What are you at?' asked Scott.

'I'm trying to put a new SIM card in my phone. You ever tried it? Bloody nightmare. Liz used to do all this kind of stuff . . .' His voice tailed off.

'Aye, well, just you sit back. There's bigger nightmares than that on the go.'

Daley sat back in his chair, which squeaked in protest. 'Okay, Brian. Do your worst.'

The driver jumped down from the cab of the large tipper truck. He'd parked in a small lay-by just on the outskirts of Kinloch.

He looked round; there was nobody to be seen, only a few

interested cows in the field opposite, and some swooping seabirds. The odd car flashed past on its way into the town, but no one took any notice of the man in the light blue boiler suit as he turned his phone this way and that, desperately trying to find a mobile signal.

He walked along the verge a bit, and without warning the full array of little bars appeared on the device. At last, he could make the call.

He pressed the screen, then held the phone to his ear, waiting for a reply.

'Aye, what do you want? Are you no' busy up at the turbine site?'

'Aye, I should be, but it's been shut doon. The polis are all over the place. They've found some skeletons, or something.'

'Oh, great. Where are you now?'

'I'm up at the quarry on the Machrie road. Listen, whoot dae you want me tae dae wae the stuff?'

The line fell silent for a few moments before the voice returned.

'Park the wagon up and meet me at the golf club. Put the stuff in a bin bag or something.'

'Right, nae bother.'

'And don't look like you've just smuggled out the crown jewels when you appear, or you'll see bugger all of that wee bonus we're talking about. Got it?'

'Nae bother. I'll be dead nonchalant an' that.'

'I can't wait tae see that. I'll meet you in about half an hour, Johnny.'

Johnny made his way back to the truck. He climbed the small ladder and was soon back in the cab, a commanding driving position high above the road.

The 'wee bonus' might mean little to the man he'd just called, but to him it was a beach holiday for the whole family – a good one, too. He revved the big diesel engine into life, drove to a farm road end, turned the vehicle and headed for Machrie.

'What're the chances?' said Daley, the dismantled mobile now scattered on the desk in front of him. 'Duncan Chisholm, too – I'd forgotten he existed.'

'Looks mair like Gandalf the Grey noo. No' a single red hair left in his heid. That's what happens when you away an' join Lothian and Borders.'

'We're all the same now, Brian. I'd better get Symington on the blower, then get up there and take a look myself.'

He stared into space, a blank expression on his face, which Scott studied with no little trepidation.

'Doesnae dae tae think too much aboot the past, Jimmy. It's done and dusted. Whoever throws thon dice flung them a long time ago.'

'But that's not the case now, Brian. You know things have moved on – DNA evidence and so on. If these remains are the three missing women – *if* – then who knows what we'll be able to get now?'

'Big leap. First of all, we're only guessing it's them. Chances are they're nothing tae dae wae the Grab a Granny case. Even if they are, there's no sayin' there's any evidence in they graves. Big Dunky didnae look too confident.'

'Big Dunky never looked too confident. Beats me how he's a DCI – and a crime scene manager in SOCO, to boot.'

'He says the same aboot you. Still thinks you're a big lanky lad, by the way,' said Scott with a smile.

'Well, he's in for a shock.' Daley patted his stomach.

Just as he was about to ask Scott more, the phone on his desk burst into life. He answered, and then cleared his throat as the call was put through from the main desk.

'Ma'am, I was just about to call you.' He listened intently, occasionally scribbling some notes on a pad of paper.

The call ended, Daley stood up.

'What's up, big man?'

'This gets more weird by the minute.'

'Who, Symington? Aye, she has her moments. I widnae call her weird, mind you,' said Scott.

'Bobby Speirs – remember him?'

'Aye, who could forget? I was at his retirement party – oh, aboot five years back, or so. He was blotto, but why change the habits o' a lifetime just cos you're retiring?'

'Well, he's not retired any longer.'

'Eh? How's that possible?'

'He's back. They've put him in charge of an experimental cold case unit. Guess where he's headed now.'

'But he was a useless bastard.'

'Yes, but he'd a good friend, didn't he – retired as an inspector in Inquiry.'

'John bloody Donald. Speirs was his best buddy, wasn't he?'

'Yup. So, now, to supplement his pension, he's left to poke about old cases and see what he can discover. Too much of a long shot for full-time detectives, but just right for an old alky who has nothing better to do. Must have been one of the last favours Donald did. I've never worked with one of these old boys' units. Can't say I'm anxious to, especially now I know who's heading it up.'

Suddenly Scott looked worried. 'They're all coming out o'

the woodwork, Jimmy. You be careful. You and Speirs have history, remember.'

'But there's one man who won't be coming out of the woodwork, isn't there?'

'Who?'

'Ian Burns, that's who.'

Scott sighed and shook his head. 'I knew this would bring that a' back tae you, Jimmy. I've just said, it's a' in the past. Best just tae let it lie, big man. Mind, you damn near lost your job o'er this before.'

Daley looked at his old friend and smiled weakly. 'But I'm older and wiser now, Brian. Plus, there's a big debt I still haven't honoured.'

5

Colin Galt examined the contents of the plastic bin bag. He was locked in a toilet cubicle at the Machrie Golf Club. It was a quiet day in terms of folk out on the course, and he needed time and space to think.

He also needed somewhere to hide what he'd just been given by his driver. Sometimes he worried that this little project had gone too far.

He double-knotted the bag, the items secure within. Stealthily he cracked the door of the cubicle open and looked around the large room. Relieved that there was no one to be seen, he hefted the bag over his shoulder and made for the exit, where he paused again to look about before sliding out of the Gents, down a short corridor past trophies and lists of club champions on wooden boards, and out into the car park.

He pressed the button on his key fob, watching as the boot of his large Mercedes saloon swung open to reveal his golf bag. Moving the clubs to the rear, he placed the plastic bag in the boot, clicked the key fob again and waited as the lid closed automatically.

'How are you today, Colin?' The voice behind him made Galt jump.

'Aye, fine, just fine, Wullie. This you off out for a round?' he replied as breezily as he could.

'Och, I'll hit a few balls wae my auld buddy, nothin' mair. An exercise in futility, but you know the game, Colin.'

'Aye, tell me about it. Listen, need to dash. Busy at the work. Enjoy your day, Wullie.'

Without waiting for the old man's reply, he jumped into the car and set off. He could feel his heart thudding in his chest, relieved to be getting away without attracting more attention. He supposed he could have had Johnny give him the stuff in the yard at work, but there were far too many prying eyes about there. And knowing his luck, if they'd arranged to meet on a remote road half of Kinloch would have sauntered round the corner just as he was taking possession of the bag. In any event, it would have looked too suspicious. No, he was happy with the decision to use the golf club as a cover, and proud of the sangfroid he'd managed to display in the face of old Wullie. No one was any the wiser.

He smiled as he swept past the first fairway on his way to Kinloch.

'How'ye, Ronnie?' Wullie was dragging his large golf bag on to the first tee.

'A nice day for it. The usual fiver wager?' Ronnie paused. 'Young Colin Galt's in a hurry, eh?'

'Och, aye. The bugger's up tae somethin', it's jeest fair lookin' oot o' him. He was stuffing a black bin bag intae the boot o' that big car of his. Aye, just as furtive as you like.'

'Jeest like his faither. He was a right sleekit bastard, tae. Widna put anything past him.'

With no further comment, the two old men commenced their weekly round of golf.

Daley stared at the skeletons in the three graves. Though each still had a powerful arc light directed down on to the remains below, it was hardly necessary, as the midday sunshine was bright, illuminating the hillside and the coast beyond in a golden light. The SOCO officers were still busy, scouring the scene for anything, however minute, that might help them discover what had happened to the people laid to rest in shallow graves only a few miles from Kinloch.

He walked away, heading back up the hill towards the canteen tent his SOCO colleagues had turned into an impromptu base. DCI Duncan Chisholm, head of the forensic team, fell into step at his side.

'You've put on a pound or two, Jimmy,' he said with a shake of his head.

'And you've not lost the knack of stating the bloody obvious,' replied Daley tetchily.

Chisholm raised his eyebrows. 'It's been a long time, right enough. How's the wife – Liz, isn't it?'

'Fine, the last time I saw her.'

'Oh, right.' Chisholm quickly changed tack, deciding the man he hadn't seen for over twenty years seemed in no mood for small talk. 'I can't believe they've managed to drag Bobby Speirs out of retirement.'

'They shouldn't have bothered. He was bugger all use when he was a proper policeman, so I'm damned if I know what they think he has to contribute now he's a cold case officer, or whatever it is they're calling him.'

'You bounced out of the wrong side of the bed this morning, Jimmy.'

Daley hesitated. 'Sorry, Duncan. It's been a difficult few

months, in and out of the office. It's good to see you after so long.'

'No change in Brian, mark you.'

'You think not? Doesn't touch a drop now – been on the wagon for months.'

Chisholm was still assimilating this astonishing fact, now confirmed, as they walked into the tent, stiflingly warm under the hot sun. In one corner, two SOCO officers had set up a table on which sat various laptops, screens and other paraphernalia.

On the far side of the tent, Daley saw a tall woman wearing shorts and a T-shirt fiddling with the zip of a large rucksack. She looked up at the new arrivals.

'This is Professor Francombe, DCI Daley. She's the on-site archaeological director,' said Chisholm.

The pair shook hands, her grip surprisingly strong. In fact, thought Daley, she looked very fit, tanned and full of life. The benefit of regularly working outdoors, he surmised.

'Pleased to meet you. I'm in charge of the sub-division down here. I'm sorry we've had to interrupt your work in this way. I promise we'll be out of your hair as quickly as possible.'

'That would be most welcome, DCI Daley. As I told your colleague, we were initially thrilled to discover the burials – stuff of archaeologists' dreams. Not so thrilled when we discovered that they weren't the kind of burials we were after. Those poor women.'

'So you think there could be other people buried on the hillside?'

'I very much hope so.' She had a soft English accent, making her deep voice seductive to the detective's ear. 'Though his abbey is further up the coast, I believe that Somerled, Lord of the Isles, may have called this home. We know his followers brought his body back here to Kintyre after he was killed at the battle of Renfrew. Everyone thinks he lived further up the coast near the abbey, but I don't agree. I think this is where he made his base. This would have been some kind of defensive structure, handy for the sea and the rest of Scotland, but even handier if he wanted access to the rest of his domains off the west coast. Just a pet theory of mine, Chief Inspector. Whatever the truth, much too important to let the site be destroyed by these bloody windmills.'

'Very interesting. I've read bits and pieces about Somerled, but I can't claim any expertise, I'm sad to say.'

'So, you know more than your sergeant about the history of this place?' she said with a smile.

'Not DS Scott's strong suit. He has many other qualities, though.'

'Well hidden, mind,' added Chisholm with a mirthless laugh.

'I'm just getting some things together. I'll be off in a few minutes,' said Francombe. 'I thought the university might recall us for a few days, but they want us to get on with admin work and stay near the site. We're under pressure to get something significant or up go the windmills and we can wave goodbye to this place for ever.'

'Not a fan of green energy, Professor? I thought an intellectual like yourself would be all for it,' said Chisholm.

'You policemen seem very interested in renewables. DS Scot asked me a similar question. Of course I'm in favour of sustainable energy – who wouldn't be? It's just that wind turbines are the least efficient and most damaging route to that. In my opinion, at least.'

Daley spotted a flash of passion in her deep brown eyes; familiar somehow, he thought. 'Have you been on any of those television shows on archaeology? I think I might've seen you somewhere before.'

'Yes, I've been on a few. As a very minor player, though. Blink and you'd have missed me. In fact, my arse has had more exposure than my face – bent over digging in some pit or other while some minor celebrity tries to sound as though he knows what he's talking about.'

'Well spotted, Jimmy. Trained observer, you see, Professor,' Chisholm put in. 'Us detectives miss nothing, you know.'

'Really?' she said, with a mischievous twinkle in her eyes. 'I'm very glad to hear it. Anyway, I'd better make tracks. If you need me for anything, we're billeted at the County Hotel, which we'll make our operational base while we're here. You'll find us between there and the Douglas Arms – the County bar is rather too cliquey for us. Besides, we have some horse fanciers among our number, and the racing's never off the box in the Douglas Arms.'

'May I have your mobile number?' asked Daley. 'Just in case we need you for something urgently.'

'Certainly.' She fished into the rucksack and produced a small handful of business cards, handing both Daley and Chisholm one. 'All my details are on there. I'll wish you a good afternoon, gentlemen.' Her expression changed. 'I hope you can find out what happened to those poor women, I really do.'

'Women? You seem very sure,' said Daley.

'As I told DS Scott, I'm an osteo-archaeologist, Inspector. It would be a poor show if I couldn't tell the skeleton of a woman from that of a man. The configuration of the skull and the synaptic notch, you know. I'm sure your colleague will fill you in on all that. Good afternoon.' She hefted the rucksack on to one shoulder and ducked out of the tent in a flash of bright sunshine that made the detectives blink.

'Clever lassie. I'm no' sure I'd like to get into a fight with her, mind you,' said Chisholm.

'Why not?'

'Did you see those muscles on her arms?'

'That's what you get if you're out digging in the ground all day, Duncan.' Daley squeezed Chisholm's forearm.

'Steady, Jimmy. I don't do any digging – leave that to the younger men. I'm here in a managerial capacity only.'

'You'll be here for a couple of days, am I right?'

'Aye, easily. We weren't sure when we came down, but it's a big job. HQ will have me put up somewhere – the County Hotel, I think.'

'I'll organise uniforms to look after things overnight. Might meet you for a pint later?'

'Now you're talking, Jimmy. We can catch up on old times. You never know, Bobby Speirs might be here, too.'

'Yes, what a treat,' said Daley, by his expression indicating the contrary. 'Maybe best to leave him out of the party.'

Chisholm thought for a second. 'Aye, right enough,' he replied awkwardly.

6

Stirlingshire, 1994

Retired Detective Chief Superintendent Ian Burns was sitting in his shed in the back garden of his home in rural Stirlingshire. The usual array of detritus was scattered over the old coffee table he'd appropriated from the house: two mugs, an overflowing ashtray, a folded copy of the day's newspaper and a golden packet of Benson and Hedges, his favoured cigarette brand.

He was listening to a piece by Mahler that filled the air, blaring from an old Hacker wireless sitting on a shelf behind him. His eyes were closed as he let the music wash over him like a warm sea of pleasure and relaxation.

This place had become his refuge in the years since he retired from the police. Unlike many officers, he had no interest in golf, sailing, boozing, hillwalking, or secret societies. He needed somewhere to give his wife space as she went about the habits of a lifetime in their solid stone-built home on the edge of the quiet village. They'd settled into a routine: he would amble down to his shed in the morning after breakfast, smoke, listen to the wireless, read the paper and gather his thoughts for two or three hours, then head back up the garden path for lunch. In the afternoons, they normally took a drive, either for shopping in Stirling, or to visit friends – mainly hers.

At first, he'd found this routine deathly dull, but he'd soon adapted to life outside the job, and now he whiled away his time quite happily, looking forward to their next trip to the south of France, where they'd bought a small holiday cottage – their only post-retirement indulgence.

There was indeed, he decided, much more to life than poking about in the worst humanity had to offer, staring at dead eyes, or eviscerated corpses. He was glad he no longer had to face shark-eyed, sneering gangsters, deranged murderers, terrorists, fraudsters, child abusers, or the rest of the long list of serious criminals, petty crooks, or the downright insane he'd had to deal with on a daily basis as a police officer. Neither did he miss the internal politics and wearisome exigencies of the job he'd toiled at for so long.

He'd kept in touch with a few friends, but now – in the main – they too were retired. He liked to keep in touch with the younger men he'd brought into the vocation that had consumed him so utterly for so long.

To this end – and with a notion he might pick his brains on a subject he found troublesome – he was waiting for a young DC to whom he was proud to be a mentor.

He looked at his watch; Daley would be with him soon. Unlike many young people, he was a meticulous timekeeper: an admirable quality, in Burns's opinion.

He pulled the stained envelope from the inside pocket of the old tweed jacket he was wearing on top of two thin jumpers and removed the contents: one foolscap page, smeared with untidy crimson script.

Despite the time of year, he could already feel the chill of autumn in his bones – hence the jumpers – and re-reading the scrawled message made his blood run even colder around his spare frame.

He wondered who'd provided the substitute for red ink on the paper he now placed on the table in front of him. He knew he should have made more of it – the second such missive he'd received. But, he'd reasoned that in the job that had occupied him for so long he'd met a selection of nutters that would easily stretch across the Campsie Fells to the city of Glasgow, where he'd spent the entirety of his career. He remembered the words of an old sergeant who'd shown him the ropes as a young probationer: *If they say it, they're no' going tae dae it.*

Just as he closed his eyes to listen to the final bars of the symphony, he heard the familiar sharp knock on the door of the shed.

'Come in, come in,' he called cheerfully, before being consumed by a rasping smoker's cough. When he recovered, a tall young man in a dark suit was standing before him. He noticed that his visitor appeared to have filled out a little since his last visit, but he still bore the loose-limbed, straight-backed deportment of youth, not yet weighed down by worry of the job, or the stress of bringing up a family.

'How are you, sir?' said his visitor with a smile. 'Still smoking, I see.'

'Here, have one yourself,' Burns replied, handing him the packet. 'Good to see you, Jim. Take a seat.'

DC Jim Daley sat on the threadbare easy chair opposite the man who had given him his chance in the CID, a man he was now proud to call his friend.

'Now, you said you had something to show me, sir.'

Kinloch, the present

Helen McNeil lay in her bed, listening to every sound: muffled voices from the street outside and cars as they swished by through puddles. She lived in a well-tended block of flats on the seafront of Kinloch. The big sandstone building, with its thick walls and double-glazed windows, usually meant that she heard little from outside her neat, two-bedroomed flat. Tonight, though, was different; her senses were heightened, brought to the peak of awareness by the message she'd received on her mobile phone earlier that morning.

She wondered how the police were getting on with tracing the heartless person who'd sent the prank text. Then darker thoughts entered her head. She banished them, picturing only the smiling face of her father, sitting in the high-backed armchair in the hospice. Even though his life had been draining away, he had still been her touchstone. She barely remembered her mother, who'd left them when she was five years old. This man – her father – had devoted his life to her, never bothering to make time for any other meaningful relationships, lest they upset his daughter. Or so she'd convinced herself; naïve, really, she thought.

Like her father, she had always gone to bed early; she supposed that correlated with being bad at getting up. For her, the dark confines of her bedroom, under a warm, comforting duvet, represented a place of refuge from the world.

Even though it was only just after ten, she closed her eyes and mercifully was soon asleep, the noises from outside now mere adjuncts to her dreams.

Stirlingshire, 1994

'You say this is the second letter, Ian,' said Daley. 'When did you get the first?'

Burns thought for a moment, then said, 'Oh, I don't know – maybe two weeks ago, something like that.'

'You don't seem very concerned, but you know the score much better than me. This isn't something you should just brush off – certainly not considering what you did for a living.'

'That's just it, Jim. Have you any idea how many people I brought to book during my time in the police? No one could investigate it all – it would be impossible. Even if you went back to the start and went through every case I ever worked on, you still couldn't be sure this has anything to do with any of them. Personally, I wouldn't be surprised if it was one of the local kids. You know what unruly wee bastards they can be these days.'

'Honestly, sir . . . Ian. Do you really think this looks like the work of a spotty twelve-year-old?' Daley spread the note on the table in front of them: *Enjoy these days of summer. They will be your last. Your end is nigh.*

'Anyone could have written that – anyone, at any age.'

'In blood? And it does look like real blood, sir. What did the other note say?'

'Oh, something about being time to pay, or some other garbage.'

'Can I see it?'

'No, Jim, that would be impossible.'

'Wasn't it you who told me nothing was impossible?'

Burns let out an amused snort. 'Well, in this case I was wrong.'

'Why so?'

'I burnt it. Never gave it a second thought until this came through the door.'

'Do you have any idea when it was delivered?'

'During the night sometime. Our post doesn't get here until after ten. Both notes were on the mat at the front door when I got up around seven. They drew my attention for that reason. The wife normally deals with the post, but I knew that wasn't what this was. Glad I picked it up and not her. You can only imagine the drama.'

'So, the envelope – do you have that? What did it say?'

Burns reached into the inside pocket of his tweed jacket. 'Here, have a look for yourself.'

Daley took the envelope from the older man. It was creased and stained with what again Daley assumed was dried blood. There was no writing, no name, nor any indication who the message was intended for on the envelope.

'It's not even addressed to you, Ian.'

'That's what I mean. If my wife had picked it off the front mat, she'd just have opened it. I'm just pleased she didn't.'

'But now you've decided to report it – that's why I'm here, right? Though we both know it will have to be handled by Stirlingshire Constabulary; this is their domain. I don't mind taking it over to Randolphfield – explain what's been happening.'

'I don't want to report it, Jim.'

'Sorry?'

'I want you to do me a favour. I want you to get it analysed – the blood, prints – anything else you pick up on. But I don't want to make it official.'

'Why on earth not? You've received what can only be termed as two threats to your life in as many weeks. This has to be reported through the proper channels.' Daley thought for a moment. 'Have you thought about Machie?' he said, referring to the city's most feared gangster, a man Burns had pursued, largely unsuccessfully, for a number of years prior to retirement.

'Not his style, is it? Maybe a gunshot in the head, or a knife in the back; this isn't direct enough for him. Far too subtle.'

Daley nodded; sending menacing letters was not James Machie's habitual MO.

'Listen, Jim,' said Burns, standing up, suddenly agitated. 'The last thing I need in my life is Amanda being frightened. She lived all those years in the police with me, you know. I watched her visibly relax when I retired. I don't want to ruin that.'

'But you agree that something has to be done? What, exactly?'

Burns shrugged his shoulders. 'You're the detective, son. I'm just an old man in a potting shed.'

Kinloch, the present

She sat bolt upright in bed, at first confused why she'd woken with such a start, but then realising that the landline phone she had on her bedside table was ringing quietly. As a district nurse, she was no stranger to being disturbed in the middle of the night. She'd set the ringtone volume low, usually just enough to rouse her, not enough to shock her into wakefulness, but tonight was different.

She picked the cordless phone from its base and said her name, without her glasses unable to see the caller's ID on the screen, just assuming it was the hospital duty sister.

There was silence on the other end of the line.

'Hello? Is that you, Dorothy?' she asked.

Still, silence.

Then she felt her heart thud in her chest. She could hear a strange rustling on the other end, for all the world like someone handing over their handset to another.

'Well, how are you tonight?'

The words made her gasp. She let the phone fall to the floor, then turned on the bedside lamp. She could hear herself sob as she rushed barefoot into the hall, then frantically delved into the pocket of her navy blue uniform, hanging from a hook on the wall, desperately looking for her work mobile.

Just as she laid her hands on it, it began to ring.

'Hello – hello?' Another pause.

Then, 'Well, how are you tonight?'

Though it was weak and distant, the voice of her dead father was again unmistakable.

Letting both coat and mobile phone drop to the floor, she rushed to the front door and wrestled with the key in the mortise lock.

The harsh light of the close flooded into her hallway as she flung the heavy door open. Clad only in her nightdress, Helen McNeil rushed out on to the landing screaming.

7

Colin Galt fretted as he paced about his office. He'd hidden the bag, but still wasn't convinced its hiding place was sufficiently secure.

He looked at his watch – almost half past ten. He needed to relax, to think of something else for a while. He needed a drink.

He picked up the phone, the receiver still warm from the last time he'd held it. The taxi number came to mind automatically; he didn't even need to concentrate as he dialled.

That done, he tidied some papers on his desk, switched off his laptop, placed it and its charger in his briefcase, then checked his pockets. Keys – two lots, here and home – phone, cash, cards . . . He thrust his hand into the left pocket of his trousers, a sudden chill in his heart. He needn't have worried; it was still there.

As he was switching off the office lights, he saw the sweep of the taxi's headlights as the cab swung through the gates and into the yard, dwarfed by some of the lorries and plant machinery there.

He set the building's alarm, locked the front doors and was off.

Instead of rubbing his hands together, eagerly anticipating a few drinks and a yarn with some of the old soaks he called friends, he looked back anxiously as the taxi made its way back on to the street beyond. In his mind, the black plastic bag and its contents still loomed large.

Daley sat down heavily, tiredness catching up with him, but he was glad to be in the busy bar at the County Hotel. Annie bustled about as usual, serving drinks and administering playful admonishments in equal measure.

The town was preparing for the first big weekend of the holiday season – and the Kinloch half marathon. From small beginnings, the event had grown into a real showpiece for the area, with thousands being raised for charity, and hundreds of runners, locals and strangers alike, keen to take part. Hotels were full, restaurants were heaving, and the bars were buzzing, as old Kinlochians returned home for the event and new visitors sampled the town's unique atmosphere.

Daley looked on and smiled. It had taken him time to feel comfortable being back in social situations – being seen to smile and enjoy himself. He'd had a few awkward moments when certain songs came on the jukebox, or his mind flashed back without warning to happy times he and Mary Dunn – even he and Liz – had enjoyed in the crowded hotel bar. But, on the whole, he'd managed to force himself from the confines of home and office to enjoy – as best a police officer could – what approximated to a normal life.

The past was the past – he had to make the best of what was to come. He sipped his pint and sighed deeply, taking the opportunity to relax for the first time that day.

His attention was drawn by a ragged cheer as the door to the bar swung open. He watched the old man leaning on two sticks hesitate, look around, then make for the policeman's table, Annie at his back, fussing like a mother hen, a large whisky in a small glass in her hand.

'Aye, but sure it's great tae see you oot and aboot,' said Hamish, beaming at Daley. 'I was fair scunnered wae you mouldering away up in the hoose on the hill thonder. I dare say you were scunnered yourself.'

Daley pulled out a chair, helping Hamish with his sticks as he made himself comfortable. 'It's nice to be amongst friends,' he said with a smile. 'How are you keeping, anyway? I haven't seen you in a while.'

'Did you no' know, Mr Daley? He was away his holidays,' said Annie, placing the glass of whisky on a bar mat after giving the table a wipe with the cloth normally draped over her shoulder.

'Hardly holidays,' said Hamish. 'I was up in Firdale wae that niece o' mine. Mair like one o' they places the celebrities go tae straighten themselves oot – you know, they footballers and pop stars. Forced tae eat like a bird, wae no' a drop o' decent whisky tae be had.'

'That's no' whoot I heard,' said Annie, flicking the towel back over her left shoulder. 'I heard you was miraculous last Saturday night – up singing and telling your tales aboot auld Sandy Hoynes, God rest him.'

'Aye, she let me oot a couple o' times,' observed Hamish ruefully. 'Even the condemned man gets tae have a decent chow before he meets his maker. An' let's be honest, it's no' long till I meet mine.'

'I thought you were on the mend – you certainly look a lot better, Hamish,' said Daley, feeling guilty again that he hadn't been able to protect the old fisherman from the assault he'd suffered a few months before.

'Don't you listen tae him, Mr Daley,' said Annie, marching off, collecting empty glasses as she went. 'Bugger's got a heid harder than stone. He'll be jeest fine. You shout oot when you want another drink, Hamish. I've had that many left behind the bar for you, I've near lost count.'

Hamish watched her go with an almost imperceptible shake of his head. 'Typical woman. They don't feel pain the way us poor men dae. That's a scientific fact, Mr Daley. They've no' got the same number o' nerves in the body – same as the ribs thing. If they could feel the full force o' a summer cauld, by Jove, they'd no' be calling it man-flu, or whootever it is they're saying. Quite simple: where there's nae sense, there's nae feeling, and that's a fact.'

'That's a bit harsh,' remarked Daley.

'I daresay. But when you've spent a few days wae my niece, you come back an' tell me your opinion o' womankind hasn't changed for the worse. It's a bit like going tae stay a whiles wae a cross between Margaret Thatcher and Attila the Hun. Aye, wae a bit o' Florence Nightingale flung in for good measure – a wee bit, mark you. It's fair hard going.'

'Remind me not to pay her a visit the next time I'm in Firdale.'

'Anyhow, I was hoping I'd see you the night, Mr Daley. I've been hearing certain things that have jeest set my mind a' on edge.'

'Like what?'

'Like there's been bodies found up on Kilmilken hill, that's whoot.'

'Now, Hamish, you know I can't say anything about that. You know the score by now.'

'Och, I'm no' right interested in these bones you've

turned up. Fae whoot I hear, they're no' that auld in any case. I'm mair concerned wae you poking aboot up there in the first place.'

'You can't hold me responsible for what's been found, Hamish. I'm just dealing with what turns up – as always.'

'Aye, but you should stay away fae the thin places.'

'Thin places?'

'Thon Somerled – aye, an' many generations afore him – knew a' aboot the thin places. It's where this world and the next jeest aboot touch. Stand on that hillside – or on Iona – och, a lot o' places like it, an' you can feel yoursel' driftin' away. Let me tell you, I know. I've felt it many times.'

'I've a job to do, thin place or not. Now get that whisky down you and I'll go up and get us both another one.'

'Mark my words. Better jeest tae leave things be in places like that. No good will come o' it, for certain sure. Do you know, there's a dark hole up there they've never found. A prison naebody can ever escape fae. When we was young, that's whoot frightened us weans tae bed at nights. *You'll end up doon the dark hole.*'

Just as he was getting to his feet, Daley noticed the bar door swing open again. This time a uniformed constable leaned his head round it, instinctively looking towards the back of the room, where the chief inspector normally sat. The young man nodded at the sight of his boss, and threaded his way through the drinkers, tables and chairs until he was standing beside Daley.

'Can I have a word, sir?'

'What about?'

The young cop looked down at the old man. 'Could we go somewhere more private?'

'What on earth has happened now?' asked Daley, becoming impatient.

The constable leaned his head into Daley's, speaking conspiratorially. 'It's the district nurse, Helen McNeil, sir. There's been another incident.'

Though Colin Galt was enjoying a large glass of brandy, his friends talking excitedly about the forthcoming weekend, he still couldn't relax. He was in the town's private club, the habitat of businessmen, teachers, doctors and lawyers; a place they could get blind drunk away from the prying eyes of employees, pupils, patients or clients. Forgetting, of course, that they still had to get home, and in Kinloch, where curtains twitched and passers-by took note, it was almost impossible to conduct a clandestine social life, no matter how discreet the behaviour.

He drained his third glass and hauled himself wearily out of the leather chair. 'Have to make a call, lads. Got a wagon on its way from England – rush job. Better make sure he's on schedule.' He scurried off to find a quiet place.

He stood in the hall, the buzz of conversation and laughter muffled behind the thick walls he'd just left. He pulled the phone from his pocket and dialled the number.

He looked up and down the hallway, his feet fidgeting on the deep red carpet as the ringtone sounded in his ear. He cleared his throat, just as he heard a reply.

'What do you want? I told you only to call me in emergencies, and I don't want any emergencies – it's your job to make sure there aren't any.'

'It's not an emergency, as such . . .'

'If it's about the bodies they found up there, I know all about it. I do follow the news, you know.'

'Aye, well, that's not helped. There's police all over the place. But that's not why I'm calling . . . I want out. I just want to be paid for what I've done, then I want out. I can't abide all this sneaking about – it's messing with my head, you know?'

'This isn't like the Saturday job you had when you were a boy. You don't just leave on a whim. You're in it up to your neck, Colin, and unless you want the water to cover your head, you'll shut up and get on with it.'

'Wait, you can't say that.' The desperation in Galt's voice was plain. 'I said I'd help you for an agreed sum of money. I haven't seen a penny of that yet. It's just not worth the stress.'

'But it's not all about the money, is it?'

'Meaning?'

'Meaning that even if I choose to give you nothing – which I do, at the moment at least – you're my creature. We both know why. Now, get back to your boozing, or whatever it is you're doing. I have other things on my mind.'

The phone went dead, and Galt knew that what he'd always suspected might happen just had. He'd lost control. Without thinking, he flung the mobile phone on to the thick carpet, where it then bounced against the wall, the screen shattering into a jigsaw of cracks.

'Bastard!' he swore loudly, then picked up the pieces and hurried off – not to rejoin his friends and have another brandy, but straight through the door and off into the night.

8

Helen McNeil was sitting in the family room at the police office, nursing a can of Coke in two shaking hands. She had composed herself, but Daley could see from her red, puffy face that she'd been crying.

She looked very different from when he'd seen her last. Then, she'd been in her uniform, her hair up, wearing a touch of make-up. Now she looked washed out; her hair was now uncombed, longer than he'd imagined, straggling down her back. Though it was dark brown, Daley could see grey roots. She was wearing a dressing gown over a pair of jeans and bright pink training shoes.

'Helen, I'm so sorry you've been put through this horrible experience again,' he said. 'Once was enough – I hear it was even worse this time.'

'Yes, yes, it was, Inspector Daley.' She bit her lip, desperately trying to ward off more tears. 'It was the shock of hearing his voice.' She bent her head forward, her shoulders sagging with the pain of it all.

'Please, try not to be upset. We're just waiting for information from your mobile phone company, as regards the text. We'll get right on to this, too. There has to be a rational explanation.'

Suddenly, she raised her head, eyes blazing. 'Oh, I'm not stupid, Inspector. I know my father hasn't sprung back from the dead. I just want to know who – how – why this is being done to me!' She shook her head and sighed. 'I'm sorry, I know it isn't your fault. I just feel like my whole world is being turned upside down.'

Daley hesitated for a moment, letting her calm herself down again. 'Would you like some tea, or coffee?'

'Do you have any hot chocolate? I can't drink tea or coffee at this time – I'll be up all night.'

'I wouldn't worry too much about that. I don't think it matters what you order from the machine we have here. It all tastes much the same. Not much substance to it, but it's a hot drink, at least.'

Daley was pleased to see the hint of a smile play across her face as he dispatched the uniformed constable to bring the beverages from the machine in the office canteen.

'Can I ask you more about your father? I hope you don't mind. I know you say you have no enemies, but all this might be something to do with some twisted person who had a grudge against him.'

He was surprised by her reaction. He had expected a staunch defence of her father's character; instead, she seemed to be considering it as a possibility, a look that said *Yes, you might be right* on her face. Daley sensed that he might be on to something.

'Did your father have anyone he was particularly at odds with?'

'Not any individual that I can think of – no, I don't think so.'

Daley was confused. 'Do you mean there might be more than one person – a group of people – a family, perhaps?'

'You think we all have enemies?' she said suddenly, a determined look on her face.

'Sadly, yes, that's probably true. For me, it's part and parcel of my job. This is very important, Helen. If I'm to find who did this, you can help us – a lot – by identifying anyone who could have made your father's life difficult.' He paused. 'Or yours, for that matter. If this had happened to one of my team, we'd have plenty of potential suspects to look at.'

'Well, my father was in the same boat.'

'Meaning?'

'Meaning that he spent almost thirty years of his life as a civil servant. Social security, they called it then – the dole.'

'Oh, so he encountered some hostility? Where did he work, if you don't mind my asking?'

'He joined before I was born. He started in Lanarkshire offices, mainly. We lived in Airdrie most of the time when I was young, though by that time he was working in Glasgow.'

'What was his job exactly?'

'Dealing with claims – hence the animosity. I hear it's all done anonymously these days. Well, then you had to look the bastards in the eye when you were telling them they couldn't have any more money. Honestly, some people have a real sense of entitlement.'

'When did he retire?' Daley asked, slightly taken aback by her opinion of people in need of help from the state.

'The late eighties. He'd had enough – was sick of how things were going, all the paperwork and so on. I'm sure I don't need to tell you about that.' She smiled. 'I think he was what you'd have called old-fashioned. He believed that people should work for the money they received. He always instilled that into me – and I'm glad he did.'

'What was his name again?'

'Stuart – Stuart McNeil. They used to call him the gambler, at work.' She smiled at the memory. 'He liked the bookies,' she added in reply to the quizzical look on Daley's face. 'Too much, as it turned out.'

'Did that cause problems at home – I mean providing for you, that kind of thing?'

'No, there was nothing like that. I was happy with him – I always had what I wanted. I was well fed and clothed, got good toys on my birthday and Christmas. I was loved. Being a child is a pretty straightforward business if you have those basic ingredients, I think.'

'And your mother left, you said?'

She looked at the floor again, her long hair covering her face.

'I'm sorry, that was insensitive of me. You have my apologies, Helen.'

'I should be apologising to you. I'm still afraid of being honest about that.'

'Oh? Why?'

'My father used to tell people that she died.'

'She didn't die?'

'She's probably dead now. Who knows – or cares? No, she left him – and me, come to that.'

'Oh,' said Daley. 'I see. So your father preferred to tell folk she was dead?'

'Yes. He was ashamed, I suppose. We moved house not long after that. The other end of town, where no one knew us. I was only small; I barely remember any of this. Just my father crying. For some reason, I remember that most vividly.'

'Was there someone else . . . I mean, did she leave with

another man? I'm sorry I have to ask these questions. I know all this must still be very upsetting for you.'

'You have your job to do, just like us all. If it will help you catch the sick—' she bit back what she had been about to say, 'sick person who is doing this to me, I'll answer anything.' She paused again, this time looking over Daley's shoulder into the middle distance. 'She was just gone one morning. My father came back from the pub . . . you know, quite early. I was in bed asleep. She'd just left a note – a very brief one – telling him she was leaving and not to try and find her, but to do his best to bring me up. That was it. She wasn't abused; it wasn't a violent marriage. Well, not from what I recall – and from what I heard subsequently from my aunts. I never heard raised voices in the house, or anything like that.'

'I see. That must have been tough for your dad. I mean, small child, difficult, responsible job. A lot to ask.'

'He did it without a single complaint. Like most children, I was adaptable; soon, I hardly thought about my mother again. He had three sisters – the aunts I mentioned – and two of them lived nearby. When he was working, one of them looked after me. As I say, Inspector, I had a happy childhood.'

'How did you find out about his gambling?'

'I was about to go to nursing college. I was always harping on at him about getting a car. You know, just a wee runabout – anything to save me from that smoky bus every morning.' She grimaced at the memory.

'Did you get the car?'

'No. I'm sure he would have bought me one if he could, but he had absolutely no savings – the bank wouldn't touch him when he applied for a loan. Not only that, he was in debt.'

'Do you know who to?'

'No, he never talked about it. Well, not until just before he died.'

'What happened then?'

'Because he'd been ill for so long – in hospital and that – I had power of attorney.'

'You mean you had access to his bank account?'

'Yes. I only paid his bills and suchlike, made sure he had some cash in hospital, clothes, toiletries – that kind of thing. But one day he asked me to take two thousand pounds from his account in cash.'

'So he had some savings by this time?'

'It just about cleaned him out. In fact, I had to pay some of his bills for a short while until his pensions accrued again. Of course he gave me that money back,' she said in a rush, clearly anxious that Daley not think her father had sponged off her.

'Yes, of course. But what happened to the two thousand pounds?'

She shifted uncomfortably in her chair, her gaze avoiding his.

'Helen, it might be important.'

'I had to take it to an address he gave me and post it through the letterbox in a plain envelope. Well, plain apart from the fact that he asked me to write his initials on it – so the recipient would know who it was from.'

'Can you remember where?'

'Wait. How will this help find this mad person who's persecuting me? We're talking about a dead man, Inspector. I can't see the relevance of this.' Again, her eyes flashed with anger.

'Trust me, Helen. The more I know, the more likely it is I can track down who's behind what's happening to you.'

She sighed. 'It was a big house in the countryside – not far from Beith in North Ayrshire, as I recall. I remember looking at it and wondering why my father should have to give away what savings he had to somebody who was obviously already wealthy. I nearly didn't post it.'

'Nearly?'

'He'd made me promise. I suppose he knew how angry I'd feel about it all. It was just after that that he told me about his gambling. I felt sorry for him. He'd lost a fortune over the years.'

'Can you remember exactly where this place was – the address?'

'No, no, I'm sorry, I can't. There was so much going on at the time. You know, what with him being ill. I wanted to see him as often as I could, but that meant I was travelling a lot, as well as working. It was quite draining.' She bit her lip, her mind suddenly propelled back into the past.

'I'm sure it was, Helen. Pity you can't remember that address. But we can add what you've told me to the investigation. You never know what will come out the other end.'

'I was using everything I had just to keep myself going, and look after my father. I'm sorry, but everything else is just a blur.'

'I understand.' Suddenly, Daley's instincts were telling him there was more to the persecution of Helen McNeil than met the eye. He sensed that she regretted admitting she'd had to pay his gambling debts. Despite her plight, it was plain that she would remain loyal to her father. His appointment for a drink with Dunky Chisholm would have to wait. He wanted to get to the bottom of this.

9

For the first time since giving up booze, Brian Scott found himself actually enjoying a night in the pub.

He'd agreed to meet Chisholm in the Douglas Arms when Daley had called off. The County Hotel, it turned out, had been fully booked, so the head of the SOCO team was staying in a guesthouse on the other side of Kinloch with the rest of his colleagues. This being a plain B&B, there was little in the way of diversion, so Scott had offered his services as a guide to the local nightlife. Hence, the Douglas Arms. It was good to catch up, especially after all these years.

Scott was also interested in meeting some of the archaeologists he'd seen on site that day, as they packed away their kit while the police investigation got under way.

'Anyhow,' said Chisholm – now on his third pint in less than an hour, Scott noted with a raised eyebrow – 'by this time we'd moved to Selkirk, so my city days were over, Brian. I hear you might be moving here full time. Am I right? I would have thought a place like this would be a bit tame for the likes of you and big Jimmy.'

'Are you kidding? You could send doon the whole o' A Division CID and they would still be struggling wae a' these buggers. If I telt you what's happened tae me doon here, you'd have nae hair. And apart fae that, they're no' happy unless you're aboot tae breathe your last on some fucking boat. They even had me sinking in a whirlpool. I'm telling you, don't think this is an easy number, cos you've no' got a clue.'

'So why haven't you moved down before?'

'Och, I've been at this perinatal thing.'

'Eh?' Chisholm looked taken aback.

'What's up wae your coupon?'

'I would have thought your Ella was a bit too old for another wean, that's all. I mean, I know they can work wonders these days . . .'

'Another wean! Are you off your heid, man?'

'What's this perinatal stuff all about, then?

'Och, you know what I mean – no' working in the one place – moving aboot in the job.'

'Peripatetic?'

'Aye, that's it, perapathetic. I was spending way too much time away fae hame, so how no' just bring hame nearer? That's the idea. And you must admit, when you're no' at the mercy o' King Neptune, it's a bonnie wee place.'

Stifling a smile, Chisholm was about to reply when he was interrupted. The tall figure of Professor Francombe appeared beside them at the bar.

'Hey, Prof, how's it going?' asked Scott.

'Anthea, please. I get enough of the "professor" when I'm up to my armpits in mud. Can I buy you gentlemen a drink?'

'That would be just the thing. Mine's a pint of lager,' said Chisholm promptly.

'Quick draw McGraw over here, eh? There no holding you back when there's a free drink on the go,' said Scott. 'A wee fresh orange will dae me, thank you.'

'Still on duty, Sergeant?' asked Francombe.

'He's on the wagon,' replied Chisholm before Scott could think of a reply. 'Fair hammering the bevvy he was, weren't you, Brian?'

'You're in the wrong profession, Duncan,' said Scott.

'Why, what do you mean?'

'You should have been a priest. They secrets o' the confessional would have been safe as hooses wae you.'

Francombe pulled up a stool beside the policemen. With drinks served she looked around the bar. 'Only a few of my charges here tonight, I see.'

'How many have you got?' asked Scott.

'Fifteen, including me. We're quite a small team. As ever, funding is a problem. This is a bit of a rush job. We had to get here as soon as we could to stop the wind farm development in its tracks. Of course, the company moved the goalposts and were on site two weeks early.' She looked around the room again. 'So I had to settle for who was available.'

'No' the A team, then,' remarked Scott.

'One doesn't live in a perfect world, Sergeant. Anyhow, if I'd to work with the worst archaeologists in the world in order to stop this project, I would.'

'You think this site is a big deal, then?' asked Chisholm.

'I think it's of massive importance. We came across it late, and only thanks to Lidar, but I'm sure we have a really substantial settlement. We know it existed because it's mentioned in historic tracts, but we never knew where it was. I think, now, we do.'

'This is a passion for you, I'm thinking,' said Scott.

She smiled wanly and looked around the room. 'Yes, certainly – a passion, granted. But I doubt I'll ever be as passionate about anything, now I've seen what's on the ground, I mean.' She swirled the drink about in her glass.

'No' wanting they big windmills buggering everything aboot, you mean.'

'Interesting terminology, Sergeant Scott, but correct, none the less.'

'C'mon, Anthea – Brian and Duncan. We're in the Douglas Arms in Kinloch, no' much point standing on ceremony in here. First names will dae.'

'I suppose you're right.'

Like many such establishments in Kinloch, the Douglas Arms consisted of the main bar area, a small back room with a pool table and two noisy slot machines, and a lounge designed for couples who wanted to enjoy a drink in less raucous surroundings – in theory, at least. Scott, Chisholm and Francombe were sitting at the main public bar, a solid construction with a tiled top. As the whoops came from the pool room, where someone had obviously won a bet, Francombe looked through the door leading from the bar to the lounge.

'Wow, Bernie and Marion. They don't venture out much.'

'Who are they when they're at home?' asked Scott, craning his neck to see Francombe's colleagues.

'Bernie – Bernard, he hates the contraction – Evans and Marion Smyth-Browne. They're our hydro-archaeological team.'

'What?' asked Scott and Chisholm in unison.

'They focus on underwater archaeology. Quite a specialised and often dangerous field. They're welcome to it, if you ask me.'

'So it's not just an on-land investigation?' asked Chisholm.

'No, indeed not. We think we may have discovered a birlinn – a Scottish version of a Viking longship. Well, the remains of it, at least. But keep that to yourselves,' she said, leaning in to her drinking companions. 'If that is the case, well, it would fund the rest of our activities.'

'This Boris and Doris are busy diving on this, then?'

'Bernard and Marion, Brian. They're not diving yet, but they'll end up doing so. There's a lot of preparatory work to get through before they can get to work on where we think the vessel is actually situated – just on the foreshore. Perfect conditions in which to preserve such an artefact, mind you.'

'How so?' asked Scott.

'Oh, peat washed down off the hillside becomes silt under the waterline at the shore. Peat is great for the preservation of just about anything. You'll have heard about the peat bog bodies in Ireland. It's a complicated process, but we kept looking, knowing the conditions were right, and by process of elimination we seem to have hit the jackpot.'

With that, one of the big fruit machines in the pool room burst into a cacophony of noise, accompanied by the clatter of coins.

'Some lucky bastard,' remarked Scott. 'I've never had any joy wae the bloody things.'

'It's not that you didn't have enough time to practise, what with the amount of time you spent in pubs over the years,' said Chisholm with a grin.

Before Scott could reply, a short, painfully thin young man with dark hair tapped Francombe on the shoulder.

'Can I have a word, Anthea?'

'Yes, sure. What is it?'

The young man looked at the two policemen nervously. 'In private, if you can manage it.' He laughed nervously as Francombe slid off her stool.

'Excuse me, guys. Duty calls,' she said, raising her eyebrows as she followed her colleague through the pub's front door.

'Strange lot, these archaeologists, eh, Brian? They all look as though they should be in primary school, too.'

'No' any stranger than us polis – and plenty these days who look as though they just left the school.' Scott was staring back to look at the couple in the lounge. The woman was in her late forties, the man younger – no more than early thirties, late twenties even, Scott reckoned.

'Penny for them, Brian.'

'You know what it's like being a cop, Duncan. You just cannae help taking stuff in.'

'You've changed.'

'Aye, just a bit. Och, just ignore me. I'm spending too much time wae oor Jimmy.'

The two veteran detectives laughed, and, almost in unison, sipped their drinks.

Glasgow, 1994

Daley was in the antiseptic surroundings of the lab, watching forensic officer Tony Barnes remove his safety mask. The room was white, with tiled walls and stainless steel worktops. The smell was almost overpowering, a mix of strong chemicals and more natural, visceral odours.

'I can tell you it's not blood, Jim,' said the man in the white coat.

'Are you sure?'

'Yes, I'm sure. More like some kind of fake blood – you know, the stage variety. Looks convincing, but then it's supposed to.'

'That's strange.'

'More clever than strange, I'd say. Real blood might have made the letter traceable. We're getting smarter all the time, and I'm willing to bet that whoever wrote this knows that.'

'Nothing to go on, then?'

'Nope – apart from two sets of prints, that is.'

'Really? That's great, Tony.'

'Listen, what's going on, Jim?'

'Sorry?'

'What's with all this cloak and dagger stuff?'

'Sensitive – you know how it is.'

'I'm doing you a big favour, you know,' Barnes said, lowering his voice.

'I know, and I'm very grateful.'

'Just you? I'd have thought the other person who spread his dabs all over this letter would be grateful, too.'

'Meaning?'

'Meaning, I've identified both sets of prints. We do keep records of all police officers – to eliminate them – remember?'

'And?'

'They belong to you.' Barnes paused. 'And DCI Ian Burns.' He looked at Daley over the rim of his glasses. 'As you know, we retain personnel information post retirement in case it becomes relevant in some cold case or other. Is Ian in some kind of trouble, Jim? He's a friend of mine, you know – a good friend.'

'Listen, Tony, I know. I can't say anything now. I'm playing this the way Burns wants. There's nothing to worry about. Do I look worried?' He forced a smile.

'You're not a good liar, Jim Daley. But I'll tell you something you should know. One day, maybe in ten, fifteen years, who knows, we'll be able to get more out of items like this. Techniques are improving all the time. We're retaining all sorts of productions, just in case we can get something out of it in the future. You wouldn't believe how quickly technology is moving.'

'But you can't tell me anything else about that letter now?'

'No, but I can give you my opinion.'

'Which is?'

'Whoever put this little message together knew what they were doing. There's no trace of anything that could incriminate them.'

'Is that unusual? With stuff like this, I mean.'

'Most people – especially the normal kind of moron who would write something like this – have no idea what we can do with forensic evidence these days. Whoever did this has been very careful not to leave us anything to work on. And that's harder to do than you would think.'

'Okay. Thanks, Tony.' Daley felt somewhat deflated, not only because the note posted through Burns's letterbox hadn't yielded more, but because perhaps it was more sinister than he'd hoped.

'Listen, if you need to do anything else like this – you know, on the QT for Ian – don't hesitate to contact me. He's a good bloke, but don't let this get out of hand, Jim.'

Daley left the lab, the note in its plastic evidence bag stuffed into his pocket. He had a bad feeling about this. Yes, it was vicious and unpleasant, but he sensed something more – a malevolence troubling in a way he couldn't put his finger on.

He got back into his car and drove. What next, he thought.

Stopped at traffic lights in the city centre, he spotted a board outside a newsagent.

Grab a Granny Murder: Another Dead Woman.

He sighed and leaned his forehead on the steering wheel.

Kinloch, the present

'I'd better go,' said Francombe, returning to the bar and pulling her coat over her shoulders.

'Oh, why so?' asked Scott, finding himself slightly dismayed that their evening was being disrupted.

'Something Simon said – my second in command.'

'You mean that boy you just went tae have a word wae? I thought he was pushing fifteen.'

'Oh no, he's twenty-six, I think. He's been qualified for a year or two now, but this is the first time he's had any managerial responsibility. Let's just say he's taking his new role very seriously indeed. I need to go and check something. Hope you guys enjoy the rest of your evening.' She rolled her eyes as she turned to leave, indicating that she thought her new errand a waste of time.

'Aye, see ya,' said Scott. He looked back through the door into the lounge, but Boris and Doris were gone.

10

Daley was at home, poring over the map he and Helen McNeil had been looking at back in the office. Quite reluctantly, he thought, she'd managed to pinpoint the address to which she'd delivered her father's last debt. It was in an isolated spot on the Renfrewshire–North Ayrshire border. In fact, he would have to check to find out which of the new divisions of Police Scotland covered it.

It was almost midnight, and he was thinking of heading off to bed, when he was startled by a firm knock on the door. He opened it to reveal a familiar figure dressed in a greasy old Breton cap, a thick fisherman's pullover, an underbib and brace dungarees, leaning on two sticks.

'Hamish! What the hell are you doing here at this time of night? Is everything okay?'

'Och, these bloody nightmares, Mr Daley. I jeest canna shift them. I canna sleep at all – fair wearing me oot, it is. No' myself, if you know whoot I mean.'

Daley felt guilty, again. His friend had been attacked as a direct result of helping him with a case earlier in the year, and for a while, things had looked very black. However, the old man had rallied, though it was clear his confidence had taken a battering.

'Listen, come in. I've been meaning to ask you something.'

'Oh aye, that sounds ominous,' said Hamish, his leathery face strangely pale in the artificial light as he stepped into the lounge.

'No, not ominous at all; I've been thinking.'

'That's the trouble wae you detectives – you think too much.' Hamish's laugh turned into a weak cough.

'I know you've had trouble sleeping. Annie told me. You're not the first and you won't be the last to find themselves a wee bit nervous after an assault. I'm actually amazed just how well you've done.'

'That Annie's got too much tae say for hersel'. I'm made o' tough stuff, Mr Daley – like generations o' us Kinloch fishermen. When you've faced up the Atlantic Ocean wae a dark face on, well, man, you can cope wae anything.'

'You know I'm knocking about here on my own so I thought you might fancy moving in here for a while – just until you're fully recovered. I could do with the company, to be honest.' Daley gestured to the capacious leather sofa. 'You'll not say no to a dram?'

'Here, I'm no' that far gone that I canna enjoy a wee sensation. In fact, I rather hoped you'd say jeest that. But a new bunk for a whiles – aye, and some company – would make a big difference. Och, it'll be jeest like *The Odd Couple*.' Despite the attempt at levity, he still looked troubled.

'What is it?'

'Och, jeest thinking aboot himself.'

'Himself?'

'You know – Hamish, the big fella.'

'Right,' said Daley, fearing he knew what was coming next.

'If I'm tae be billeted way up here on the hill, I'll need tae bring him wae me. Och, I know folk think he's a big bruiser, but he's jeest nervous o' people, you know.'

Daley recalled Hamish the cat's sharp talons digging into the back of his head on one occasion, and wondered just how nervous this huge half-breed Scottish wildcat actually was.

'I suppose he'll have plenty of room to roam up on the hill here.'

'Aye, he will that. Fair enjoy himsel', so he will.' Hamish smiled as Daley poured him a large dram in a squat crystal glass. 'Nice whisky glasses, tae. It'll be just like a wee holiday for the pair o' us – aye, a grand break, right enough.' Again, his expression changed.

'What's up now?'

'Och, I'm jeest thinking. I've never lived this side o' the toon. It'll be right emotional, that's for sure.'

'What do you mean? It's not exactly Manhattan, Hamish. You're not about to swap continents! In fact, you can just about see your house from here.'

'Aye, I dare say – but for us, it's a big step. This used tae be two toons, Mr Daley. Years ago, they reclaimed a big part o' the loch and united the two places, but, well, sometimes I feel a stranger o'er this end.'

They sat in silence for a while as Daley assimilated this information.

'It must have been a while ago, Hamish.'

'No' that long ago.'

'When?'

'Seventeen hunner an' fifteen, or thereabouts. I'm no' right sure, now you're putting me under so much pressure tae remember.'

'You'll be fine. You can go back home during the day and just sleep here at night.'

'Och no, that wid make the big fella even mair unsettled. In for a penny, in for a pound, says I.' He looked around, patting the leather couch with his gnarled old hand. 'Aye, hame sweet hame, right enough.'

They chatted for a while and then Daley showed the old man into one of the spare bedrooms. It smelt a bit musky, but Hamish said he wasn't worried about a bit of stale air and would be happy to just open a window. 'Nae time like the present. I can pick up my kitbag in the morning,' he said happily.

Once his old friend was settled, Daley returned to the lounge. The map was still spread over the coffee table, but he ignored it and began to switch off the lamps in the room one by one.

Beyond the big picture window, the lights of Kinloch twinkled under their counterparts in the midnight blue sky. The loch rippled in this light, the new moon illuminating the island at its head in a shaft of light, as though by celestial design.

He wondered how many before him had stared down from this hill on the scene below, and thought of the changes that had taken place since men inhabited the place they now called Kinloch. He gazed at the twinkling panorama, his mind wandering aimlessly for a few minutes.

He was jerked out of his reverie when, without warning, there came a noise like thunder which rooted him to the spot. It was a few seconds before he realised from where this cacophony was emanating.

From behind the door of the room he had settled Hamish in came a racket that could have woken the dead. The old man's snoring was quite unlike anything he'd ever heard; it seemed to echo around the house. Unexpectedly, it would cease for a few moments; then, with renewed vigour, the deep rumbling, followed by a keening whine, would begin again.

Daley stood for a while, then shrugged his shoulders in resignation and sighed. He hadn't planned on gaining a housemate, but now he had one. As he wandered into his own bedroom, the snores of the new arrival grew in intensity. Just for a moment, the big detective wondered exactly what he'd let himself in for.

Greenock, 1994

The boy sat in the café, sucking at his Coke through a striped straw.

Daley observed him. The lad's grandmother was fussing around him, her face tear-stained, while the grandfather sat across the table, showing no emotion, though it was obvious that he was finding it difficult to maintain the stereotypical façade expected of males from the west of Scotland when faced with personal tragedy.

A young WPC, also sitting at the table, was looking at the little boy with a smile, her hand outstretched, holding his.

Daley supposed that a seven-year-old couldn't possibly process the enormity of what he'd just witnessed, hence the lad's expressionless self-possession. Maybe he was just in shock. The detective attempted to think himself back into his own childhood, trying to imagine how he'd have reacted if he'd seen his mother's lifeless body washed up on the shore. Despite the effort, he couldn't conjure up the boy he'd been.

Across the street and down on to the pier he could see the

flash of blue police lights, as a body wrapped in a black bag was carried into a private ambulance on a stretcher. He saw the familiar figure of Brian Scott gesticulating to another man he didn't know, a member of the Greenock CID, he assumed.

As though he sensed this, the young boy stood up, gazing at the distant vehicles, his eyes wide, but still with no discernible expression on his face.

'Can we go now?' he said softly.

'But you've not finished your drink, Derek,' said the WPC, looking at him, tears in her eyes.

'Aye, son,' said his grandmother, grabbing at his sleeve. 'You sit down. There's another policeman would like to talk to you. We're just waiting on him.'

Without warning, the boy stamped his foot and threw the Coke over the WPC, drenching her. He shrieked at the top of his voice, 'My mummy's gone, and now I want to go too!'

Stirlingshire, 1994

Ian Burns was halfway down the broad stairway of his house when the phone began to ring.

His old instincts started to spark. It was only just six-thirty in the morning. Who would be calling at this time of day? He walked to the hall table upon which sat the cream-coloured phone and picked up the receiver.

'Good morning. Burns,' he said, then listened for a few moments. 'Yes, tell him that's no problem. What time did you say again? Hold on, let me write this down.' He opened a notebook on the table and scribbled the pen he picked out of a brass holder on a blank page to bring it back to life. 'Right, twelve thirty. I know the place, just on the main road to

Milngavie, not far from the distillery. Tell Jim I'll meet him there as per his instructions. Where is he, by the way?' Again, Ian Burns listened for a moment. 'Ah, yes. Terrible, just terrible. It's times like this I'm glad to have hung up my spurs. Thank you, Constable.' He put the phone down and rewrote the note he'd scribbled, to make sure he could read his own writing.

Jim Daley. The old stile, bottom of Dumgoyne. 12.30 p.m.

He drew in a deep sigh. He knew why Daley had chosen this meeting place. When the lad had only been a matter of weeks in CID, they had attended that very spot together, where the body of a young man had been found. It was quiet, and though not far from the road quite secluded – clearly why the unfortunate young man had picked the location as the place to cut his wrists.

He suspected Daley had something delicate to communicate to him about the two anonymous notes he'd received – hence the clandestine approach. He tore the piece of paper he'd written on out of the notebook, folded it and put it into the pocket of his dressing gown.

Well, he thought, at least today will be different. A change is as good as a rest.

He shuffled off in his slippers to make his wife a cup of tea and smoke his first cigarette of the day.

11

Colin Galt stretched as he woke. He rubbed his eyes and looked round the room. They were still there – his luminous green running shoes sitting boldly on the floor beside the chest of drawers as though they were calling out to him. The Kinloch half marathon was only a day away, and he really wanted to get in a quick 5K run before he had to go to work.

He staggered off to the shower, ran it as hot as he could bear, then stood under the powerful jet of water. As always, its blast helped him to collect his thoughts ahead of another busy day. He had to phone the accountant to make sure she could meet him the following Monday. He had to find holiday cover for the driver who normally took the delivery van to Glasgow on weekday afternoons. He had to speak to his so-called business partner about new opportunities, away from Kinloch. Expansion – that dreaded word.

His father's old partner, whom he'd inherited along with his half of the business, was slow to accept change. Left to Geordie McKay, they would still have one tipper truck, a couple of delivery vans and a digger or two. It was he, Colin Galt, who'd built things up.

He looked at his watch, then got dressed in an old grey sweatshirt and running pants. With his wife and children off on a short break during the long weekend, he only had his own needs to worry about. He could please himself. He bounded out of his front door, turned left and headed along the rough track that led from his house to the main road.

It was a beautiful day. He could see the Paps of Jura, hazy in the distance as they shimmered in the warm morning air. He heard the call of gulls soaring high into the blue sky on thermals. He felt strong as he picked up the pace, turning on to the main road. It was quiet at this time of day. Those travelling between Machrie and Kinloch wouldn't be on the go for another hour or so, by which time he'd be back home getting ready for work.

A long black shape raced across the road in front of him in a blur. A mink, he realised, slowing down, his heart racing. It was then he heard it, the distant whine of a car making its way towards him on the other side of the rise.

Glad of the chance of a rest, he stopped on the verge, leaning against an old drystone dyke in order to get his breath back and allow the vehicle room to pass on the narrow road. As it appeared over the hill, though, he frowned, the joy of being out in the fresh air and away from his problems replaced by the sense of impending doom that had been haunting him for weeks. He wasn't surprised when the battered SUV slowed down.

'You're very predictable, Colin,' said the woman in the driver's seat.

'And you're very bloody annoying – do you never give up? This has to stop. I can't take all this sneaking about.'

'Get in!' She leaned across to the passenger side of the vehicle and swung open the door.

Galt sighed. 'This is the last time. You know what's at stake here, don't you?'

She smiled.

They drove for a few moments, the question left unanswered by his companion as she turned on to a rough track, leading to an abandoned quarry on the far side of a small hill.

Within moments, she was straddling him on the passenger seat, one arm on the headrest at his back, the other against the car's roof, thrusting down on him while he searched desperately for her small breasts through the denim shirt she was wearing.

Roughly, he pulled the garment apart, sending a button spinning into the back seat, searching for her taut nipple with his tongue.

On top of the rise, hidden from view by a large boulder, stood a silent figure. He stared down at the SUV in the heart of the old quarry, as though framed there by the rough amphitheatre created over decades of work at the site. It rocked to and fro, and even from this distance he could hear the muffled cries of a woman – cries of pleasure.

A pale palm of a hand was suddenly plastered against the passenger window, leaving a smear as it slid down the steamed-up smoked glass in time to the motion being generated from within the vehicle.

Having seen enough, the watcher turned, bounded down the rocky slope, jumped on to a quad bike and raced across the rough track in the field until he was out of sight.

Galt was still breathing heavily when the woman pulled over and left him on the road, only yards from where she'd picked him up.

He considered continuing his run, but couldn't stop his right leg from shaking after his exertions in the SUV.

He decided to turn back for home, figuring that, in one way or another, he'd had sufficient cardiovascular exercise for the day. At the same time he cursed his lack of willpower. He'd promised himself not to mix business and pleasure again, yet here he was, still panting from their lovemaking, the smell of her strong on his clothes, her dampness making his jogging pants stick to his leg.

'Bastard!' He swore loudly, sending an unseen creature scurrying through the undergrowth on the verge.

When Daley awoke, he was surprised to hear a radio playing accordion music in the kitchen. The distinctive aroma of bacon and strong coffee came wafting into his room.

'Bloody hell, Hamish, I'm not used to this.' He looked at his watch. 'It's only half six!'

'Aye, no time for hanging aboot in my bunk, Mr Daley. Up an' at 'em, the fish'll no' catch themselves, so tae speak – no' that I've got any fish tae catch these days. But you know whoot I mean.'

Before Daley could reply, the smoke alarm in the hall began to wail, making Hamish burst the yolk of the egg he was turning over in the pan. 'Whoot on earth . . .'

Daley reset the alarm and then opened the kitchen windows, setting the extractor fan above the cooker to its highest setting.

'Sorry, Hamish – life in the modern home. I know it must be strange to you.'

'My niece has a' that carry on, tae. When I go and visit, I jeest wait till she goes oot, then I take a' the batteries oot o' these contraptions. I canna be footered wae that nonsense every time you set a pot on the stove. It's nae wonder every bugger goes on aboot stress these days – it's as though the hooses have a mind o' their ain.' He shook his head as he lifted the skillet of sizzling bacon and eggs off the cooker and began portioning out breakfast on two plates.

'Looks wonderful, Hamish, thank you. But don't think you have to do this every morning.'

'I'd be up cooking for myself, so why no' the baith o' us? Breakfast is the maist important meal o' the day. I'm sure Mrs Daley always sent you oot wae a good fry-up in the morning.' He paused for a moment. 'No' that I'm prying intae your nuptial occurrences, mark you.'

'I wouldn't worry too much about that, Hamish. If I was lucky enough to get breakfast made for me, it was likely to be muesli and a very skinny latte. Liz was always trying her best to reduce my waistline, not expand it.' For what seemed like the first time in months, he suddenly felt a pang of sadness, missing his wife and young son. He knew he'd ended their marriage when he'd chosen his colleague Mary Dunn over Liz, but he needed to try harder to maintain some kind of relationship, if only for the sake of James Daley junior.

As though he'd picked up on these melancholy thoughts, Hamish began to shake his head. 'You canna afford to dwell on it, Mr Daley. No, life has its ain way o' steering you on the course that wiz plotted for you fae the start. That's a fact.'

Bobby Speirs stared out of the window of the small plane as it came in to land at Kinloch. The town seemed to huddle between the hills and the loch, which twinkled far below in the bright sunlight.

He'd missed being a policeman. Not the actual work – never that – more the camaraderie. Also the position: to retire as a detective inspector was no small achievement, something that made him proud, despite those who were critical of his style and efficacy. Not bad for a lad from the wrong side of the tracks who'd left school at fifteen and joined the police cadets. He knew his father, also a cop, would have been proud.

And now here he was. Retired for almost five years and he had it all back – well, the closest approximation of being an actual officer.

One part of this trip he wasn't looking forward to was his reunion with Jim Daley. He'd almost forgotten about the young DC. Now the memories were flooding back. Too keen, too explosive, and too straight. Daley would turn a blind eye to nothing, he remembered. A sanctimonious prick, he thought – a time bomb, too.

Then darker thoughts took hold. He quickly banished them.

He'd heard about Daley's career as time went on, but their paths hadn't crossed again. Lucky for him, he thought, draining the last of his bottle of water then running his hand across his bald head.

As the plane bumped across the tarmac, Speirs's thoughts drifted to matters in hand. The Midweek Murders, or, as he'd always known them, Grab a Granny. How strange life was, he thought. He of all people was left to resurrect a case that had caused him so much worry so many years ago. Not to mention Jim Daley. But he knew how to handle that boy.

When he stepped on to the runway at Kinloch, he raised his face to the bright sun and thanked his lucky stars they'd sent for him.

12

Dumgoyne, Stirlingshire, 1994

Ian Burns pulled his car into the lay-by and lit yet another cigarette.

He remembered the last time he'd been there, the bleached white face of the tragic youth who'd taken his own life. The lad had cut his wrists and calmly sat down by a stream to die. Something in Burns admired the quiet dignity of the act, while most of his being recoiled at the needless waste of life. But he'd seen lots of wasted lives, one way or another.

He shielded his eyes against the sun as he stepped out of the car and waited to cross the busy road. Black smoke issued from the tall chimney of the little distillery nestled near the road to his left. He carried on, taking a rickety stile over a barbed wire fence and beginning a slow plod across a rolling green field.

The weather had been mercifully dry, so he'd decided not to put on the pair of old wellingtons that resided in the boot of his car, yet another hangover from his long police career. In the beginning, he'd ruined too many pairs of shoes in mud, water, snow, oil, or the many other underfoot conditions he'd had to endure as a young detective. Burns had soon learned to keep three items in the boot: his wellingtons, a large rain jacket and a heavy torch. He'd passed the tip on many times – including to the man he was about to meet. He was glad, though, of the warm scarf round his neck. He was painfully thin and always felt the cold.

He crossed a tiny bridge on to a rough track that took him uphill. He had to stop after a few long strides in order to cough. It was cold in the shade of the trees that covered the hillside; he drew the scarf closer about his neck.

As he wheezed in more air, he sighed at the habit he couldn't quit and reached into the pocket of his jacket for his cigarettes and gold lighter, cursing when he realised he'd left the latter in the car. Thankfully, in another pocket, he found a small book of matches, emblazoned with the name 'Germond', the tiny bistro he and his wife visited when they were in France. He smiled at the thought of the little brasserie. He resolved to book flights and return soon.

It was in a cloud of blue cigarette smoke that he emerged from the canopy of pine trees into a clearing. The steep dome of the hill loomed over the scene as he looked around. There was no sign of the man he'd come to meet, so he took the weight from his lean frame by leaning against a fence in order to finish his smoke, staring about idly. A single white trail from a passenger jet meandered across the blue sky, while an unkindness of ravens tumbled just above the treeline.

An unkindness. A strange name for a collection of birds, but not for much he had seen in his life: far too much thought-lessness, cruelty, violence, death and pointless wickedness. They left a mark on any police officer, the size and shape of the stain dictated by the soul of the individual concerned. The blemish Burns carried around was broad, ink-black and, despite his best efforts since retirement, stubbornly ever-present.

He heard something move to his right and turned to face the noise.

'Jim, is that you?'

When there was no reply he ambled across to where the thick forest of spruce trees met the path, in the general direction of the noise he'd heard. A collared dove flapped from the curtain of evergreens, making his heart thud in his chest with surprise. He shivered, the sun now shaded behind the high green canopy.

Burns heard footsteps behind him.

'Jim, there you—' The blow caught him hard on the side of the head, stopping the words in his throat as he swivelled round. He managed to catch his assailant's lip, making him grunt.

But the man was too strong for him. As Ian Burns's strength ebbed away, high above the trees, the ravens cawed at yet more unkindness in the world.

Kinloch, the present

Speirs stared down at the graves as the slow process of removing the remains for forensic investigation got under way. Duncan Chisholm was fussing over a large plastic box – like an oversized version of the Tupperware affair his wife used to put his lunchtime sandwiches in, Speirs thought.

'Calm down, man. You'll have a bloody heart attack,' he said. 'Trust me, this bloody job's no' worth it.'

'But you're not in the job now, Bobby,' replied Chisholm, a strand of his white hair flopping over his sweaty brow as he toiled away in the white forensic suit.

'Oh aye, here we go. I'm here, aren't I? I'm investigating this, so relax. I'll deal with young Jimmy, too.'

'Young Jimmy? You're behind the times, Bobby. Big lump of a man now.'

'Does he still walk about quoting from Force Standing Orders? Prick.'

'All I'm saying is watch how you go. Remember, he's not forgotten what happened the last time – not by a long, long chalk, I'd say.'

'Someone told me he was a fat bastard now. That bonnie wife o' his fucked off. Man, she was a cracker. Went over the jumps with half of Paisley CID, I heard, the tart.'

'Would you shut up!' said Chisholm, plodding towards him, his voice urgent. 'This is his little kingdom down here. If I were you, I'd keep him onside. He's no wet-behind-the-ears laddie now.'

'Huh! Nah, he's a fat late-forty-something that can't keep his wife satisfied. Remember, I'm not part of the command structure down here, or anywhere else. I answer tae ACC Cunningham, end of. I don't care how big Jim Daley's boots have become.'

'Well, you'll be able to judge for yourself in a minute.' Chisholm nodded over Speirs's shoulder.

He turned. Sure enough, striding up the hill came two figures: one tall, his shirt tail hanging from the front of his dark suit trousers, the other man smaller, hair close-cropped and hands in his pockets as he sauntered towards them.

'Is that Brian bloody Scott?'

'Sure is.'

'No show without Punch.'

'Aye, literally. He's just the same – apart from not boozing any more.'

'Steady on,' said Speirs, feigning surprise. 'I don't think I can take any mair shocks.'

'I hope you won't have to,' said Chisholm.

Glasgow, 1994

On Daley's desk was a picture of the murdered woman who'd been washed ashore at Greenock. Denise Milton was young and pretty; dark hair and dark eyes above a winning smile. She stared out of the photograph, oblivious of the horror that lay in wait for her. The thoughts that always plagued him when he looked at images of murder victims flooded into his brain yet again. The many smiling faces, blissfully ignorant of their future. It always made Daley shudder.

Yet again, his job weighed down his soul. Not for the first time, he questioned his decision to become a police officer. It wasn't too late. He was still young, could easily change tack and do something else. Though what *something else* was eluded him.

He saw the little boy's features in his dead mother's face. The poor child was pathetically stubborn in the face of tragedy, railing against the loss of the touchstone of his young life with an upturned chin and a determined expression.

The awful twist of fate that had led him to see his dead mother when she washed up on a tiny stretch of sand would cause a feeding frenzy within the ranks of the press. The Midweek Murders were already a cause célèbre.

Though they couldn't be sure at this stage, the chances that this woman was the latest victim were strong – the same modus operandi. Young woman, unattached, last seen in one of the city's nightclubs on a Wednesday night. Despite the best efforts of the team of detectives dedicated to the case, they had been unable to discover anything about the other woman, the friend who'd accompanied her on her last night out. The chances of a breakthrough were little aided by the sketchy description the mother of this victim had given the police.

'She was just a friend; I'd never seen her before. Tae be honest I was watching *Coronation Street* so I wisnae paying much attention,' the older woman had sobbed.

The phone on his desk rang.

'Daley.'

'A call for you, Jim. Mrs Burns.'

Daley waited while the call was put through.

'Hello, Jim, is that you?'

'Mrs Burns, what can I do for you?'

'Oh, I'm just wondering, Ian isn't with you by any chance?'

'No,' replied Daley, puzzled by the question. In the years since his retirement, despite many invitations, Ian Burns hadn't crossed the threshold of his former place of employment. 'I'm sorry. What makes you think he would be here?'

'He said he was meeting you. That was about three hours ago. To be honest, I'd expected him back by now. I just thought perhaps something had turned up that required him to go to Glasgow with you. I mean, I know you normally meet in the potting shed.' She laughed, but Daley could hear the concern in her voice.

'I had no meeting arranged with Ian. Are you sure it wasn't someone else? I know he sometimes sees Mike Allen, his old DS.'

'No, it was definitely you he mentioned. Unless he made a mistake – us old folk do, you know.' Again, the attempt at humour was strained.

Daley felt his heart pound in his chest. He could see the note written in 'blood', threatening the life of his old mentor. 'You're sure it was me he said he was meeting?'

'Yes, most certainly it was you. He's always happy to see you, so he was quite bright about it.'

'Did he take the car?'

'Oh, gosh, yes. You know Ian – rarely walks the length of himself.'

'Okay. Well, give me a wee while with this. I'm sure there's a reasonable explanation. Possibly got side-tracked by Mike, and they're getting into a dram or two in that wee room of his. He's got some collection of whisky.'

'I've been married to a detective all these years, Jim Daley. Some things rub off, you know. You're not telling me everything. I can hear it in your voice.'

'Oh, just this case I'm working on. Difficult stuff,' he lied.

'Okay, if you say so, Jim,' she replied doubtfully.

'Leave it with me. I'll phone you as soon as I've found him.'

Daley ended the call, then immediately rushed from his desk, across the foyer and into the control room.

'Donnie,' he said to the controller sitting in the low light, a set of headphones with attached microphone on his head. 'I need you to put out a vehicle search – urgent.' From memory, he recited the registration number.

'That's vaguely familiar. Isn't that Ian Burns's car?'

'Yes, it is,' replied Daley, grim-faced.

'I'll get on to it now. I'll make it force wide and pass it on to Central Scotland. He still lives up in Stirlingshire, right?'

As Jim Daley heard the registration being broadcast to every police officer in Strathclyde and beyond, he cursed his foolishness. He shouldn't have listened to Burns. He should have alerted his superiors to the threats being made to the former DCI. He'd suspected they were not idle mischief all along. He should have listened to that voice in his head, his instinct – the things Burns himself had taught him.

The controller looked him straight in the face. 'You're white as a sheet, Jim.'

No wonder, he thought. In his heart, he felt something was very wrong.

The door to the control room opened.

'Why are we searching for Ian Burns's car?' John Donald was framed in the doorway, wearing a well-cut suit, his hair slicked back. 'Daley. Might have known you'd be at the root of this. Can't bear to be without the old boy. Aw, how touching.'

'That's not what's happening.'

'Well, what *is* happening?'

Daley sighed. 'I need to speak to you. Now.'

Daley's tone wiped the smug smile from Donald's face. 'Come with me,' he commanded.

Kinloch, the present

Brian Scott emerged from the shower room, rubbing his hair with a towel. He'd begun his run at the County Hotel and ended it back at the office, where he left a suit, shirt, tie and shoes into which he would change after his run.

He looked at his watch as he sauntered through the CID suite, nodding to the detectives hard at work there.

He chapped on the door of Daley's glass box, opening it slightly to see the big man sitting behind his desk, phone to his ear and a deadly serious look on his face. He waved his DS in. Still rubbing his hair dry, Scott took a seat opposite him just as he was ending the call.

'Yeah, sure. Okay, Bobby, I'll be up within the hour. Cheers, mate.'

As Scott looked on, he noticed the face didn't match the words. 'Don't tell me, Bobby Speirs.'

'Yup,' replied Daley. 'Telling everyone he's *directing operations*, if you please.' He shook his head in disgust. 'Nothing I can do, of course. I mean, who's in charge of these bloody cold case officers? You saw the arrogance of him earlier.'

'Buggered if I know. Mind you, that bastard never paid any attention tae orders when he needed tae. I cannae see he'll be any different now, Jimmy.'

'Do you know, that was the first time I've actually seen him face to face since . . .'

'Aye, I know, big man. I know how you feel. How can any o' us forget? I met him a few times – mind I was on secondment tae the north for a murder case? Och, must be ten years ago noo. And that retirement shindig I telt you aboot.'

'Yes, I do, funnily enough. They took you off the case we were working on in Paisley, if I remember.'

'Aye, that's right. Anyhow, I was there for nearly a month. Speirs was a DI at Baird Street then. Never looked the road I was on. You'd have sworn he didnae know who I was.' Scott looked as though he could spit.

'He got a shock when he saw me, didn't he?'

'You've no' changed that much. The hair's no' the same colour as it was, but you've still got your youthful charm, Jimmy.'

'Oh aye. By the way, you had your head down when I saw you earlier. Pounding around the esplanade. What on earth were you wearing?'

'I never saw you. I was starting tae get cramp there. And you should know – a road safety issue – you have tae wear bright clothes when you're oot running, so as folk see you.'

'See you? You were visible from space. Running about like a superannuated budgie.'

'This bloody marathon is the morrow. I don't want tae let the side doon. I'm representing Police Scotland, mind.'

'And don't worry. We'll have someone at this monumental event to get some pictures for posterity. I won't be surprised if you end up getting a promotion out of this, Bri.' Daley smiled at the look on his colleague's face.

'You know fine I'd have tae beat thon Usain Bolt tae sniff a promotion. No, I'm running for the honour o' the job, remember. I'm no' angling for a bloody promotion. Too late in the day noo.'

As Daley laughed, the phone on his desk burst into life again.

'Kinloch Hospital for you, sir,' said Sergeant Shaw.

Daley waited for the call to be put through.

'Chief Inspector, it's Adam Keiller, nursing manager here at the hospital. We talked earlier.'

'Yes, Mr Keiller, how can I help you?'

'It's Helen McNeil, one of our district nurses. I know you're aware of the problems she's been having.'

'Yes, I am. We're still investigating the case, so I'm afraid I've nothing to tell you at the moment. I know you must be concerned.'

'No, no, it's not that – though of course we're concerned,' Keiller added quickly. 'It's just, well . . .'

'I'm quite busy, Mr Keiller. Can you get to the point, please? I know this will be difficult for Nurse McNeil. But a spell working in the hospital where we can keep an eye on her until this unpleasantness is resolved is better for her, I assure you.'

'Right, now that's where we have a problem.' Keiller sounded unsure.

'What kind of problem?'

'We had a call this morning – just after Helen started her shift, in fact. One of the visitors here for the marathon tomorrow, staying in a cottage near Machrie, had a fall, apparently. Knocked themselves about a bit – damaged leg, I think. Nothing life-threatening, you understand, but needed attention and the ambulance was out on an emergency.'

'And?' Daley's expression darkened.

'Well, Helen insisted. I mean, Machrie's not far and it was broad daylight by this time. We sent her to help the patient.'

'You did what!' Daley sprang from his chair. 'I left strict instructions that Nurse McNeil was to stay in the hospital during her working day, and be escorted back to her flat when she finished. Where is she now?'

'Well, that's the thing. That was almost two hours ago, and she hasn't returned. We tried to call her on her mobile, but no reply. Also, no reply from the person who made the call for assistance in the first place. It's probably just the signal – you know how bad things are here. But we thought we'd better get you in the loop, just in case.'

'Stay where you are, Mr Keiller. I'll be at the hospital in a few minutes. I can't believe you've been so casual with the safety of one of your charges.' He slammed the phone down. 'Right, Brian. Bobby Speirs will have to wait. Come with me.'

13

Stirlingshire, 1994

As he climbed the hill under the shadow of Dumgoyne, Daley's mind scrolled through the many times he'd felt this way. Being taken out of class to be told by the headmaster that his granny had died and somebody would drive him home; the news that his best friend in primary seven had been killed in a car accident; the look in his father's eyes as they caught his for the last time before cancer took his life. It was that same empty feeling, a mixture of hopelessness and displacement that gnawed at his heart.

He had it now.

He'd heard the words only an hour ago, but they were still playing in his head.

'I'm sorry, he's gone, Jim,' said DS Bright.

'Who's gone – gone where?'

'Ian Burns. He's dead.'

As he crested the top of the hill, he turned to stare back down at the lay-by where Ian Burns's Volvo estate was parked, now flanked by two police vehicles, lights flashing.

He swallowed hard as he set foot on the path which swung into the trees and was met by the familiar sight of a group of police officers, some uniformed, the others forensic detectives. Two men in white paper overalls were erecting a blue police incident tent within the bounds of the yellow *Police – Do Not Cross* tape.

He'd walked into scenes like this literally hundreds of times. Although it was never pleasant, it normally lacked this heightened sense of horror and loss.

He flashed his warrant card at a young cop, who let him approach the knot of his colleagues with a grim nod.

DCI Sanderson was standing over the body, his mouth, as always, agape. Suddenly, Daley felt utter revulsion for the man. He stood beside another elderly detective Daley didn't recognise. This man was shaking his head, a pained look on his face.

Sanderson looked up. 'Daley, come here!'

The young detective did as he was bid, weaving his way through the quiet ranks of his colleagues until he was standing beside the two senior men.

At first, he couldn't bear to look down at the figure lying in the storm ditch. But a glance was enough for him to recognise the worn beige raincoat, the scarf half covering the face of the spare, motionless frame. This was the lifeless body of the man who had been not only his boss and mentor, but also his friend.

Ian Burns was dead.

'This is where ignoring the rules gets you, Daley,' said Sanderson, spitting out the words. 'I've spoken to DI Donald. Your actions – or lack of them – are the cause of this. DCI Burns was respected by us all – a cop to his bootstraps. This is his reward for all those years of toil, fighting against the shite we face every day. And it's your fault.'

Daley couldn't speak. He opened his mouth but the words would not come.

'Say something!' roared Sanderson.

'I . . . I was keeping Ian's confidence. He didn't want anyone to know . . .'

'He'd received a written threat. Your friend in Forensics was smart enough to come forward with that little nugget as soon as he heard. The one we know of, of course. What else don't we know that you've kept secret?' The question was rhetorical – for now. 'You, of course, didn't see fit to go through the proper channels. No, all you thought about was licking his arse the way you did when he was in my job. You should have come to me immediately, you prick!' Flecks of spittle showered from Sanderson's mouth as he spoke. 'You might as well have stuck the fucking knife in his throat yourself!'

Daley cracked. He flung himself bodily at the DCI, fists clenched. He caught Sanderson a blow on the shoulder before the phalanx of other officers managed to subdue him.

'Well, if it wasn't obvious already, that's your job fucked now, son,' said Sanderson, rubbing his shoulder where Daley had connected and trying to regain his composure.

'Now, that's enough!' shouted a man beside Sanderson. 'Daley, pull yourself together, man. Let him go,' he continued, gesturing to the officers restraining the young detective. 'I'm Superintendent Ronald Alford, DC Daley. I might be a mere Central Scotland Police officer, but this is my patch and I'm the ranking officer here. What you do in Glasgow is up to you, but I won't have this behaviour here. Got it?' He looked from Daley to Sanderson. 'I only met DCI Burns on a few occasions during his career, but I knew him sufficiently well to know that he was a thoroughgoing professional. Please afford him the courtesy of handling this – this tragedy – in a manner of which he would approve. I'm sure he would wish nothing else.

I know there are many questions to be asked and answered, but at the moment we're standing over a fallen colleague. Show some respect!'

A forensic officer spoke quietly to Alford.

'Right, gentlemen. Let's us away and leave these men to get on with their jobs. Sergeant Cowan, I want the hill sealed off at all its access points, with uniformed officers at intervals around the locus here. See to it.'

As the small group of detectives made their way down the hill Alford continued to speak.

'I will want a statement from you, DC Daley. All that DCI Burns told you, as well as the whereabouts of any evidence he may have given you. I intend to play this absolutely down the line, DCI Sanderson. I'm sure you understand. We also have the vexed question of who will break the news to his wife. I should be the one, but from what I can gather you're a family friend, Daley. I want you to come with me.'

'Then you make sure you hand Daley back to me,' said Sanderson, the bile in his voice obvious.

'*Hand him back* sounds rather over the top, DCI Sanderson. But of course, when we've been to see Mrs Burns, and DC Daley has given me his statement, he will be free to return to Glasgow.'

'Aye, just make sure you do return to Glasgow – straight back to Stewart Street, Daley,' said Sanderson. 'We'll not go through the formalities here, but consider yourself under arrest.'

Kinloch, the present

After an acrimonious meeting with Keiller at Kinloch Hospital, Daley, with Scott at his side, was driving the short distance to Machrie. He dropped the speed of his SUV as he drove through the village, following the directions he'd been given by Keiller's assistant.

The little cottage nestled in the lee of a small hill, about half a mile out of the village along a single-track road. Three expensive-looking mountain bikes were propped up against the wall: two adult cycles and a tiny child's bike.

Daley pulled the car to a halt and he and Scott made their way up the shingle path, past several fish boxes, half a dozen yellow net-floats and a lobster creel, all painted and prettified to provide a feature in the tiny front garden.

As Daley knocked on the door he could hear the tinkling laughter of a child – a toddler, he reckoned – which instantly brought a picture of his own young son to mind. Banishing the thought, he stepped back to stand beside Scott, who was idly taking in the scene as they waited for a response. Gulls soared above a blue sea bordered by rugged clumps of rocks, which gave way via rough machair to small bays of white sand dotted along the coast. A sandpiper flew low over the house, its baleful call adding to Daley's feeling of unease.

The door opened to reveal a tall young man dressed in a T-shirt and chinos, his bare toes poking from a pair of sandy flip-flops.

'Can I help you?' he asked, passing his hand across his short dark hair, a puzzled look on his face.

'I'm DCI Daley from Kinloch Police Office, and this is DS Scott,' replied Daley, showing the man his warrant card. 'I'm sorry to disturb your holiday – it's really nothing to worry about. I'm just looking for some information.'

The man shrugged. 'Yes, of course.' He looked surprised,

but he stepped back from the door, letting the detectives enter the cottage.

Sitting at a dining table, a young woman was feeding a toddler. The little girl, sitting on her knee, had food plastered across her face.

'Dan, what's this?' asked the woman, looking just as confused as her partner.

Daley got straight to the point. 'I think I'm right in saying that none of you has had the need of any medical assistance since you arrived?'

'No, not at all. The little one here has had the sniffles, but it's just the change of air. Nothing this fresh in London, I'm sad to say. This is Daisy's first holiday and she's just acclimatising.' The father smiled at his little girl. 'Can I ask what, or who, you're looking for?'

'Can I have your name, sir?' said Scott, notebook in hand.

'Sorry, how rude of me. I'm Dan Wilks, this is my wife Terri, and you've met Daisy,' he replied, smiling again at the toddler.

Scott took a note of their permanent address – in an upmarket London suburb – and let Daley continue.

'Dan, Terri, the reason we're here is because apparently a call was made from this cottage to the local hospital in Kinloch earlier today.'

'There must be some mistake. We've had no cause to call for medical assistance. In fact, I'm a doctor, so I think I'll be able to cope with most holiday emergencies.'

'Nae landline here, eh?' asked Scott.

'Sorry? You'll have to say that more slowly, I'm afraid.'

'Oh, for goodness' sake!' Terri Wilks made her first contribution to the conversation. 'No, we've not been in need of any medical help, and yes, there is a landline – it goes with the broadband, which, incidentally, is crap. There's the router over there.' She pointed to a phone sitting in its cradle on a table beside a sofa.

'I'm sorry,' said Dan, frowning at his wife. 'We both have very demanding careers. This is the first holiday we've had since Daisy was born. No offence intended, but people keep popping in out of the blue. It's a bit unsettling when you're trying to relax. I mean, this is a beautiful place, and we just want time to enjoy it.'

'Can you tell me, who has been popping in apart from us?' Daley asked.

'Oh, the owner of this place has been here no less than three times in four days, as well as a bloody cheeky archaeologist, of all things.'

'Who owns the cottage, Dr Wilks?' asked Scott.

'A local guy – he lives at the other end of the village. Galt is his name – Colin Galt.'

'I thought the owners of places like this always did their best to stay out of the way, let guests enjoy their holiday,' said Daley.

'Not in this case. He's not been coming to see us, just taking things up to the loft.'

Scott looked up. 'Cannae be very big,' he observed quietly.

'Don't get us wrong, we love the cottage, and Mr Galt is a very pleasant chap . . .'

'Bit of a sleaze, if you ask me,' said Terri, raising her brows.

'Sleaze?' asked Daley and Scott in unison.

'Come on, Terri, he's not that bad. You spend too much time with those creeps in Whitehall.'

'Wandering eyes, Mr Daley. Ask any woman. You can always spot them.'

'You work in Whitehall, Mrs Wilks?' asked Daley.

'Yes, I'm director of communications in a government department. I spend a lot of time dealing with senior police officers, as it happens. I didn't envisage doing it on holiday.' She spat out the comment, making the little girl on her knee cry. 'Come on, poppet, we'll go for a little walk – come back when things are quieter.' She glared at the police officers, picked up the child and strode from the room, muttering under her breath.

'I must apologise. My wife isn't normally as spiky as this. As I say, she has a difficult job and I think she hoped that her time here would be more . . . peaceful,' Dan said, flashing a weak smile.

'Don't worry, sir. We'll leave you to enjoy your holiday. I'm sure we can get hold of Mr Galt quite easily. I want to get to the bottom of this call to the hospital, as I'm sure you understand. Before we go, though, could you tell me about this archaeologist?'

'Nothing to tell, really. Young man – a bit older than me. Scruffy, maybe, but in my experience from uni, most of that calling are. Wanted to dig up the front garden there and then. He was very insistent – rude, as I said. I told him that he would have to go and see Mr Galt, and that we didn't fancy being part of an archaeological dig on our holiday. Terri left him with rather a flea in his ear, I'm afraid.'

'You don't say,' said Scott under his breath.

'Did you get his name?' asked Daley quickly.

'No, I didn't get the chance to ask. Sorry.'

'Okay. We'll leave you to the rest of your holiday. I hope you'll be left in peace for what remains of it.'

'I'm running in the race tomorrow. Then, I'm sad to say, we're off back to London the day after.'

'Me tae. I'm running as well,' said Scott, the second half of his sentence more slow and deliberate in case Wilks didn't understand him.

'Good effort! Especially for a man of your age.'

'Eh?' exclaimed Scott. 'I'm in the prime of life, mate. I widnae go back tae my thirties even if I could.'

Daley interrupted before Scott managed to get the bit between his teeth and started wasting valuable time regaling them with the science of running, a subject in which Daley had absolutely no interest. 'I'm sure this archaeologist will have contacted Mr Galt. I'll ask him what he was after.'

'Look, here's Colin's card,' said Wilks, handing Daley a small rectangle of cardboard. 'It has his mobile, home and work numbers, as well as his email address. He left it with us when we arrived. Sorry I can't be of more help.'

Daley wished him well for the run and the rest of his holiday, and soon he and Scott were back in the SUV.

'I wonder who this bloody archaeologist is, Bri?'

'Boris, I shouldnae wonder.'

'Who?'

'Och, I cannae remember his name. Bernie something or other – he was in the pub last night when I was wae Dunky Chisholm and thon Francombe lassie.'

'Why are you so sure it was him?'

'He's based here in Machrie. Looking for some kind o' Viking longship, or something. Here, Jimmy, we missed a trick there. We should've been right up in that loft tae see what this Galt bloke was up tae.'

'Great idea, Brian. So, just jump into the loft without a warrant and piss off Mrs Wilks more than she's pissed off already. Then, in the unlikely event we do find something untoward we've not even been looking for, we're buggered because of evidence protocols. Good plan. We have a missing nurse, remember. When we find her we can ask this Bernie what he was up to. But I'd like you to give Galt a call. I'll go back to the hospital, get as much on Helen McNeil as I can. Maybe she's surfaced.'

'You think so?'

'Maybe. Give the office a call and see if anything's been reported. We might get a fix on her mobile, or maybe her car'll be spotted. I'm sure she'll surface eventually.'

Daley put his foot down and sped along the straight road to Kinloch. She's not going to turn up, he thought to himself.

14

Sergeant Shaw took Daley aside when they arrived back at the office. As he'd expected, there had been no sign of Helen McNeil back at the hospital, nor had any contact been made, despite Keiller's calling her mobile every fifteen minutes, or as much time between calls as his guilty conscience would permit. It appeared the device was switched off, making tracing it virtually impossible.

'There's Mr Speirs to see you, sir. He's waiting in the family room,' said Shaw with a frown.

'That'll please him.'

'No, it won't. He wanted to sit in the CID suite, but as a civilian I told him that wasn't really appropriate.'

Daley grinned to himself as he strode down the corridor. Shaw was a good judge of character, and it appeared, despite the brevity of their first meeting, the wily desk sergeant had already spotted Speirs for the rotten apple he was.

Daley swung the door open to find the cold case officer fast asleep, stretched out on a couch in the family room. He watched the retired cop's large gut rise and fall as he snored softly.

'Sleeping on the job, Bobby? Some things never change,' said Daley in a voice slightly louder than required.

The older man stirred, opening his eyes, looking momentarily disoriented.

'Jimmy Daley,' he said. 'Never got the reception I was hoping for here. That bloody sergeant wouldn't let me in the CID office. I'd nothing better tae do than catch a wee bit of shut-eye. I thought you – of all people – would be keen tae find out what's lying up on that hill.'

'Me of all people – what do you mean, Bobby?'

'Ach, come on, son. Every bastard Glasgow cop o'er the age of thirty-five knows about you and the Grab a Granny case. I reckon they buggers at the training college teach it – you know, how not to conduct yourself as a police officer.' He sneered at Daley, swinging his legs back on to the floor and straightening his tie.

'For a start, Mr Speirs, I'm not "son". If these are the remains of the missing three women from the Midweek Murders case, then I'm pleased to say any involvement you have will be over.'

'How so?'

'You're a cold case civilian investigator, remember?'

'Oh aye.'

'And once it ceases to be cold and becomes a fully fledged investigation, your services will no longer be required.'

Speirs shook his head and smiled. 'I had a wee word wae Assistant Chief Constable Cunningham before I came doon. He's right intae these cold case units. "Why discard experienced detectives just because they've had tae give up the badge?" says he. Aye, that's what he thinks. "Just you see this tae its conclusion, Bobby – no matter where it leads you." Good bloke, as far as I'm concerned.' Though his smile was benign, there was something behind his grey eyes of another complexion entirely.

'Well, we'll see what happens.'

'Aye, that you will, Jimmy. The remains have just been flown tae Glasgow. We should know within the next few hours.'

'I know that, I read it online. Some bastard's leaking like a burst drain.'

'Really? Bad form, Jimmy. You'll no be happy aboot that. I didn't have you down as someone who'd paddle a leaky boat, so tae speak.'

'An old speciality of yours, if I remember. Now, what was it you used to say? "The papers pay my holidays every year. You should try it."'

Speirs laughed. 'That was then, this is now, Jimmy. Mind I've got a pension as well as a nice lump sum under my belt these days. All the kids have flown the nest – just me and the wife. No need tae supplement my income – unless you count this wee number, that is.'

'I'm sure.'

'Dae you know who put me ontae this? Wasn't sure about it myself, but the man was very persuasive – as you know.'

'John Donald.'

'Aye, the very chap. Sadly missed, sadly missed, indeed. I for one didn't believe half the shite they said about him. Brave, tae; got between you and a bullet, did he no'?'

'Something like that.'

'Anyhow, just calling it as I see it.' Speirs got to his feet and coughed throatily. 'Nothing much tae be done until they bones get analysed. If you don't mind, though, I'd like access tae a desk and a computer.' He winked. 'Just want tae reacquaint myself wae the case. Lot on my plate in this game. Lots o' cold cases.'

'Speak to Sergeant Shaw at the bar office. He'll find you a cubbyhole somewhere.'

'We'll see, son. I'm no' too keen on cubbyholes. I remember the one I put you in – mind?'

Daley walked up to the rotund man. 'Difference is, Bobby, these days, I call the shots.' He turned on his heel. 'We'll hold off until we hear from SOCO.'

'Aye, whatever you say, *son.*'

Daley hesitated in the doorway. He could feel his right eye twitching and his heart rate rise. 'First time I've ever heard you say anything that was remotely correct, Bobby. I'm glad you've picked things up so quickly.'

Before Speirs could answer, Daley stepped out of the room, slamming the door in his wake.

The first pain she felt was in her knees. It was an ache, but sharper. It reminded her of the times she'd fallen off her bike as a child, the agony of a bare knee impacting with the hard pavement, followed by the scrape of skin being ripped off by an unforgiving surface. Tentatively, she reached out with her hand; sure enough, she could feel a gash and a dampness she assumed was blood. She sniffed at it – yes, the unmistakable metallic odour. Both knees were the same. Yet she had no memory of how these minor injuries had occurred

It was dark, though there seemed to be a grey luminescence, enabling her to just about see her hand in front of her face, if not the walls of the room she was in. She began to panic, but forced herself to remain calm by taking deep, slow breaths.

She pulled herself up painfully from the cold rough ground. Come to think of it, she was really cold. Only when she had processed this thought did she begin to shiver.

Holding her arm out in front of her, her hand held up flat, she walked forward with tiny steps until her outstretched palm met something hard – the wall, she presumed. She reached up tentatively, pushing both hands as high as she could up the roughly hewn surface – on tiptoes now. Slowly, she moved along, hoping to locate something on the face of the structure – but something was wrong. Maybe she was losing her mind, perhaps it was the darkness, but this wall seemed to curve.

She breathed deeply again, desperately trying to collect her thoughts. A door, yes, where there was a wall there had to be a door!

Again she shuffled, more purposefully now, following the curve of the wall, repeatedly running her hand up and down its cold, damp surface. Somehow, there was a sense of time-lessness about this place. It was as though she had slipped into a dark chasm where nothing made sense.

She kept moving slowly sideways. The space seemed never-ending. Either it was huge and she just hadn't come across the door yet, or there wasn't one. But surely that was impossible!

She looked up. The source of the dim illumination was two tiny pinpricks of light. Glowing dimly back, just enough for the room not to be completely dark, but not enough to see anything clearly. There was no way of gauging how far above her it was. She stood on her tiptoes, reaching high above her head, desperately trying to lay hands on the source of this meagre light.

She gave up, her deep breaths echoing from the cold stone walls.

Another idea popped into her mind. In an attempt to estimate the rough size of the room, she would place her back against the curved wall then walk straight ahead. Without the aid of sight, the biting cold, darkness and echo made the space appear huge. In her mind, she already imagined she was at the bottom of a large tower. Find a door and she would be free – at the very least, if it was locked, she could bang and shout for help with some hope of rescue. Even the sound of a human voice would be of some comfort, malevolent or not.

She cursed her muddled thoughts. Her mind was like cotton wool. The more she tried to think straight, the more her attention would drift to something else: her home; work; colleagues; old loves, childhood; hopes; fears. This all made her angry, eventually forcing her to cry out in frustration, a desperate wail that echoed so loudly about her in the darkness that she cowered into herself.

She pulled herself up, placed her back flat against the wall, and took a deep breath, feeling her hand shake as she held it out as a guide.

She walked slowly, barely lifting her feet, rather shuffling in case she fell over something on the uneven ground. Then it dawned on her: what if the floor fell away? What if she was near a vertiginous drop, a plummet into oblivion? She had already counted three steps – she now resolved to push her front foot out, sliding it as best she could upon the ground, inch by inch, just to make sure that her next stride didn't see her topple into an abyss.

She counted again: three, four, five, six, seven, eight . . . When her hand collided with the unyielding wall she was momentarily shocked. That she had walked in a straight line she was almost certain. But how could this be a tiny place? Again, through the cotton wool confusion of her thoughts, she tried to process the discovery.

She turned round and shuffled back the way she had come – or hoped she was doing so. Sure enough, in just over ten paces she was back against the wall.

Things were beginning to make terrifying sense. She stopped for a moment, thinking. She slid off the sturdy black shoe was wearing, left it on a point near the wall, and began to shuffle again, this time using the cold stone as her curving guide. She tried desperately to keep her stride length even, so that by each step she was measuring a similar distance.

In the process of taking her sixteenth shuffle, her front foot collided with something light, pushing it along the ground with a tiny scraping noise. She knelt down and picked it up – her left shoe.

This was no vaulted cathedral, no infinite space – barely any space at all, in fact. There was no door she could hammer on to call for assistance – she was trapped in some hellish prison with no way out.

Helen McNeil screamed. The sound of her desperation echoing around the cold, hard walls was the only response.

15

Stirlingshire, 1994

Daley looked at Amanda Burns as she sat in the neat living room of the house she'd shared with her husband for so long. Her eyes were red with tears, but the crying had stopped now. In fact, Daley was impressed by her self-possession given that she had just been informed about the murder of her soulmate.

'Of course, Amanda, it goes without saying that should you need anything all you have to do is call my office – day or night,' said Superintendent Alford. 'I've stationed two men outside the house, and there they'll stay until we get to the bottom of what happened to Ian. And we will find out who did this, I promise.'

'Thank you, Ronald. It's so strange. I lived with the fear that something like this would happen all the time Ian was in the police. Stupidly, when he retired, I felt as though a world of care had been lifted from my shoulders. How naïve I was.' She shook her head.

'Remember, we have no idea why this happened to Ian. Of course, it could be something to do with his past. Equally, he could just be the victim of some random, sick individual. Goodness knows, there's more than enough of them about,

I can tell you.' Alford paused, turning his gaze towards Daley. 'We should go – get you back to Glasgow, DC Daley.'

Amanda Burns looked up suddenly, focusing on Daley as though this was the first time she'd realised he was there. 'Jim, can I have a word with you before you go? In private, if possible – would that be in order, Ronald?'

Alford cleared his throat. 'As I've said, anything you want. Of course you can have a chat with young Daley here. I know he's a family friend as well as a former colleague. I'll wait for you in the car, DC Daley.'

He left the room, leaving the young DC feeling momentarily confused. In the main, it had been Alford who had imparted the bad news. Daley had just sat holding Amanda Burns's hand, trying his best to be of comfort to her. He had admired the professional, no-nonsense way the Central Scotland superintendent had handled the situation, almost as much as he admired the way she was bearing up. Now he was left alone with the newly widowed woman he felt awkward, despite having known her for so many years.

Amanda Burns cocked her head as the front door closed, and looked up at him. 'Jim, I have something to give to you. I know what Ian was doing now; he must have known he was in danger.' She shook her head and sighed deeply. 'Why didn't I pick up on any of this before?'

Daley processed the information with surprise. 'What did he give you?' he blurted out, sounding impatient, which made him angry with himself.

'He was very fond of you, Jim, as you well know. Always said you had the brain of a proper detective, and the heart,' she replied, stressing the last three words. 'Ian always maintained that one without the other was worthless. I know he expected big things from you – in your career, I mean.' She stood up and walked across the room to a long sideboard made of dark wood polished to a shine. She opened the drawer and searched through some papers. 'Here it is,' she said, brandishing an envelope. She walked over to Daley and handed it to him. 'He gave me this about three months ago. Made the excuse that it was best for me to pass it on if anything should happen to him. Made a joke about cigarettes and heart attacks. I just thought it was some parting words of advice that would moulder away in the drawer for years – until you were retired yourself,' she continued, smiling at the thought. 'Now I fear that he had some notion of what was going to happen to him. Do you think that's possible, Jim?'

Daley felt guilt gnawing at his heart. Of course Ian Burns had been afraid something terrible might happen; perhaps he was more frightened than he'd made out when he revealed the receipt of the threatening notes. Though Daley wanted to tell her everything, he knew it would be too much for her. 'Who knows,' he said lamely, again at odds with himself. If this letter was anything other than some personal advice, or best wishes, he'd have no choice other than to turn it over to the investigation into Ian Burns's death. 'Thank you, Amanda,' he said at last, his eyes filling with tears. 'I'm sorry. I don't know what to say.'

'One thing he did stress to me was that I should give this to you when you were on your own – just the two of us. He didn't want colleagues, or even Liz come to that, to know about it. That's why I asked Ronald to leave us just now.'

That made sense, he thought, as he held the envelope between the thumb and forefinger of his left hand. 'I think I'll open it later. I have to get back to Glasgow and start working on finding who did this' – he looked at the floor – 'who did this terrible thing.'

Amanda Burns put her hand on his shoulder, smiling up into his face. Despite the shock of the murder of her husband, she was trying to comfort the younger man, who now had tears streaming down his cheeks. 'I'm not sure it's my business to know what's in it, Jim. Better that you read whatever it contains when you're on your own. Now, you should get back to work.'

Daley hugged the widow of the man he'd admired so much, said his goodbyes and was walking from the room when she stopped him.

'Please remember one thing Ian always said, Jim.'

'What was that?'

'His mantra, I suppose – daft, really. Fight the darkness – always fight the darkness. You must have heard it many times, I suppose.'

He couldn't speak, so just walked away, closing the heavy oak front door gently behind him before taking the steps down to the garden path. As he walked to where Superintendent Alford had parked his car, he looked down at the letter Amanda Burns had given him.

In the familiar spidery hand, written in blue fountain pen ink it read simply: *Jim Daley.*

Daley tucked the letter into the inside pocket of his jacket and got in the car, ready to be driven to Glasgow – to face the music.

Kinloch, the present

Chief Superintendent Carrie Symington looked different. Instead of the uniform he was used to, liberally adorned with braid, she was wearing a smart trouser suit, her dark hair loose over her shoulders.

Daley watched her as she studied the files on her desk, familiarising herself with the Midweek Murders case.

After almost half an hour of silence, she looked up and sighed, ran her hand through her hair. 'There's no doubt now. The dental records of two sets of remains match those of missing women from ninety-four – the last supposed victims. Though we don't have confirmation yet, it's a bit of a stretch to suppose the third is unconnected. You worked on this case, I see.' She looked at Daley levelly.

'Yes, I did. First in divisional CID, then the Serious Crime Squad.'

'But not all plain sailing, from what I've gleaned elsewhere.'

'No, not plain sailing, I think it's fair to say that, ma'am.'

'Care to elaborate?'

'Not really. If it's an order, I'll comply. If not . . .'

She stood, walking across what had been the sub-divisional commander's office, once reserved for John Donald, now hers, since Daley preferred to base himself in the glass box in the CID suite. 'I'm not interested in what happened then. I just want your word that whatever problems you encountered at the time won't colour your judgement this time round.'

'Will it make a difference what I do? I mean, Bobby Speirs tells me he's had the nod to head up the case regardless of what the conclusions of SOCO may be. I must confess that I'm astonished we're leaving the investigation of a high-profile case of long standing such as this to a man who is no longer a police officer, and in my opinion should never have been one in the first place.'

'That's not strictly true, Jim.'

'No?'

'No. I had a meeting with the ACC earlier today. He wants this to be a joint effort. You, naturally, will take charge of the police side of things – you know, try to discover why and how these three victims ended up on a hillside near Kinloch. Mr Speirs will pull it all together. He was second in command of the inquiry the last time round, and the bosses are keen that we make the most of senior officers in retirement. An untapped resource; think of all that experience going to waste the minute they hang up their warrant cards. It will make us more efficient, while at the same time giving men about to end their careers as police officers proper a goal to aim at if they want. A better prospect than becoming a store detective or private investigator. I would have thought you'd welcome such a development.'

He sniffed. 'For me, the sentence containing the words "Speirs" and "welcome" doesn't exist, unless it also contains the word "dismissal". The other downside is that instead of recruiting new, young, enthusiastic police officers we'll have the same old dross living on for ever.' But as he spoke the words, he wondered how different things would have been if Ian Burns had had the chance to impart his experience as a cold case officer, rather than wasting away in his potting shed.

'Matter of opinion, Jim, and as you know, our opinion doesn't matter.' She smiled. 'It's not as though you don't have enough to do. You have this missing nurse, and it's the marathon tomorrow. As sub-divisional commander you'll be head and ears into that. Quite a spectacle, so I hear.'

Daley didn't take the bait, just shook his head. 'I've got half of everyone I have on finding Helen McNeil, the rest on the bodies.'

'You know a case like this will take on a life of its own. Once the press get a whiff that these are actually the missing victims from the nineties, the landscape may change. Meanwhile – Speirs aside – what's your plan?'

'Well, the first thing we have to do is try to find the nurse – she's my priority. Second, find out how the remains got here – and why. Let's be honest, Kinloch isn't the automatic choice of burial sites if you're operating in Glasgow somewhere. I have men out trying to ascertain who regularly travelled up and down at that time. If we can get to the bottom of that, we'll be much nearer solving the whole thing. It's hard going, though – in terms of numbers, I mean.'

'Don't worry, I'm sending extra bodies your way. Just give me a few hours to get it fixed.' She thought for a moment. 'I'm worried about Helen McNeil, Jim. These texts and calls. Do we have some bloody stalker – or worse?'

'How worse? It's no coincidence that she's gone missing after the messages. I'm furious that her boss at the hospital let her go. Absolutely against my instructions, I can assure you.'

'Maybe she shouldn't have been at work – given the circumstances, I mean.'

'She was determined that whoever was doing this to her, she wasn't going to let it get to her, or change her life. I admired her, in a way.' He rubbed his temple. 'I must admit, I wish I'd been more forceful with her now – but we all know what *wish* did. I've got two detectives going through everything we can find on her. SOCO are searching through her flat for anything that might give us a clue. I have some leads to look at, too. But in the main, we have to let Speirs do what he does at the moment with the Midweek Murders case – until everything's firmed up, I mean.'

'I understand, Jim. Leave this all with me. I'll liaise with Speirs, get things moving on that front. You, quite rightly, prioritise Helen McNeil.' She looked at her desk for a moment, drumming her fingers. 'Is it just me, or is it a bit strange that these things are happening concurrently?'

'You mean McNeil and the bodies?'

'Yes.'

'I don't know what possible connection there could be, but, well, we'll look at everything, obviously.'

'Just a thought,' she added absently.

16

Daley left his boss to organise extra manpower, troubled by the train of thought Symington had sparked in his mind. Was it really a coincidence that the remains had been uncovered just when the district nurse began getting messages from her dead father? In his line of work, coincidences happened all the time; some were connected, some were not. However, they always raised his hackles.

He went in search of Brian Scott.

As he had expected, the redoubtable DS was in the small canteen, eating a large bowl of pasta washed down by a glass of milk.

'Should you be eating that? You've got to pound the pavements tomorrow, remember.'

'Oh aye, this is what you need tae get you up tae scratch, Jimmy. All they top athletes fuel up on this kind o' stuff before a big race,' he said, before taking another forkful.

Quietly, Daley had been impressed by the change in Scott since he'd given up booze. He looked trim – not that he'd ever carried much extra weight – and sharper, more alive. It had been a clever idea to combine his abstinence with regular physical exercise. As Scott said himself, this had a lot to do with filling the time that used to be devoted to drinking. Daley had wondered if his friend would keep it up for more than a few weeks, but here he was, sober and fit, seemingly as addicted to healthy living as he had been to alcohol. Daley had seen it before; reformed drug users throwing themselves into good works, becoming evangelists for health, spirituality, charity, sport – all manner of things.

As he noticed the changes in Scott, he felt even more disgusted by his own failings. Since he'd split with Liz and Mary had died he was certainly drinking much more than was good for him, as well as eating unhealthily and getting no exercise. His meals consisted of sandwiches on the run, takeaway meals, or microwaved fare that all tasted much the same. He could barely remember the last time he'd sat down to a home cooked meal – apart from the excellent breakfast Hamish had made for him, that was.

'They've sent a special kit down for you to wear,' he told Scott.

'What?'

'You know, running vest and shorts, all emblazoned with the new jaggy thistle.'

'The Polis Scotland logo?'

'Yes, that's the one. You're to be the feature of the next in-house magazine. The perfect example to new recruits: a detective in his fifties, making sure he stays fit and healthy in order to be able to carry out his duties to optimum efficiency. We're all very proud.'

'Bollocks. They should have come tae see me a few months ago, when I was howling at the moon and seeing the walls move. Fuck me, I'll be like a walking recruitment board.'

'Who'd have thought it, the new force poster boy!'

'They should use you, tae – me and you – before and after.'

'Touché, Brian.'

'I knew fine you was going tae say that, Jimmy. I don't know how many times you've come oot wae it o'er the years and I've still no' got a clue what it means.'

'Come on, Mo Farah, we need to go and have a wee chat with this Colin Galt. Then we want to start collating what the lads are getting door-to-door.'

'Mo Farah? I think I'm mair a Steve Ovett kind o' guy.'

The pair left the office and headed out into the warm afternoon. Men in council boiler suits were busy hanging bunting across Main Street, while the little roundabout at the bottom of the road beside the grand sandstone hotel on the seafront was a blaze of floral colour: red, purple, yellow and white flowers all caught the eye. Just beyond, along the esplanade, flags of various colours and designs flapped lazily in the sea breeze while a flock of seagulls descended on a couple of holiday-makers who had made the mistake of eating fish and chips beside their lochside patch. Yellow traffic cones were arranged on both sides of the road, marking the route of the marathon the next day.

Some shopkeepers were busy erecting pop-up stalls, ready to serve pizzas, burgers, drinks, fancy goods, hats, flags, toys, balloons, and anything else of which the fine entrepreneurs of Kinloch could conceive. Apart from local spectators, a large crowd of tourists was expected for what had become an annual event: a homecoming, as well as an opportunity for tourists to sample the allure of this west coast town for themselves.

'Right bonnie, Jimmy, eh?'

'Yup, they do a good job,' replied Daley as he swung the car left on to what was known locally as the back road.

They drove past the town's swimming pool and leisure centre until they came to a yard where sat three lorries and some plant equipment. An old cattle float, stripped of its awning, was being painted by a couple of workmen, no doubt for the pageant that was due to precede the race the next day.

'Is Mr Galt aboot?' enquired Scott.

'Doon there in the offices,' replied a man brandishing a paint brush. 'He's in there noo – there's his car.'

Daley and Scott walked towards a one-storey office block at the very end of the yard, skirting past the brown puddles slicked with rainbow films of oil from the vehicles that were kept there. In front of the building sat a few parked cars and an orange van bearing the company logo. Scott shaded his eyes as he peered through the windows of a large Mercedes.

'Very nice,' he said, nodding his head in approval. 'Ever think you're in the wrong job, Jimmy?'

'Every day, Brian.'

Daley pressed a buzzer on the door entry system, and after establishing their identities and that they wanted to speak to Colin Galt, gained admittance and walked into a small reception area.

Behind a curved workstation sat a young man in a cheap-looking two-piece suit. His tie was loose, the collar crumpled and like the rest of the shirt he was wearing badly in need of the attentions of an iron.

'Mr Galt doesnae normally see folk unless they've got an appointment. Can I ask whoot it is yous are wanting?'

'Just you tell him we're here, son, and that we want tae talk tae him tout suite – got it?' said Scott impatiently.

Flustered, the young receptionist made the call. 'Mr Galt, that's the polis here. They want tae talk tae you right noo.'

He hesitated, listening to the reply. 'Something aboot sweets, I think.'

Though the detectives couldn't hear the other end of the conversation, the young man's face reddened sufficiently to assume he'd been in receipt of a flea in the ear.

'Jeest go through – along that corridor, the door facing yous at the end.' He went back to his work, muttering under his breath.

Galt was already standing in the doorway of his office when Daley and Scott appeared. 'Gentlemen, sorry about the lad – my sister's boy, I'm unhappy to say. You know how it is with family – you can't pick and choose,' he said ruefully.

He showed the policemen into his plush office. A huge picture window framed the yard, ensuring that, as boss, Galt had a good view of what his employees were getting up to.

'Now, how can I help you?' he asked, biting his lip.

'To cut a long story short, Mr Galt, we had reason to visit a property you own. The holiday cottage just outside Machrie.'

'That old place. It used to belong to my granny. We didn't have the heart to sell it when she died, so now it pays its own way. More bloody trouble than it's worth, mind you.' He wiped a bead of sweat from his brow.

'Still, we discovered that you make regular visits to the place, even when there are visitors in situ,' said Daley.

'They weren't very chuffed, neither,' added Scott, for good measure.

'N-no, I, I dare say.' Galt stumbled over his words. 'In fact, there's nothing sinister about it – the loft, I mean,' he continued with a nervous laugh. 'Fact is, the boiler there is a bit temperamental. Always mean to get the bloody thing replaced, but I never get the damned time. That sister of mine is worse than useless, never lifts a hand, but likes half of the money at the end of the year. I'm sure you know how it is.' The words were rushed.

'Did I say there was anything sinister, or mention a loft?' asked Daley, letting the question hang in the air as Galt struggled to get out a coherent sentence. 'So, your only reason for being there was to check the boiler?'

'Yes. Didn't want my guests getting showered with water. The last bloody thing I need is a compensation claim, I assure you.'

'In that case, what were you taking up tae this loft?' asked Scott.

'Sorry?'

'We were told you were leaving items up there, or perhaps removing them,' said Daley, making Galt look between the two officers nervously.

'Nothing unusual about that. I merely store some of my things there.' More beads of perspiration were now obvious on Galt's brow. 'It is my property, after all. I have every right to visit whenever I see fit. If the guests look carefully at the small print they'll see that clearly mentioned in the holiday rental agreement.'

'If you don't mind, we'd like to take a look in the loft, Mr Galt,' said Daley.

'Sorry, but what on earth for? Since when has storing items in the loft space of your own property been a crime? This is outrageous – an invasion of privacy. I do have a lawyer, you know – a good one, too.'

'Put simply, your property is connected to a missing persons inquiry. Of course, you are at liberty to call your lawyer at any time. However, at present, I'm just asking you if you'll let us see what is in the loft of the property at Machrie. If you refuse, then I will leave DS Scott here while I request a search warrant. Trust me, because of the connection to the missing persons case we're investigating, I'll be issued with one immediately.' Daley smiled.

'In other words, get your coat on an' come wae us tae Machrie,' said Scott. 'Either way, we'll be up in that loft whether you like it or not.'

'Very well, but I'm calling my lawyer just the same.'

'Here,' said Scott, fishing his mobile from his jacket pocket and offering it to the businessman. 'Use this. I've got free minutes, face time, unlimited texts – all sorts. I've no' got a clue what they a' mean, but you're welcome tae them.'

Shaking his head, Galt lifted the phone on his desk, dialled a number quickly and after a few moments spent drumming his fingers on his desk, spoke. 'Chris, it's Colin Galt. Meet me at the cottage in Machrie.' Then, after a pause, 'Now – just do it, man!'

Helen McNeil shivered as she lay curled up on the cold, hard floor of what had become her prison.

At first, not trusting the results of her investigation into the size and shape of the place, she had gone through the whole routine again, a quest that resulted in the same conclusion. She was stuck in some stone tube with no doors or windows, only pale, barely visible slits of light an unknowable distance above her head.

She sobbed quietly to herself, desperately trying to piece together the events that had placed her here. She thought of the text and the phone call, both apparently from her dead father. She could barely think of anything else, however hard she tried to focus her mind, to think, to try to find some way out of her predicament.

She'd driven away from Kinloch Hospital, enjoying the feeling of being free from its bonds, back out on the road. The police had recommended that she work within the safer confines of the building until light had been shone upon those sick messages, but she'd opted to be a district nurse in order to be out and about in the community, not stuck within the antiseptic, unhealthy, stressful confines of the hospital.

How ironic that her need for freedom has led directly to the dark confines of her prison.

She'd been driving along the long straight road to Machrie when she'd spotted something in the ditch at the side of the road. Too big to be a dog or a deer, and the colour was wrong. This was a person, and whether he was simply drunk – which was not unusual – or unfortunately injured in some way, it was her duty to help. She stopped the car.

Then everything happened quickly.

She bent over the figure and began to speak, trying to elicit a response from the stricken individual. The question was left unfinished, as, after a blinding pain that literally cast a red flash across her vision, she blacked out. Now, here she was, still in darkness.

Her mind was a fog. The instinct to escape, to be free of this place had been replaced by a kind of torpor – an exhaustion of hope and will now that it was obvious that there was no escape.

As she struggled to keep her eyes open, she could taste bitterness in her mouth, and despite the slough of despair into which she had fallen she reasoned that she had been drugged in some way. No doubt that was why she could recall nothing about being cast into this living tomb.

Yes, she thought, it's a tomb. I'm dead and this is my grave – that's why I can't get out, why there's no door. I'm just not dead yet.

Horribly galvanised by the thought, she struggled to her feet, using the curved wall as a support, and screamed, a high-pitched wail like that of a trapped creature. The noise echoed around her, but nothing happened.

She slumped to the ground again, her heart thumping in her chest. She couldn't be dead, she reasoned. Death has no heartbeat.

She screamed again, this time less desperately. This was the whimper of lost hope, which quickly turned into convulsive sobs.

As she opened her eyes to set tears free, she was conscious of a change. She could see the pale shade of her leg and the flash of reflected light on her gold bracelet.

Slowly, her surroundings brightened. There was an accompanying scrape, iron on stone, she thought – a sliding noise.

Quickly, she craned her neck upwards. The pale slits of light were now replaced by a glowing orb, shining brightly above her head. To Helen McNeil, now used to the dark, it seemed like a summer sun – so much so, she had to shade her eyes from its incandescence.

Then, there was the voice.

17

Brian Scott poked his head above the lip of the loft. He was on a rickety stepladder, feeling less than secure, even at this relatively modest distance from the ground.

'Hand me up that torch, Jim,' he said, reaching as far down with his left arm as he could. This was a small house, but the ceiling was more than high enough for his liking. 'So, this is the next torture I'm being put through. Nae doubt there's a boat waiting for me oot in the bay tae finish it a' off,' he mumbled under his breath.

'I really must protest,' said Chris Hill, a leading local solicitor, standing beside his client Colin Galt. 'I know Mr Galt gave you his permission to search the loft space, but this is all really quite unnecessary. My client has his guests to think about. If nothing else, please consider their feelings.'

'Mr Galt's guests were the ones who told us about his regular visits to this loft, Mr Hill. They're quite accustomed to it, I assure you,' said Daley.

'There's a bag o' something here, Jim. It's away in a corner. Looks like a sack – hessian – I'll need tae get right in. You keep a haud o' this ladder.' Scott's feet disappeared into the roof space as he hauled himself up with a groan and a mumbled expletive.

'I can explain,' said Galt, ignoring a warning look from his brief.

'Explain what, exactly?' asked Daley.

'I can explain what's in the bag. I'm a collector – plain and simple. The items in it are my personal property. Nothing to do with any missing person, nothing to do with my guests, and most certainly nothing to do with the police!'

Daley watched as Hill whispered to his agitated client, who growled back an incoherent reply.

'Are you a fan of the Bard, Mr Galt?' asked Daley.

'What?' said Galt, a look of incredulity on his red face.

'Methinks he doth protest too much. Now, I'm no Shakespeare scholar, but I do find he had a keen eye for the frailties of the human condition.'

After much scrabbling and swearing, Scott's feet appeared back on the ladder. 'Here, grab this, will you? It's heavier than it looks.'

Daley stood on his toes and grabbed the old hessian sack from his colleague. As his sergeant descended the ladder, he opened it and peered inside. Instantly, a flash of gold caught his eye. He fished for the phone in his pocket, selected the torch app and shone it on the bag's contents.

'Well, well,' said Daley, the irony heavy in his voice. 'What do we have here?'

'I can explain,' said Galt, sudden desperation in his voice.

'I rather think you'll have to. I'm sure you won't mind accompanying us back to Kinloch Police Office. If this is your property, it will just be a formality.'

Galt looked at his solicitor, who shook his head then nodded with a sigh.

'Let me out of here!' shouted Helen McNeil, desperation plain in her voice.

'I'm sorry. That's not going to happen.' The reply was short, the voice horribly distorted, modulating in tone, timbre and pitch and echoing eerily around her.

'Why are you doing this to me?'

No reply.

'You're the evil bastard who sent those messages. I hate you – hate you for what you've done.'

Still there was no reply from the bright circle of light above her head.

She breathed deeply, trying to remain calm. She realised that she was vulnerable, but had, somehow, to make this person understand that there would be consequences. She thought of her father; his advice had never wavered. *If you're bullied, fight back!*

'The police know about you. If you harm me, they'll find you.'

'You place a lot of faith in the police. You should know better.' The voice was still horribly distorted, but slow and deliberate, no sign of emotion, or anger.

'What do you mean?' She tried to keep her voice steady, but she could feel sobs welling up in her throat.

Though she received no reply to this question, she could hear movement from above. A shadow passed across the bright light above her head. Something metallic was bouncing off the walls; an object was being lowered down towards her.

'What is this?' she called.

'Eat. Then use the bucket as you please. You will have need of it soon enough.'

A metal bucket landed on the hard floor just beyond her

reach. As she struggled to her feet to see what it held, the light disappeared with the sliding, scraping sound she'd heard only moments before. She cried out, the sudden darkness making her heart lurch in fear. 'Please, no – come back! Let me out!'

There was no reply, only the echo of her pleas. Gradually, as she stood shivering, she could again make out the pale slits of light.

Despite her fear, the cold and the apparent hopelessness of her circumstances, she felt pangs of hunger. She'd had no time for breakfast before leaving for work – she had no idea how long it had been since she'd last eaten. Come to that, she had no idea how much time had passed since her capture.

She slumped to the ground, colliding with the bucket. She reached inside and pulled two items from within. Though she couldn't see, she could feel the shape of a packet of sandwiches, triangular as though from a supermarket or garage. Now really hungry, she groped at the film lid, almost sightless, but managed to rip it clear of the cardboard container.

She stuffed the first sandwich into her mouth, beyond caring what its filling was. Ravenously she chewed on cheese, tomato and bread. The other item she had pulled from the bucket was a plastic bottle. She wound off the lid and sniffed. It smelled of strawberries. Desperately, she gulped down half the contents, intending to consume the other sandwich next.

Almost immediately, she felt her lips tingle, then a burning, constricted feeling in her throat.

Frantically, she struggled to her feet, grabbing at her neck, coughing weakly to try to clear her airways.

The pale slits of light above her head swayed as she fell painfully to the floor, wheezing.

In seconds, she lost consciousness.

Above, iron scraped on stone again as the light flooded back into the chamber, illuminating the motionless figure below.

Daley had the items from the bag set out in front of him on an evidence tray in the interview room at Kinloch Police Office. With Scott beside him, he stared wordlessly at Galt, who sat across the desk with his solicitor. He let silence fill the room, watching as Galt shifted uncomfortably in his seat, sighing and clearing his throat nervously.

'Really, Mr Daley,' said Hill. 'You brought my client here to ask him questions about the contents of that bag. Please be good enough to begin your questioning.'

Daley smiled. 'I'm sure you – like me – have been in the company of many people who been guilty of some offence or other, Mr Hill. Now, I don't expect you to reply, but does your client look like a man with a clear conscience, a man with nothing to hide?'

'This is ridiculous!' shouted Galt. 'Why am I being persecuted in this way?'

'A call was made by someone purporting to be from your holiday cottage in Machrie asking for medical assistance.'

'And? Anyone can say they're anywhere, doesn't make it true.'

'But why your cottage?'

'How the hell should I know?'

'For anyone from Kinloch the workings of the hospital, the doctors and the district nurses must be well known, wouldn't you say?'

'Meaning?'

'Meaning, because of its remote location and the small number of doctors, the community nurses play a large part in ensuring the health and wellbeing of the population.'

Galt started to speak, but Daley held up his hand. 'At the time the call was made, someone who knows how these things work would also be aware that no doctors would be on duty, therefore it was reasonable to assume that a district nurse would be called to assist. Particularly, as in this instance, when the matter in hand is not life-threatening, but still requires prompt attention.'

Galt swallowed hard, and gripped at the collar of his shirt as though he found it suddenly constricting. 'What the hell are you on about?'

'Prior to her disappearance, the missing woman in question had been receiving calls and texts of a threatening nature – indeed, it was almost as though her tormentor knew where she was and what she was doing.'

'Again, I must protest, DCI Daley. You brought my client here to ask him questions about the contents of the bag that we now have spread out before us. The whereabouts of your missing person – troubling as it is – has nothing to do with him, nor are these items suspicious,' said Hill, waving his hand at the bag's contents.

Daley looked down. Thirty or so rings, shining buttery gold under the lights of the interview room; three heavy torcs, also gold, all bearing precious stones at both ends; silver bracelets and three goblets, also of silver. A tangled variety of jewellery. Not only did they look expensive, they looked old – very old.

'Okay, Mr Hill, we'll get to the nitty-gritty, if you like. These items, Mr Galt, how did you come by them?' In the wake of Daley's talk about the missing nurse, this question came almost out of the blue.

'Well, yes, of course,' replied Galt, stumbling over his words.

'These items are mine. Family jewels – literally,' he said with a nervous laugh.

'Looks tae me as though they'd be better off in some museum,' observed Scott, making his first contribution to the conversation. 'How did your family come across stuff like this, eh?'

'Well, my grandfather was a collector. I inherited these bits and pieces. What's wrong with that?'

'Would anyone else in your family corroborate this?' Daley asked.

'Sadly they're all dead and gone. My mother died last year. I can't help you on that score.'

'But you've got a sister, right?' asked Scott.

'How did you know that?' Galt was momentarily confused.

'You telt us aboot her in your office. Do you no' remember?'

'Ah, yes, yes, of course – my sister.' He gulped again, further loosening his tie. 'Well, you know, she wouldn't remember anything about this. She's younger than me by quite some way. All of this probably went right over her head.'

'Aye, right,' said Scott. 'Half o' the British Museum up in the loft and your sister doesnae know anything aboot it. I'm no' buying that, buddy. What aboot you, sir?' He looked at Daley.

'Agreed, DS Scott.' Daley nodded sagely. 'In any case, we'll bring her in. Your wife, too – I take it she must know about this little treasure trove?'

'No – well, not really – she doesn't get involved in my business affairs. And she's on holiday, so you won't be able to contact her.' A bead of sweat meandered down Galt's nose and dripped on to his white shirt.

'As the family solicitor, you'll have a record of these items being bequeathed to your client, is that right, Mr Hill?'

It was the solicitor's turn to stumble over his words, until Galt came to his rescue.

'There was no bequest – no will. My grandfather hated writing anything down – didn't trust anyone, including lawyers. It was word of mouth, plain and simple.'

Daley leaned back from his desk, drumming his fingers on it for a few moments. 'You'll forgive me if I find this explanation rather far-fetched, Mr Galt. I'd like you to stay as our guest while we check out the provenance of the artefacts in front of us. Fortunately, we have a team of archaeologists with us in Kinloch right now. I'm sure Professor Francombe and her colleagues will be happy to assist.'

Without warning, Galt jumped out of his chair and banged his fist on the table, making some of the glittering haul clink together. 'There's no need to involve them, absolutely none. I want to make a complaint. See to it, Chris!'

'Not a problem,' said Daley. 'I'll make sure that your brief is given the appropriate forms. Now, let's end this interview . . .'

'I have a business to run. This is ridiculous!' Galt was still on his feet.

'Oh, while we're still recording, I might as well ask,' said Daley, pointing Galt back into his chair, an order which he obeyed meekly.

'What now?'

'I know you run the family business these days. But what were you doing in nineteen ninety-four?'

'What has this to do with the matter in hand, DCI Daley?' interrupted Hill. 'I really do not like the way this interview has been handled. Not at all.'

'Just answer the question,' said Scott, backing up his boss.

'I was at college, if you must know.'

'College where?'

'Paisley. I studied civil engineering at Paisley Tech. Best civil engineering course in the country. What of it?'

'Did you live in Paisley?'

'No. I lived in the West End of Glasgow in a family flat. I can give you the address if you want!'

'So you were up and down the road to Kinloch – you know, for holidays, weekends, and the like, Mr Galt?' asked Daley.

'Yes, yes, of course I was. What the hell . . .'

Ignoring Galt's protestations, Daley ended the interview and left the interview room with Scott in search of Sergeant Shaw, who would officially place Galt in custody.

'Something no' right there, Jimmy. No' right at all,' said Scott, then paused. 'Here, what gave you the idea tae ask about nineteen ninety-four?'

'Oh, just something Symington said earlier – about coincidences.'

'Don't know aboot you, but I'm no' so sure he's anything tae dae with Helen McNeil going missing.'

'No, I'm not either – well, not directly.'

'What dae you mean, big man?'

'I'm not sure, Bri. I'm just not sure. But one thing's certain, he's guilty of something.'

18

Glasgow, 1994

Daley sat with his arms folded tightly across his chest. Sitting across the desk in the interview room in the Stewart Street Police Office were DCI Sanderson and Inspector Campbell from the Complaints and Discipline branch.

He'd been sitting there for a good five minutes as Sanderson and his colleague silently went through paperwork, speaking neither to each other nor to him. Daley knew this was a tactic designed to make him feel ill at ease, but he was still irritated by it.

Eventually, Sanderson cleared his throat. 'Right, DC Daley, you find yourself in hot water – very hot water indeed.' He consulted a document on the desk in front of him. 'By your own account, information was passed to you by former DCI Burns regarding threatening letters that were being delivered to his address anonymously. Rather than follow the proper channels and report this to me, you chose to follow your nose – a very inexperienced nose at that. The result is that our old friend and colleague lies on a mortuary slab.' He looked at Daley with his mouth gaping, the reason for his nickname: the Flycatcher.

'I admit to not following procedure, but informing you would not have been the right thing to do, even if I had been willing to go against Ian's wishes.'

'DCI Burns to you!' shouted Sanderson, flecks of spittle showing white at the corners of his mouth.

'I was handed this information as a friend, not in the course of my duties. So, Ian, not DCI Burns. Who was, if I may remind you, long retired at this point.' Daley's tone was defiant. 'Had I felt it appropriate, my next course of action would have been to report the incidents to Central Scotland Police. After all, Ian lived in that force area, not in Strathclyde.'

'*Had I felt it appropriate!* You're an insufferable shit, Daley. Just because you married into money doesn't mean you can patronise me!' Sanderson was suddenly shouting at the top of his voice. 'You do as I fucking say you do, got it?'

'Now now,' said DI Campbell, raising his hand. 'This is getting us nowhere, sir. I know we're talking about the murder of one of our own, but we'll not get far if this just descends into a shouting match. DC Daley, if you could go through how you came to know about the threats to Ian Burns, step by step.'

Campbell was calm and authoritative, and despite glaring at him over the rim of his thick spectacles, Sanderson fell silent.

With as much composure as he could muster, Daley began to relate the circumstances behind his knowledge of the threatening letters.

Kinloch, the present

Brian Scott was standing beside a seven-foot-tall blue chicken, replete with crimson coxcomb, long green beak and massive yellow feet. At another time, he'd have shaken his head and cursed alcohol, but he knew this vision was very real. On his other side, an elderly woman in a blue tracksuit was going through an elaborate warm-up routine, including stretches, deep breathing and other bodily contortions the detective could never have contemplated.

He jogged on the spot self-consciously, to appear similarly motivated. Just my luck, he thought – stuck between a massive cock and Supergran.

The start of the Kinloch marathon was crowded, so much so, in fact, that the race had a staggered start. A handful of professional runners, plus amateurs boasting good personal best times, were in the most spacious group right behind the start line. Scott was in the far more crowded section of 'also-rans', populated by keen hobbyists and those doing their bit for charity.

'That's a hoora-lookin' kit you've got on there,' said the chicken, with a shake of its beak. Scott was in his newly minted Police Scotland running kit: dark blue shorts and a blue-and-white check running vest, complete with the force's angular thistle logo in the centre.

'Eh?' replied Scott in disbelief. 'You're a fuckin' chicken. Behave yoursel'!'

'Aye, you never thought you'd see a massive chookie running up an' doon Main Street, I bet.'

'Listen, son, you're certainly the biggest chookie I've ever seen. But just you drink a bottle o' whisky a night and poultry running up and doon the street will seem like an everyday occurrence, trust me.'

'He's raising hunners for charity, aren't you, Josie?' said the older woman, who had dispensed with her complex warm-up and was now making do with jumping up and down energetically on her toes.

'Aye, damn near four hunner pounds, jeest fae sponsors,' replied the chicken, now aping his elderly companion by leaping up and down on the spot, his beak flapping alarmingly. 'Whoot are you runnin' for?'

'The Police Benevolent Fund, if you must know,' Scott lied. He'd been encouraged by his superiors to think of this as essential participation in a community event, designed to aid police/community relations. He was also keen to see how he'd fare on a race of this length. He regularly managed 10K runs now, but this was of another order entirely. The thought of sponsorship hadn't crossed his mind until the last minute. His fiscal reward for running would now be change from the deep pockets of his colleagues. Still, he thought, he was a newcomer to this type of thing, and could surely be forgiven. After all, only a few short months ago, he'd have been much more likely to be found draining a pint glass in some boozy dive rather than out in the fresh air, satisfying his latest, albeit healthy, addiction.

He resolved to make a donation to charity after the race. In fact, now he wasn't shelling out on alcohol, he was astonished by the amount of money he'd accrued. Initially, the realisation had given him great pleasure, until he calculated just how much dosh he must have wasted over a lifetime of heavy drinking. But you couldn't go back and live your life again, he reasoned. At least he'd stopped before booze had stopped him.

Buoyed by this consoling thought, he drew a deep breath and took in the scene around him.

They were on the town's esplanade, which curved round

the head of the loch. Today, mercifully, its blue water reflected the azure sky, punctuated here and there by white, fluffy clouds scudding overhead in the light, salty breeze. A swan was being pursued by a gaggle of cygnets, all brown-feathered with little spots, paddling furiously to keep up with the effortless progress of their graceful mother as she surveyed the crowd with interest from the edge of the loch.

In the distance, the pipe band could be heard, blowing a fine rendition of 'Campbeltown Loch', the rattle of the snares echoing amongst the buildings, boats and hills. Despite its being only midday, a drunk man, small in stature and of a certain venerability, capered along in time to the march, swigging from a soft drink bottle that had once contained Scotland's other national drink, but was now much more likely filled with the original water of life.

As he tumbled to the ground, cursing volubly, some members of the band were forced to stride over him, which they did with élan.

A group of young boys on bikes were threading their way through the gathered runners, passing comment on the more outrageous costumes, or speculating upon whether or not some of the more portly or geriatric participants would live to see the end of the race.

Alistair the butcher bundled a parcel of his special 'marathon' sausages in white paper, then popped them into a bag for a woman in a headscarf, while on the stall next door an old farmer waxed lyrical on the benefits of using the correct variety of potato to make the perfect mash, before selling five kilos of same to a bemused tourist, who hefted the heavy hessian bag gingerly.

A pretty girl on roller blades was handing out flyers announcing the performance of her folk group in the George

Hall that evening, while two young men on saxophones provided an interesting counterpoint to the mournful lament the pipe band had now embarked upon.

'Gie us another, Art,' shouted a middle-aged man, as his companion burst into song. Whether this was to the accompaniment of the band or the saxophones was unclear; either way, his ribald words soared into the air to join the cacophony: the music, the deep murmur of the large crowd, the lapping of the loch at the harbour wall, the excited chatter of the runners, the bell at the end of the pontoons, the shouts of the vendors from their stalls, and the intermittent bursts of laughter emanating from the happy people of Kinloch and the many tourists who had come to join in the fun.

When Scott checked his watch, he noticed there was only a few minutes until the race started. He began to take deep breaths, but was disturbed by a tap on the shoulder.

'My, Brian, you're looking jeest the part, right enough,' said Hamish, his pipe billowing out blue tobacco smoke. 'Mark you, it's a long way tae run. I hope you're up tae it.'

'Dae you think I'm going tae croak? You're a right cheery bastard, Hamish.'

'Mind, you'll be up near the thin places, so keep your mind on the road and your hand on your ha'penny.'

'What's this thin places guff?'

'The thin places are few and far between. But you know when you come across them. In this particular case, jeest aboot three miles oot o' the toon – you know, where yous found they bodies. Man, you're as close tae heaven – aye, or hell – as you'll get anywhere in this world in places like that. So take heed, an' jeest keep your heid doon and pound your plonker, or whootever it is joggers dae.'

'We pound the pavement!' replied Scott indignantly. 'And I'm a runner, no' a bloody jogger.'

'Aye, whootever you say, Brian, whootever you say.'

'Get away wae that pipe. The old dear here doesnae need your smoke filling her lungs before we start.'

'I'll *old dear* you,' said Supergran. 'I'm jeest turned eighty, an' I'm willing tae bet I'll make better time than you.'

'You will so, Jean,' said Hamish. 'Sure, these poor buggers that's got tae live up in Glasgow alongside a' they fumes fae traffic, factories and the like. They never get the chance tae breathe God's clean air the way we've been lucky tae, all oor lives. Och, he doesnae stand a chance.'

One of the small boys on his bike drew up beside them.

'How'ye, Auntie Jeanie? Josie – cool chicken, by the way – hope yous get on okay.'

'Thanks, son,' replied Jean. 'You tell your mammy tae get some photies o' me at the finish.'

'Aye, I will,' he said, turning his gaze on Scott. 'Here, are you thon polis?'

'Naw, son. This says fire brigade, can you no' read?' said Scott.

'Hell mend you! My faither says yous are nothing but a bunch o' wankers, anyhow. I hope you trip o'er an' dunt your knee.' He rode off, taking time only to turn round and flick Scott the V-sign.

'Weans these days,' observed Hamish.

Mercifully, Brian Scott's reply was rendered inaudible by a loud claxon, indicating that the start of the race was imminent.

Glasgow, 1994

'The letter given to you by Ian Burns is still with the forensics unit, am I right?' said Campbell, pausing in his note-taking and glancing at Daley.

'Yes, sir. Not that they could glean much from it.'

'I'll tell you what I can *glean*,' spat Sanderson with no little vitriol. 'It's not hard to work out that your career in CID is over, Daley. I wouldn't be surprised if you end up facing criminal charges over this. You'll *glean* plenty when you're locked up in a cell with some psycho eighteen hours a day, that's for sure.'

Campbell turned to the DCI. 'I need a word with Daley alone, sir.'

'What? I don't know what you think you need to say to my detective, but whatever it is, you say it in front of me in my station. Got it?' snapped Sanderson.

'On the orders of ACC Taylor, sir. I can ask him to call you for confirmation, should you wish.'

'Ach, I've wasted enough time on this idiot,' said Sanderson, knowing when he was beaten. 'Just you mark my words, Daley. As far as I'm concerned, you're finished!' He picked up his notes and left the interview room, banging the door for good measure.

'That went well,' Daley remarked, almost to himself.

'You've been a fool, Constable. Of that there is no doubt. But you did what you did with the best of intentions, following the instructions of a man to whom you felt great loyalty.' Suddenly Campbell's tone had changed, the deadpan face of a few moments ago replaced by a much more friendly mien. 'You have a fairy godmother, Jim. Admittedly, a big hairy-arsed one, but a fairy godmother none the less.'

'Just what I need, I think.' Daley was now utterly confused.

'ACC Taylor is my boss. He oversees Complaints and Discipline, as well as some more covert operations within the force.'

'I see – well, I don't, really.'

'Your move to the Serious Crime Squad is effective as from tomorrow.'

'It is?'

'Also, you will be an acting detective sergeant. That is, for the time being. In the fullness of time we aim to make the promotion permanent.'

Daley looked at Campbell in disbelief. 'This is a wind-up, right?'

'No, not at all. I'm not in the habit of perpetrating windups. This is all deadly serious, as I'm sure you must realise, considering we've just lost an old colleague.'

'Yes – yes, I'm sorry. But I don't understand what's just happened. When I walked into this room, I envisaged handing over my warrant card and walking out as a civilian.'

'You will have a dual role in the Squad.'

'I will?'

'You'll report directly to me on matters contained within this file.' Campbell handed a grey folder across the desk to Daley. 'Take it home, read it all carefully and don't bring it back into any police station – well, not for the time being, at least.'

'Isn't this all a bit cloak and dagger?'

'Yes. It has to be. You'll understand why when you read the file.'

'And what about Sanderson?'

'I'll deal with him. Get back downstairs and clear your desk. Tomorrow you report to me at HQ in Pitt Street.

Make sure you're fully briefed on the contents of that file.' He removed his spectacles and began writing. 'That will be all, DS Daley.'

Still mystified, Daley left the room with the file tucked under his arm and the letter from Ian Burns in the pocket of his jacket. He would be spending the evening reading; there was no doubt about that.

As he remembered Burns, he looked along the corridor to where his old boss had had his office, now occupied by Sanderson. In his mind's eye, he could see the old beige raincoat – and scarf more often than not – hanging from the coat stand, as Burns sat behind his desk dispensing words of wisdom through a fug of cigarette smoke.

He thudded downstairs, his eyes filled with tears.

He went to the office janitor and found a cardboard box, into which he began packing personal items from his desk in the general CID room.

'Hey, big man, you're having a laugh?' said the familiar voice. 'I knew things was bad, but no' as bad as this! Surely they've no' sacked you, Jimmy?' Scott's tone was all concern.

'You'll have heard about DCI Burns, Bri?'

'Aye, aye, I did. Poor bastard. I'm still in shock here, man – all of us are. If I ever catch the—'

He stopped in mid-sentence when the door swung open to reveal DI Donald. He stood in the doorway for a moment, looking round the room. When he was sure it contained only Daley and Scott, he strode in and closed the door.

'Well, well. Leaving so soon, DS Daley?'

Scott looked from one to the other, his face a picture of confusion.

'Yes, sir. Won't be in tomorrow, as you obviously know.'

Donald hesitated, running a hand through his hair. 'Fuck off, Brian,' he said in a low, aggressive tone.

'Eh? I'm buggered if I know what's going on. DS Daley – what's that all aboot? I thought you was upstairs getting your jotters.'

'Do one, DC Scott!' Donald shouted.

Scott scuttled out of the room, leaving Daley and Donald standing almost toe to toe.

Donald leaned into Daley's face. 'I don't know what wire you have to Pitt Street, but rest assured I'll make it my business to end this little charade and see you back here as a cop on the beat. Trust me.'

'You do your best, *John*,' replied Daley, deliberately using his superior's Christian name to irritate him. 'But let's be honest, your best isn't really up to much, so I'm not holding my breath.'

Just as Donald was about to reply, two DCs entered the room, talking animatedly about the murder of Ian Burns.

'This isn't over, Jim Daley. This won't be over for a long time,' Donald whispered into Daley's ear. He swept back his hair, turned on the heels of his well-polished shoes and departed.

19

Kinloch, the present

The crack of the starting gun echoed from the hills that held Kinloch in their embrace. The crowd of runners set off, banging and barging into each other as they jostled for position.

The huge chicken flapped its wing in Scott's face as he tried to navigate his way past.

'You should have chosen tae be a duck,' said Scott, wrestling the fabric wing from his line of sight.

'Why?' came the muffled voice of Josie inside the large suit.

'Cos if you get in my way once mair, I'm going tae fling you in that loch. I'm no' sure chickens can swim.' He barged his way past, making sure he trod on the large yellow toes of the chicken's costume, making the bird stumble, its head lurching perilously from side to side.

'Aye, and there's the polis getting knocked intae Josie Thomson in his chicken costume!' shouted Councillor Charlie Murray through the tannoy. 'Any mair o' that an' your goose will be cooked, DS Scott,' he continued gleefully, to laughs and cheers from the spectators.

Scott threaded his way through the crowd, ready to take the long, punishing hill on the first part of the course.

'He's got a fine pair o' legs, right enough,' said Annie dreamily, as she watched Scott disappear in the crowd of participants.

'I'm thinking it's mair than his legs you're thinking on, missus,' replied her friend Nancy, a broad smile on her face.

'Here, I'll have nane o' that. Brian's jeest a good friend. Sure, his wife's coming doon soon tae have a look aboot and see if she wants tae move tae Kinloch – for a whiles, at least.'

'Ach, you must be fair devastated. Mind you, she'll be daein' well tae have as good a figure as you. For a woman o' your age, it has tae be said, you're no' too bad on the weight front, Annie.'

It took Annie a few moments to assimilate this information before she turned to look at her companion. 'I beg your pardon? Bugger me, you've got an arse there like a small island, Nancy. I widna go aboot casting expurtions on anyone else's physique!'

'Woo! Now who's the touchy one? Och, his wife will likely be o' the model variety. I mean, look at his boss, thon Daley – his wife was a right looker.'

'She's a bonnie lassie, right enough. But remember one thing, Nancy.'

'Whoot?'

'She's no' here.'

'How long have I known you for now? Aye, it must be forty years since we first met at primary school.'

'So?'

'In all that time, Annie, I've never seen you jealous. Aye, but I see it noo!' Nancy laughed heartily.

For once, the formidable hotel manageress had nothing to say as she stared at the distant figure of Scott, disappearing round the corner and up the hill, half obscured by a massive blue chicken.

'You bastard!' shouted Nancy, staring down at a large seagull dropping on the right shoulder of her red coat. 'They bloody gulls! I swear, these tourists are feeding them till they burst. There's half a fish supper on my coat.'

'They're right whoot they say at the Highlan' Kirk, Nancy: God does indeed work in mysterious ways.' Annie laughed at her friend's plight as she tried to remove the unwanted deposit with a small paper hanky. In truth though, she asked herself, was she looking forward to the arrival of Mrs Scott? No, not one bit.

Glasgow, 1994

The nightclub was winding down. Very drunk men were doing their best to prop themselves up on their partners as they shuffled around the floor in what could only be described as an approximation of the last dance.

'Here, have one mair for the road, Anne Marie,' said her friend. She looked around, then pulled a half bottle of vodka from her handbag and surreptitiously poured two large measures into their glasses of Coke, all the time hiding the manoeuvre behind her oversized handbag.

'Thank fuck I've nae work tomorrow,' her companion replied, grabbing the glass and glugging down the spirit. 'Mind you, that mother o' mine likes tae wake me up wae a slap in the face when I've had a skinful – just cos she's got a miserable life, like.' Anne Marie McKean fiddled with the gold locket at her neck.

It was a shock to the system when the DJ eventually wound things up with a scattergun delivery list of what attractions the nightclub had to offer for the upcoming weekend. 'Hope you've had a fantastic Wednesday evening – but now it's

Thursday morning, so cheerio for now!' he finished with his usual flourish.

Anne Marie squinted as the bright lights were turned on and the music disappeared, to be replaced by the gabbled banter of the tired and emotional crowd. Even though she was three sheets to the wind, she marvelled at how the magical, inviting place she had paid hard cash to enter a few hours ago now looked so mundane – tatty, even – under normal light.

Soon they were outside, shivering in the early morning air. A young man in his late teens pushed past Anne Marie, then spewed copiously into the gutter. A slight girl of about the same age – his companion – looked on in disgust.

As she leaned over the flickering flame of her new friend's lighter, Anne Marie saw two lads squaring up to each other in the middle of the road. They were being goaded by a handful of onlookers. Without warning, there was a distinct snap, followed by a yell, as a forehead connected with the bridge of a nose. One of the youths fell back clutching at his face, blood pouring down his chin. His opponent took the chance to land a couple of kicks into the unprotected ribs of his victim, now helpless on the ground, before he and his friends ran off down the street, yelling and screaming their delight at their inhumanity.

The aroma of beefburgers from the fast food van beside them and sizzling kebabs from the shop across the street, mixed with the scent of cheap perfume, alcohol, diesel taxi fumes and youthful hormones, filled the air. Woman screamed and giggled, men roared and guffawed. Distantly, a police siren sounded, as a girl in a red dress pleaded with a lad in a light blue suit not to leave her. All life played out under the orange glow of sodium lights on the Glasgow city centre street, the silver flow of the Clyde just visible through a small lane.

The girls were arm in arm now as they passed an alleyway. A woman in her late forties, her overly thick make-up obvious under the bright pool of the street light, had her back against a wall, dress rucked up to her waist, her bare legs entwined around the back of a muscular young man no more than twenty years of age. He grunted every time he thrust himself inside her, trousers at his ankles, his white socks splashed with mud. 'What the fuck are yous lookin' at?' she shouted over the shoulder of her energetic lover as he went about his business, sending the girls giggling past the scene, their high heels clicking and scraping on the rough pavement.

'Och, let's make a night of it. I've got a full bottle at hame.'

'Aye,' said Anne Marie. 'If you've got mair vodka, I'm yer woman. How far away dae you live? I love a party, me.'

The pair staggered on until a black cab appeared round the corner.

Kinloch, the present

Scott wheezed as he struggled up the hill, and was then overtaken by a woman with a ponytail wearing a dark blue tracksuit and orange wrap-around sunglasses.

Despite himself, he had to stop in order to lean on his knees and take huge lungfuls of air. The hill seemed to go on for ever, and though he knew its full extent, he'd only ever travelled its length by car. Now he was doing so as part of a race, and regretting every minute of it.

'I must be mad aff my heid,' he said to himself in breathless gasps, filling his lungs and starting the fifty or so yards to the top of the rise.

The race was strung out now. As Scott looked ahead, he could see a long line of brightly clad runners, snaking down the hill into a small valley, back up another hill and round a corner out of sight. Though it looked steeper, he knew the climb to be considerably shorter in distance than the one he'd just tackled.

'C'mon, you,' said a voice from behind.

Scott looked back to see the thin figure of the pensioner who'd been at the start with him and the chicken.

Determined not to be outrun by the old woman, he kicked on and was soon on the slope heading down into the little glen. He looked at the pedometer he had on his wrist – almost two and a quarter miles, though the long hill had made it feel three times that distance. As a general rule, he stayed away from hills if he could when out on his training runs. Though he'd given up booze, he was still a smoker. Hills and smoking didn't mix, as he realised he was now proving to himself.

He took another deep breath, just as he was passed again, this time by a man approximately his own age. He dug in, his running shoes slapping into the tarmac as he made his way down the steep hill, his bad knee aching.

Time to stop the fags, he thought to himself, as he ploughed on. From behind, he could hear the panting of the old woman. It occurred to him to feign cramp, but his wily fellow participant would probably clock the deceit.

The honour of Police Scotland was at stake: he would not be beaten by a grandmother.

Glasgow, 1994

The taxi ride had taken longer than she thought. But she knew that if drivers thought they could get away with it when carrying inebriated passengers, they'd take creative routes.

'That's us here,' said her companion, as they finally pulled up in a nondescript street of sandstone tenement flats.

Anne Marie watched as her new best friend paid the fare then crouched out of the cab. Maybe because the journey had been longer than expected, or perhaps thanks to the cool night air that now flooded into the taxi, she felt squeamish. She wasn't sure whether she wanted to go to this woman's house for more alcohol – after all, she hardly knew her. In fact, she was yearning now for the cosy embrace of her own bed.

'I'm going tae pass,' she slurred.

Her new friend wouldn't take no for an answer, though, and hauled at the sleeve of Anne Marie's coat, pulling her sprawling across the back seat.

Despite her protests, she found herself being half dragged, half cajoled up a path and through a big red close door. With no little effort, the two young women made it to the second floor. They had to suppress their laughter as one of them managed to kick over three empty milk bottles sitting on a mat outside a neighbouring front door. Luckily, the bottles chinked and rattled against each other but didn't break.

Her friend nimbly produced a key, which she used to access her flat.

Once inside, Anne Marie did as she was told, stumbling straight through to the lounge, while her friend went off to get some drinks.

As she sat down on a long leather sofa, her head began to nod with tiredness.

Just as she was about to fall into a drunken sleep, her synapses sprang back into wakefulness, sickeningly prompted by the constricting pain in her neck.

Wildly, eyes bulging, she grabbed at whatever was cutting off her breath and circulation and sending flashes across her vision.

The last thing Anne Marie McKean saw was the blood on her hands as she fell forward into oblivion.

The man stood over the body for a few moments. He heard the front door slam, but didn't react.

He removed the garrotte from the dead girl's neck, closed the lids over her bulging eyes with his thumb and forefinger, and went about his grim business.

20

Kinloch, the present

Scott made it to the top of the second hill, just over three miles into the race. In a mile or two, the route doubled back on itself. Already, fit young men and women were passing him on the other side of the road, heading back down into the town to complete the next leg of the challenge.

Scott stopped, again breathing heavily. He noticed he was only a few steps away from the narrow forestry road that wound to the site where the graves had been found. He walked to the fence and sat down on a grassy hummock above a ditch, fishing into his shorts pocket. He hated being parted from his smokes. With a nod of defeat, he took a slim cigarette from the ten-pack he'd bought especially for the occasion and lit it with the tiny lighter stowed away in his sock.

As he drew deeply on the sweet tobacco, he squinted up the hill, shading his eyes with one hand. Silhouetted in front of the sun, he could see two figures gesticulating. He cocked his head and was sure he could make out a distant expletive carried on the breeze.

At the moment he was a runner, but for some reason what was taking place up on the hill fascinated him. The detective in him overcame the athlete.

He made his way up the rough track, crouching low enough to make his back ache so that the couple on the hill couldn't follow his progress, and managed to slouch to a position behind a gorse bush a few yards from where they were arguing.

He cocked his head to one side, trying to keep his breathlessness at bay and calm the thud in his chest the race had engendered. Down the track, he could see runners heading in both directions. Ironically, the participants heading back into Kinloch, having completed more of the race, looked much fresher than those who had just toiled up the twin hills.

A snatched part of the conversation in the field caught his attention.

'And just how do you think I'll manage that?' The voice was male. He knew he should recognise it, but something wasn't right – tone, timbre – it was like a shouted whisper. Try as he might, he couldn't place who was saying the words.

Scott edged his way forward and had to bite his lip to prevent himself from crying out in pain when he accidentally knelt on a thorn. The little sliver of sharpness penetrated his left knee and the pain was excruciating. Eyes streaming, he swore silently as he pulled out the offending thorn with a grimace. Collecting himself, he cupped his hand to his ear, much in the way he'd seen his grandmother do when her hearing began to fail.

Sure enough, he thought, still wincing in pain, he could hear more.

'I'm telling you. How this happened, I'll never know. How someone found out about it is almost impossible to imagine. But that's where we are. You'd better get that fucking brain of yours into gear and fix this, now!'

Scott was even more convinced that he should recognise

the voice, but whether because of the pain in his knee, or the exertion of the race, his mind was blank.

Without warning, he heard footsteps on the forestry track behind him. He was already partially hidden by the gorse bush, so he slowly edged himself as far round it as he could, hoping not to be spotted.

As Scott held his breath, one of the young archaeologists he'd seen in the Douglas Arms trudged past, rucksack on his back. More intent on listening to whatever was coming out of his earphones than on examining his surroundings, he didn't spot the detective.

As the newcomer headed further up the hill, Scott noticed that the conversation on which he'd been eavesdropping had stopped. He waited for a few heartbeats before edging his head above the bush to have a look. Squinting into the early afternoon sunshine, he could only make out a bare hillside. Whoever the arguing pair had been, they had disappeared.

With his many years behind the mast, Scott's suspicions were now fully aroused. What had begun with a couple of shadows gesticulating to each other on top of a hill had turned into something altogether more sinister.

He resolved to abandon the race, wait a few moments, then take a walk further up the track to where the shallow graves had been discovered. He'd make some excuse about the half marathon being too much for him and beg a lift back from one of the forensic team, presumably still on site examining the crime scene. In reality, he'd have a poke about to see just who was up there and try to place that voice.

Scott hoped something would jog his memory further than his legs had managed to take him.

Glasgow, 1994

As always after the act, the man was disgusted with himself. He stared at the naked corpse of the woman who lay face down on the lounge floor.

He went to the kitchen and returned with some heavy, black builder's film, walking back to where the pale young woman's eviscerated body lay. He pulled thin rubber gloves from his pocket and began to unroll the film beside the corpse – as always, just over twice the length of the body, equidistant at either end.

As he turned her over on to the plastic sheeting, it wasn't the absence of life in her face that caught his attention, rather the gold locket that flopped on its chain between the cleft of her breasts, now bloody and mottled grey in death.

As he made to grab it, three loud knocks sounded on his front door.

He froze, panic making it difficult to breathe.

Kinloch, the present

Daley paced around his glass box. He bent over his desk again, checking the message on the screen once more. To add to the dental records, the DNA of the first set of remains had been identified. They belonged to Anne Marie McKean, divorced mother of two, who had been missing since 1994, one of the three missing women presumed to be the last victims of the Midweek Murderer.

He sat down again, restlessly swivelling from side to side on his chair. Somehow, seeing her face again had been a shock. He'd always argued that she had been a victim of the Midweek

Murderer. The three women had disappeared under exactly the same circumstances as those whose bodies had been discovered discarded around the city in ditches or lanes, or simply flung in the Clyde. The only difference was that while the previous remains had been carelessly disposed of, those he'd always reckoned to be the final three had never been found – until now. For some reason, the modus operandi had altered. Something had made the murderer change his approach.

Daley swivelled round and stared at the large map of the area on the back wall of his office. Why did they end up here? Why Kintyre?

He felt the same rush as all those many years ago. How ironic that he should end up here in Kinloch, less than a handful of miles away from the last victims of a killer whose case he had worked on for so long – the case that had nearly ended his police career almost before it began.

Without the courtesy of a knock, Bobby Speirs burst into Daley's office.

'There, we have it now. No doubt possible, eh?'

'You mean Anne Marie McKean's DNA? Yes, I've just read the email.'

'No' sure if that makes you happy or sad, Jimmy boy,' said Speirs, smirking.

'Sad, obviously. A young woman lost her life, her children lost their mother – that will never change. We know now what we always suspected. Why on earth would the memory make me feel happy?'

'Proves you right, son, does it no'? After all, you banged on about this for long and weary.'

'Yes, and you weren't listening, if I remember.'

'Oh, come on, son, get off your fucking high horse! We were fighting a losing battle. We'd mair deid women than we could handle. You must remember that. Aye, and you were doing your best to add to that number.'

'No one wanted to know.'

'Is it any wonder? The way you were behaving wasn't designed tae win friends and influence people, I can tell you that right now.'

'But it's not what you told me at the time, is it?'

'Still at this – after a' this time – I can hardly believe it. If you want some advice, leave the past be, Jimmy. You damn near went tae jail o'er it the last time round. Don't make the same mistake again.'

'Oh, Bobby, but you forget, things are different now. I'm not the rookie detective, wet behind the ears, and you've been put out to pasture. Your threats aren't worth shit.'

'Is that so? Why am I here, then?'

'Good question. I have no idea. But I aim to make your stay as short as possible.'

The door burst open, revealing Symington, this time in full uniform.

'Gentlemen, please. I can hear you right down the corridor. I wouldn't tolerate this type of behaviour from probationers, never mind two senior men. Enough!' She stared from one to the other, imperious under her braided hat, her Yorkshire accent suddenly strong.

'Och, ma'am, just a bit o' banter with an auld colleague here. Is that no' right, son?'

'I may be an old colleague,' replied Daley, his face still red with anger, 'but I'm not your son. Just get out. I want to speak to the divisional commander in private.'

Speirs snorted in derision. 'Okay. You'll remember that I don't have to have any truck wae rank these days. Keep that in mind, *son.*' With that he nodded to Symington and left Daley's office.

'And clean your feet before you come in here!' shouted Daley at the closed door, looking down at the muddy footprints Speirs had left on the carpet. 'What a bloody mess.'

'Never mind that,' said Symington, her eyes alight. 'Now they've managed to harvest identifiable DNA from the victim, they're hoping something in these graves'll identify the perpetrator. We need to make progress here, Jim – and quickly. I'm sure we'd rather get a handle on this with the resources we have on the ground. You've no idea how many beans I have to count to justify our every move. This is good.'

'I agree it's good news, ma'am. But, how likely is it that the murderer's DNA will have survived for more than two decades? Slim, I would say.' Daley walked to his desk, taking a seat and keying his desktop computer. 'I've been going through old files. They've been digitalised now, which is handy. Just got this from Gartcosh.'

Symington stood behind his chair as Daley typed. A photograph of a woman appeared on the screen. Though the resolution wasn't good, they could see she had an open, pretty face, a broad smile and blue eyes. Her hair was long; brown ringlets, with a touch of auburn. A link in the long gold chain she was wearing had caught the flash of the camera, twinkling as it held what looked like a locket in place between the cleft of her breasts.

Anne Marie McKean held a wine glass up to the camera into which she was beaming. She would have passed for any age between twenty and thirty but for the lines on her forehead and crinkles around her eyes that placed her nearer to her fourth decade than her second.

'One of the victims?' asked Symington, her hand on the back of Daley's chair.

'Anne Marie McKean, almost twenty-nine when she was murdered. Had two small children – a girl and a boy, from memory. I'll check.'

'From Glasgow, I take it?'

'Yes. Lived in Maryhill Road in the west of the city, ma'am.' Despite Symington's presence, something was working in his brain, telling him that this image was of significance. He stared again, trying to take in every part of the picture. His train of thought was interrupted by the chief superintendent.

'And she ended up on a remote hillside near Kinloch in a shallow grave.'

'Yes, she did,' replied Daley with a sigh.

'Listen, Jim. You're not the only one who's been reading up on this case. I knew you were involved the last time around, and I now know to what extent. If you feel this will be too traumatic, just say. Now we have a positive ID, we can import extra resources quite quickly.'

'No, I'm fine, ma'am. One favour you could do me, though. This is no longer a cold case, is it?' He nodded purposefully at the door.

'Get rid of Mr Speirs? I don't think that will be quite as easy, Jim.'

21

Glasgow, 1994

He had been going to read the letter from Ian Burns at home. But as Daley sat in his vehicle in the car park opposite Stewart Street, he decided he could wait no longer.

It had been one of the saddest days of his life – one of the most traumatic. He'd learned that his old boss, mentor and friend had been brutally murdered, then faced the awful task of telling Burns's widow. If that wasn't hard enough, he'd travelled back to Glasgow convinced he'd lose his job, only to end up with a new posting and a change of rank, albeit temporary.

He held the envelope bearing the familiar handwriting at arm's length, propping it up against the steering wheel in the dim light. It was as though Burns himself was bursting to tell him something.

Daley ripped open the envelope, removed the single sheet of paper within, and began to read.

Dear Jim,
It is with a heavy heart that I write these words. Heavy, because you must know that now you are reading them it is certain that I have failed miserably in my intentions.

When I joined the old Glasgow police force so long ago, or so it seems now, I walked into a very different job when compared to the one I walked out of a few years ago. In those far-off days, most experienced police officers had served during the Second World War. They had seen and done things that even we as modern police officers couldn't comprehend – were lucky that we never had to face.

That horrendous experience brought out the best in many brave men, who fought and died to save our country, and our rights, and to preserve the way we live. It also engendered a strong camaraderie – an esprit de corps – that the many who swapped a military uniform for that of a police officer brought with them to their new job.

Of course, in the main, this comradeship was a good, commendable quality; the forces of law and order require each officer to rely on his or her colleagues as they face the many challenges that are out there, as you well know. Sadly, however, in some cases it was taken too far, stretching the bounds of friendship and loyalty into another, much darker realm.

You will be unaware that I have kept a close eye on matters involving my old department since I handed in my warrant card. We all know that my replacement isn't up to the job, and so, through a small number of people I utterly trust, I have been able to help out in some of the more pressing cases with which you all have been involved.

The Midweek Murders have caused me great concern. Not only because of thoughts of such horror being perpetrated on young women, but also from another worrying perspective.

In 1963, as a young detective, I faced two murders

bearing very similar hallmarks. Airdrie or thereabouts, I think it was. Two young women – late twenties, early thirties – out on the town in the middle of the week. Both had been strangled, and their sexual assaults perpetrated upon them near or after death. The resemblance to the Midweek Murderer case is striking.

In those days, if we were unable to find a perpetrator within a few weeks, the case would be slowly wound down. We lacked the modern crime-solving techniques that will further improve and widen in scope as time rolls on. Never forget this, Jim. I'm willing to bet this part of our job will become more and more pivotal in the years to come.

On a cold night shift though, only a few years later, some information came into my possession which implicated someone close to (or actually) a serving police officer in the murders of '63. No name, just the suggestion that the case of the murdered women had been covered up. The bounds of comradeship had been taken too far.

Of course, with the limited resources at my disposal then, I tried to make sense of what I had found and reopen the case. I came up against a formidable wall of silence and obstruction that stopped me in my tracks. Indeed, I had almost forgotten about the case until these poor, tragic women began disappearing in what had been my own patch.

I will not commit the details of my theory to this page, but ask you rather to seek out ACC Taylor. He is a man you can absolutely trust. Like you, he was once one of my protégés. He has done well and is an honest man who shares the same aims for the modern police force as I.

Who knows, if things have gone so badly that I cannot

communicate this to you personally, maybe he has already made contact with you. He can provide all my case notes from 1963 to the present day, as regards this matter.

Good luck, Jim. You are a good man, a clever, honourable young detective. The future of the job I love depends on men like you.

No matter how tempting, never take the easy route. Always fight the darkness.

Your friend, always,

Ian Burns

As Daley re-read the letter, it was all he could do to make out the words through the tears streaming down his face.

He tucked the letter back into the envelope, then into his jacket pocket.

Burns had been right – Taylor had made contact, and quickly too. Daley would meet the assistant chief constable the next day. He was the man who had apparently saved his career.

He swore loudly, sitting at a traffic light on his way out of the city. If Burns had told him of his suspicions, the links to the threatening letters would have been obvious.

But why hadn't his old boss made him aware of his concerns? He had a feeling that Burns would have liked to alert him, but that the time had never been right. Daley honestly had had no idea his former boss had kept such a close eye on police matters after his retirement. Though, he reasoned, Burns had been so devoted to duty for almost forty years, it would have come to him as naturally as breathing.

As the lights turned green and the cars in front of his began to move, he glanced at the file he'd laid on the passenger seat.

He still had a lot more reading to do. Now, at least, he had some idea where he was going.

Daley turned up the radio and drove from the bright lights of the city into the darkness of the countryside.

Kinloch, the present

The blue dome of the bright afternoon sky was now streaked with the purple clouds of evening as Daley and Scott trudged down to where two very different sets of people were busily at work.

In the second and third of the shallow graves that had held the victims of the Midweek Murderer, SOCO personnel toiled under their familiar arc lights. Their white protective suits, hoods and masks gave them an ethereal, wraith-like appearance as they worked away in the artificial brightness. There was something otherwordly about the whole thing, thought Daley as he strode towards them.

At the first burial site – the one nearest to the detectives – the rag-tag team of archaeologists were busy back-filling the grave with the small pile of earth that had hidden the remains for over twenty years. Even this material had been sifted through by the officers before being replaced, just in case there were some tiny pieces of evidence to be uncovered. Nothing had been found.

'I'm wae you, big chap,' said Scott as they neared the graves. 'No way will they find the murderer's DNA noo. I'm no expert, but it's one thing getting that kind o' evidence fae bone marrow or tooth enamel, and another entirely hoping some will be left behind on the remains. Pity the soil's so acidic roond here.'

Daley looked at his companion. 'You've been spending too

much time with Dunky Chisholm, Bri. I've never known you expostulate on the vagaries of forensic evidence before.'

Scott thought for a moment. 'See, if I understood what you just said, I would resign fae the polis right noo and get a job on the papers – or maybe the TV. I'm buggered if I know where you get a' they words fae, Jimmy. You've always been the same.'

'No leisure time tonight, Brian. We've got to interview the locals turned up by uniform. They'll be reporting to the office in an hour or so.'

'You mean the folk that were up and doon tae Glasgow at aboot the time o' the murders? Reckon we'll get any no-shows?'

'Now that would just be too easy.'

Scott sighed as they approached the first grave, where Professor Francombe was hefting a large shovel as she helped with the task of backfilling.

'Gentlemen, how nice to see you back at our little dig – well, the dig that was once ours,' she continued, nodding across at the SOCO team. 'No social call, I suppose, given the pressure you're under from various directions, or so I hear.'

'You're well informed, Professor,' said Daley.

'Oh, one thing I've discovered since I've been in your small community, DCI Daley, is that there aren't many secrets.'

'Plenty secrets, Prof,' replied Scott. 'They're the things you never hear aboot, mind.'

'Which is why we're here, in fact,' said Daley. 'I need your help.'

'Fire away.' She brushed a strand of hair from her forehead.

'As part of our investigations into the missing district nurse you'll have heard all about, we uncovered some items you may be interested in.'

'Such as?'

'Rings, bracelets, bangles, neck chains – that sort of thing. Mostly gold, I think, but some other metals, silver, maybe. I'm no expert, but they all look quite old.'

Francombe let the shovel fall to the floor, removed the heavy protective gloves she'd been wearing and rubbed her hands on the back pockets of her jeans. 'I'm intrigued. So, you want me to have a look?'

'Yes, please. I'm making no assumptions now, but I'm willing to bet there's a chance these pieces have come into the possession of their owner feloniously. I'd very much value your opinion.'

'Tell me where and when.'

'Brian, could you see how DCI Chisholm is doing? Keep him up to speed with developments.'

'Aye, nae bother,' replied Scott, and plodded his way towards the men and women in white suits.

'I'm convinced that the items are from around the period you're looking for here.'

Francombe shrugged. 'But you're not confident enough of that to speculate in front of your sergeant.'

'No, not that. If I'm right, there are very few places where this little haul could have come from – get me?'

'One of my team, do you mean?' Francombe raised her voice, attracting some attention from the busy archaeologists. Then, more quietly, 'If you're remotely on track with this – *if* – then I'm willing to vouch for my colleagues, here and now – all of them. I'll come with you now, shall I?'

'Yes, that would be best, I think. It won't take too long. I'm sure you'll be able to see these things for what they are very quickly.'

'Oh, I'm sure, too.' She hesitated. 'Have you anything more

on the whereabouts of that poor nurse? I must admit, we heard about it in the pub yesterday. Very disturbing.'

'No, very little progress, I'm sad to say.'

'From what I've been hearing she's a bit of an oddball. The locals aren't surprised she's gone.'

'Really? Why would that be the case?'

'Oh, you know, fifty-something and never been kissed, from what I can gather. Bit of a loner, prefers her own company. You know how people gossip.'

'Well, take some advice, Professor. Pay very little attention to things you hear in the Douglas Arms – or any of the watering holes hereabouts. Gossip is bad enough, but when it's fuelled by booze, well . . .'

'Rather closed-minded, DCI Daley, don't you think? I thought you'd be taking a more rounded view of this. Any information gladly received, that sort of thing.'

'You get an instinct for things once you've been doing them for as long as I've been toiling away at this. Trust me.'

But as Daley hailed Scott and made his way back up the hill to his SUV, Francombe in tow, he bit his lip, deep in thought. Had he been blind to all the nuances surrounding McNeil's disappearance just because he felt sorry for her? There was no doubt that his first impressions were of a woman devoted utterly to her job; early to bed, early to rise.

He brought to mind the interior of her flat. He'd taken a look at it when it was clear she had vanished, and it had struck him on entering the place how devoid of warmth it was. There were a few random prints in frames on the wall, but no family photographs, knick-knacks, keepsakes. The whole place seemed perfunctory; functional, not personal. Almost as though her past had been erased.

He chastised himself for paying too much attention to her father and his past, and not enough to the woman herself. He knew that she'd been in no relationships since coming to Kinloch, and that she rarely left the town, seemingly reluctant to take holidays at all. But that was the sum of his knowledge.

He should have probed deeper – discovered more about Helen McNeil herself.

As they sped towards Kinloch, Daley driving while beside him Scott carried on a rambling conversation with Francombe in the back seat, he could feel rising desperation, a distress that grew as they travelled on.

He did and would always blame himself for the death of Ian Burns. He'd been too close to his former boss to have perspective; too embroiled in the Midweek Murders case to pay attention to the real danger communicated in the threatening letters sent to Burns.

Here he was, all these years later; was it possible the same thing was happening? He should have been more assiduous regarding the safety of McNeil, a vulnerable woman who had felt threatened by the malicious calls to her home and mobile.

As soon as he'd realised there could be a connection between the remains found on the hillside at Kinloch and the case that had all but consumed him in 1994, he knew his eye had been off the ball – again.

'Hey, steady on, Jimmy,' exclaimed Scott, bringing him back to his senses. 'That poor lassie in the back will need a sick bag the way you're driving.'

Daley apologised with a smile. But as they drove into Kinloch the churning feeling in his stomach spoke of the fear of failure and letting people down. It had been his unwanted companion for many years now.

22

The world seemed to spin as Helen McNeil regained consciousness.

Her mouth was so dry she could feel her lips crack as she tried to cry out. Nothing but a parched croak issued from her throat as she winced at the pain in her legs.

As she slowly came to her senses, the worsening of her predicament became apparent.

She could see above her the dim slits of light, and she noticed that they appeared different somehow: larger, so most likely closer, she reasoned.

The explanation for this was soon obvious. She held her hand out and felt the cold, pitted bars of a cage. Looking up again, she could see this was a place of imprisonment within a prison. The cage appeared to be suspended from the curved wall with which she'd become so familiar.

Helen remembered the sandwich and the sweet smell of the strawberry juice she'd been given to drink. She'd been drugged, and whoever her captor was had placed her in the cage while she was still unconscious.

There was something else, though. She could hear noise coming from the space below her cage – the space she presumed was the floor where she'd first tried to work out the dimensions of her cell.

It was running water: a trickle, nothing more, but running water all the same.

It didn't take her long to determine the new horror of her situation. She was captive within this iron cage, itself within the stone cylinder where she'd been incarcerated; below her, the slow trickle of water was like a bath being filled from a low-pressure tap.

Slow, but unrelenting, the trickle grew louder in her ears.

She was about to call out again when a new thought stopped her. It was only when she'd begun to protest that she'd been drugged and her circumstances had become even more uncomfortable. Whoever had entrapped her was vindictive. The more she railed against her captivity, the worse things would become – it was an obvious conclusion. She shifted forward, sending her barred cell rocking alarmingly, making her whimper in fear. The transfer to this cage had been a punishment for calling out.

She tried to control her breathing – tried to think.

Whoever it was who had her at their mercy wanted her to stay quiet. It followed that there must be a reason for this. She remembered her father's words. 'Everyone has an agenda – we all do things for a reason.' It made sense that her captor worked on the same principle. Either her protests were simply an irritant, or there was another reason. Whoever had taken her prisoner had gone to a lot of trouble to make sure she remained quiet and compliant.

For the first time, Helen felt a glimmer of hope. No, she wouldn't try to scream randomly – with her parched throat there was little point anyway. She would conserve her energy. She would listen.

Daley let Scott and DC Potts begin the task of interviewing those in Kinloch and the surrounding area who had been regular travellers up and down the road to Glasgow around 1994, the year the victims of the Midweek Murderer had been interred on the hillside just outside the town.

It turned out to be a bigger task than they'd expected. The small reception area was crowded with chattering locals, all being marshalled by the redoubtable Sergeant Shaw.

'This is just the first batch, sir. I've had to split them into two – because of numbers,' he said, a weary expression on his face.

'Why so many?' asked Daley.

'You'd be surprised how many people from the area travel up to Glasgow on a regular basis. We've got bus drivers, hauliers, doctors, lawyers, fish buyers, students, undertakers . . .'

'Aye, a' right,' said Scott. 'We get the picture. Near half the toon, in other words.'

Shaw was nodding his head as an older man, who'd perhaps had one drink too many, piped up.

'I know fine whoot's happening here,' he slurred. 'Yous polis think we're a' daft, but yous are jeest trying tae fit one o' us up for kidnapping thon Nurse McNeil. Ach, I've seen it a' on the telly – you know, in thon *CSI Miami*, an' that.' He turned to the woman sitting on his left then got to his feet. 'Well, I'm wanting a . . . an . . . anutturney, or whootever it is they get in tae make sure there's nane o' that hokey-pokey going on. I'm no' taking the rap!'

A younger man wearing a replica Scotland football top looked up pleadingly. 'Can yous no' dae us a favour an' jeest pull him in anyway? You'd be doing us all a public service.'

'Ach, don't worry, son,' said Scott. 'If he doesnae shut up, I'm just going tae shoot him.'

As the drunken man stared about the room with a startled look on his face, the rest of the assembled interviewees guffawed.

'Oh, by the way, sir,' said Shaw, weaving his way through the crowd. 'Mrs Daley was on the phone a couple of times. She said she called your mobile, but couldn't get a signal. I tried too. You must have been out of range.'

Daley checked his phone – sure enough, three missed calls and two messages. The last thing he needed now was for his estranged wife to start playing up.

He would find out what she wanted later. He thrust the phone back in his jacket pocket.

Once things were organised, Daley took Professor Francombe to his glass box and waited while a young uniformed officer signed out the stash of jewellery found in the Machrie holiday cottage loft, and fetched it from the evidence safe.

'Here you are, sir,' she said as, with no little effort, she hefted the hessian sack on to Daley's desk.

'Thank you, PC Martin.' Daley waited until she was out of the room before tipping the contents on to the evidence tray in front of him.

Francombe's eyes widened as the trinkets sparkled before her in the harsh neon light of the office.

'Impressed?'

'That's not the right word, DCI Daley. Astonished – flabbergasted – would be more appropriate. Do you mind?' She reached out to pick one item from the jumble of rings, torcs, bracelets and necklaces.

'Absolutely. Be my guest.'

Daley watched as the archaeologist examined one item after another, sometimes shaking her head in disbelief, or dropping her jaw in sheer amazement.

'So, what do you think?'

'I *think* this is one of the most significant hauls of early medieval Norse jewellery that's ever been uncovered. This isn't just any find; this has historical significance – real, genuine historical significance. Not just for Scotland, either – for the world.'

'That big?'

'Oh yes, *that* big.' She stared at the gold and silver before her, her face pale with shock and surprise, Daley noted.

'The question is, how did the person we're interviewing come into possession of this treasure trove?'

'I know you're saying treasure trove lightly, but that's exactly what this is. For a start, it's the property of the crown, so whoever turned this up has already committed an offence.' She paused, for the first time her expression changing from sheer excitement to one of deflation and disappointment.

'What's up?'

'Well, of course some of these bloody pain-in-the-arse metal detector freaks sometimes happen upon stuff like this. But even the most greedy and stupid of them would have the good sense to turn this in. It's not just about the items themselves, it's the context, DCI Daley. As no doubt you do yourself, we're trying to piece an entire story together here. Out of context, these items can't tell us their part properly.' The passion for her subject flashed in her dark eyes.

'But I don't understand, what would make these guys give up their finds – I mean, who would know?'

'Could you sit on something like this that is literally

priceless?'

'Literally priceless? Really?'

'Oh, yes.' She nodded enthusiastically. 'I have never seen anything like this in my time in the business. We know that Kintyre was a centre of ancient populations – the famous jet necklace and the Iron Age fort above Kinloch are evidence enough of that. But we could never have expected to have so much of this kind of thing.'

'So where might this have come from?' asked Daley.

'I know what I said earlier – about my team, I mean. I'm not blaming anyone – I want to make that clear. But these artefacts are absolutely consistent with the period we are investigating up on Kilmilken hill. I mean, they couldn't be a more perfect fit.'

'I see. So I guess the evidence safe here at the station isn't exactly the right place to keep them?'

'No! We'll have to inform the relevant authorities – Historic Scotland, Crown Office – the whole battalion of people. I can deal with that for you.'

'It is possible that all this could have been discovered by an amateur, though.'

'Yes, it's possible, I suppose. But who would be in the places you might find the likes of this? This little lot was probably hidden away by somebody . . . oh, over eight hundred years ago. It wasn't *meant* to be found; the likelihood of its just sitting at the side of the road ready to be picked up by a lucky individual is way, *way* out there.'

'How well do you know the company who began the ground works at Kilmilken hill, Professor Francombe?'

'The local boys, not too well. Much of the site was closed to them when we declared an interest. Closed, as in restricted for a defined period to give us a chance to discover what we think is there. The main contractors are a company called Demar Environmental Solutions – Americans. Specialists in the construction of wind turbines.'

'Who are the local sub-contractors?'

'Oh, NG Groundworks. It's their tipper trucks that have flung all that bloody mud about. The boss is an odious little shit . . .'

'Colin Galt,' said Daley, before Francombe had the chance to finish her sentence.

'The very man,' she said. 'I can see by your expression that you share the same low opinion of him.'

'Something like that. Tell me, if any individual took it into their head not to turn this find in to the authorities, what could they do with it?'

'I'm very sad to say, DCI Daley, that there is an unhealthy global market for stolen or undeclared historical artefacts. Some of the richest people in the world these days have very . . . *unconventional* backgrounds. They see owning items of massive historical interest as a matter of entitlement. Money can buy anything, so why not buy your surgically enhanced bimbo wife a necklace that once adorned the wife of a Roman emperor? That kind of thing. Big money changes hands on the black market, but the risks are enormous. You have to have the right contacts, and those kinds of people are few and far between.'

'Yes, I've read about cases like this. Just never thought I'd actually come across one.'

They both remained silent for a few moments, as though mesmerised by the artefacts.

'Oh!' said Daley suddenly, extricating an item of jewellery from the tumble of precious metal in front of them.

'What?'

'This necklace here, the one with the rather ugly locket.'

'Yes?' she replied absently, taking it from him reluctantly.

'It's an odd one out, isn't it? Looks very different compared to the rest.'

'Different, as in it's modern – well, relatively, in any case. I'm no expert, but I'd say anywhere between the fifties and the late seventies.'

'Which century?'

'The twentieth, of course!' she exclaimed.

She handed the item back to Daley and picked up a more antiquated piece, clearly not interested in the locket Daley was now examining through his reading glasses. There was something very familiar about it, something about the gold chain and the rather confused design of the locket itself.

It came to him in a flash.

'Excuse me, please, Professor,' he said, keying his ID code into his desktop computer, and scrolling down the emails. In seconds the open smile of Mary Anne McKean beamed at him from the large screen.

He looked between the cleft of her breasts and held up the locket Francombe had just examined. There was little doubt. The locket round the neck of the woman whose remains had just been discovered on the hillside near Kinloch and the one he had in his hand were identical.

He picked up the phone. 'Get me DS Scott, please.'

Francombe looked on, an enquiring expression on her face. 'Something wrong, DCI Daley? You've gone as white as snow.'

'I've just spotted something of interest.'

'I see. I thought you'd just seen a ghost.'

'In a way, I have.'

As Daley continued to stare at the piece, Francombe quietly examined every detail on the policeman's face. The expression on her own face had completely changed.

23

Glasgow, 1994

ACC Taylor sat behind his desk shaking his head.

Daley reckoned him to be in his early forties. Unlike their mentor Ian Burns, he was a stocky, powerful figure, but he did share Burns's intense, probing stare and clear devotion to his duty.

'This is Ian and me when I was promoted to DI,' he said, handing Daley a framed photograph. Taylor looked much the same, but Burns looked noticeably younger than Daley remembered him, less stooped, with an almost youthful bloom on his face. 'I can tell you, DS Daley, I wouldn't be sitting here today if it wasn't for Ian Burns.'

'Yes, I know what you mean. Looks like the job took its toll.'

'No doubt about it. I always thought stress or the fags would finish him. I could never have predicted . . .' He stopped, staring at the picture. 'We will find them, Jim.'

'I hope so, sir.'

'Hope, nothing – we *will*. In fact, that's part of the reason you're here. Ian Burns had great hopes for you. Prompted by him, I've been watching your progress in the CID, and I share his view. It's just ironic that you'll be entrusted with making sure the investigation into his death is all it can be.'

'I'm not sure I know what you mean, all it can be?'

'Let me explain, Jim.' Taylor stood, then leaned on his desk. 'As you know, because Ian was one of our own, the Squad has taken direct responsibility for investigating his death. Central Scotland Police have called us in.'

'Yes, sir.'

'You'll be working with the team. It's to be headed up by DI Graham. He's a good, steady man – a clever detective. One of the best we have, in fact.' Suddenly he sounded uncertain.

'Sir?'

'Though DI Graham is clever – gifted, even – he lacks certain qualities. Mainly, he's a lone wolf, happiest when he's out digging around himself, rather than running the department. But there's no one more likely to find Ian's killer, so he is the automatic choice. In short, though, team management is not his strong suit.'

'What will my function be, sir?'

'Yes, I'm just coming to that.' Taylor cleared his throat. 'Because DI Graham lacks management skills, his deputy – as usual – will be coordinating everything. I want you to get involved with that side of things, Jim.'

'Help out with admin?'

'No, not just that. I want you to make sure that no information turned up by DI Graham manages to go missing, or fails to be communicated to the right people.' Taylor eyed Daley unsmilingly.

'Is that likely? I mean, is it likely that evidence concerning the murder of DCI Burns will go astray? I would have thought that every cop out there would be desperate to find the bastard who did this.'

'Yes, so you would have thought – and I'm not saying that

isn't the case.' He walked to the window of his office, high in Strathclyde Police HQ on Pitt Street. 'Ian was working with me on a little theory.'

'Yes?'

'I know what he wrote to you in the letter Amanda gave you. We discussed it. Ian had major concerns about how the Midweek Murders case was being run by his old divisional CID. It's one of the reasons – plus the growing number of victims – that we have taken over the task. That, and the lack of leadership at Stewart Street.'

'Sanderson?'

'No, not directly, but certainly his ineptitude doesn't help.'

'Are we talking about the misguided loyalty Ian mentioned in his letter to me?'

'Yes, I'm afraid we are. As the letter says, there are suspicions that a police officer, serving or retired, or someone close to him or her, is closely involved with the murder of these women.'

'How do we know?'

'We have intelligence, that's all I can say right now. You'll have to trust me on it, Jim – for the time being, at any rate.'

'So what's my role?'

'Taking nothing at face value – nothing. Get in with the team – play the part if you have to.'

'Play the part?'

'Go along with things, even if you know it's wrong. Then report back to me. We'll organise some way we can meet regularly, away from prying eyes.'

'Can I ask a question? With the greatest respect, sir.'

'You mean why don't I just come down with a heavy hand and go through things like a hurricane?'

'Yes, something like that.'

'You know how police officers work, Jim. Once you have this shit on your shoulder you're no longer an operational policeman – almost the enemy, in fact. Certainly true as far as many of our colleagues are concerned, wouldn't you say? Even straight, decent cops would baulk at knocking at my door and telling me about any misgivings. Ian Burns told me you were the man to solve this problem – a man we could trust implicitly. If you feel you can't do it for me, *please*, do it for Ian Burns. Only a fool would think that what happened to him isn't connected with the suspicions we have. I don't buy the old adversary with a grudge explanation.'

'Does that mean that – one way or the other – you're in danger too?'

Taylor shrugged his shoulders. 'Logically, yes, that would appear to be the case.'

'And following that logic, sir, where does that leave me?'

'Not hard to work out, Jim. I'll do my best to help you – to protect you. But I'd be lying if I said there was no risk. Now you're a DS – acting, at any rate – I'm willing to consider a temporary appointment of a DC to help you. You need someone to watch your back – safety in numbers and all that. Do you have anyone in mind?'

'DC Brian Scott, sir,' said Daley, without hesitation.

For the first time in the conversation Taylor smiled. 'I was afraid you might say that.'

'He's a good man, sir – a bit rough and ready, I grant you, but in these circumstances there's nobody I'd rather have with me.'

'Very well, I'll make the necessary arrangements. Best you get down to the incident room. DI Graham is off somewhere, but the rest of the team are there.'

'Thank you, sir.' Daley stood to leave, then paused. 'One thing, sir: who is the coordinating officer you mentioned? DI Graham's deputy, I mean?'

'Oh, yes. His name's Bobby Speirs.'

Kinloch, the present

Daley stared at the large map on the wall. Scott had been dispatched to re-arrest Colin Galt, who had been released from custody, mainly to see what he would do. Now, with new evidence, it was time for him to return to custody. He suspected the businessman was involved with the felonious possession of historical artefacts, but the discovery of Anne Marie MacKean's locket in amongst the stash was something else entirely.

Sergeant Shaw stood with him as they pored over the depiction of the Kintyre Peninsula.

'Right, so the last sighting we have of Helen McNeil was here,' said Daley, pointing to the straight road almost two thirds of the way to Machrie from Kinloch.

'Yes, sir. The guy who saw her was driving into town. He recognised the car. She's been attending his elderly wife recently, so they exchanged a wave – he said it was definitely her behind the wheel.'

Daley stared at the terrain: beach, machair, rocky bays and the village itself, all framed by the hills beyond. This wasn't going to be easy to search, but he had to do something to move the investigation on. Even though he suspected they'd turn up nothing, he hoped a search using police officers and members of the public would be enough to panic anyone who was holding Helen against her will. That was *if* she was being held in the area, *if* they were searching in the right place, and *if* she was still alive. 'No sign of the car, or signal from her mobile, I take it?'

'No, sir, not a thing.'

He turned thoughts over in his mind. It didn't bear too much scrutiny. Daley had railed against the hospital boss for allowing her to attend the call, given her circumstances, but really he blamed himself. However, he couldn't help but wonder what this quiet, self-effacing nurse had done to attract such vitriol. He had no doubt in his mind that her disappearance and the fake calls she'd been receiving were connected.

Coincidence – it happens, but be aware. Again he recalled the old mantra his first boss had taught him.

As Shaw was relating how difficult the search across some of the rugged hillside above Machrie might prove, Daley felt his mobile vibrate in his pocket. *Liz*, the screen read. How typical of her, he thought. Almost like a second sense, she seemed to be able – even now – to know when he was under most stress and proceed to make his life even more difficult. It had happened throughout their marriage, now it was happening even though they were no longer together.

He clicked the call off with a flourish, and turned his attention back to the map.

Scott and DC Potts were on their way to Machrie and the home of Colin Galt.

The streets of Kinloch had been thronged with people, all celebrating the marathon weekend. But Machrie was quiet, save for the last flames of a magnificent sunset as it popped beneath the horizon, an explosion of red, yellow and orange, followed by green and purple hues reflected on the mighty Atlantic until the dark of night turned the sea black, ready to reflect the waxing moon and the ancient light from billions of stars.

They drove up a hill and through a set of open ornamental gates. Though the house was designed to look old, it was modern, and clashed with the bare hillside. No illumination showed from within save for one of the upstairs rooms, from which a dim light flickered, almost like candlelight.

'Right, son. You know the scoop,' said Scott as they exited the car. 'You cloak roond the back, just in case this slippery bastard decides tae get on his toes. I'll go and gie the front door a hefty chap.' He watched as Potts slid round the back of the building, then took the three steps up to the front door. A security lamp burst into life above his head. He grabbed a heavy cast-iron knocker and thudded it against the stout oak door in four sharp raps.

As he waited, he listened for movement from within, slipping open the heavy letterbox with one finger the better to hear what was going on inside.

Though he held his breath, there was no sound of footfall on the stairs, nor bustle along the hall towards the door. He knocked again, though this time with more force.

'Mr Galt, it's the police. We want tae talk to you, now!' he shouted. Still he could discern no movement from within the property.

He was about to lift the knocker again, when he heard Potts cry out.

'Sergeant, quick!'

Scott raced round the side of the house, just in time to see Potts disappearing into the gloom towards the hill behind.

'What the hell's happening?' called Scott, taking to his heels after his colleague.

'Look – up the hill!' shouted Potts breathlessly.

Scott squinted ahead as he took the first steps on to the rise. Sure enough, he could make out two figures making their way further up the hill. The larger of the two – Galt, Scott reckoned – appeared to be almost dragging his companion along after him.

The detective nearly lost his footing, regaining his balance just in time to see his younger colleague vault agilely over a fence, using one hand on a post to propel himself over. Fuck that, Scott wheezed to himself.

As he paused to take the fence in a less spectacular fashion, he could see that Potts was gaining ground on their quarry, one of whom appeared to have stumbled and was being hauled back to his or her feet.

'Shit!' shouted Scott, his breathing rapid now as he jumped down from the fence and hurried after Potts. This might be Helen McNeil; certainly, the figure being pulled up the hill looked to be female, and unsteady enough to make Scott think she might be under duress in some way. 'Keep going, son. We have to get to them before we lose the light!'

Even as he spoke, Potts's pale grey jacket was fading into the hill in the darkness. Scott was scrambling now, his tan brogues no match for this rough hillside, slick with mud and damp grass.

As he stumbled on to his hands and knees, a scream rent the darkness, followed by more shouting and the sounds of a scuffle.

Running in the direction of the noise now, Scott, almost sightless in the velvet darkness, tried to orient himself by staring over at the sliver of moonlight now streaking across the sea towards the looming coast of County Antrim. The sun had fully set, leaving a bright, almost full moon to hold sway in the sky.

Up ahead, there was the unmistakable crack of fist hitting flesh and bone, followed by cry of pain.

He saw movement to his left, rushed towards it and saw Potts rolling on the rocky hillside with another man.

Slipping and sliding, he scrabbled across the slick heather, and was only a matter of yards away from the fracas when a sharp crack issued from somewhere in the darkness. There was a cry of pain followed by a groan, as one of the figures went limp, lying still in the moonlight.

'Potts – son!' shouted Scott, fearing the worst. But as he reached the scene, he almost jumped as he saw a beam of white light dart across the hillside.

'Get down, Sergeant,' roared Potts, as he directed his torch towards the saddle between two peaks.

'Are you okay, Potts?'

'Yes, but I'm not sure about our friend here. Quick, can you call the cavalry?'

As Scott removed the phone from his jacket, he peered at the figure now curled at his feet. A cross between a wheeze and a desperate cry of pain was emanating from Colin Galt as he lay almost motionless save for a desperate twitch in his right hand, now pinned underneath him.

'Jimmy, it's me. Get an ambulance oot here quick! We're on the hill behind Galt's hoose at Machrie. He's taken a bullet. Oh aye, an' bring a torch – a big one!' Scott listened to the response for a few heartbeats then hung up.

'Are they on their way, Sergeant?' asked Potts, still searching the hillside with his powerful torch.

'Aye. But put that bloody torch doon. You're turnin' us

intae sitting ducks. Whoever fired that gun only has tae take aim at the beam and you're a goner.'

Before the DS could finish the sentence, the light was extinguished and both detectives knelt over the stricken man.

'He's still got a strong enough pulse,' said Scott, removing his fingers from Galt's neck. 'I think he took the blow on the shoulder.' He held his hand close to his face in the darkness, smelling the distinctive tang of fresh blood. 'Here, help me put pressure on the wound. He's bleeding heavily.'

As Potts did as he was told, another shot rang out, whining as it ricocheted off a boulder.

'Hit the deck!' screamed Scott.

As he looked tentatively back up the hill, a shaft of moonlight illuminated two figures making their way upwards.

Galt groaned, suddenly regaining consciousness. 'Help her – please help her,' he managed to whisper before his head rolled sideways.

'Colin – Mr Galt,' said Scott, checking for the pulse on the stricken man's neck. 'How the hell have you got yourself in this mess?'

Though Galt's pulse was weak, it was steady, but answer came there none.

24

Glasgow, 1994

Every face turned to Daley as he entered the room. It was a typical CID office, dotted with desks groaning under the weight of paper and cardboard files. Each bore a typewriter, some word processors and a phone, with various framed photographs of wives, girlfriends and children scattered about. This wasn't just any CID office, though; it was the home of Strathclyde's Serious Crime Squad.

Daley noted that there were signs of this. No smutty calendars on the walls, and the office had its own coffee machine – most unusual.

'Can we help you?' asked a rugged old detective from behind his newspaper. His face was deeply etched with lines, no doubt a testament to many years of hard drinking, smoking and insufficient sleep. The familiar blue haze of sweet tobacco smoke hung just below the ceiling.

'I'm looking for DS Speirs. I was told he was in,' said Daley confidently.

'How come I know your face?' asked his interlocutor with a quizzical look.

'You tell me,' Daley replied, not willing to play the usual

game of hide and seek so common when you started a new job with a change of police colleagues. Soon, he'd be asked his name, favourite colour and place of birth – almost anything, in fact, rather than a direct question as to, which side of Glasgow's religious divide he happened to fall on.

Before the detective could respond, another voice sounded from the back of the room.

'You be careful, Kenny. You're talking tae a superior.' A balding man with a round face was propped up against the door jamb of an adjoining office. He looked Daley up and down with an expression of weary distain.

Kenny looked from one to the other, not sure if he should take the second-in-command of his section seriously, or not.

'This here is young DC – I mean, *acting* DS Jim Daley. The darling of A Division – I'm right, am I not?' He directed an insincere smile in Daley's direction.

'Sorry, Sergeant,' said Kenny with little contrition, as he turned his attention back to the newspaper.

'So, you've come tae teach us all what we should be doing, son, eh?'

'DS Speirs?' asked Daley, unmoved by the sarcasm.

'Well done! Did they gie you my photo?'

'Can I have a word with you, please?'

'You can have as may words as you want, son. Ask away.'

'In private, I mean.'

'Oh, come on. This isnae the refined atmosphere o' Stewart Street. We're a team – close-knit. We trust each other here – don't we, lads?'

Daley sighed. He was always surprised by the way police officers seemed to be constantly at odds with each other. Tension between individuals, shifts, divisions, squads, forces

– it never ended. Without comment, he pushed his way past Speirs and into the office.

DS Jim Daley was in no mood to play games.

The present

Helen concentrated on her breathing, trying to keep it slow and steady: in through her nose, out through her mouth. After a few minutes she was convinced that she could smell something of which hitherto she hadn't been aware. The nurse concentrated hard, screwing up her eyes to try to focus on this new smell.

Then, it came to her: she was near the sea.

The salty tang of the sea was ever-present in the lives of Kintyre's citizens, so most were desensitised to the underlying aroma that pervaded their environment. Unless they were very close to the element itself.

She calmed her breathing again, feeling her heart rate slow. There, through the musty smell of earth and decay was the unmistakable smell of the sea, she was convinced.

However, Helen wasn't too sure just how this new discovery could help. She supposed it narrowed down the potential places in which she could be contained, but it wasn't a solution in itself.

Then it came to her. Suddenly, without warning, the subconscious part of her brain had calculated her most likely location.

But surely it couldn't be!

She strived to keep her breathing slow and steady, but the heady mixture of excitement and horror she felt made this temporarily impossible.

All she had to do now was turn this new knowledge to her own advantage. The question was, how?

Doctors and nurses rushed to and fro as Daley and Scott sat in the corridor outside Kinloch Hospital's intensive care unit. So far, despite Daley's attempts to glean information, they were none the wiser as to the condition of Colin Galt.

As a doctor he knew rushed down the corridor towards them, Daley opened his mouth ready to ask again, but was waved away.

'All in good time, DCI Daley. I'll let you know how things are as soon as I know.' With that, the medic hurried by, crashing through the swing doors into intensive care.

'You'll no' get anything oot o' them until they work oot whether he's fit enough tae go up tae Glasgow,' said Scott matter-of-factly.

'Okay, Dr Finlay, exactly how do you know that?'

'If you'll remember, it's no' that long ago since I was fighting for my ain life after bein' shot – or have you forgotten?'

'No.'

'So, you'll concede, I know a wee bit aboot what's going on in there.'

'No. You were spark out the whole time, Bri. In fact, if memory serves me right, you didn't regain consciousness until the second day you were in Glasgow ICU. Unless you had one of those out of body experiences.' Daley raised an eyebrow.

'Och, I had plenty o' them when I was on the booze, Jimmy.'

'I can imagine.'

'Anyhow, you'll just have tae cool your jets until the docs have done their job. Mind you, he wasnae looking too clever when he went in there.' Scott fished into his pocket, produced a bag of salted peanuts and proceeded to pour a small mountain of them into his right palm before transferring them into his mouth. 'Here, you wa' a peanu'?' he said through a mouthful.

'And having expressed his gloomy medical prognosis, Dr Brian Scott moved on to the more important matter of feeding his face.'

'You're right in the doldrums again, big chap. You're no' still mooning aboot that poor wee lassie, I hope?' Scott's speech was clearer now that he'd swallowed the mouthful of peanuts.

Daley's expression made it plain that part of the conversation was at an end.

They sat in silence for a while, Daley observing the busy hospital staff, while Scott, having shaken the remains of the peanuts vigorously into his hand, decided he'd hold the open end of the bag to his left eye, just to make sure he hadn't missed any. Suddenly, he yelped in pain. 'Bastard!' he shouted, drawing a disapproving look from a staff nurse.

'What on earth's wrong?'

'I knew fine one o' they peanuts was left in the packet. Bloody thing just donked right intae my eye. Oh, you bandit,' Scott exclaimed, sitting forward in his seat, rubbing his eye furiously with his forefinger.

'Rubbing will make it worse,' said Daley.

'Oh, fuck, it's bloody agony,' groaned Scott. He stood, attempting to open the stricken eye, which only led to another bout of expletives.

'Please!' said the staff nurse, on her way back past the detectives. 'What on earth is wrong?'

'He took one in the eye, nurse,' Daley informed her dispassionately.

'Oh my . . . not a bullet fragment, I hope? I know he was with poor Mr Galt when he was shot.'

'No, a peanut,' said Daley.

'Aye, nurse, any chance you can take a swatch at this?' Scott leaned his head towards her, one eye closed as though he was attempting a particularly pronounced stage wink.

'Don't be ridiculous. Get into the Gents and rinse it out with some water, man. And don't be such a baby!' She bustled off, shaking her head in exasperation.

'Angels in uniform, my arse. That bloody peanut hit me a fair wallop right on the eyeball. You would think she wid have the professional courtesy tae take a look – in case I've got a detached retina, or that,' Scott added, squinting despairingly at Daley through one eye.

'I've just remembered something you said, Brian.'

'What?'

'You said that Galt appeared to be dragging a female up the hill when you and Potts started chasing them. Am I right?'

'Aye, that's what I said.'

'So how come she recovered her composure sufficiently to escape?'

'He's a lucky bastard. If he'd been shot wae a peanut they widnae gie a fuck in here. I'm off tae the bogs tae administer self-help. It's true what they say aboot hospitals these days – nae care any mair, just a job.' He plodded off in the general direction of the toilets, left hand covering its corresponding eye. Daley noted he managed to take time to explain his plight to an old man wearing a tartan dressing gown and pushing a walking trolley before disappearing through the door of the Gents.

Daley watched him absently, deep in thought. Who was

the shooter? And why take such drastic measures? Whoever it was, Daley would bet his pension it was they who had fired on the injured man, and not Galt's female companion. If she was his companion – if she was Helen. However Galt had come across the hoard of Norse jewellery, he hadn't done so alone.

He thought again about the unfortunate nurse.

'Ya bastard!' came a muffled shout from the Gents, just as a young doctor walked towards him.

'How's Mr Galt?' asked Daley anxiously.

'Holding his own. We've stabilised him sufficiently to be able to helicopter him to Glasgow. He's not out of the woods yet, but things could have been so much worse. I'm confident they'll be able to put him on the road to recovery up there, though it'll take an operation or two, and he's lost a lot of blood. You can never be sure.'

'Is he conscious? You must be aware that I think Mr Galt might be able to help me to find your missing colleague Nurse McNeil.'

'I understand why you want to talk to our patient. And, of course, finding Helen's very important to us all. But at this stage, DCI Daley, even if he was conscious, Mr Galt would be in no condition to be questioned by you. That'll have to wait, I'm afraid.' He stopped suddenly, cocking his head to one side like a confused dog. 'What is going on in the toilet?'

Daley gave him a grave look. 'Nasty peanut injury, I'm afraid.'

Glasgow, 1994

Brian Scott was sitting in front of his friend in the canteen in Pitt Street, the Strathclyde force headquarters. He looked about nervously, the large mug of coffee in front of him as yet untouched. His eyes followed the progress of an assistant chief constable as he weaved his way between tables, cup and saucer in one hand, briefcase in the other.

'Is that no' MacPartland?' he said to Daley in a loud whisper.

'I think you're right, Bri. ACC MacPartland.'

'Do you know what his nickname is?'

'No.'

'They call him the bastard. Aye, and he's no' alone in here – this building's full o' them.'

'So, you don't want the job?'

'Wait noo, big man. I never said that. It'll just take me a wee while tae get used tae my surroundings.'

Daley smiled. 'I don't know why, Brian. You've spent more time here than anyone I know.'

'Aye, getting hauled o'er the coals by some so-and-so wantin' tae put me on the dole. I never thought I'd actually find myself working here.'

Daley looked about absently, stirring his coffee. 'It's not going to be a cushy number, that's for sure. Speirs is a prick – that was obvious as soon as I met him.'

'No surprise, Jimmy. His good mate's oor John Donald – nae need tae say mair than that. But I'm no' worried aboot arses like him. What's this DI Graham like?'

'I'm about to find out.' He looked at his watch. 'I'm meeting him in half an hour. I'm to brief him on what I know about . . .'

'I see. Well, if it's any consolation, they tell me he's a good bloke. Proper auld-school detective. Doesnae rest until he gets his man – that sort o' thing. Wyatt Earp type.'

'Not like his number two. Speirs doesn't rest until he gets a pint, by the looks of things.'

'Beats me how these guys get tae where they are.'

'Simple. He runs the team, Graham gets on with doing his job. You must have seen that before, Brian.'

'Sure have, buddy. Keeps the gaffer sweet, has his own little kingdom in return. These are the guys that always make it tae the top. Go on, Jimmy, tell me I'm no' right.'

'Sadly, you're spot on. Hopefully it won't be like this for ever.'

'Don't hold your breath.' Scott eyed him for a few seconds. 'Who would have thought it?' He grinned.

'Thought what?'

'You a DS in the Serious Crime Squad. I bet your Lizzie's right chuffed.'

'She will be when I tell her. But remember, it's only an acting promotion. I'll be back on the desk before you know it.'

'Nah, that's no' going tae happen. You'll be right up there. Here, don't forget your auld pal when you're Chief Constable.'

'Talking of which, I want you to get up there – introduce yourself. Speirs is in court, so have a poke around and see what you can find out from the troops. You're better at that than me.'

'Only cos I'm no' a threat. Nae bugger's worried aboot their job when Brian Scott rides o'er the horizon, that's for sure.'

'You're too hard on yourself, Brian. It's horses for courses.'

'Here, is that no' what Burns used tae say?'

'Yes, I suppose it is,' said Daley, sadness in his voice.

Machrie, the present

The tiny bothy – more of a shepherd's hut – was in the hills about three miles from Machrie. He'd struggled to get her across the rough terrain in the darkness. But the cool night air appeared to clear her head, so the last mile or so was easier.

She was sitting cross-legged on the floor, wrapped in a thick woollen blanket, rocking gently to and fro.

He eyed her with a mixture of love and loathing. He could picture the car rocking in the quarry, as the palm of her hand slid down the misted window. He remembered them in the remote rocky cove, naked, never dreaming anyone was there to witness their lovemaking. These and so many other instances that had driven him to insanity over the last few months; it tore at his soul.

'You've fucked this up big style,' she said, her diction still lazy after the alcohol.

'How do you know? Your boyfriend looked pretty lifeless through the night-sight of my rifle. You know the fix we're in. I merely did it.'

'*I merely did it*,' she mocked in an effeminate voice.

'What was *your* plan?' he shouted in response.

'Not to blow his brains out in front of the constabulary, that's for sure.' She stood, still holding the blanket around her shoulders. 'I should never have involved you in this. I knew it right from the start. You must be one of the most immature men I've ever met.' She angled her head back and laughed.

'What's so funny?'

'You being associated with the word *man*. You're no more of a man than I am,' she snorted. 'Why do you think I've had to get my jollies elsewhere?'

'Your jollies! You mean slake your unnatural desire for sex. It's you who's not normal, trust me!'

He looked at her in the flickering light of the fire. She dyed her hair, and it looked false somehow; too dark for her complexion. There were lines around her eyes and the corners of her mouth. Her cheeks were hollowed slightly, making her features sharper, more pronounced. Her hand holding the blanket tight at her neck was the hand of a middle-aged woman, wrinkled, fingers not bony yet, but they would be one day.

She was still beautiful, though. She was still beautiful enough for him to desire her: still beautiful enough for the thought of her being with another man to torture him, night and day.

'So, what's the plan now?' he asked weakly.

She glared at him, the fire reflecting in her dark eyes. 'The plan was that you would let me do things my own way. I knew how to handle Galt.'

'Oh yes, we know all about your *handling* of Mr Galt.'

'I know you know. You surely weren't stupid enough to think for a moment that I didn't know you were following me, watching me with him?'

'What?' He took a step away from her.

'That's your problem. You're still a bloody child. You have no idea how the real world works. I wish to hell I'd never asked for your help with all this.' She turned away, huddling back on to the floor nearer the fire.

'We were going to be rich, remember? We were going to live somewhere in the Med – dig for what we wanted, not ever worry about who was going to be our boss, or how we would fund it. You told me this job would lead us to millions!'

She shrugged her shoulders. 'It would have done – it should have done. Now, though, we're trapped in a bloody hut waiting for the police to descend on us, and you've shot someone. Someone who will put us in jail as soon as he opens his mouth.'

'Only if he's alive. He can't identify us if he's dead, can he?'

'What, really?' It was her turn to shout. 'So if he's dead, the police will just put it down to bad luck? You shot at them – you hit Galt! If he dies they'll come after us, if he lives they'll come after us. How many people do you think are up in the hills here tonight?' She stared ahead. 'We only have two feasible options.'

'And they are?'

She shook her head and stared into the flames of the fire. 'Let me think.' She paused, turning to look right into his eyes. 'Remember, the police and Galt – they're the least of our worries.'

Suddenly, despite the warmth of the fire in the little room, he felt a shock of cold. 'Our customers, you mean?'

'What do you think, arsehole?'

25

Daley was frustrated. He felt as though an opportunity had been missed, and that was one of the feelings he hated most in his job.

He and Scott were sitting at their usual table at the rear of the County Hotel bar. Even Annie had noticed the big detective's expression and served them their drinks with little of the cheery banter she habitually imparted.

The place was quiet, save for three noisy fishermen sitting on stools at the bar. Normally, this would have irritated Daley, but tonight he was grateful that they were keeping Annie busy, giving him time to think, as well as question Scott more fully about the chase.

'So, tell me again. You got there, knocked on the door, and after that Potts shouted that they were on their toes up the hill.'

'Aye, Jimmy. As I telt you, that's just what happened.'

'You're definitely sure it was a woman?'

'Yes! How many times are you going tae ask me that? Mind, I've been looking at women for a long time now. I recognise them quite easily, big man.'

'And Potts agrees.'

'Aye, he agrees. But, like me, he didnae get a right look at her, so he cannae say if it was Helen or no'. How many times are you going tae go through this?'

Daley looked at his watch. 'The helicopter should be on its way by now. They found that missing child in the Campsies over an hour ago.'

'Listen, I know you're anxious tae get moving on the search, but the chopper is the only way in the dark. It's just oor luck they were busy trying tae find a wean when we needed them. But I tell you this, it's a brave man – or woman, come tae that – that will try moving far on that hill tonight. Cannae see your hand in front o' your face.'

'They could have a torch – or a vehicle. Have you thought of that?'

'Who in their right mind is going tae take off up a hill wae a missing woman, shoot at us, then allow themselves to be caught because they're plodding aboot wae a great torch beam lighting their way? They cannae know that the chopper's delayed. And mind, we've got every track off that hill covered.'

'Symington should have let me send up a search team. We've searched in more dangerous conditions than this.'

'Not since they brought in Health and Safety officers. Different world, Jimmy. She just did as she had tae. You should know that fine by noo. How many decisions have you made just because you had tae follow the book now you're a gaffer?'

'As few as possible.'

'Ach, there's nae talkin' tae you the night. I suppose you're getting back up the office tae coordinate this search when it's light enough?'

'Of course. It's my job.'

'So what's Symington doing?'

'She's up there now, but how much experience can she have

in incidents like this? I mean, she's probably spent most of her time at Health and Safety seminars, the rest climbing the greasy pole.'

'I hope you don't let any of the gaffers hear you at that – you'll be oot the door quick smart. And, I might add, she's nae stranger tae outdoor pursuits, if you remember. Much less o' a stranger than you and me, that's for sure. When's the last time you scaled a rock face, Jimmy?'

'Every time I go to work.' He paused and sighed. 'Point taken, Brian.'

'You're supposed tae be taking this down time tae get some shut-eye. I'm off tae bed. Mind, I've got the wife arriving tomorrow.'

'How are you going to break the news about your injury?' Daley nodded to Scott's bloodshot eye.

'I'm telling you, that was sheer agony. All the salt 'n' all. Ye didn't think o' that. Just bliss when that wee doctor skooshed it oot wae thon water jet thing. You try it, see how you get on!'

'Get to your bed. See you bright and early, remember.'

Scott hesitated. 'And you're really back off up tae the office?'

Daley nodded his head. 'We still don't know if Galt's going to pull through. He's off in one helicopter while we wait for another. I've got a duty to Helen McNeil. I feel responsible – you know how it is.'

'Come on, then. Let's get back up tae the ranch, Jimmy. We've had oor break.'

Daley smiled at his old friend. 'I knew you wouldn't let me down, Brian.'

They said goodnight to Annie, left the County Hotel and trudged up the hill to Kinloch Police Office.

Glasgow, 1994

Daley walked slowly into the Horseshoe Bar in Glasgow city centre. Not far from Central Station, it was always thronged with customers. People from all walks of life congregated around the eponymously named bar of the public house, the barriers of class and social standing almost forgotten. Within moments of entering the premises, he recognised a retired sheriff and a couple of the city's less upstanding citizens, one, an elderly but notorious housebreaker, the other, a former hard man, now too addled by alcohol and drugs to intimidate anyone. They were all enjoying a drink in relative conviviality, watching the racing on television sets placed at strategic viewing points throughout the large room.

It was all dark wood, thick cigarette smoke, the sweet smell of alcohol and the rather subdued, familiar murmur emanating from lunchtime drinkers, so different from the noise and clamour that would fill the establishment after five p.m.

The young detective looked about, eventually spotting the man he was looking for sitting at a small iron-legged table under a window.

'Excuse me, sir. DC – acting DS Daley.' He still hadn't become accustomed to his new title. Better not to, as it was merely a temporary advancement, he reasoned.

'Yes, Daley. Thanks for coming here to meet me,' replied the man at the table, tapping his pipe out in a tin ashtray bearing the trademark of a well-known lager. 'I should have come back to the office. But, as you probably know, as soon as you set foot back in that bloody place you're assailed by problems and stupid requests from all and sundry. I swear, the buggers just like to look as though they're busy.'

'Can I get you a drink, sir?'

'Yes, just a half pint of light, please. My lunch, you know.'

Daley returned with the drink for DI Graham and a soda water for himself.

'You not a drinker, Daley?'

'Not on duty, sir.'

Graham nodded his head gloomily. 'I should give you a pat on the back for that, young man. But it just makes me feel as though I'm rapidly becoming an anachronism in the job. When I joined up, if you didn't take a drink you didn't last long. Nobody trusted you. Different days, mark you – better in many ways.'

'How long have you been in the job, sir?'

'Nearly thirty years – and no, the time has not flown. Joined up just after my national service. I suppose I couldn't imagine a working life out of uniform. I'd have stayed in the army, but they were cutting back, so I joined the thin blue line. Irony is, I've spent the great majority of my police career in civvies.'

'I'm pleased to be joining the team, sir.'

'Pleased to have you. Just what Speirs and his merry men need, a good kick up the arse from some younger men. They're all damn good detectives, but too independently minded. I should be at their heels like a bloody terrier, but I'm too busy trying to work things out in my head. As you'll discover, when it comes to investigating leads, they're top notch. Just don't ask them to produce original thought.' He eyed Daley as he relit his pipe. 'But that's why you're here, young James. You come highly recommended. Not least by poor Ian Burns.'

It was Daley's turn to assess his new boss as he tamped down a new pinch of tobacco in his pipe, then took a long match to it, initiating a series of puffs and billows of pungent smoke. He was a neat man; had a tidy collar as Daley's mother would have it. He wore a well-pressed dark grey suit and a white shirt, with a dark blue tie buttoned up in a tight knot. He had no hair on the top of his head, merely a monkish fringe, which was probably why he wore his trademark trilby, presently sitting beside him atop a neatly folded trench coat. His eyes were dark and watchful, and he had a spray of small purple veins on both cheeks that reminded Daley of Ian Burns. Again, his heart sank.

'You want to ask me what I think about what happened to your old boss, don't you?' said Graham, as though he'd read Daley's thoughts. 'Well, I don't think for one minute that it was your fault, if you're worried about that. I knew Ian reasonably well, and any man less likely to take off for a spot of hill walking I cannot conceive.'

'DCI Sanderson doesn't share that opinion, sir.'

'You'll find that DCI Sanderson and I have few opinions in common, Daley. The very fact he has reached the rank he has makes me despair about the way things are going. He couldn't catch a bloody cold, as far as I'm concerned. I'm sorry to be so frank; I know you'll have some residual loyalty to him having just left his charge.'

'Absolutely no need to worry on that score, sir,' said Daley without hesitation.

'Good. Wisely assessed.' DI Graham took a couple more puffs of his pipe as he surveyed the room. 'I know about the threatening letters,' he offered suddenly.

'You do?'

'Oh, yes. I've known about them for as long as you have.'

'Really, sir?' Daley was again surprised. He'd thought that

Ian Burns had confided solely in him. Though he was pleased not to have to explain the situation to Graham, he was slightly disappointed that his old mentor had found it necessary to trust someone besides him with the information.

'No need to feel down about it, son. Ian – as you know – wanted it kept quiet. I can do nothing quietly now that I'm in the Squad. He – we – needed someone we could trust, who could work behind the scenes without too much scrutiny. You were that man. Sadly, it turns out we were wrong.' Noting the sudden look of desolation on Daley's face, he changed tack slightly. 'Not wrong about you, Daley, wrong about the real level of threat those missives represented.'

Daley was going to ask DI Graham if he was aware of ACC Taylor's interest in the case, but something stopped him before the words could form in his mouth. Taylor had made no mention of Graham's having knowledge of the letters. And, knowing Ian Burns as he had, the young detective was sure that he would have had a number of contacts with whom he would share various bits and pieces; contacts who might not necessarily be aware of each other. He decided to bide his time in finding the answer to that particular question.

'Here's another reason Ian and I shared this information that you should know about.' He reached into the inside pocket of his jacket and removed a brown envelope. 'Here, take a look.'

Daley took the envelope and looked inside. He fished out a letter, written on expensive paper in what looked like blood. It read, simply, *Time you were gone*. For a moment or two, Daley was nonplussed. 'This is exactly the same as the ones DCI Burns received,' he said, not really wanting to give the thought voice, but doing so all the same.

'Yes. Interesting, isn't it? I must say, like your old gaffer, I was inclined to view this as the work of some crank with whom we'd had some forgotten mutual contact over the years. But, I'm very sad to say, the recent tragic events have rather made that theory redundant.'

'I don't know what to say,' said Daley, absolutely meaning it.

'Yes, it's a hard one, that's for sure. However, I think that one thing is definitely clear.'

'What, sir?'

'These letters have something to do with the Midweek Murders.'

'But how, sir? I mean Ian – DCI Burns – was retired long before these crimes began. I know he had a theory about the past, but does that stand up?'

'Before the most recent crimes, yes, you're right. But, as I think you are aware, DS Daley, Ian Burns thought that what is happening now had its roots in the past – going as far back as his early years in the job. I believe he was correct in that assumption.'

'But how does that involve you, sir, if you don't mind my asking?'

'No, I don't mind at all. But tell me what you know first.'

Daley thought for a moment. 'Just that DCI Burns felt that similar murders had taken place years ago, while he was still a beat cop. He thought the MO then and now were too similar to be a coincidence. I think he tried to pursue this, but came up against a brick wall.' Daley bit his lip.

'Spit it out, son.'

'He thought a cop – or cops – were involved, sir.'

Graham took a few more puffs on his pipe, then upended it, patting glowing tobacco out into the ashtray using the palm of his hand.

The noise level in the bar had risen, as a race was about to begin. Punters fiddled nervously with bookies' lines, or ordered another quick drink as the horses were being ushered to the starting gate.

The DI leaned forward. 'Ian told his sergeant of his concerns at the time, but nothing came of them,' he said quietly. 'He then turned to someone he thought he could trust. Someone new to it all, untainted by any possible corruption, or whatever it was he thought was going on.'

'Who?'

'A young DC, just in the job, and lucky enough to get a break in CID because his old captain in the army was now the DI.'

Daley furrowed his brow, still none the wiser.

'Oh, come on, DS Daley. I've been told to have high expectations of you. Bright, the future of the force.'

'I'm sorry, sir. I don't know too much about the early part of DCI Burns's career – only what he told me.'

'That young DC was me, Jim.'

26

Kinloch, the present

Daley was working on the clear board in the main CID suite when a sudden gust rattled the windows, prompting him to gaze out into the darkness. The street light danced in the strong wind and rain, illuminating tumbling litter on Main Street and sending the good citizens of the town scurrying into cars; early on the go, perhaps a baker or a nurse, thought Daley. Like his own, occupations to which normal working hours were strangers. He stood still, watching a white plastic bag with absent fascination as it rose into the air, tugged to and fro as though by an invisible hand. It reminded him of a film Liz had liked, but for the life of him he couldn't remember its name.

Then he pondered upon just how tiny things, mere snippets of conversation, or memories of fleeting seconds in the past, could remain rooted in the mind for no apparent reason.

Behind him, a young DC swore as he typed furiously on a computer keyboard, bringing Daley back to the here and now. The young detective apologised when he realised his boss was in the room.

'You've been spending too much time listening to DS

Scott,' remarked Daley before he turned his attention back to the board and the images that had been roaring silently in his head for days.

A large black-and-white photograph of Helen McNeil in her district nurse's uniform stared back at him. Alongside, in a colour image, a smiling Colin Galt looked more youthful than the strained individual with whom Daley had become familiar.

Above, various shots of three graves on a lonely Kintyre hillside appeared at odds with one of a happy woman wearing a golden locket in a faded photograph; this was the photograph that had immediately transported him painfully back more than twenty years. A thin red line ran between her image and the skeletal remains lying at the bottom of the impromptu grave nearest the sea: her resting place for all those years. That is, if the brutally murdered could ever truly rest.

The big detective barely registered the opening of the door. He almost jumped when Symington spoke.

'An old governor I used to work with in Wandsworth nick used to do that, Jim. He stared just the way you're doing, sometimes for half an hour at a time.'

'Did it help?'

'Not really. He was one of the least successful detectives I've ever known. I think they call it mindfulness now.'

Daley sighed. 'I hope you don't think I'm wasting my time, ma'am.'

'No, not at all. We all have our own methods. I worry more about manning levels, HR and budgets these days. It's almost like not being in the police at all.' It was her turn to stare out on to the windswept streets of the town. 'Sometimes I feel I'm more akin to a second-rate accountant than a police officer.'

'Can I have a word with you?'

The two of them walked into Daley's glass box, and the DCI pushed the door shut with more force than he intended, making it rattle.

'I know you're frustrated, Jim. What's happened to Galt, on top of losing McNeil, is a blow. I've just had to explain the circumstances to the ACC. But, you must agree, there's no way I could authorise a search – especially in these conditions.'

'I take it the chopper's still grounded, too?'

'Yes. They're here, but can't fly in this wind. We're hoping there'll be a window in the weather about eight.'

'We need people on the hill before then, ma'am – as soon as it gets light.'

'Yes. I've been organising a team. We've some bodies coming from Division to help out. They're on their way, plus the Tactical Firearms Unit, of course. By road, so don't hold your breath.'

'I'd better get out there and get ready to coordinate. It'll start getting light soon.'

She sat down heavily on the chair opposite his, staring at him across the large desk. 'Let me do that, Jim. I want you to keep thinking, keep working things through. I'm sure there's something we're missing.'

'It's strange ground for you, Carrie. We've a couple of local guys retained as Specials. One of them is a local farmer; bit of a hill climber, too. He tells me that he knows the area reasonably well. We'll take our lead from him until we can get eyes from the helicopter.'

'Good. You've just justified my taking charge of it. What difference will it make that I don't know the hill? Are you seriously telling me you've been rambling about up there since you arrived here?' She smiled.

'No, indeed.'

'Where's Brian?'

'He's off with Potts to knock up those two archaeologists working on a project in Machrie. A villager told us she'd seen Galt with one of them on a couple of occasions.'

'Accomplices?'

'Surely not. I mean, if they're pilfering their own site, it's pretty bloody obvious, isn't it?'

'Nowt as queer as folks,' replied Symington, suddenly adopting her native Yorkshire accent. 'It would be reckless, but then again, how often have you arrested reckless people?'

'Good point.' Daley leaned back in his chair, neck craned back, staring at the ceiling.

'Just tell me, Jim. I don't care how daft it sounds, just run it past me – please.'

'You know I have to be extra careful with this. I know you've read the old case notes. I can't afford to lose credibility the way . . . well, the way I did then.'

'Who's going to find out? This is between you and me.'

Daley got to his feet, taking time to tuck his recalcitrant shirt tail back into his waistband. 'I'm thinking about connections.'

'Go on.'

'Okay. All of a sudden these remains are found, then McNeil is abducted – or whatever.'

'Or whatever – what do you mean?'

'Okay,' said Daley, leaning on his desk, looking down at Symington. 'The locket; it could connect Galt to the Midweek Murders – in what way, we don't know. Now we think Galt may have abducted McNeil. If so, why is he where he is now? And, thinking logically, he looks to have been doing a roaring trade selling historical artefacts – handling a hoard that just happens to include the locket. How did he come across that piece in particular? Was it from the current dig, or has he – or someone else – been up to some amateur archaeology?'

'Or has he had it for much longer?' They both paused, thinking about this. 'What does Francombe say?'

'She doesn't recognise any of the pieces Galt was hiding. I mean, apart from the locket they're broadly of the right age to have been part of the site she's working on, but she swears that none of the three graves had been tampered with prior to her team's arrival.'

'And it stands to reason that the only place the locket could have come from is the grave of its owner.'

'Yes – but as you say, does it? How can it have come from a grave that hadn't been touched?'

'And Professor Francombe is certain about that?'

'Not just her, the rest of the team, too.' Daley sat back down. 'So, there we have it. We have a piece of personal jewellery belonging to a murder victim turning up amongst a pile of looted artefacts, but apparently not from her grave.'

'So, are you saying what I think you're saying?'

'You tell me. Please reassure me I'm not clutching at straws.'

'Galt is the Midweek Murderer?'

'He's old enough. He studied in Glasgow at the time of the murders. He travelled regularly between here and the city. The list goes on, ma'am.'

'Doesn't do much for your old mentor's theory that the murderer had a connection to the police.'

'Everyone makes mistakes. And let's be honest, we've not had the chance to look properly into Galt's past, have we?'

Chief Superintendent Carrie Symington thought for a few moments, then got to her feet with a yawn. 'You keep thinking,

Jim. I'd better get going and arrange that search party. We'll have to be careful. For a start, there are firearms involved. We need to know who else is up on that hill, and what connection they have to Galt.'

'Yes. I've already stepped up to an armed guard at the hospital. He's still touch and go. But going back, we always thought that whoever the murderer was they had an accomplice.'

Symington strode to the door. 'I need to borrow Brian, if I can, Jim,' she said over her shoulder.

'Of course, but do me a favour.'

'Which is?'

'Make sure he wears a bloody vest, ma'am.' Daley hesitated. 'Oh, and do I have your permission to run background checks on the archaeological team, as well as Galt's employees? We need to try to work out how he came into possession of all this priceless treasure.'

'Of course, go ahead. Keep me up to speed, will you?'

Before he could reply, she was gone.

Daley thought about his theory. If he was right, it stood to reason that Ian Burns was wrong. Colin Galt may well be a serial killer, but he wasn't a police officer.

As always, doubt – that great enemy of reason – clouded his thoughts.

The strong wind tugged at the machair, sending sand and sea spray into the air. Scott and Potts had driven almost two miles down a potholed single-track road as the growing storm rocked their SUV. Now, parked next to the low fisherman's cottage that was the temporary residence of the maritime archaeological team, Scott eyed the slanting rain with distaste.

'You should've brought a rain jacket, Sergeant.'

'Nae need. You're here, son. Just you get oot there and chap the door. If you think someone's inside, gie me the thumbs up and I'll jump oot the motor.'

'Aye, right,' replied Potts ruefully.

'See one day, you'll be a DS. Then you can send some daft bastard oot intae the rain. Stands tae reason, a man wae brains like you, that knows aboot Vikings and big words. Come on, jump to it, young man.' He smiled with quiet satisfaction; another point scored.

As the unfortunate Potts stumbled out into the deluge, Scott rubbed the condensation from the passenger window with his sleeve. He stared out into the rain, the dark shadow of the tall hill to his left just about visible through the downpour and darkness. Though it was barely four in the morning, and despite the heavy rain clouds, Scott detected a grey light framing the horizon. Daylight was on its way, though the rain showed no signs of abating. A line of pale light appeared in the wing mirror of the car as the sun hauled itself up to banish the black of night.

As he squinted into the gloom, something caught his eye. At first he thought it was a reflection from inside the vehicle on to the window, but looking around the car's interior he could see nothing that could be causing this to happen. He looked again – there it was.

Scott pulled the radio from his pocket and called Kinloch. Soon, he was patched through to Daley. 'I've got something here, Jimmy.'

'What, with the archaeologists?'

'Nah, up on the hillside. I'm sure I can see a light – tiny, but it's there.'

As the radio crackled, the driver's door of the SUV swung open, revealing a drenched Potts.

'Can you get up there, Brian?' Daley asked through the static.

'Who do you think I am, Ranulph Fiennes? It's sheer from here. Aye, and it's pouring and blowing a gale, too.'

'Anything from the archaeologists?'

Scott looked at Potts, who shook his head miserably as he tried to dry his hair with a paper tissue. 'No sign, Jimmy. The birds have flown.'

'Stand by, Brian. The Chief Super is organising the search. I'll get her to call you. In the meantime, keep eyes on that light.' The radio crackled off.

'Get that heater on, son. We're standing by.'

'Great,' said Potts, doing his best to wring out the sodden paper tissue. 'Just great.'

27

Glasgow, 1994

Anne Marie McKean's parents lived in a nondescript housing scheme in the north of Glasgow. The street was grey and drab, with the inevitable gang tags scrawled across walls, bus shelters and the boarded-up windows of empty properties.

Daley and DI Graham found the right close and took the stairs to the second floor. Graham knocked on the door, and both detectives stood back awaiting a reply.

A small, plump woman appeared, squeezing herself between the heavy door and its jamb. When Graham flashed his warrant card and introduced them as police officers, she visibly shrank, her head bowed towards the floor. 'Aye, I suppose yous better come in.'

She led them along a bright, old-fashioned hallway, with patterned paper, a telephone on a small table, and a thinning floral carpet. She swung open the door at the end of the hall, revealing a small lounge, where an old electric fire buzzed in a hearth below a tiled mantelpiece, bookended by two china dogs, or wally dugs as they were known.

Two blue budgies twittered in a cage on a stand, and a small transistor radio played on a light wooden sideboard. Beside it stood a whisky decanter, to which Mrs McKean plodded before turning to offer the policemen a drink.

'I'd offer yous tea, but tae be honest, I just don't have the energy tae make any. There's no' much tea been drunk in this place o'er the last couple o' days,' she said as she switched off the radio.

Daley was about to reply, intent on politely refusing the offer, but Graham spoke first. 'Aye, the very thing, Mrs McKean. There's still a chill in the air. Just straight for me – I'm sure my colleague will have the same.' He glanced at Daley, who nodded in response.

There came the sound of footsteps in the hall, and a rather dishevelled man entered the room. He was in late middle age, and sported a stained vest over which a pair of grey braces held up his baggy black trousers. He too was stout, but like his wife the lines and shadows on his face spoke of long hours without sleep. 'Mair polis! I want tae know how come yous are wasting your time coming tae my hoose instead o' finding my daughter.'

'I'm DI Graham and this is DS Daley. We're from the Serious Crime Squad, Mr McKean.'

'Huh,' he snorted dismissively. 'Yous fair love your titles in the cops these days. The last bloke that came tae see us telt me that he was the heid o' CID at Stewart Street. Didnae look much o' a detective tae me. Sat there with his mouth gaping the whole time. Looked like a fucking deid fish. Did I no' say that, Margaret?' he said, taking a seat in an armchair beside the fire, as his wife handed Daley and Graham two large measures of whisky. 'Here, I'll have one o' them, tae. Make it a big yin.'

'Did you no' have enough last night?' his wife asked, clearly not expecting a reply.

'Well, have you got news for us?' he asked belligerently; then, as though suddenly realising just what the police might have to relate, he changed his manner, crumbling slightly. 'Take a seat, the pair o' you,' he said, pointing at an old leather sofa.

'I just want to know about your daughter's friends,' said Graham. 'I'll need a list of them. I see you hadn't met the girl she was going out with on Wednesday. You've no idea at all who she was?'

'No. If we had we'd have telt your colleagues. All I know is that her name was Janet.'

'Or Jane,' added his wife wearily.

'Och, you know young people. Always meeting new friends at that age – at work, or on nights oot . . .' He fell silent.

'So, you've no idea where this friend lived, or worked, for example?'

'Not a clue. The first time I'd heard aboot her was the day afore they went for their night oot. I cannae say I was paying that much attention. It's no' as though Anne Marie was a daft wee lassie. She just couldnae settle doon.'

'She was tall,' said Mrs McKean suddenly.

'Have you mentioned this before, Mrs McKean?' asked Graham, fishing out his notebook and flicking back a few pages.

'No, I just minded there. Anne Marie telt me she was wearing her highest heels, just so she didnae look like a short arse beside her new mate.'

'And the nightclub was the Palace down near the river, yes?'

'Aye, it was that. But I've gied a' this tae the other polis that came.'

'No, you didn't. The fact we now know she's tall is a help. Please try to think of anything else you might not have related to my colleagues.'

The McKeans looked at each other, sadness reflected in both faces. Their daughter had disappeared from a nightclub in the middle of the week. At the moment in Glasgow, this amounted to an almost certain death sentence.

Mr McKean shook his head. 'Nah, I cannae think o' anythin' else.'

'Me neither,' said Mrs McKean. 'Did I mention that the lassie was a student?'

Graham checked his notes, running his finger down the relevant pages as he read the details of Sanderson's interview of the pair. 'No, not that I can see here. How do you know this?'

'The wee yin telt me. She said that she was thinking o' going tae college herself. You cannae get anywhere wae no qualifications these days, that's for sure.'

'You don't happen to know which college she attended?' asked Daley, more in hope than expectation.

'No. Well, it was in the toon centre somewhere. I mind she got the train intae Queen Street every morning, so it stands tae reason the college was in the toon.'

'This is very important information, Mrs McKean,' said Graham. 'I want you to do me a favour.'

'Aye, what?'

'When we go away, I want you to get some paper and a pen, sit back, try to relax and think hard. You've remembered two important pieces of information – you may have more that you haven't thought of yet. I know it's a pain, but you'll be helping us immensely if you can conjure up anything more.'

'Aye, I will. I'll do it the minute you're away.' A spark of hope appeared in her eyes, replacing the hollow stare she had worn on their arrival.

'Dae you think this will help you find her?' asked Mr McKean.

'In this job, the smallest piece of information can make a huge difference.'

'Can you do me a favour, Inspector?' asked Mrs McKean, a sudden passion in her voice.

'Yes, of course.'

'Bring my wee lassie hame.'

The twittering of budgies filled the small room.

Machrie, the present

The large group of police officers in the golf club car park climbed into various vans, cars and people carriers. The wind was still strong though the rain had mercifully abated – at least for the time being.

Her uniform-issue fleece zipped up over her mouth, Chief Superintendent Symington shivered as she climbed into the front of the van beside DS Brian Scott, also dressed for the weather, his form bulked out by a flak jacket. Behind them, fifteen police officers laughed and joked as they readied themselves to take one of the routes up into the hills above Machrie.

The beam from Rathlin island lighthouse light flashed across a dark stretch of the restless sea from its perch on the very edge of Northern Ireland. The brightness of its sweeping light only served to highlight the paucity of the steel-grey dawn breaking weakly from the east.

Scott shivered as he looked at the dark Atlantic. 'You'd think that at my time o' life I'd be given a pass when it comes tae this type o' nonsense,' he moaned.

'Try and stay up-beat, DS Scott,' replied Symington. 'You're the man with the local knowledge here. Plus, you were the one who chased them into the hills last night.'

'Aye, I suppose so.'

'And you're my right-hand man.'

'What aboot Inspector Blake fae the Tactical Firearms Unit? He ranks above me.'

'He has his hands full positioning his men as we move the search forward – doing his thing. You're on the operational side with me.'

'While oor Jimmy's reclining in that glass box o' his, enjoying the central heating and the coffee.'

'He has a meeting with the ACC and Speirs later this morning. I'm sure he'd rather be here with us – despite the bloody weather,' she said, a stiff gust rocking the vehicle as they made their way through the village.

'I cannae understand this bloody Speirs, ma'am. He was bugger a' use when he was in the polis. Now he's a civvy and he's still heading up an inquiry? Wouldnae have happened in the good old days. The very worst man tae pair up wae Jimmy – I can tell you that without fear or favour.'

Symington sighed. 'It's a new approach, Brian. We can give cold cases to retired detectives with experience, freeing up serving officers to deal with the here and now. The way things were, officers – like yourself when you hand in your warrant card – ended up as store detectives, or working part time on building sites on security. It's a waste, especially with all the training and experience that's been invested in them.'

'But this isnae a cauld case, ma'am,' Scott persisted. 'As soon as it turned back intae a live inquiry your man should have been sent back tae Glasgow tae find some other ghosts tae resurrect. Dae you know how much history he's got wae the big man?'

Symington looked out of the window, deep in thought. She was constantly surprised by the small world of Scottish policing. Despite now being part of the wider Police Scotland, she was regularly involved with officers under her charge who knew their opposite numbers in Edinburgh, Aberdeen, or even further afield. And, it seemed, almost inevitably, there was always some kind of history. In her experience in the Met, while you might have heard of members of the new team, you rarely knew them.

She supposed that since Scottish police trainees all attended the same college there were bound to be connections. Mercifully, though, the type of enmity that existed between Daley and Speirs was a rare occurrence.

'Two miles o' this!' exclaimed Scott as the van jolted off down a rough forestry path. There were five main access points on to the hill. This one would lead them to a point closest to where Scott had spotted the light only a short time before.

'Well, I think we can be pretty sure they're still up there. We sealed off all the ways out and there's been no sign.'

'Ach, they could just have made a run for it across the fields. Scale a few barbed wire fences and Bob's your uncle. If you're prepared tae take pot shots at folk in the dark, ripping your troosers on a fence or two is no' going tae gie you a problem. They're likely halfway tae Peru by this time.'

'Peru?'

'I can never say Venezuela, ma'am.' He winked.

'Anyway, if that's true, what light did you see?'

'You don't know the folk here. They're forever cloaking aboot the countryside. Do you know that there's a whole bunch of guys here who get a big carry-oot of beer and whisky and wander across the hills until they get tae some auld shepherd's hut or something, light a fire and get pissed a' weekend. Wife an' the weans sat at hame, mark you.'

'Oh, that's not unusual, Brian. Where I come from they call it golf,' replied Symington drily.

'It's a' the fun o' the fair roon here, let me tell you.' He stared out as the view of the sea disappeared. 'And I know fine I'll end up in a boat before much longer.' He paused. 'Shit, my lovely wife's arriving today!'

'Oh dear. I'm sure they'll make her comfortable back at the office if you're still out on the hill.'

As Scott pondered the arrival of his significant other, the van bumped and jolted until they slowed into a clearing – no more than a vehicle turning point – amid a coppice of tightly spaced fir trees.

'Ah, this is our embarkation point,' announced Symington. 'Everybody out!'

As they stepped out into the cold grey dawn, a spray of rain that quickly turned into a downpour began to drench the search party of police officers. They all struggled into the hooded plastic bags that were grandly entitled 'emergency rainwear'.

'Happy days,' opined Scott as the rain thudded off Symington's cap.

Daley was drinking yet another coffee when his mobile rang. He'd managed to snooze in his reclining office chair for an hour or so, but this rest had done little to banish his fatigue.

He squinted at the screen. 'No way,' he said to himself when he saw Liz's name emblazoned across it. He declined the call and switched on his computer. Colin Galt's face appeared on the monitor, though looking much younger than the man Daley knew. A youth with dark curls stared out at him, an image taken from an old Paisley College of Technology matriculation card. As it turned out, Galt had attended this institution prior to moving to Strathclyde University around the time women began to go missing midweek from Glasgow nightclubs.

As Daley studied the features, he tried to place himself in the young Galt's shoes. He'd been brought up well, at the heart of a decent family. It transpired that his father had very worked hard to build up the business Colin now ran. Despite its small size, the company back then was still profitable. Colin and his sister had had a rather privileged childhood when compared with their peers in Kinloch. Foreign holidays, junior membership of the local tennis and golf clubs, private tutors – all of this spilled off the screen as Daley read the background report compiled by one of his detectives.

There was little that pointed to a young man with the capacity to murder women; but then again, there rarely was. Daley matched up what was known of Galt's movements to the dates and times the nine women had disappeared.

Suddenly, as he scrolled down this list of information, a photograph appeared. It was the same young Galt, dressed in a gaudy orange tracksuit top, typical of its time. He was standing beside a striking-looking young woman. Both were giving a thumbs-up to the camera. She had light-coloured hair, and although she was wearing large round sunglasses, Daley found something about her very familiar.

The scene behind was that of a seafront – not Kinloch, but definitely Scotland, Daley thought, as he looked at cars and passers-by, inadvertently frozen in the image.

He called the mobile belonging to DC Martin, the young detective who was working on Galt's profile.

'Aye, what's up?' said a tired voice.

'DC Martin, it's DCI Daley.'

'Oh . . . oh, sorry, sir. I'm just at home catching a couple of hours' sleep.'

'Don't worry about that. I'm looking at the Galt file.'

'Yes?' The voice on the other end of the line was wary, the young man no doubt concerned he'd made a mistake.

'The image of him with a woman in sunglasses?'

There was a pause while Martin desperately searched his newly alert memory. 'That one's from Galt's house, sir. It was loose in a drawer. We found it last night, after he'd been shot.'

'You have no idea who she is? I mean, there was nothing on the back of the image to identify her? I'm thinking of a name written on the back of a photo, or something like that.'

'No, sir. If there had been, I'd have noted it down. There were a lot of photos, but mainly more recent ones. Mostly Galt and his wife and kids. I wasn't sure you'd be very interested in them, sir. This one just jumped out.'

'And do you have any idea where it was taken?'

'I'd have to take another look, but I don't think so.'

'You've done well, Martin. If you feel up to it, I'd like you back in as soon as possible.'

Daley ended the call and looked back at the image that now filled his screen. From memory, Galt was above average height, perhaps five feet ten or eleven. In the photograph, the girl beside him looked around the same size.

Suddenly, in his mind, Daley was back in Glasgow, more than twenty years ago.

28

Glasgow, 1994

A group of detectives sat in the muster room at Pitt Street, Strathclyde Police HQ in Glasgow.

This room had been newly designated smoke free, and there were disgruntled murmurs as hardened smokers suddenly found nothing to do with their hands. By way of compensation, the coffee machine was much busier, the beverage being used in the absence of tobacco.

At the head of the large room, DI Graham was flanked by DS Speirs and acting DS Daley. Behind him, a carousel projector hummed as it beamed a square white patch onto a screen on the wall.

'Right, ladies and gentlemen, let's settle down, shall we?' As the room came to order Graham alighted from his seat and walked to the projector, picked up a small remote control and pressed a button. One by one, the faces of women reckoned to be victims of the Midweek Murderer flashed by. The final three images were accompanied by thick crosses in red felt pen, indicating that their remains were as yet undiscovered, though the circumstances under which they had disappeared were identical to those of the wretched women whose bodies had been found. Graham left the last image on the screen.

'This is Anne Marie McKean. As you know, she disappeared last Wednesday from the Palace Club. Same MO as the rest, but as yet – as you also know – we have no body.'

'You're convinced she's a victim, gaffer?'

'Yes, DS Speirs. I know we found the earlier victims very easily – too easily, in my opinion. But I think this poor girl and the previous two women are also victims.'

'So what's changed, sir?' asked a voice from the floor.

'What's changed, Charlie, is that I believe our killer has had a close shave. He was taunting us before; now, for some reason, he has to be more careful.'

'You sure he's no' just fed up sneaking corpses intae various parts of the city, sir?' asked Speirs. 'Might even be a copycat.'

'As you know, Bobby, it's hard to fathom the mind of a killer. But from all the advice we've had from our profiler guy, we're sure the same hand is at work.'

'So, it's not some other sick bastard, sir?' came another voice from the floor.

'No, not in my opinion, Amy.'

'Or the guy fae California,' opined Speirs somewhat dismissively.

DI Graham clicked the button on the remote control once more. On screen the frontages of five Glasgow nightclubs appeared. 'Again, as you know, these are the places from where our victims went missing. We've tried discreet observation at each of the premises over the last few weeks, but come up with nothing. However, we have new information.' There was a murmur of interest from the collected detectives. 'DS Daley, the floor is yours.'

Daley cleared his throat and stood. 'As we know, examination of the victims we have prove that sexual intercourse with a male took place near or soon after death. We've always believed that the victims were entrapped, coerced in some way to leave the clubs by the killer himself. Now we're not sure. We think he might be using a proxy.'

Speirs leaned forward in his chair and addressed Daley, his head craning up to look the tall detective directly in the face. 'You mean *you* think a proxy might be being used. I think that theory is pish.' This elicited sniggers from the floor.

Undaunted, Daley continued. 'The information we have is pretty conclusive. It would appear that our victims are being led to the killer by a third party, or parties. We have a number of theories as to how this is happening, but we now reckon each of these women has somehow been befriended by someone working in concert with our killer.'

Quiet chatter now filled the room. Until now, it had been assumed that the unfortunate victims had been picked up by the murderer himself. After all, this was the pattern with which detectives across the globe had become familiar. A charismatic psychopath charming an unsuspecting victim to death: it was a classic scenario.

'I want tae make a point,' said Speirs, standing and indicating to Daley that he should resume his seat. His young colleague shrugged, but remained standing. 'Anyhow,' Speirs continued, glaring at the acting DS, 'this is the opinion o' this new-fangled profiler young Daley here was keen tae employ. In my opinion, it's mistaken. I mean, the guy's never even been tae Glasgow. We fax him, and he faxes back.' He paused. 'Wae the greatest o' respect, sir,' he turned to DI Graham, 'I don't think this is the right way tae go about things. I want my opposition to this line of inquiry noted.'

Graham addressed his number two in the Serious Crime Squad. 'We've been through this. These profilers are used all the time in the States, aye, and down south by the Met. Times change, Bobby. If the generations of police officers that came before us hadn't been receptive to change – progress – we'd still be back in the dark ages in terms of detection. We're standing at the threshold of new procedures and techniques that will transform the way we do our job. This is one of them. Just sit down and listen, DS Speirs.'

Again, Daley cleared his throat, emboldened by a wink from Brian Scott sitting in the third row, thoroughly enjoying Speirs's humiliation.

'We intend to set a trap for this third party.' Daley turned back to the projector. 'And this is what we'll do.'

Kinloch, the present

History teacher Allan Gilligan had been taking students from Kinloch Academy to the ruins of the old castle high on the hills just outside the town for almost thirty years. Still, he worried that one of his more headstrong pupils would ignore the warnings and plummet down the sheer drop on to the rocky shoreline far below. The proximity of the high cliffs with the broiling sea eating at their base always worried him.

Along with his colleague, he drilled the importance of staying close together and – for once – doing what they were told. There had been an incident only four years ago, when in order to impress his female classmates a testosterone-fuelled teenage boy had jumped from what was left of a wall, only to break his ankle on the uneven ground below. A nurse and ambulance had arrived very quickly to save the day, but now, staring out over the restless sound under the lowering grey sky, Gilligan began to worry that another disaster was imminent.

This kind of fretting was part of who he was. The very trait he'd chastised his late father for had now become his own bête noir. In short, he was a worrier, much happier imparting wisdom in the classroom than being responsible for field trips. However, he realised that such visits could spark a passion for history in a young mind that could last for ever; something a dusty old book, or even a flickering computer screen, could never do.

'Right, you lot, stay here within the ruins. Do not climb, do not wander off, do not damage anything – just behave!' This admonishment was greeted by the same collective groan he'd been hearing for almost three decades, but he hoped that the glare he directed at each of his fifteen charges would emphasise the warning. 'Now, gather round.' Somewhat reluctantly the small group of teenagers arranged themselves in a rough circle around himself and his teaching assistant Courtenay Sharp.

'As you know, these are the fourteenth-century remains of Killcallan Castle. To whom did this once fine fortification belong?' He looked around the group, unsurprised when a stout girl with dark brown hair and thick glasses raised her hand almost immediately. 'Yes, Sheridan, enlighten us all.'

'Archibald Campbell, the third earl, sir.'

'Absolutely correct, Sheridan, well done. And it is rumoured that that infamous family helped themselves to this place when its previous occupant, Somerled, Lord of the Isles, was killed by the crown. That's still speculation, mark you.' Noticing that the attention of his charges was already on the wane, he changed tack. 'Now, what are we *really* looking for?'

He looked around again. 'No, not you this time, Sheridan. Let's try someone else . . . you, Malcolm McConnachie.'

The young man with red hair looked about, then grinned. 'Is it buried treasure, sir?' he said, sniggering at the intentional simplicity of his reply.

'No. Try again, McConnachie.'

The boy rolled his eyes. 'It's the hole thing.'

'The *hole thing*? No need to guess what's on your mind most of the day.' Gilligan paused to enjoy the giggling this elicited. 'What *hole thing*?'

'Ach, I canna mind whoot it's called – something French, sir.'

'Anyone?' asked Gilligan, opening the question to the floor, knowing from where the answer would come.

'Oubliette, sir,' shouted Sheridan, a smug look on her face.

'I sometimes wonder if you're the only person who listens to what I'm saying, my dear. Yes, the famous oubliette. A particularly secure form of medieval dungeon. Tell me why it's so secure, McConnachie.'

'Whoot?'

'Why is it almost impossible to escape from an oubliette?'

'Oh, right – even I know the answer tae that yin, sir. It's cos there's nae door.'

'Well done, Mr McConnachie. *There's nae door*. We know Killcallan had a particularly claustrophobic oubliette, very narrow in circumference and very deep. It is immortalised in the *Annals* of Thomas Whey, an unfortunate English visitor who spent almost a year in it. There's also a reference in Barbour's poem to the "dark hole o' Killcallan". I knew you'd find that funny, McConnachie. Maybe you can tell us what's unusual about this notorious prison cell?'

'I know that tae, sir.'

'Wonders will indeed never cease. Pray, do enlighten us, Malcolm.'

'Nae bugger knows where it is, sir.'

'How well put. However, you're right. The oubliette, though much discussed by historians and local folk, has never been found. So, it's time to make a name for yourselves and Kinloch Academy by finding this semi-mythical structure, while Miss Sharp and I enjoy a cup of coffee.'

'Whoot aboot the ghost, sir?' asked a timid-looking girl, the hood of her rain jacket pulled forward over her forehead. 'I heard it's the earl's wife.'

Hearing this, a number of her classmates – notably Malcolm McConnachie – burst into gales of laughter.

'Okay, calm down, you lot. Let me tell you, Mandy. There's not a castle in the world that isn't populated by some sort of ghost or other. I've been coming here for thirty years and rest assured I've never seen any ghosts. Just enthusiastic students taking in what they're seeing and writing sensible essays on same to help them with the continuous assessment part of their exams. So, my advice is to brave the ghost, remember the oubliette, think of your grades and get on with it!'

As his students headed off to explore what was left of Killcallan Castle, the young teaching assistant poured steaming coffee into two plastic mugs from a thermos flask.

'Wouldn't it be great if they found it, Allan,' she said, handing him a mug.

'What, the ghost?'

'No, the oubliette.'

'Oh, I wouldn't worry too much about that. I'm not really sure it ever existed. And even if it did, it's likely buried under a few feet of earth and grass. It'll take more than the fine young girls and boys of S4 to find that; the archaeologists have been searching for decades. Still, it'll keep them amused for a while.' He looked up at the dark grey sky, mirrored by the waves in the sound. 'At least the rain's still off. Oh, we have biscuits. Thank you, Courtenay, how thoughtful.'

29

The line of dark-clad police officers stretched across the high moor atop the majestic sea cliffs. It was almost 10 a.m., and no sign of the two people for whom they were searching.

Symington stopped to answer her phone, nodding silently then ending the call with a word of thanks.

'Don't tell me, ma'am. Nae joy – am I right?' said Scott, drawing deeply on a cigarette.

'No, not at the moment, but plenty of time, Brian.'

'Plenty o' time for me tae freeze and be soaked to death by turns. I'm just drying off, then another bloody shower of rain appears o'er the horizon.'

'Much more likely smoking will kill you first. We're hardly slogging across the tundra, are we? It's springtime, after all.'

'I've always hated bloody searches. Nine times oot o' ten we find nothing, and all you get for your pains is blisters on your feet, an' a cauld.' He flicked his cigarette away and watched it tumbling in the strong wind.

'Very environmentally friendly, DS Scott. If you were anyone else, I'd make sure you were given a fixed penalty fine for that.'

'I'd happily pay the fine if this wind would just drop and we could get the chopper up here.'

Symington shrugged her shoulders then plodded on. They were walking across a broad clifftop. 'So you reckon these marine archaeologists have something to do with this?'

'Best guess, ma'am. It's all a bit coincidental, is it no'? Big find o' illicit booty, no sign o' them. Looks tae me as though Francombe's no' been paying enough attention to her staff.'

'You can hardly blame her if some of her charges have gone rogue. It's like me taking the hit for the actions of one of my more wayward officers.' She smiled at Scott, knowing she had much to do in order to regain his trust, having had reason to reinforce her authority over him a few weeks before. Though she liked and respected Scott – was indebted to him, even – it was easy to foresee a scenario whereby she had to answer for some of his less conventional methods.

'Aye, touché,' said Scott.

There was a distant crack, which made the heads of every officer on the hillside turn towards the noise. In seconds, the chief superintendent's radio burst into life.

'Two-twenty. We've got them, ma'am. One shot fired by the suspects, no injuries.'

'Give me the coordinates, two-twenty.' Hurriedly, she typed numbers into her navigation device, looking to her left towards a small rise. 'Roger, got it, two-twenty. Make sure everyone is safe – leave this to the firearms officers. I'll send more your way. We'll follow, but my priority is the safety of all those on the ground. We know that whoever is using this weapon is pretty competent.' She ended the conversation and briefed the inspector of the firearms detachment.

Soon, led by the armed officers, the entire search party focused its attention on a broad stretch of boggy ground at the foot of a steep incline.

'Who says we never find anything, Brian?'

'As long as they don't find us, ma'am. Keep your heid doon and let the boys wae the guns sort this.'

'Once they've secured this piece of ground here, you and I will move forward. I'm in charge of the operation, remember.'

'I'm no'!'

'But you have the experience, DS Scott.'

'Aye, the experience o' getting shot – no' one I want tae repeat. Is there no' a boat I can go on?'

Symington listened to another brief message and the pair crouched forward, one much more willingly than the other.

Malcolm McConnachie looked about. When he realised neither Mr Gilligan nor Miss Sharp was in his eyeline, he fished a battered packet of cigarettes from his pocket.

He looked round for a suitable location in which to enjoy a quick smoke undetected. It was too risky to chance it within the confines of the ruins, but looking across to his left he noticed a line of gorse bushes, their yellow flowers bright in the dull light. He slouched towards the end of the hedge, looking back to make sure neither Mr Gilligan nor his assistant could see him.

Soon he was on the other side of the bush, searching about for a suitable perch. He frowned when all he could find was a moss-covered flagstone, but it beat sitting on the wet ground, and he was delighted to note that despite the slimy moss the ground here was not as saturated as the rest of the field.

He took off his jacket and used it to cover the stone, then sat down, placing a cigarette between his lips and setting the tip aglow with a lighter from his pocket. He'd only been smoking for a few months, but already the effect of the bitter smoke was to make him relax as he sighed at the pleasures of nicotine, too young to give a moment's thought to its more lethal properties. He was young, and therefore immortal.

His mobile phone began to buzz in his pocket, banishing this existential peace. He wrestled it from his jacket, and smiled when he saw the name on the screen. 'Pogo, man, how's it hangin'?' The response sent him into a fit of laughter. 'She's so hot! How did an ugly bastard like you manage tae pull a chick like her?'

Almost forgetting the illicit nature of what he was doing, McConnachie let rip with a belly laugh, which sent him into a paroxysm of coughing. 'Aw, stop, Pogo, man. I'm up at that auld castle wae auld Gilligan and Miss Sharp. Having a fly fag, man.'

As he said this, McConnachie became aware of another sound. At first he thought it was the wind groaning off the nearby cliffs. But as he ended the call and listened more intently, what he was hearing seemed more akin to wailing. He shot up off the flagstone, flicking the cigarette across the wet field and letting his mobile tumble on to the ground. Quickly, he picked it up and ran full pelt round to the other side of the gorse and back towards the ruins of the castle.

'No running, McConnachie,' roared Gilligan, seeing his errant pupil vaulting a short wall. 'What on earth's wrong with you?' Then he noticed that McConnachie seemed unable to speak. 'Good grief, boy, I know you're normally pale under that red hair, but you're white as sheet. If you've been taking drugs . . .'

'I think I heard the ghost, s-sir.'

'The what? I don't expect much from you, McConnachie, but even so I didn't think you'd display this ridiculous hysteria.'

Hearing what was going on, and seeing the state of alarm

afflicting her normally cool classmate, Mandy began to scream, and was soon joined by other members of the class, wondering what had happened to their red-haired companion.

'Right! Everyone calm down,' Gilligan snapped. 'Now, McConnachie, get your wits about you, man, and tell me what you think you heard.'

'O'er there, s-sir,' replied the schoolboy, his voice wavering and finger shaking as he pointed towards the gorse bushes.

'And let me think, just what were you doing over there? Against my specific instructions about not leaving the grounds of the castle, too.'

'It's like a screeching, sir. Like a lassie screaming, man.'

'Probably the collective voices of long-dead teachers bemoaning the hopeless nature of their chosen profession.'

'Shouldn't we take a look?' said Miss Sharp.

'Oh, all right. Come with me, McConnachie, and show us all where you heard this – this nonsense.'

'You go first, sir,' said McConnachie, holding back.

'I don't know what's happening to young men these days,' muttered Gilligan, following his pupil's directions. He made his way around the gorse, his class trailing after him in a long line, headed by Miss Sharp.

'O'er there,' said McConnachie. 'Jeest on that stone – the one wae the moss on it, sir.'

Gilligan plodded off through the thick wet grass until he reached the large flagstone, quite surprised when his feet settled on less sodden ground. He cocked his head, a pained expression on his face. 'Be quiet! Let me hear this.' He knelt down on the stone, rubbing around the mossy surface with his gloved hand. 'What the hell is this?' he said, turning to Miss Sharp, now at his side.

From beneath the large flat stone, the voice was muffled, distant, but frantic and unmistakable. 'Help me, please God, help me!'

30

What Daley saw first was a white minibus, windows steamed up with condensation caused by the breath of the excited chatter of the pupils within. He noticed two figures standing by the bus, one of whom he recognised as a teacher from the local secondary school.

'Mr Gilchrist, is that right?' he asked.

'Gilligan, DCI Daley. But not a bad effort, considering you and I only met briefly at the school when you addressed my class – a talk on the dangers of legal highs, if I recall.'

'Ah, yes. Apologies. I meet so many people in the course of my work that names tend to drift away.'

As he spoke, the personnel from Kinloch's Fire and Rescue service appeared over the rise, complete with what looked like digging equipment and a generator, all pulled behind a stout red Land Rover.

'Can you point us to the spot you first heard the shouting, Mr Gilligan?'

'Yes, just follow me. The worrying aspect to all this is that though I heard the voice myself – quite distinctly, in fact – it was only once. Despite my calls, I heard nothing else in return.' He stepped awkwardly over the remnant of an ancient wall as they made their way towards the line of gorse bushes.

'Who was the first person to hear this calling, Mr Gilligan?'

'Oh, young McConnachie. One of our less enthusiastic pupils and more disruptive influences, I'm sad to say. I must confess, I enjoyed the look of terror on his face rather more than I should have when he came rushing to tell his tale. I hope that doesn't sound too unworthy of my profession, Chief Inspector?'

'Not at all. I know all about dealing with difficult adolescents. Large part of a young cop's life – usually wrestling with them outside some licensed premises or other.'

Once Gilligan had circumnavigated the bushes he stopped. 'Here we are. You'll note that the conditions underfoot feel rather different here.'

Daley stared down, taking in every detail of the scene before him. 'I also notice this,' he replied, kneeling down stiffly on one knee. He pushed his big hands into the rough grass, and as though he was peeling off a sticker from some packaging hauled up a great piece of turf. Though covered by wild grass on top, the great sod was squarely cut, with neat edges. Beneath it lay another grey flagstone.

'Well, bugger me,' spluttered Gilligan, who then looked around nervously lest his pupils had heard such profanity from the mouth of their teacher.

After a few words between Daley and the officer in charge, the Fire and Rescue service got to work.

Glasgow, 1994

WPC Margaret Baird had ten years' police service, and despite not being a full-time CID officer was used to being seconded to various units for this or that operation. Indeed, she had been offered a permanent position as a detective on numerous occasions, but preferred her role as a uniformed beat officer. She liked her old haunts where she had illicit tea breaks: her visits to the old folks' home, the high school, and the homeless hostel, all to be found on her beat. Her regular patrol of the row of shops she was responsible for provided her with tip-offs that had led to the capture of many a petty criminal – and indeed, some not so petty.

Only a few years ago, she had gleaned information at the local hairdressers leading to the arrest of one of Glasgow's most feared crime lord's favourite lieutenants. In turn, this had brought her face to face with the man himself, when he hopped out of a large black German sports car and – breathing whisky fumes into her face as he challenged her toe to toe – intimated that a repeat of this feat of detection would lead to her untimely and viscerally painful demise.

This had worried her for a while – not the threat, but how James Machie had come to know of her involvement. Her name had purposely been left out of the case notes, and as far as she knew, no one apart from the investigating team had been aware of her role in the conviction.

It could mean only one thing, of course: Machie had been alerted by one of her colleagues.

This, as well as making her doubt the career she had chosen, confirmed her gut feeling that she was happy being a good, old-fashioned community cop.

Yet here she was in the main office of the Serious Crime Squad, make-up plastered on her face, wearing a skirt that barely merited the name, given the paucity of cloth used to make it.

'Aye, you scrub up well, Maggie,' said Speirs.

'Beats me how you can't use one of your own WDCs for this,' she replied.

'Their faces are too well known, kid. We have tae assume

that oor killer – or this imaginary friend of his oor *acting* DS is so keen on – may have knowledge of the squad. Naebody outside the Toonheid knows who the fuck you are.'

'You've a lovely turn o' phrase,' observed DC Scott.

'You've a lovely turn o' phrase, *Sergeant*, son. Don't come the auld soldier wae me – got it?' he spat.

'Now, now, boys. Let's keep it civil,' said Baird, adjusting her black stockings. 'Here, don't you think I look more like a hooker than a lassie off on a night out?'

'Nah. Mind it's Grab a Granny night. You auld birds have to display mair plumage tae pull a mate,' said Speirs.

'I'll have you know I'm no' even forty yet!' she protested.

'Is that no' the average age of a granny up in the Toonheid?'

Before she could reply, Daley entered the room, eyes fixed on the file he was reading.

'Watch oot, Maggie, here's Hercule. This crap is all his idea.' This time Speirs's sneer was plain to see.

Daley looked up from his reading material and smiled. 'You'll do the job nicely, Maggie,' he said. The pair had worked together when he was a probationer, and he had a lot of respect for her as a person and as a police officer.

'Right, Jimmy, son. Can we go through this again?'

'Of course.'

'I go into the club on my tod – sit at the bar, or whatever, right?'

'Yup.'

'How come you've chosen that dive on Clyde Street?' she enquired.

'Our killer never uses the same club twice. Even Glasgow has a limited number of establishments that have these kinds of nights. We just had to make an educated guess.'

'Whit, based on your long experience in the job? You're barely oot the wrapper,' scoffed Speirs.

'Based on the fact that we know our killer likes seedier establishments away from the likes of Sauchiehall Street. Based on the fact that he has used mostly backstreet clubs in the area near the river, away from CCTV coverage. And based on a discussion with the ACC.'

Speirs shook his head, his face bearing a mirthless grin. 'Fucking smart arse,' he said under his breath as he left the room, slamming the door behind him.

'He sure failed at charm school, eh?' suggested Scott. 'I bet you the trees are full o' birds where he stays.'

'He's always been like that,' said Baird. 'Story is that his uncle was an ACC in the old Lanarkshire Constabulary. Otherwise he'd never have sniffed the job.'

'The cleansing department's loss is oor gain.'

Daley looked at his watch. 'Right, Maggie, let's go for it. And remember, there's cops watching your back – some of them armed – both inside and outside the club.'

'Is that supposed to cheer me up? Mind, I did a stint doon at the shooting range in Oxford Street – och, back in the days they couldn't think o' anything for us women to do. None o' them could hit a barn door at two paces!'

'I've failed three times,' said Scott ruefully.

'That's because you've usually been on a bender the night before,' said Daley.

'Och, you know fine how I hate loud bangs. Do you know, Maggie? I've this recurring dream o' being shot and falling headlong intae the sand.' He shook his head.

'Well, son, you know my advice,' said Baird.

'What?'

'Don't go to Largs for your holidays. Noo, Jimmy, can we get going, or I'll need the cludgie again.'

The hills above Machrie, the present

There they were, two figures on the sheep-dotted hillside, across a small valley. Though the pair were crouching on the ground behind some bulky tufts of grass, they were visible to the police officers who faced them, four high-powered rifles trained on them, red dots playing a game of catch me if you can in the gun sights.

'Right, Inspector, well done.'

'They must be cold, wet and exhausted, ma'am.'

'Which may lead to a certain desperation? I hear you,' she replied.

'Oh, here we go,' muttered Scott. 'Me in the path of another desperado wae a shooter determined tae blow my heid off.'

Symington glared at him. 'Please shut up, DS Scott. If you don't have what it takes to do your duty here, get back to Kinloch and we'll find you a cosy desk job.' She spat out the words, leaving Scott in no doubt who was in charge.

Scott's face shone red and he turned to face his young superior. 'I've been near killed twice by men wae guns. I'm sure none of us here doesn't have something from their past that scares them.' He paused, staring at her with a blank expression. 'Is that no' right, *ma'am*?'

The rage she felt at the use of the exaggerated title almost made her rise to her feet in anger. Sensing this, Scott put his arm on her shoulder.

'I apologise, ma'am. Fear can dae nasty things tae a man.'

'And a woman,' she said emphatically, turning her head from him, eyes blazing.

The crack of a gunshot screamed overhead, sending all those but the firearm's unit forcing their faces into the ground.

'We have him in our sights, ma'am. I strongly advise that we take him out.'

'Not a kill shot, if possible.'

'If that's an order, I can't comply, ma'am. We'll do our best, but this is no exact science. The call and its consequences are yours.'

For a moment, Scott felt a pang of sympathy for this woman forced to make life or death decisions on this windswept hillside. Then he thought about her attitude towards him since he'd saved her career, her big salary, her pension and her position of authority over experienced men like himself. Aye, this is why the big cheque lands on your doorstep, my dear, he thought to himself. Hell mend you.

Another shot made them duck for cover.

'At your discretion, Inspector. Try your best.'

'Will do, ma'am.' He spoke into his lapel mic. 'A4 defensive return of fire – non-fatal if possible.'

These words had barely left his lips when a shot rang out and one of the figures across the valley went limp and began to slide from behind a protective tuft, accompanied by a high-pitched scream.

Scott shuddered. He knew how that felt. It was a pain he could never forget.

31

To the obvious disappointment of the pupils – and their teachers – Daley asked that the school party return to Kinloch as the Fire and Rescue service got to work. The pursuit on the hills above Machrie and the dangers involved were on his mind.

He watched the minibus make its way along the rough track away from the castle, then switched his attention to the careful lifting of great sods of turf that was revealing more flagstones.

Then, as they pulled away another layer of turf, there was a collective gasp when a very modern-looking iron cover was revealed; round, painted black, with a diameter of about three feet. It was a simple wrought-iron drain cover, unremarkable, to be found across the land.

'Looks as though the teacher wasn't the first to happen upon this well, or whatever it is,' remarked Stacey Marr, the senior fire officer.

'Indeed,' replied Daley. He kneeled on the flagstones and ran his hand across the iron circle. 'Who owns this land, does anyone know?'

'Kevin Finnerty, I think,' said Marr. 'His farmhouse is just up on the rise. Robertson, take a quick hike up there and see if he knows anything about this. Mind you, if it is as it looks

– a drain cover – how on earth did Gilligan and his pupils hear someone calling out?'

'And why cover it with turf?' said Daley. 'Not just that, but freshly laid turf, if I'm not mistaken.'

'Indeed,' said Marr. 'Also, as you might guess, I'm no stranger to fire hydrants – much the same thing – and that cover has been removed recently.'

'How can you tell?' asked Daley.

'Simple detection, DCI Daley.' She smiled. 'Look at these two slots.' She pointed to two rectangular gaps, each a few centimetres long by a couple wide, situated on either side of the middle of the iron construction and equidistant from it.

'They're there to yank the thing out, right?'

'Yup, DCI Daley – well put,' she said with a laugh.

'Sorry, I've never been a very practical man. Much to my father's chagrin,' he added more quietly. The sudden memory of his father showing him around the intricacies of plumbing suddenly sprang to mind. It was one of several other such attempted tutorials that had bored him to tears – one of the many reasons he'd joined the police rather than learn a trade.

'Well, I'd hazard a guess that this is a relatively new drain cover. In fact, I had to remove an almost identical one a few months ago when we had that flood in Kinloch.'

'Oh yes, I remember. Brian – my sergeant – was out buying rolls. To cut a long story short, he stepped off the kerb into the flooded street only to land in a pothole in the road, fall over, and watch our breakfast floating down Main Street.'

'Well, anyway,' said Marr, clearly anxious to get on. 'Look at the slots. The metal inside is bare; the protective paint has been scraped off with use.'

'Sorry to sound ignorant, but is that not to be expected?'

'Certainly, but to a drain cover hidden under a mound of turf? I would say unlikely. This cover has been removed recently – aye, and not just once or twice.'

Just as the words issued from her mouth, everyone froze as a piercing scream sounded beneath the drain cover.

'Quick, lads,' shouted Marr. 'Get this off!'

Glasgow, 1994

Maggie Baird had always hated nightclubs, even when she was young. Noisy, smelly places, where the drink was too expensive, more than likely watered down and where you spent half the night in the queue for the Ladies. She always reasoned that the chance of meeting the man of her dreams in such places was almost non-existent.

The man of her dreams. This individual still eluded her. In her heart, she realised that the tall, handsome, kind, faithful companion she craved didn't, in all probability, exist. She had a number of failed – badly failed – relationships under her belt, and had more or less given up hope of ever meeting the person with whom she could settle down.

She looked absently about the bar at which she sat on a high stool. The dance floor was in the next room, accessed by a few deep steps, the entrance a tacky faux proscenium arch. Despite this, even down here the music was almost deafening, and she was doubtful whether if anyone were to try to engage her in conversation she would be able to hear what was being said.

The bar was covered in a paint that made it sparkle under the array of coloured lights. She drained her glass and held it out, mouthing 'vodka and tonic' to a young barman with a nice arse. He smiled, took the glass from her and returned with a newly filled one, hand held out, intent on payment.

'Two pounds seventy – you should hang your head in shame,' she shouted above the din. 'Sixth o' a gill measure, tae.' He smiled and winked back at her before rushing off to serve the next customer.

The room was mostly occupied by women in their late thirties and – in many cases – well beyond. She'd considered her own make-up gaudy, but now, seeing some of her fellow clubbers, decided that she looked almost dowdy. One woman, whom Baird reckoned to be in her mid-fifties, was so caked in make-up it would have been impossible to recognise her without it. Light blue glittering eye shadow above false lashes, silver-tipped and at least an inch long, fought for attention against the backdrop of the thick orange carapace covering her face. Her lips were plastered in the brightest red lipstick Baird had ever seen, while her eyebrows were mere thin lines, drawn unevenly on to her forehead, one higher and more arched than the other. Her little black number revealed a plunging neckline and a pendulous belly, all propped up by thin legs with small ankles but burgeoning calf muscles, giving her an almost masculine aspect. In fact, Maggie genuinely wondered if she was in fact male.

I'll do anything not to end up like these sad bastards, she thought to herself. When I turn forty I'm just going to sit at home and read self-improvement books.

As she stirred her extra long drink – doubtless poured into such a glass to convince the imbiber that he or she was getting value for money – Baird was aware that someone had occupied the stool beside her.

Casually she turned to have a look, seeing a tall, awkward-looking woman with curly ginger hair and the minimum adornment of make-up and other decorative trimmings, wearing an unattractive, ill-fitting yellow dress that gaped at the neck, revealing an off-white bra that had clearly seen better days. For some reason, it struck Baird as strange that she had opted to paint her nails black while wearing this outfit, but after what she'd seen so far it seemed almost anything was possible in this parade of fading, failing vanity and self-delusion.

The woman, a good few years younger than herself, Maggie reckoned, made eye contact with her, smiled and shouted a greeting.

'Hi, I'm Alison. Are you here alone too?'

'Yes,' replied Baird, wondering whether the woman who was sharing the bar with her thought she was gay. 'Not many men about,' she hollered back, making sure there was no misunderstanding.

Her new companion shrugged. 'They won't be in for another hour or so. Filling up on Dutch courage at more reasonable prices.'

'Ah, good thinking. Wish I'd done the same.'

Daley and Scott were watching proceedings via a number of CCTV screens in the manager's office.

'Tall lassie, Jimmy. This could be oor women. That would be a bit o' luck, eh?'

'Too lucky, Bri. But, I suppose you never know – stranger things have happened. We'll just observe for the moment.'

'Should we no' alert Speirs? I mean, if things look likely, you know.'

'Nah, that mob would rush in and ruin it. We need

evidence. All we have just now is a tall lassie. We can't move on that.'

Scott nodded, his and Daley's eyes still fixed on the screens.

'Fancy a seat?' Alison pointed to an empty table at the back of the room. 'Might be a bit quieter.'

'Yes, why not? I'm Tina, by the way,' said Maggie casually. 'Pleased to meet you.'

They shook hands, ordered fresh drinks for which Alison insisted on paying, then made their way through the preening, screeching, gaudy crowd to a quiet table.

At least I can see the whole room, thought Maggie, as they took their seats. She opened her handbag to a slit, taking comfort from her small police radio within.

She reasoned that she would look less conspicuous with a companion; and at the very least she would have someone to talk to, as the operation, in all probability, would fizzle out and come to nothing.

She'd done this before.

Kinloch, the present

The figure that emerged from the deep hole on the end of two stout ropes was in a cage of thin, rusting flat-bar iron, untidily welded, clearly an amateur job. Helen McNeil was pale, her hair stood in filthy clumps, and the stench of her body was plain in the cool damp air. She looked around as though reborn, almost as though she was seeing life for the first time, having been removed from the horrors of her squalid confinement.

Helen squinted up at the grey sky through the bars of her

tiny cage. Mercifully it had stopped raining, but even though the ground was still saturated she fell to her knees sobbing uncontrollably, staring up at the faces looking down at her through long hair that straggled over her face.

A fireman got to work with a burning torch, and soon freed her from the ill-constructed cage.

'Thank . . . thank you all so much,' she managed to say through sobs, the thick blanket she had been given wrapped tightly around her.

Daley gestured to the Fire and Rescue personnel to give him and the liberated nurse space.

As they moved off, Daley said, 'Helen, we need to get you to the hospital. An ambulance is on its way from Kinloch.'

For a few moments she just looked straight at him, her eyes suddenly wild with terror, and then she said, 'What if it's one of them?'

'What do you mean?'

'One of my colleagues – the people I've worked with all these years. What if they did this to me?'

'Why would they do that?'

'You don't know the people of Kinloch. You think you do, Mr Daley, but you've not been here long enough. They resent anyone who isn't local – think of them as second-class citizens.'

'But you're well respected and liked – both in the hospital and by those in the community, from what I can gauge. I know Kinloch's tight-knit, but this is on the extreme side even for here.'

'You reckon?' A new determination flashed across her features. 'You're never part of the community here unless everyone can trace you back to a great-grandmother from Machrie, or a room and kitchen in the Glebe Fields. I got this job ahead of a local nurse. I'm sure that's what's behind all this.' She stopped and jabbed her right forefinger repeatedly into her temple, making Daley wince. 'I've had a lot of time to think in there, Mr Daley. Oh yes, you don't have much else to do when you're trapped in absolute darkness waiting to die.'

As if on cue, the distant sound of an ambulance siren echoed round the hillside, and she flung herself at the policeman, grabbing him tightly as the blanket fell on to the thick grass. Daley automatically shrank back from her odour.

'Don't let them put me back in there. They'll inject me with something and say it was a mistake. Please, please, DCI Daley.'

'If anyone is at fault, it's me. I left strict instructions you were to work only within the confines of the hospital. I should have made sure that those instructions were adhered to.'

'See, I'm right!'

'You insisted on attending the Machrie call, I believe.'

She said nothing, simply burying her head in Daley's chest as the ambulance swayed and bumped up the rough track to the castle and its newly uncovered dark secret.

As a paramedic tried to help McNeil into the vehicle she struggled wildly, holding her hand out to Daley and screaming his name. The detective realised just how gravely her imprisonment had affected this fragile woman.

Before he joined her in the ambulance, he stared down at the gaping black hole that had been her prison. The darkness seemed to pull him in, the same feeling he had when standing on a cliff's edge.

Her screams broke the spell, and he left the once legendary, newly discovered oubliette to be secured by the Fire and Rescue team.

'Poor Helen,' said a paramedic he vaguely recognised from his trips to the hospital and the bar at the County Hotel. 'She's lost her mind – thinks we're going to put her back in there.'

'Maybe she's not thinking straight,' said Daley. 'But one thing is for sure, someone imprisoned her in that hole.' He nodded at the medic and stepped into the ambulance beside the shivering, dishevelled, stinking figure of Nurse Helen McNeil.

32

The bar of the County was busy. As always, whenever some event of note took place in the area, the locals headed to their hostelry of choice in order to find out the real truth behind what was going on.

'They tell me she was gnawing at a rat when they found her,' said Hamish. Uncharacteristically, he was propped up on a stool at the bar, there being no spare seats at any of the tables on his arrival. 'The blood wiz fair dripping doon her chin – aye, absolutely that. They tell me she was jeest sucking up the tail like a piece on thon spaghetti they Italians like so much.'

'Oh, the poor woman,' said Annie. 'She must have been beside hersel' tae go tae such lengths.'

'It's hellish whoot starvation will dae tae a man – aye, and a woman as weel come tae that,' said Hamish, puffing at his unlit pipe.

'I mind she came up tae change a dressing on my faither's leg – och, this was years ago. Do you know, I'm sure we were having a bolognese when she arrived.'

'There you are,' replied Hamish, raising his eyes to the heavens. 'That incident was likely tae the forefront o' her mind when she was incarcerated doon in that great hole in the darkness, and managed tae trap a rat for her dinner. Aye, I can jeest imagine her sayin tae herself, "Noo that's just how Annie fae the County eats her pasta. I'll dae the same wae this rat's tail."'

'I'm not saying anything,' interrupted Malky, the paramedic who had taken the stricken nurse back to Kinloch Hospital and spoken to Daley. 'It's mair than my job's worth tae be spreading gossip, but I can tell you this, there were nae rats involved. I'm sure that doesn't contravene the Hippocratic oath.'

'Och, but you're a decent soul right enough, Malky Ramsay,' said Hamish. 'When – like me – you've pitched your life against the great Atlantic Ocean day after day, you know whoot awful necessities desperation can bring aboot. Sure, I'd tae eat an uncooked mackerel one day when I forgot my pieces. My auld skipper Sandy Hoynes said that the Japanese swore by eating raw fish.'

'Sashimi – have you never heard o' it?' said Annie.

'Aye, well, whootever they call it, it wisnae tae my taste. Food's no' right unless there's been a bit o' fire aboot it . . . or some other legitimate cooking method, you understand. In any event, I widna be sooking up a rat's tail as though it was a length o' spaghetti, no, no matter how bleak things were. A man has tae have his limits.'

'Funny we've never found whoot your limit is when it comes tae downing drams,' observed Annie.

'Ach, that's another matter entirely. How can you compare the consumption of the water o' life tae munching on an uncooked rat? Makes me wonder jeest whoot passes for standards in the kitchen here.'

Just as Annie was opening her mouth to let fly with a volley of expletives, the door swung open to reveal two figures. One tall, unkempt, in a crumpled suit and bearing an unhealthy pallor; the other shorter, with his neatly cut salt and pepper hair still wet, sticking up in spikes as though it had just been roughly towelled.

'Whoot on earth are you wearing, Brian?' enquired Annie, looking at the grey jogging pants and hooded top her new customer had on.

'It's the only thing I could find in the office tae change intae. One o' they young fellas gave me a loan o' it. I've been soaked all day . . .' He was about to say more when he paused, sniffled, panted, then let out a tremendous sneeze. 'See,' he said, wiping his dripping nose on his sleeve. 'I've caught double pneumonia – aye, and a' doon tae the shite job I've tae dae.'

'One large malt and a ginger beer,' said Daley, wincing suddenly as he passed his right hand across his chest.

'Here, you're as pale as a ghost, Mr Daley,' said Annie, a look of concern on her face.

'Indigestion,' he replied. 'I'd fish for my lunch. I'm always the same, but I can't resist mackerel.'

'Was it cooked?' asked Hamish.

'Indigestion doesnae make you pale in the face,' said paramedic Malky Ramsay. 'Sure you don't want me tae check you out?'

'Indigestion might not make you peelly-wally, but no sleep will do it every time,' said Scott. 'And too many drams.'

'Well, would you listen tae that,' came a familiar female voice from behind. 'This fae the man that never so much as touched a drink. Don't you listen tae him, Jimmy. Same wrong wae you as always – you work and worry too much. It's been like that all the years I've known you.' She returned her gaze to Brian. 'What on earth have you got on? I know polis uniforms are getting mair casual, but . . .'

'Ella, dear. How are you?' said Scott. He hugged his wife as Annie looked on from behind the bar, a forced smile on her face.

Glasgow, 1994

Though she'd been asked to blend in, WPC Maggie Baird felt she was maybe enjoying herself too much. Though she'd only had three vodkas, she felt as though she'd consumed much more. She was even finding her new companion surprisingly good company. Since she'd visited the Ladies, the evening seemed much more tolerable.

A small balding man sidled up to their table. His clothes were at least a decade out of fashion, and the Cuban-heeled boots that stuck out from below wide-bottomed trousers were clearly an attempt to make up for lack of height.

At least he wasn't wearing a toupee, thought Maggie, though it took her a few seconds to remember why she was in this place dressed as she was. She squinted at the man and tried to concentrate. Who knew? This could be the murderer – or at least his assistant.

As it turned out, the man – who introduced himself as Dougie – seemed much more interested in the younger Alison. She slid her large frame nearer to Maggie as her admirer helped himself to a seat beside them.

It wasn't long before Maggie noticed that Alison looked increasingly discomforted by the attentions of the middle-aged man. She decided to intervene.

'Listen, you,' she said. 'Who invited you tae shit wae ush?' She broke into a fit of the giggles when she realised how the slur in her voice had made her sound. Alison grabbed her hand under the table, trembling.

'How come yous are here if yous don't fancy a bit o' chat an' a stagger aboot the dance floor wae me? Are yous a pair o' dykes, or what?'

Maggie sat back, a mean look spreading across her face. 'See me, I've never been tempted by a member o' the shame shex as me in my life. Not that there's anything wrang wae that, mind you. What folk dae in their personal lives is their business, none o' mine.' She straightened her back and composed herself, her gaudily painted lips pursed in a prim, schoolmistress-like thin line. 'But I tell you thish for nothing. I'd rather mate wae a fucking scabby donkey than have anything tae dae wae a wee shite like you.'

'And dae you speak for your granddaughter, auld yin?' said Dougie, smiling at his own wit.

'Naw, but she doeshn't want anything tae dae wae you neithers. Sure you don't, Alison?'

Maggie's companion shook her head and said, 'Please leave us alone.'

'Aw, c'mon, lassie, gie a guy a chance. I mean, you're not exactly belle o' the ball yersel'. I would have thought you'd be happy wae any kind o' attention, cos you sure don't look like you're getting much, if you get my drift. You and your granny.'

Unsteadily, Maggie got to her feet and leaned across the table, watching Dougie's eyes flash as he spied her plunging neckline. 'Fuck off, pervert!' she shouted, attracting looks from around the bar, despite the general din.

'Aye, aw right – keep your girdle on, auld yin,' said Dougie, holding his hands up in a gesture of surrender and backing away from the table.

When she sat back down, Maggie couldn't understand why she'd just landed on her backside on the floor.

'Fuck me, Alison. The vodka's strong in here, eh?' She laughed as the younger woman hauled her to her feet with powerful arms.

Looking on from the nightclub office on a flickering black-and-white CCTV screen, Brian Scott raised one eyebrow. 'Are you sure you chose the right woman for this, Jimmy? She's no' looking too clever.'

'Probably an act,' his colleague replied, though he looked less than convinced.

'If you say so, boss. But mind you, if she can act as good as this she should be on the stage, no' pounding the beat up in the Toonheid.'

Scott had barely finished speaking when the screen registered a flurry of flailing bodies: a fight had broken out. A group of about six young men who had been drinking quietly together had suddenly turned on two newcomers. Daley watched a blade flash under the lights, as a stool was cracked over a young man's head.

'Call Stewart Street, Bri,' he said as he watched a team of doormen enter the fray.

As Scott called for uniformed officers to attend the fracas, Daley returned his attention to the table where Maggie Baird and her companion had been sitting. It was empty.

'Delta Alpha One to all units, I've lost visual on Maggie. Report, over.'

Scott looked at Daley with a puzzled expression, and said, 'They've probably gone for a waz, Jimmy. You worry too much.'

'Check out the toilets, please, Delta Alpha Five.'

'Roger, Jim. Stand by.' The voice was barely audible above

the shouting that accompanied the fight. After less than a minute: 'That's a negative, Delta Alpha One.'

Daley grabbed his radio. 'To all stations outside premises, we've lost sight of subject. Anything to report, over?'

Through background noise and crackle of the radio, the silence was deafening

33

'So you're wae us the night then, Mrs Scott,' said Annie in her best Sunday voice.

'Ella, please – I'm no' royalty.' She looked across the room to a table where Daley and her husband were deep in conversation. 'Nor am I likely to be, neither.'

They both laughed.

'So, Jimmy,' Scott was saying, 'what's happening with oor three bodies up in the hospital?'

'Symington's up there now. Helen's in a state of collapse. I don't know how this is going to affect her.'

'I'm no' surprised, after being banged up doon that hole.' Scott shuddered. 'I cannae even imagine what that was like.'

'As for our archaeologists, your Boris was lucky. He was hit in the shoulder; he'll survive. Mind you, they won't let us talk to him – any of them, come to that.'

'The gaffer will sort that out; I widnae worry aboot that. They'll no' be able to say no tae her for long. What aboot Galt?'

'Not sure. He's in Glasgow now; got helicoptered out about half an hour ago. I'll check up later.' He thought for a few moments. 'I'd love to know how that necklace got where it did.'

'Oor patients up the road will be able to throw some light on that.'

Daley looked meaningfully at the bar, where Annie and Ella were deep in conversation. 'Could this become a problem?'

'Eh? Why, Jimmy?'

'Don't give me the daft laddie routine. Half of Kinloch thinks you've been involved with our friendly host.'

'Aye, well, half o' Kinloch are wrong.'

As Annie waved across at them, Daley watched Scott drain his glass of ginger beer, his face a picture of innocence. The detective wondered if he would ever be able to stop worrying about his old friend and his uncanny knack of attracting trouble. It had been happening ever since he'd known him: Daley wasn't convinced his recently found sobriety had altered his propensity for making mistakes.

Glasgow, 1994

Daley rushed out of the nightclub. The street was a scene of confusion, with the lights and sirens of police vehicles arriving to attend the fight within. Meanwhile, detectives in his squad rushed to and fro under the orange glow of the street lights, their gleam reflected in the silver Clyde just across the street.

'All stations, do we have anything? Yes, DS Speirs, go ahead, over,' said Daley over the crackle of the radio and the din surrounding him.

'She's with me. Perfectly safe, but pissed as a rat.'

'What's your position, over?'

'Turn round, son.'

Daley did as he was asked. Standing under a tall lamppost was Speirs, holding up the bedraggled figure of WPC Maggie Baird.

'But she hardly had anything to drink in there.'

'How would you know? Probably too busy with your boyfriend tae watch the CCTV.' Two DCs smirked as Speirs gestured to them to relieve him of the drunk policewoman.

As they grabbed her and walked her to an unmarked police car, Daley stepped forward almost toe to toe with Speirs.

'What's this? If you're after a kiss you picked the wrong guy. Get back to your ain man,' said Speirs, in a taunting voice. Before he uttered another word, Daley drew his head back and in a flash head-butted him, sending him falling to the ground.

'Oh dear, son.' Speirs was holding his nose in an effort to stem the flow of blood. 'Oh deary, deary me. I think your stellar career has just hit the buffers.'

'Where's the woman who was with Maggie in the club?'

'How should I know? I was too busy rescuing a colleague tae do your job as well.'

Daley glared at him for a moment, and walked away.

The woman moved briskly but unhurriedly along Clyde Street, looking round cautiously before striding round the corner into a dark, dank lane. Distantly, in the shadows, she made out the figure of a fat man bent over spewing a surfeit of alcohol into the gutter.

With one hand, she pulled off her curly ginger wig and shook down her long dark hair. She stuffed her cheap coat into a skip across the lane, covering it with some of the builders' debris it contained. Checking the man was still oblivious of what was going on, she took a few deep breaths and stepped back out into Glasgow's bright lights, disappearing into a crowd of revellers in her yellow dress, and heading for the nearest taxi rank.

'I cannae believe you're so taken wae this place,' said Ella, taking in the run-down hotel room her husband called home when he wasn't with her in his real domicile in Kirkintilloch. 'They net curtains look as though they've been up since the war.'

'Likely they have,' replied Scott as he pulled the hooded sweatshirt over his head, discarding it on the floor beside the small double bed they were sharing. 'It's no' the Ritz, honey, but they're a friendly bunch – make you feel at home, you know?'

Ella raised her eyebrow and laughed ironically. 'I'm right sure thon hussy behind the bar makes you feel mair than welcome.'

'Come on, Ella, I thought yous were getting on like a hoose on fire.'

'Aye, typical man; no' a clue aboot the world and how it spins.'

'You're right there. What passes for the way you understand things and the way I do are totally different.'

'And big Jimmy, tae. Look at the state o' him.'

'Eh? You said he just looked like he was working too hard.'

'Well, I wisnae going tae declare *Oh for fuck's sake, you look like you're aboot tae keel over at any minute*, am I? Think aboot it, man.'

'He just looks the same tae me.'

'Sherlock Holmes o'er here,' she said, shaking her head.

'Eh?'

'Thon detective wae the hat. Mind me an' you used tae watch it on the telly? Before . . .'

'Before what?'

'Before you started capering up an' doon the road here. It's like being a widow.'

'Och, not at all. You'd be much better off for a start. You'd get a great pension – especially when you consider how long I've been in the job.'

She didn't reply for a while, then said, 'That's kind o' what I'm getting at.'

Scott looked at his wife. The flaming red of her hair had faded, but her eyes were just as green. Despite middle age, she hadn't run to fat, still possessing the same lithe figure he'd lusted after so long ago. But he detected something new. 'It must be the sea air, cos I swear, since you've appeared here, you seem like a different person, Ella. The whole idea o' you coming doon was so we could have a look for a place tae rent. So you wouldnae feel so alone. That's what I thought, anyhow.'

'Dae you no' think it's time you considered retiring?' She turned to him, staring him squarely in the face.

'Very good . . . what would I dae then, mope aboot the hoose? You'll mind the last time I was confined tae quarters after being shot. Me and you just got under each other's feet. I got so bored I got well knocked intae the bevvy, tae.'

'But retirement's different. Anyway, you're aff the drink – aye, and you'll stay that way, tae.' She paused, then kissed him on the cheek. 'We've been lucky, me and you, love. How many times have you survived through situations that could have killed you? You're still in good health!'

'It's a wonder the drink never carted me off afore noo, mind you,' he replied thoughtfully.

'So, think o' what we could dae. As you say, you've got a decent pension; the weans are fine and independent – they don't need us any mair. We could get a wee villa on one o' the

Costas, or that. Soak up the sun an' enjoy ourselves while we can. Fuck knows, we've earned it.'

'What aboot oor Jimmy?'

'He's got his ain life tae lead – aye, and he's no' making too good a stab at it right noo, if you ask me.'

'Aye, I suppose.'

'Just picture you and me in the sunshine. Maybe you could get a hobby.'

'Like what, basket weaving, or thon ty foo?'

'What on earth is ty foo – tea, dae you mean?'

'Och, you know – when these Chinese hang aboot in parks cloaking aboot in slow motion. Like geriatric karate; I cannae see myself at that kind o' caper, Ella darling.'

'That's t'ai chi, you daft bastard.'

'Is that no' a fruit? Well, it can be ty foo or typhoon – I'm no' prancing aboot in my jammies making an arse o' mysel' in some park, Spain or no Spain!'

'What aboot golf? Great thing tae dae. Gets you oot the hoose, nice walk, exercise.'

Scott shook his head. 'You know fine the only time I tried that I missed the ball and it clonked off John Donald's napper. He always thought I did it on purpose. Me an' him was nearly at fisticuffs, if you remember. It was that charity day in Troon. You were there!'

'Well, maybe no' golf,' she said, images of the day in question flashing through her mind. 'We could start up a wee business, or something.'

'I could be a private detective,' he said, snorting with derision.

'Naw, I wisnae meaning that. You've done plenty detection. Something different. What aboot buying a wee pub, for instance? They punters still love a drink in the pub o'er there

– no' like here wae folk stuck in the hoose drinking supermarket booze. The sun brings them oot – gies them a right drooth, tae.'

'Great idea!' he said, sitting up in bed.

'Really?'

'Absolutely. I can just see it noo. You behind the bar chatting up some good-lookin' Spanish waiter half your age, while I'm lying in my ain vomit, seeing pixies at the bottom o' the bed. Dae you really think the life o' a publican's for me?'

'Right enough . . . maybe no' a pub.'

He plumped his pillows and turned over, his back to his wife. 'You wait, this place'll grow on you – you'll see. You'll get a proper look aboot the morrow.'

'Aye, well, night night, Brian.'

He was already snoring as she turned to switch off the bedside light. 'No night o' passion for me then,' she said quietly to herself with a sigh.

34

Marion Smyth-Browne's complexion was white against the light blue hospital pillow. Her dark hair was streaked with flecks of grey, brown eyes hollow in their sockets, her high cheekbones exaggerated by her drawn face.

When Chief Superintendent Symington began to speak, she turned her head slowly to face her interlocutor.

'How's Bernie? Please tell me he's not dead,' she said, gazing desperately at Symington.

'No, he's not dead, Ms Smyth-Browne, but no thanks to your actions. You've both been really stupid. I'll reiterate what my constable said to you. You really must retain the services of a lawyer.'

'Why? I've done nothing wrong.'

'You sound very sure.'

The archaeologist made to speak, but remained silent, clearly considering her reply. Then, after a few moments, she said, 'I really don't know what you mean.'

Having cautioned her, Symington pulled up a chair, seating herself as close to the bedside as possible. 'Come on, Marion, we know what you've been up to. You and Bernie have been helping Colin Galt plunder archaeological artefacts in order to sell them on the black market.'

'No!' She tried to raise her head from the bed, but grimaced in pain, letting her head flop back on to the pillow. 'I have no idea what you're talking about. This is complete nonsense.'

'I have a little theory, Marion.'

'Oh, do you now? *How interesting*.'

'I ask myself what connects you and Bernard to Colin Galt – apart from your clandestine archaeology, that is.'

'I'm not up to listening to some second-rate Agatha Christie impersonation.'

'Since you've nothing better to do, please indulge me.'

Smyth-Browne waved her hand dismissively. 'I'm in no position to stop you, so if you must, say what you like. You'll get nothing in response from me.'

'I think that you and our friend and local entrepreneur Galt have been having a fling.' Symington studied Smyth-Browne's pale face, seeing not a flicker of emotion. 'Now, your Bernie, being a rather switched-on, possessive type of chap, cottoned on to this. In short, he was less than chuffed, to say the least.' Again, no response. Symington stood up, placing her braided cap back on her head. 'Of course, if Galt survives – which is far from guaranteed – you can rest assured that we'll pose similar questions to him. From what I hear, he doesn't appear to have your cool resolve, Marion.'

This time the response was different. Despite her aches and pains, Marion shot up in bed and stared intently at the police officer. 'You have to tell me what condition he's in. I demand . . .'

'Now, there's a thing; great concern for a man that you don't know intimately. Though I do mean what I say. As far as I know, he's struggling for his life in Glasgow.' She paused. 'Don't you think it's time to tell the truth?'

'I've told you all I'm going to. Now, I've changed my mind. Until I have legal representation, please don't bother me again.' She lay back on the bed, turning her head away from the police officer.

'Fair enough. That is, of course, your right.' Symington picked up the chair and placed it back against the wall where she had found it. She walked to the door of the hospital side room and opened it, ready to leave.

She hesitated, turning to face the woman in the hospital bed. 'One more thing, Marion. When my detectives discovered Colin's little stash . . . I'm sure you know where I mean; even Bernie worked that out, as he visited the cottage doubtless on some flimsy pretext to find out what was going on . . . but I digress; when we found the stash, among all that precious Viking jewellery was a more modern piece – much more modern.'

'And what's that got to do with me?'

'Well, it turns out to have belonged to one of the unfortunate women whose remains were discovered at the site at Kilmilken hill.' She smiled. 'Let me be entirely frank: when you are charged – and you will be charged – it won't be merely for theft. You'll be charged as an accomplice to murder. At the very least.'

Smyth-Browne turned to her, unable to keep the look of shock from her face.

'So I think you're right, Marion. Seek out the services of a legal representative as soon as you can – I promise you, you'll need them.'

Before Marion could reply, Chief Superintendent Symington swept out of the room.

Glasgow, 1994

DI Graham sat behind his desk, drumming his fingers on a blotting pad. His face was red with anger, a pulsing vein plainly showing on his neck. Before him stood Daley and Speirs, both looking grim.

'So, this is it! All we have to show from our operation at the nightclub is a WPC in hospital after being poisoned, plus very brief, poor quality CCTV footage of the woman who could very well be the accomplice we've been looking for.' He paused to reach for a packet of cigarettes. Remembering HQ was now a smoke-free zone, he threw the packet down in frustration. 'As you know, I will have to answer to the top floor. And let me tell you, the bosses are pissed off, to say the least. I've read your reports – now tell me the bloody truth!'

'With respect, sir,' said Speirs, 'this is what happens when inexperienced officers are left in charge of an operation like this – stands tae reason. I mean, who the fuck would monitor the situation on the club's CCTV system and no' make sure it was all being recorded.' He shook his head, a sarcastic smile on his face, a large plaster across the bridge of his nose and bruising to both eyes testament to Daley's head butt.

'I was told that the recording equipment was in order and working properly. As you know, sir, it stopped shortly after WPC Baird was in position – *mysteriously*,' he added, pointedly looking at Speirs.

'You're a cheeky bastard,' said Speirs, his voice raised. 'I hope you're not going to let comments like that go, sir. Bad enough I was assaulted by an *acting* DS at the locus in front of the public in the middle of the street. Now, if the papers were tae get hold o' that . . .'

'Shut up, the pair of you! I'm well aware what passed between you and DS Daley, Bobby. I also know what was said prior to the fracas. I had hoped a man of your experience would have behaved in a more professional manner – regardless of your opinion of DS Daley. Be certain of this: upstairs won't care that you've got a sore nose – or what insults were directed at you, Daley, perceived or otherwise. They are however, I assure you, greatly concerned about the loss of a suspect who could have brought this bloody Midweek Murderer to justice!'

Speirs snorted with derision, while Daley looked as though he was about to add to what he had to say, but then thought better of it and remained silent.

'Make no mistake, gentlemen, your careers are at stake here. I'll do my best. But the very fact that one of our female officers, vulnerable, working under cover, was slipped a Mickey and placed in obvious danger, is of huge concern. So, if any of this appears in the papers – from whatever source,' he added, staring at Speirs, 'the person who leaks it can rest assured that they will also see their name in print, with a P45 in the post.'

'What now, sir?' asked Daley, expecting the worst.

'What happens now is that you and the team pore through any evidence this Alison woman may have left behind. I know the glasses she was drinking from were washed and the table cleaned while you were busy trying to find Maggie, so we have no obvious prints. But I want everyone who was in that nightclub interviewed, and every scintilla of evidence examined with a fine toothcomb. I include CCTV evidence from street cameras – anything that might help.'

'Aye, get yourself in front o' a screen wae that mate of yours, son. See if you can find out where she went.'

'I'm more interested in how she went,' replied Daley, his

fists balled at his sides. 'I mean, we have a witness who spotted them leaving the club, our suspect supporting WPC Baird as they left.'

'What are you saying, son? Come on, out wae it!'

'I would have thought that was obvious. When you "rescued" Maggie, where was this Alison?'

'You bastard!' shouted Speirs, making for Daley.

'Enough!' shouted DI Graham. 'DS Speirs, get out and put people on the CCTV trail – if there proves to be one. Then go to the locus yourself; get a hold of the taxi drivers who were working that night – anyone who could have seen her. I want her found.'

'But, sir . . .'

'Now, DS Speirs! Daley, you stay here for the moment.'

The two men watched Speirs march out of the room.

'Take a seat, DS Daley.' Graham's tone had moderated.

'First car back to Stewart Street, and pick up my uniform on the way. I think that's what you're about to say, sir.'

'Don't think that hasn't crossed my mind, young man.' Graham passed his hand over his bald head, sighing deeply. 'However, this incident has left me even more troubled. The club's CCTV recording stopping for no apparent reason, no sign of this Alison character leaving with Maggie, despite the presence of officers placed around the building. Let me make it clear, Jim. I'm very unhappy at the way you conducted yourself last night. I will not condone fights between my officers in the street, regardless of the circumstances.'

'Sorry, sir.'

'But, as I know you suspect, it's all too convenient – even down to this fight that broke out of nowhere. Far too convenient.'

'You think the fight was pre-arranged?' Daley looked surprised. Even he hadn't thought of that.

'That's exactly what I mean.' He stood up, taking his raincoat from a peg and donning his trilby hat. 'But what has happened has happened. I blame myself – I should have taken direct charge of the operation. In the meantime, before I have to face the bosses, we have to take a trip to the lab.'

'What for, sir?'

'Something to do with Ian's murder. Come with me, Daley. But please, be aware your career – all of our careers – are on a knife edge.'

'Yes, sir,' replied Daley, struggling to believe he wasn't already back walking the beat.

35

Kinloch, the present

Daley still had detectives checking out locals who'd had cause to travel regularly to Glasgow during the time of the Midweek Murders – and there were many, as Sergeant Shaw had pointed out. So while his team concentrated on this he decided to check the credentials – and anything else known – of the archaeological team.

In the main, he found them to be young graduates bolstered by a couple of undergraduate volunteers. Bernard Evans was still recovering from his wounds at the local hospital. Despite being in no real danger health-wise, police were still being denied access to interview him, something that irritated the chief inspector. However, Daley now knew where he'd gained his prowess with a rifle: Evans had spent three years in the army.

Having lost interest in military life, he trained as an archaeologist and took a diving course. From then on, he'd worked on underwater sites, meeting his partner in work and life – Marion – on his first proper job. It appeared they'd been together for three years, and were well respected in the archaeological community.

Despite the difference in ages – he'd just turned thirty, she was almost forty-eight – their relationship appeared to have been strong and enduring. Until now, that was.

Daley couldn't help but wonder how his own relationship with Mary Dunn might have turned out. He'd always suspected that he'd become less and less appealing to her as he entered late middle age. As it turned out, heartbreakingly, there had been no need to worry.

He dragged his thoughts back to the task in hand, and turned to the information on Marion.

He was surprised to note that she didn't hail from an upper-class family, despite her lofty accent and double-barrelled surname. As it turned out, her father, Arthur Browne, a shipbuilder from Tyneside, had married her mother, Doreen Smyth, then employed at the same yard as a typist. Both came from working-class stock. Marion had changed her name by deed-poll when she went up to Oxford.

Clearly Marion had done what she thought was her best to cover up her humble origins by the change of name and accent, which in itself was revealing, Daley thought.

Her work had taken her across the globe, and she was highly respected in her field. There seemed to be nothing to indicate she would become involved in an elaborate scheme to rob the nation of its antiquities – or maybe this was just the first time she'd been caught.

As ever, the cynical mind of the world-weary copper pondered the worst.

Daley was just about to read what had been found on the formidable site director, Professor Anthea Francombe, when his mobile buzzed into life in his pocket.

Liz was again emblazoned on the screen.

As he clicked the call off without answering he instantly felt guilty. What if something had happened to his son? Reasoning this through, he realised that he'd have heard of it by now. Most likely the persistent calls were another attempt by his estranged wife to make him feel worthless and unhappy. He'd felt that for long enough; he wanted more than anything to put an end to those feelings.

Liz would have to take her bile out on someone else.

He clicked the mouse on his computer and began to read what his team had managed to find out about Professor Francombe.

Glasgow, 1994

The forensic lab exuded the usual mixture of smells, both chemical and biological. The mix was heady and unpleasant; as always, Daley could feel his stomach churn in the same way it did when he was called to the scene of a murder, or the mortuary.

He remembered a dinner party he'd attended with Liz a few weeks before. One of her old university friends – arrogant and obnoxious by turns – wondered how Daley could possibly be squeamish about such things given the years he'd spent in the police.

'I'm a bloody dentist – if you can't get used to staring into the rotting abyss of some knuckle-dragger's mouth, you wouldn't last long,' an unpleasant young man had said, looking round the table with a chuckle.

'Perhaps slightly different from dragging what's left of a child from under a bus,' replied Daley, simultaneously silencing the room and earning a glower from Liz.

He felt sicker than normal now. Lying on a stainless steel table, spread out like a garment ready to be ironed, lay Ian Burns's tatty raincoat. Daley recognised it instantly. It brought with it so many memories – images of the man who'd been his mentor and friend.

DI Graham looked at the coat and sighed. 'You know, in all the time I knew him he never wore any other coats but these. He must have had a number over the years. But no matter where he went – work or play – there would be the beige raincoat.'

Daley pictured it hanging on the coat stand in Burns's old office in Stewart Street, his old black scarf draped over its collar.

'Now, DC Chisholm, what have you been able to find out using these new bloody miracles of yours?'

A stocky young man with a shock of red hair, wearing a white lab coat, stroked his chin. 'Very little, I'm afraid, sir. There was some blood on the collar . . .' He paused. 'It turned out to be that of Mr Burns himself. Apart from that, just the usual grass and dirt stains associated with the locus.'

'What about the body? Nothing from under the fingernails, say?' asked Graham, glancing at Daley, who looked as though he was about to pass out.

'No, nothing. You remember Ian – DCI Burns,' said Chisholm, correcting himself. 'Fingernails bitten to the quick. From what I've seen of the body and what Mr Crichton from the mortuary tells us in the pathology report, it doesn't seem as though he had the chance to put up much of a fight. Plus, I would say the murderer has been careful – knew what he was doing – as with the letters, sir.' This time Chisholm looked at Daley.

Daley's mind was spinning. He could smell pine needles, hear the ragged cries of ravens, the trickle of the tiny burn beside the stile, all under the looming shadow of Dumgoyne, as there lay Ian Burns's lifeless body on the damp grass, surrounded by police officers. It all seemed unreal, like a scene from a film, or a particularly vivid dream.

Silence prevailed in the sterile room for a few moments, all three of them deep in thought.

'I must confess to being a tad disappointed, Duncan,' said Graham. 'I was under the impression that you guys could work wonders these days. Spirit bloody perpetrators out of test tubes, as they told us at the forensic lecture at a seminar I was forced to endure recently.'

'Not quite, sir,' replied Chisholm. 'One day – one day soon, I would imagine – but though we can pull some rabbits out of hats, the forensics surrounding DCI Burns has little to offer. Things are improving all the time, though, sir. One day – well, who knows?' He looked at them both apologetically.

'What happens to his stuff now?' asked Daley, gesturing to the raincoat.

'Oh, yes – good question. Such are the advances we're making year on year, everything is retained.'

'All of the case forensic evidence?' asked Graham.

'Yes, sir. This has been in our protocols for some time.'

'But you've no idea when some new test will turn up that could glean something from this evidence?'

'No, not yet, sir.'

Graham and Daley left Chisholm to his work. Stepping out into the car fumes and noise of a busy Glasgow street was a genuine relief for Daley. He looked at DI Graham and said, 'You were expecting that, sir, I think?'

'Yes,' replied Graham resignedly. 'Like DC Chisholm, I spoke to the pathologist – what's his name? The one who smokes that infernal bloody pipe.'

'Crichton, sir.'

'Yes, that's the man. If the body yielded nothing, I was pretty sure the clothes wouldn't.'

'Back to the office, sir?'

'You go, Jim. I want to go somewhere quiet to think.'

The young DS knew this to be shorthand for a visit to the Horseshoe Bar, so took his leave of DI Graham, heading back to his office with a leaden heart.

Kinloch, the present

After being disturbed by Liz's call, Daley felt the need of a coffee, so he returned to his desk with a steaming mug from the machine and laid it on his desk.

He was pondering how people change over the years – not just physically, but in almost every aspect. He pictured the Speirs he'd known years ago. He – like Brian Scott – was much the same to look at. Indeed, apart from Scott's miraculous abandonment of alcohol, they had little changed in attitude, either. But that's where the comparison ended. While Scott was the same rebellious but steady man every police officer would want at his side, Speirs remained sullen, arrogant and devious.

Daley caught sight of his reflection on the glass of his office door. The years had certainly changed him. The face of a careworn middle-aged man stared back at him: overweight, unfulfilled and becoming unkempt – especially now that he had no significant other in his life.

Duncan Chisholm had changed physically, too. From a powerfully built ladies' man, with a shock of red hair, he'd gone grey, almost white, in the intervening years. His muscular physique had turned to fat and flab – much like himself, he thought, gloomily.

He passed his hand across his chest, cursing the huge cooked meal Hamish had concocted for breakfast. If this continues, I'll need the doors widened, he thought, making a note to tell his new guest that he'd enjoy coffee and a grapefruit to break his fast for the next few weeks.

Then, from nowhere, came another memory of Chisholm. He made a mental note to act on it at the first opportunity.

Back to the task in hand, he keyed the case number in to his computer and soon returned to the information on Francombe.

She was a professor at a Cambridge college – a high-flyer – young for such a position, but highly respected. She'd been responsible for the discovery of some significant Roman archaeology in the last two years, and was considered a future star of the profession. Certainly, from his own experience, he knew her to be smart, methodical and in possession of the perfect personality with which to manage her team. She remained aloof, yet approachable – there was no doubt as to who was in charge when she was on site.

Yet Daley wondered. She hadn't been able to see through Bernie and Marion's clandestine business.

He scrolled down further, looking for her own qualifications and other educational and personal details provided by her present college.

He was surprised to note that these had been redacted, thick black lines running through much of the text, leaving most of what had been provided unintelligible.

He stepped out of his glass box and looked around the CID office. Four detectives were busy at their workstations. 'Anyone know where DC Potts is?'

'On night shift for the next two nights, sir. Giving him a rest after all that wandering about hillsides in the rain,' replied a DC from a division Daley didn't know.

'Ping me his mobile number,' said Daley. 'Am I right in saying it was he who collated the background info on our archaeologists?'

'Yes, I think so, sir.'

He returned to his office and waited for the phone to ring.

There was a sharp knock on his door. He looked up to see Speirs entering the room.

'Yes?'

'Charming, DCI Daley – no' even the courtesy of a "good morning".'

'If you have something to contribute, take a seat. If you're just here for some more verbals, you can . . . well, you know what you can do.' Daley managed to hold his temper.

'I give up. I was just going to tell you I was heading back to Glasgow on tonight's flight.'

'Well, I'd like to say it's been a pleasure, but it hasn't, so I won't lie.'

'You, lie? No' the saintly Jim Daley. That could never happen.'

'I'm just glad the bosses have seen sense and directed you to waste your time on something less challenging. Best to leave this to those of us who are still real police officers.'

'That's a sharp tongue, Jimmy. Mind you, you've never changed. As a matter of fact, I'm going for a meeting with the ACC. He wants an update – in person, if you please.' Speirs smiled sickeningly.

'Happy landings then,' said Daley. His computer pinged, announcing Potts's number on his screen.

'Same to you.'

As Speirs opened the door to leave the office, Daley called him to a halt.

'While you're up there, you might as well do something useful.'

'Like what?'

'I want you to have any forensic evidence on Ian Burns's murder case re-examined.'

'Och, they did that a few years ago – found nothing. Is it no' about time you got rid o' this obsession? I mean, it's well o'er twenty years ago now, man!'

'I think it has a connection to this case.'

'Fuck, no' this again. Anyhow, I cannae authorise stuff like that. Remember, I'm no' a cop any more.'

'Don't worry, Bobby, I still am. I'll phone ahead and authorise it. I want to hear back from you tomorrow on any progress. Oh, and while you're with the ACC, please tell him I'd like a word – in person.' It was his turn to smile.

Speirs stared at Daley for a few heartbeats, saying nothing, shook his head, then turned on his heel and left, leaving Daley's office door swinging open.

He'd been able to act on his memory of Duncan Chisholm sooner than he'd thought.

Daley was about to call Potts when his office phone rang.

'Yes, DS Shaw, how can I help you?'

'I've got Hamish for you, sir.'

'Erm, I'm quite busy right now. Tell him I'll phone him back.'

Shaw hesitated on the other end of the line. 'Actually, he sounds quite agitated, sir.'

'Okay, put him through,' Daley replied reluctantly.

After a few clicks: 'Hamish, what's up? I'm a wee bit busy here. Can I give you a ring in an hour or so?'

'Aye, well, you could, but the situation here's no' ideal, if you know what I mean.'

Daley was sure he could hear a child crying in the background. 'What's happening – don't tell me you've started a crèche?'

'Now, well, you see, that's no' as daft as it sounds. I'm in your hoose.'

'So what's the problem – and who's crying?'

'I canna stay long on the phone, Mr Daley. Like you, I'm kind o' busy; trying tae keep the big fella here from having a go at the wean. Oh, he's a right jealous crater, right enough. Hates me paying any attention tae anyone but him – particularly weans.'

'What wean – child – what's going on up there?'

'You mean you don't know? For the love o' the wee man, I can hardly credit it.'

'Know what?'

'I'd a visitor aboot an hour ago. She left me in charge o' her wean.'

'Well, I don't know what you want me to do, Hamish. You should have said no. I'm afraid this hasn't got anything to do with me. It's not part of your boarding agreement, either.'

'Aye, noo, that's where you're wrong, Mr Daley.'

'Eh?'

'I'm currently in charge o' your son and heir, if you please. Mrs Daley said you knew all aboot it. She left him here aboot an hour ago. Went skidding off doon the drive in a big fancy motor. And she wasna at the wheel, if you get my drift.'

It suddenly dawned on Daley what all the calls and messages he'd been ignoring were about. 'Give me ten minutes, Hamish. I'll be right up.'

'As quick as you can. Oor Hamish is on the prowl. Fair wild he is, tae – fit tae rip oot a throat. An' I'm no' as fast on my toes as I once was, you know. Forby that, I've no' had much experience with weans, an' whoot I have had – well, it's no' been pleasant.'

The thought of his son being mauled by Hamish's wildcat sent Daley leaping from his chair and heading for the door.

36

Professor Anthea Francombe paced to and fro across the threadbare carpet in her small room in the County Hotel. She'd had breakfast, which basically consisted of too much coffee and a few mouthfuls of muesli.

How I hate this bloody place, she thought.

She was to have a Skype meeting with her bosses, the college's directors of archaeology, in the afternoon, and was at a loss as to what to tell them. Her career was in the balance.

She cursed Evans and Smyth-Browne. They'd ruined everything.

Of course, she should have realised there was something wrong; but the necessary pace of the research caused by the imminent destruction of the site, plus the usual paucity of manpower, had left her stretched to her very limit.

Be honest, that's got bugger all to with it. You know that. The words echoed unbidden in her head.

She was failing on all levels – plain and simple. Failure was something she was not only unused to, she actively despised it.

She reached for the room's tiny kettle, filling it from the tap over the sink in the en suite bathroom. She walked back into the room, sat it on the top of the old chest of drawers, plugged it in, then cursed the fact she'd run out of instant coffee; the little jar beside the kettle now contained only teabags and sachets of artificial sweetener.

She flopped back on her bed, staring at the cracks in the ceiling, subconsciously counting them. When she got to seven she paused and sighed.

How had the necklace from the dead woman come to be amongst the Viking jewellery? It was a question she'd gone over time and time again, coming up with the same answer.

University had changed her: taught her many things, instilled self-confidence, an ability to trust her instincts and logical processes.

It was that inescapable logic that tortured her now.

There was someone else – someone she failed to legislate for. Not the hapless Galt; she realised very quickly he'd merely been prey to greed and the dubious charms of Marion. No, there was another mind at work here. Someone who had more knowledge of her objectives than she was comfortable they should have; someone with more on their mind than mere archaeology. Of this she was utterly convinced.

What to tell the directors? That question now occupied her completely.

Brian Scott was dozing on a chair in Kinloch Hospital, waiting for a chance to talk to Helen McNeil.

He'd been roused by his alarm at five a.m., fumbling about in the dark, his wife breathing softly beside him. Daley had given him time off later in the day to show her the house the force had earmarked to be their temporary home, but meanwhile she'd be happy wandering about Kinloch, getting a sense of the place and the people.

His only advice to her that morning as she'd wished him a tired goodbye was to steer clear of boats and the hotel's black pudding, which always gave him heartburn.

He yawned now and stretched.

'You look as though you need this,' said a nurse, bearing a steaming mug of tea.

'Oh, you beauty! You're an angel.' He accepted the mug with both hands, taking a sip of the hot, sweet beverage that seemed to invigorate him almost instantly.

The nurse stood over him, smiling. 'I know exactly how you feel. Normal people – members of the public, I mean – don't realise what shifts are like. I thought I'd get used to it, but they still turn my life upside down.'

'Tell me about it,' said Scott, gulping down more tea. 'They normal folk don't know they're living.'

The nurse sat on the chair beside him, leaning her head into his conspiratorially. 'Can I ask you a wee favour, DS Scott?'

'Aye, sure. If it's legal, definitely – if no' I'll have tae think aboot it.'

'We were wondering – you know, us nurses – if you could tell us more about what happened to Helen. We're all very worried about her. Even though we've been in and out doing the usual checks and things, we're not allowed to ask her anything.'

'I know the feeling.'

'Oh.' She looked surprised.

'What, lassie?'

'Just that when I saw your colleague in with her earlier, I assumed you would know a bit more about what happened.'

'What colleague? Big Jimmy – I mean DCI Daley?'

'No, I know him. This was another policeman I've never seen before. The hospital manager gave him permission to speak to Helen.' She looked at the watch she wore on her uniform top. 'Must have been about an hour ago.'

'Right, where's this manager of yours?'

'In his office, just down the corridor.' She stood, looking startled. 'I'm so sorry, I hope I haven't got anyone in trouble. It's just we've been so worried . . .'

'No' your fault, lassie. In fact, you've been a great help.' Scott left the mug of tea at the side of his chair and marched off in the direction of the hospital manager's office.

A scene of carnage met Daley when he swept into his lounge.

Hamish was sitting on a wooden chair, wailing toddler held on his knee with one hand, while in the other he brandished a walking stick at his huge cat Hamish, the animal hissing menacingly, ears flattened onto its head. Plants were knocked over in their pots, a vase lay cracked on the floor carpet, a mug of tea had been spilled on the table, and a modernist porcelain figurine that belonged to Liz lay smashed in the fireplace. In short, the room looked as though it had suffered the attentions of professional looters.

'Jeest in the very nick o' time, Mr Daley,' said Hamish breathlessly above the din. 'The big fella's been trying tae execute a flanking manoeuvre, but I've managed tae fight him off wae my stick. It's been touch and go, mind.'

Daley met his son's gaze, making the child bawl even more volubly.

'Give him to me, Hamish. You deal with that bloody cat!'

'Noo, that's a bit harsh, don't you think. I mean, it's no' as though me and the big fella signed up for babysitting duties. The mood your good lady was in, it's jeest as well I was here.'

'Sorry, Hamish. This is all a bit of a shock to me too, I assure you.'

Hamish handed him the toddler.

'She telt me you'd been ignoring her calls and messages for days, so it's your ain fault. She's away on holiday – she left a note for you on thon ugly table in the lobby. I'm going tae fling some fish oot the back door. Himself canna resist a piece o' herring. That'll get him oot the road.' Hamish ushered his formidable pet out of the room, while Daley tried to placate his son, with little success. James Daley junior was crying fit to burst, his only discernible comment 'I want Mummy!'

Shortly, after much screaming and wailing, Hamish sauntered back into the room, a white envelope in his big hand. 'Here, I'll show the wean the boats oot the window, while you get your glimmers on whoot Mrs Daley's had tae say. I don't ken a wean that doesna like boats, and that's a fact.' He handed Daley the note.

As his son began to quieten, taking note of the loch and the sailing craft upon it through the room's huge picture window, Daley felt free to open the letter left by his estranged wife.

Dear Jim,

I know your instant reaction will be one of anger and hatred, directed at me. In my defence, may I say, I am just as angry that you've failed to answer my calls and messages in the last few days. It appears you have little regard for your own son's welfare. Whatever has passed between us, I cannot forgive this.

You have no idea how tough it is bringing up a child single-handed. I know my mother helps, and money is of no concern, but it's unhealthy for James not to have contact with his father. That is, assuming you want to remain in your son's life, which, I must regretfully say, looks most unlikely at the moment.

I really hope that will change – for the sake of our child, not me.

I know you'll be busy – there's never been a time in our lives when you haven't placed your work before our marriage. However, I've had to make so many sacrifices in my life in order to accommodate our son, I think it only fair that you take your turn.

You may have guessed that I've met somebody – despite the drudgery of my domestic routine. We simply want a holiday in order to become better acquainted. I'm sure you know the feeling. Such a pity you and young Mary didn't get much of a chance to really get to know each other.

Or perhaps that was a blessing in disguise. I'm sure the scales of Cupid would have rapidly fallen from her eyes once she got to know the real Jim Daley.

I'll be gone for three weeks. If there's a problem with James, my mother knows how to contact me – you have her number.

Look after my son and live up to your responsibilities!
Liz

The note ended as abruptly as many of their conversations over the years had.

Not that long ago, the tone of her letter, the thought of her with another man – his loss – would have been crushing. Now his lack of emotion surprised him.

'See, there's your faither,' said Hamish, taking the child by the hand as they both, each rather unsteadily, made their way across the room in Daley's direction.

He took his son in his arms, embracing him. 'Well, James, what are we going to do with you for three weeks, eh?'

The boy looked him squarely in the face, tears gone, and said quite calmly, 'I want to see my mummy.'

Daley jiggled him on his knee, his eye catching the smashed figurine on the grate.

For the big policeman, it was uncannily emblematic.

Brian Scott burst into Kinloch Hospital manager's office without knocking.

'What do you think you're doing?' said the figure behind the desk, recognising Scott, and knowing something of his reputation.

'What I'm up to is wondering who you gave permission to question Helen McNeil? You know I've been sitting for hours waiting tae speak tae her.'

'You were sound asleep, Sergeant Scott – when your colleague arrived, I mean. He told me not to bother you. And as he was senior to you in rank, I did as he asked.'

'What?' Scott sounded exasperated. 'I know it wasn't DCI Daley, so who was this senior officer?'

'I took a note of his name. Yes, here it is.' He produced a pad from his desk. 'Chisholm – DCI Chisholm. He left about an hour ago. I . . .' The hospital's manager was given no time to reply as Scott strode out of the office.

He walked to the side room where Helen was being treated. A young uniformed officer was sitting by the door reading a newspaper.

'McGougan, were you here when DCI Chisholm arrived?'

'Yes, Sergeant,' McGougan replied, immediately on his guard thanks to the look of extreme agitation on Scott's face. 'I mean, he's a DCI – I had to let him in.'

'So you did. But didn't you think o' taking a walk tae tell me? You knew fine where I was; I spoke tae you when I arrived.'

'I was going to, but DCI Chisholm said you were getting some shut-eye, and he was helping out.' PC McGougan looked perplexed.

Scott stood for a moment thinking, then scrolled down his phone, finding the mobile number Chisholm had given him recently. He let the phone ring for a few moments, but no reply was forthcoming.

Scott pushed past McGougan and entered Helen McNeil's room. He gasped, finding her bed empty. Heart thumping, he checked the adjoining toilet and shower room, but Helen was nowhere to be seen.

He went back into the corridor, where PC McGougan was still standing, looking concerned.

'When did she leave the room, son?'

'Who?'

'Beyoncé, who dae you fucking think?'

'I thought she was in there – she must have gone out of a window, or something.'

'We're on the second floor. She's a district nurse, no' a mountaineer.'

'I swear, she's never left the room since I've been here.'

'Well, she must be able tae disappear at will in a puff o' smoke, cos she ain't in that room, son.'

'Wait,' said McGougan, his face crimson.

'I'm listening.'

'When DCI Chisholm went in – you know, to question Ms McNeil . . .'

'Aye, and?'

'Well, he told me to go and grab a bite tae eat fae the canteen. I've been on since two, so I was a bit hungry. You know how it is, Sergeant.'

'Great. So when you came back fae the canteen, you didn't check inside the room?'

'I was only away for ten minutes. I assumed that DCI Chisholm had questioned her and gone. I mean, there was no sound of voices from the room, sir.'

Scott shook his head. 'I'll have tae get hold o' DCI Daley.'

'He'll not be happy, I take it.'

'Och, I widnae worry. He'll be jumping for joy, cracking jokes, an' all sorts. What dae you think?'

As PC McGougan began to mumble a reply, he was disturbed by the hospital manager running along the corridor towards them waving a sheet of paper.

'What's this, peace for oor time?' said Scott.

'It's a copy of an email I've just received. It's from Helen. I thought I'd better print it out for you.'

Scott grabbed the piece of paper and began to read.

I'm so sorry to have left without telling anyone. I'll be in touch later today. I just have to get my head round what's happened to me.

Don't worry, please tell DCI Daley I'm safe. DCI Chisholm will explain.

Regards,
Helen McNeil

Scott sighed. 'If she's as good at nursing as she is at disappearing, she must be bloody Florence Nightingale.'

He dialled Jim Daley's mobile number.

37

Glasgow, 1994

Daley trudged through the underground car park, his footsteps echoing in the big concrete space. It reeked of fuel, damp and urine, as these places always did. The walls were covered with various graffiti tags, sprayed to identify some of the city's many gangs.

He could hear water dripping before its sound was cancelled out by a vehicle leaving the car park from the floor above, via the narrow, twisting access ramp.

He was surprised to see someone sitting on the bonnet of his car: a female, with her back to him.

'Here, get off my motor!' he shouted, suspecting this woman to be one of the prostitutes who occasionally used this place for their clandestine business.

When she turned round, he was surprised to see that the woman was WPC Maggie Baird, erstwhile undercover cop.

'Maggie, aren't you meant to be in hospital?'

'Nah, Jimmy, signed myself oot. Nothing more than a bit o' a sore heid from whatever she slipped me.'

'So you think it was definitely this Alison, yeah?'

'Bet my pension on it. You know, now I'm thinking straight.'

Daley nodded, appreciating her confirmation of the theory he'd suspected all along. 'Pity we lost her, Maggie.'

'That's why I'm here, Jimmy.'

'I did wonder.'

'I'm no' in the habit o' hanging about car parks, son. Unless there's a cosy caretaker's office wae a boiling kettle an' a decent biscuit on offer. You cannae beat a good doss, Jimmy. Or have you forgotten that since you left your uniform hung up in the cupboard at home?'

'The way things are going I'll be getting it back out. The last few days haven't been the highlight of my police career to date.'

'Aye, I dare say. But that's what I want tae talk to you about.'

'What?'

'Right, even though I looked drunk, I didn't feel as bad as I probably appeared. You know when you're pissed – you cannae remember bugger all. Well, I cannae, anyhow.'

'So you realised you'd been slipped a Mickey?'

'No, not really, but things stuck in my mind.'

'Like what?'

'Like when that fight started, this Alison pulled me oot the club.'

'Okay.'

'I remember being in the street. She telt me we should go tae her hoose an' get a cup o' coffee tae sober me up.' She shook her head. 'I wasn't thinking right, but it seemed like a bonnie idea – under the influence, you know.'

'So you couldn't get a taxi? Just as well, Maggie.'

'Not just that, Jimmy. I mind someone grabbing her and pulling her away.'

'Must have been the rest of the team when they found you.'

'Aye, it was.' She bit her lip, the expression on her face troubled.

'Come on, Maggie. You've not been sitting out here in the cold just to tell me that.'

'I've been a cop for a long time – too long. The bloody job's all I've got in my life, I'm sad to say. Time for a change, I reckon.'

'Oh, come on, you're good at what you do.'

'That's the thing, Jimmy. Something wasn't right that night. Och, maybe I'm imagining it, me full o' whatever drugs got slipped tae me, but you know what instincts are in this job by now, eh?'

'What are you getting at?'

'Well – between you and me, mind, promise!' She looked pleadingly at Daley.

'Of course – between you and me, that's a promise, Maggie.'

'Well, I think they let her go – this Alison.'

'What, on purpose?' Daley was astonished.

'Yes. We were surrounded by your lot and I remember her being caught by the arm and pulled away from the rest of us, and then I didn't see her again.'

'And who was doing the pulling – I mean who had her by the arm?'

WPC Maggie Baird was silent for a while, staring across the car park. One of the neon lights, ready to break down, began to flicker. 'I've never grassed up a colleague – never, Jimmy. Aye, an' I've seen plenty in my time, I can tell you.'

'Haven't we all,' replied Daley, meaning it. 'So why now?'

'This is serious. These poor lassies are being killed near every week. They've husbands, mothers – weans tae look after. But for the grace of God, I could have been one o' them.'

'So who was it you think let Alison go, Maggie?'

She stared straight into his face, a tear running down her cheek, smudging her mascara. 'Bobby. Bobby Speirs. I'm sure o' it, Jimmy.'

Kinloch, the present

Brian Scott winced as Daley hurled an empty mug of tea to the floor, watching it smash into tiny pieces. Another officer, Duncan Chisholm, the object of Daley's wrath, ignored the smashed crockery, attempting to weather the storm.

Scott glimpsed raised eyebrows and astonished looks from the team of detectives in the general office outside. Daley's glass box was soundproofed enough to mute general conversation, but not the onslaught being directed at the unfortunate Crime Scene Manager.

Scott flicked the blinds closed; not that this would mask Daley's roaring, but at least those outside couldn't see what was going on. Maybe that's worse, Scott mused for a moment, then cast the thought aside, determined to stop his old friend doing something he would regret.

'I just wanted to know about what happened down that hole, Jim. I've got the boys on to it now. We're hoping to be able to get some DNA. This could mark a huge breakthrough in the case.' Chisholm was trying desperately to fight his corner.

'Why not take Brian in with you?'

'He was having a kip!'

Daley glared at Scott, then redirected the glare to Chisholm. 'That's no excuse. You knew she was vulnerable – you knew she was at risk. What did you say to her to make her think doing a runner would be a good idea? Fuck, it's not as though you're wet behind the ears. You've behaved like a bloody clueless probationer!'

Chisholm straightened his back, his expression flicking from one of subservience to determined defiance. 'You've no right to speak to me like that. I'm a bloody DCI too – it's not just you. Watch yourself, Jimmy. From what I hear, your jacket's on a shoogly nail after what happened to that wee lassie you were shagging. So don't come the high and bloody mighty with me!'

Guessing what Daley's reaction was likely to be, Scott put himself between the two burly detectives, now both standing. 'Wait, you pair. The troops out there can hear every word o' this. There's no war getting won this way – no, nor finding Helen McNeil, neither.'

At that, the door swung open. Dressed in a red trouser suit stood Chief Superintendent Symington, a look of fury on her face. 'Sit down, all of you,' she said, firmly, though the anger in her voice was plain. She watched as they silently obeyed. 'I could hear your little exchange down the corridor. Senior men like – like all three of you – are supposed to be setting an example, not turning this investigation into some testosterone-fuelled side show. If you have points to make, please do so in a manner befitting your respective ranks and seniority. I'll not have this from my officers!' Now her voice was raised.

Silence reigned in the office for a few moments, as Symington pulled up a chair and looked at all three of her colleagues one by one. 'I've just been summoned to HQ by the ACC. Though he had the decency to make his point in a professional manner, his message was very clear. It was a question, in fact.'

Silence, until Scott spoke. 'What was that?'

'It was: what on earth is going on in Kinloch? Not a question I could answer at the time, but the answer is now glaringly obvious. I have three highly experienced detectives having a stand-up fight because, yet again, someone in our charge has disappeared.' She stared at them. 'Well, am I right?'

This question was met with a muted response.

'Well, the upshot of it is that I now have to take direct control of all operations relating to the Midweek Murder investigation, the case concerning Galt, Evans and Smyth-Browne, plus the second disappearance of Helen McNeil. From this end, at any rate.'

'Bobby Speirs is behind this,' said Daley angrily.

'No, I'm behind it, DCI Daley.' She paused. 'It has become very obvious to me that there are too many axes being ground – too many ghosts at work here with you all. You all share a past – and from what I can decipher, not a harmonious one. I should have been on top of that from the start.'

'Right. Now you're in charge, ma'am, what do you want us to do?' asked Daley, pulling himself together.

'First of all, we start from scratch. I want a detailed report from each of you on the progress of the various investigations, to date. Then I want us all to sit down and coordinate a plan. Meanwhile, I want bodies out looking for Helen. How did she appear to you when you spoke to her, DCI Chisholm?'

'Actually, I was surprised. She was quite bright. I'd heard she was a bag of nerves. She seemed, well, confident, assured. As though she'd managed to put her incarceration behind her already. She even cracked a joke or two.'

'I've seen that kind o' thing afore,' said Scott.

'What?' asked Symington.

'Och, a few times now, but one that sticks oot. A wee mate o' mine – I'd been to school with him – great man for the doos.'

'Pigeons, ma'am,' said Daley, noting Symington's puzzled look.

'Aye, the pigeons – you know, racing them, ma'am. Big thing when I was growing up. You'd see they doocots all o'er the city. Big black jobs – mostly made o' auld sheds an' that . . .'

'Do get to the point, DS Scott.'

'Do – aye, very good, ma'am.' Scott cleared his throat, realising that no one else seemed in a humorous frame of mind but deciding to press on regardless. 'Well, tae cut a long story short, wee Geordie had a whole rack o' problems. Och, his wife was having it off wae the bloke doon the street, his daughter was up the duff – aye, only fifteen, tae – money worries. I felt right sorry for him, but what can you dae?' Scott paused, but seeing only nods of encouragement to conclude his tale, carried on. 'Anyhow, after weeks o' moping aboot he appears in the pub this night, all laughs and jokes, like. He spent a fortune buying drinks. Happy as a sand boy, so he was.' Scott shook his head.

'I'm sorry, I'm missing something here,' said Symington.

'Och, they found him the next day. Flex o' the light roond his neck – he'd jumped off the kitchen table.'

'Oh, how sad. Taking your own life is always a tragedy.'

'He didnae die, ma'am. You want tae have seen the state o' the wiring in they council hooses back then. Bloody scandalous, it was. The wire just came through the ceiling – brought the auld boiler doon and it landed right on his leg. Poor bugger walks wae a limp tae this day.'

'I'm struggling here, Brian,' said Daley. 'What's your point?'

'Well, even though he didnae die, he meant tae. That's how he was so chirpy the night afore. As I say, I've seen it wae folk that were mair successful. Once they've made their mind up tae dae the business, it takes a' the weight off their shoulders. I'm betting that's what's brightened up this Helen.' He nodded sagely, convinced that his story had been a worthwhile contribution.

'You have a way of really cheering people up, Brian, do you know that?' said Symington.

'Nae bother. *Semper Vigilo*, I live tae serve – it's the force motto.'

'That's not what it means,' said Daley.

'What? I've thought that for thirty bloody years! What does it mean?'

Before Daley could reply, Symington barked, 'Reports, gentlemen. I'll expect them in an hour. In the meantime, I'll make sure our search for Nurse McNeil intensifies.' She swept from the office, followed by Chisholm.

'How well do you know Chisholm, Bri?' Daley asked once they'd gone. 'I didn't really have much to do with him back in the day.'

'Och, he was okay. Had an eye for the women, right enough. Quite successful he was. Him a ginger, tae.'

'I want you to ask about – phone some old mates, see what they know about him.'

'What about my report for Symington?'

'What are you going to say? I fell asleep in the hospital and let Helen do one?'

'Aye, good point, Jimmy. I'll get on the blower now.' He stared at the floor. 'Will I get a brush and shovel and sweep up your favourite mug?'

Anthea Francombe sat on a boulder, high on the hill overlooking the Kilmilken site. Inevitably, she'd had a hard time from the directors of archaeology at the faculty. She didn't blame them, but needed time by herself. She'd always been proud of her organisational abilities, the talent to get things done. Yet here she was in the midst of a shambles.

In front of her, the wind was pushing dark rain clouds across the Kilbrannon Sound, already discharging their load over the Isle of Arran. The waves were now white-tipped and angry. A small shellfish boat was being tossed around at the mercy of their peaks and troughs, its diesel engine puffing black fumes as it struggled to push the vessel through swell and tide.

Near her, a gull had its head under a wing, grey and white plumage ruffled by the rising wind. Today there was no sign of the Ayrshire coast; it was hidden behind a curtain of grey cloud framing the mound of Ailsa Craig, an eerie shadow in the gloom.

She stared down at the dig, particularly the three rough graves of the victims of the Midweek Murderer. She sighed, and out of nowhere a memory of her nose pressed against the window flashed into her mind.

She was about to get up when she felt a crushing blow to her head. Though she saw stars and the world appeared to turn upside down, she managed to hold on to consciousness through the pain and shock, trying to stagger to her feet. She was strong, and swung round, albeit unsteadily, to face her attacker, fists bunched, instinct for survival taking over of its own accord.

Just before the next blow sent her into darkness, her mouth fell open in recognition.

The gull removed its head from under its wing and soared into the slate-grey sky, wind doing the work of wings, its plaintive call an ancient intimation of danger.

38

Glasgow, 1994

Daley arrived home, thoughts of what Maggie Baird had told him in the car park still echoing round his head.

Suddenly, everything made sense. Speirs – it had to be! He had connections with the army, Daley was sure. But the fog of recollection was thick and he would have to dig to confirm this. He recalled Burns's theory regarding the murders he'd encountered as a young officer, and his warning about ex-army cliques who remained fiercely loyal to each other even though they were now wearing police uniforms.

As he locked his car and searched for his house keys, he reasoned that, given he had a good few years' more service than he had himself, Speirs could easily have fallen in with a group of old-school policemen, ex-soldiers covering for one of their own. Now he was at the heart of the Crime Squad, it would be easy for Speirs to deflect the course of an investigation, especially under the slack reins of DI Graham's regime. Daley admired Graham's skills as a detective, but his management of a team left a great deal to be desired.

As he opened the front door, he encountered his wife. She was wearing the expensive dress he'd bought her for Christmas, her immaculately made-up face pointing to the fact that she was heading out somewhere.

'Must be a posh party if you're wearing that dress,' he said.

'Oh, Jim, I told you about this weeks ago. It's a girls' night out – the old badminton crowd from uni. We're going to the Fox and Hounds in Houston for a meal, a few drinks and a boogie.' She sidled up to him, kissing his neck. 'Mind you, the taxi doesn't arrive for half an hour.' She winked, directing her gaze to the stairs.

'You've been on the wine already,' he observed, smelling it on her breath.

'Oh, is that a crime, Detective Sergeant? In that case, you'd better wallop those cuffs on me now.' She held her hands out, lips pouting. 'Bad girls have to be punished, don't they?'

He stared at her. She was always beautiful, but the smoky eye shadow and mascara highlighting her hypnotic eyes made her almost irresistible – almost.

'Sorry, Liz. You go out and have a good time. I'm not feeling like . . . well, you know.'

'You're turning into a bore, Jim,' she said, the seductive tone suddenly banished. 'I know you're depressed about Ian Burns – we all are. But you can't mourn for ever. It's not healthy – for you, or for me.'

He stared back at her. 'I'm sorry. I've other things on my mind, too.'

'Clearly.'

She stomped upstairs, no doubt to apply the finishing touches to her make-up.

He poured himself a large whisky and sat at the table in the kitchen, sad and furious at the same time. He heard her footsteps on the floor above. She looked a million dollars – far too good for a pub in the next village. He often wondered about what she did when he worked the long hours that were the stuff of any police officer's life.

It was jealousy, pure and simple, and he had to banish it. Returning thoughts of Speirs soon refocused his mind on the hatred he now felt for the man.

He was halfway through his second dram when he heard Liz rushing down the stairs. When she found him in the kitchen, she sighed.

'Why don't you sit in the lounge, darling? That's what it's for. This idea of your mother's of keeping the front room for special occasions is so . . .'

'So what – common? That's what you were going to say, wasn't it?'

'Bloody hell, she kept the plastic wrapping on her suite! I mean, what's the point?'

He sighed, shaking his head. 'I'm not in the mood for this, Liz. Go and have a nice time. I've got things to do.'

A taxi horn sounded outside.

She kissed him on the cheek and clicked out of the kitchen in her red high-heeled shoes. 'Don't wait up, misery guts.' The door opened then slammed shut and she was gone.

Daley poured himself another dram. A large one.

Kinloch, the present

'I've left messages wae a couple o' mates who know Dunky Chisholm. They'll get back tae me shortly,' said Scott.

'Right, good,' replied Daley distractedly, staring at a clear board bearing photos of victims and suspects, joined by the usual lines of connection and scribbled notes. Though all the collected information lay in the limitless mind of a computer, Daley still liked to augment it with the old-style board. Yes, information on possible suspects could be gleaned at the touch of a keyboard from any force in the country and beyond, but this was something tangible. He focused on it now, desperately trying to force his synapses to make a connection, find the solution to the problem.

'If there's anything tae tell they'll know about it. After all, me an' you've no' seen him for years.'

'Until now.'

'No, right enough, Jim.' Scott shuffled from foot to foot, clearing his throat loudly.

'What's up? Ants in your pants?'

'Nah, Jimmy, no ants. Mind you said I could take a bit o' time oot tae view this hoose wae oor Ella? I mean, I know we're busy and a' . . .'

'You've asked me once, Brian. You should know me well enough by now. It's not as though you don't put in the hours.'

'Aye, true. I'll be off, then. No' be mair than an hour or so.'

'I'm not counting. Have a lovely time,' said Daley with a grin, returning his attention to the clear board.

Scott decided not to drive. Though there had been a shower or two, they'd soon blown over in the strong wind. After all, everywhere in Kinloch was within walking distance of the County. Going to their proposed new house on foot would acquaint his wife more readily with the town than swishing through the streets in a car.

Though he'd arranged to meet her in the bar, he was surprised to see her in the vestibule, walking a toddler up and down by the hand.

'Is that who I think it is, Ella?' he asked, somewhat bemused.

'Yes, this is James Daley junior. Well spotted, Brian. It's no' like you to recognise weans.'

'What dae you mean? I am a detective, after a'.'

'Don't you remember the time you took all they photos of oor weans at the sports day?'

'Ach, that was years ago. Plus I'd had a pint or two.'

'No' one o' them was oors. You'd a picture o' near every other child in the school. Mind you, I'm no' surprised you recognise this one. Eyes just like his mother. She should be ashamed of herself. What's Jimmy saying aboot it?'

'He never mentioned it tae me. Where is she, anyhow?'

'Come wae me an' you'll hear a' aboot it.'

They walked into the County's wood-panelled bar, Ella leading James Daley junior by the hand.

'Don't tell me,' said Hamish. 'You're here tae arrest me for child cruelty.'

'Eh?' said Scott.

'Tell him what you were doing wae the wean,' piped up Annie, polishing a glass while shaking her head at the old man.

'Och, well now, you see, the wee fella was fair scunnered sitting in that hoose a' day, so we went for a walk doon the pier.'

'As did I, as luck would have it,' said Ella.

'Och, I don't claim tae be an expert wae children. I thought he'd enjoy it – like the fun fair.'

'They had him on a breeches buoy, being swung to and fro between two fishing boats. The poor kid was greeting fit tae burst,' said Ella.

'No, no' greetin'. Sure, the wean was fair enjoying himsel'. Those were cries o' laughter you heard.' Hamish tutted in disgust.

'Tell him whoot you fed the boy,' said Annie.

'A roll, square sausage an' a tatty scone – aye, wae a wee bit brown sauce. Fine, wholesome food. He couldna quite manage

314

it whole, but once I'd chewed a wee bit off it for him, he was in fine trim. Fair wolfed it doon, so he did.'

'Damn near choked,' said Annie. 'And anyhow, how unhygienic is that, you chewing food wae they auld falsers o' yours and then handing it tae a child?'

'Sure, the gulls dae it a' the time, and there's nae shortage o' them aboot. You jeest need tae open a poke o' chips doon on the esplanade an' it's like that Hitchcock film. Frightened the hell oot o' me when I first saw it doon the wee pictures. Aye, me that had tae work amongst they vicious birds while fighting off the great Atlantic.'

'Well, you're lucky Liz Daley never clocked any o' this,' said Ella. 'You'd be diving intae the Atlantic for cover. She's no' a woman tae mess aboot, I'll tell you that for nothing.'

'I've always liked her,' observed Annie.

'Right, one wean saved. No doubt I'll hear a' aboot why he's here and where his mother is in due course,' said Scott. 'We need tae get on oor toes and go see this hoose.'

'We'll take young Jimmy with us,' said Ella, putting the toddler in his pushchair. 'Doesn't it make you feel a bit broody, Brian? It does me.'

'No' in the slightest,' said Scott.

They said goodbye to Hamish and Annie, leaving the hotel with Jim Daley's son in his pushchair, humming away happily to himself.

Annie watched them as they walked through the big swing doors. 'A bit broody! Did you hear that, Hamish? Her days o' having weans are long gone.'

'Right enough whoot they say,' said Hamish quietly to himself, as he watched Annie head through into her little office. 'Isn't jealousy a terrible thing.'

39

Glasgow, 1994

Daley swirled the remains of his dram in the glass. He knew if he had another he would never carry on with what his mind screamed at him to do.

He slammed the glass down on the table and reached for the bottle.

He paused. Despite his best efforts, the whisky had heightened the dark shadows of his temper. He could see the lifeless body of his mentor and friend Ian Burns lying on the rough grass under the big hill, as the ravens cawed and tumbled above the trees. He could see the flecks of spittle flying from Sanderson's gaping mouth as he berated him. And he saw the letter Ian had written to him – the face of his grieving, devastated widow as she solemnly handed the envelope over. He thought of the life they could have had together – deserved to have – now Burns had come to the end of his dedicated and distinguished career of public service.

He pictured Speirs's condescending sneer. He suspected more than one man on the team had aided the suspect Alison in her escape, but thanks to Maggie Baird he had no doubt who was at the root of it.

Speirs – and whomever he was working with – had let one of the main suspects in the Midweek Murder case disappear into thin air. This act alone would condemn more innocent women to suffer and die, see more children lose a mother.

He remembered Ian Burns's suspicions. Speirs fitted his theory on every level.

Pushing the whisky glass away, Daley walked into the hall, removed his car keys from the table, and closed the door behind him.

Bobby Speirs was watching a comedy show on the television in his lounge in Milngavie, tomato sauce from his spaghetti bolognese dripping down his chin.

His wife sighed, but said nothing. Both of them had come from poor backgrounds in the worst parts of Glasgow. Now here they were in their detached bungalow in one of its more leafy suburbs.

A sharp knock on the door made Speirs turn round. 'Who the hell is that at this time o' night?'

'How should I know?'

'Why don't you go and see who it is, honey?'

'Why don't you?'

He cursed as he struggled to put the tray of food safely on the coffee table in front of him, an action made difficult by the collection of his wife's magazines liberally scattered atop it.

As he walked down the short hallway, another knock sounded at the door, louder this time. Frantic, even.

Bobby Speirs had been a policeman for a long time, and had made his fair share of enemies. He reached into the umbrella stand and hefted the iron poker he kept there unseen, just in case someone he'd locked up, cheated or mistreated decided to look him up. 'Who is it?' he called.

The voice behind the door was muffled, but he could make out the words. 'Wait a minute,' he replied, placing the poker back in its hiding place, confident this visitor posed no threat.

He removed the chain then unlocked the door, opening it wide. 'Right, if you're here for a dram and a wee catch-up, you can forget it. I reserve my whisky for my friends, and you're no' one of them.'

'I want answers, and I want them now,' said the tall young man on his doorstep. 'No hiding behind the bosses, or your greasy pals back at the office – just you and me, man to man, that's all I want.'

Speirs took a step forward, taking him out of the bright warmth of his hallway on to the top step at his front door, enabling him to stare directly into the eyes of his visitor, who stood on the step below. 'You know what you can do, Jimmy Daley? Sleep off your Dutch courage – I can smell the whisky on your breath, son – and fuck off.'

The pair stood stock-still for a few moments, their eyes locked.

'Is everything all right?' asked Mrs Speirs, poking her head round the lounge door. 'I thought I heard shouting.'

'Och, just one of the young boys I work with has had one too many. Just go back and finish your dinner, dear.'

Mumbling something about what an inconsiderate time it was to call, she did as she was bid and disappeared.

'Okay, I hope we're straight here, son. We've all done it – had too much o' the bevvy then thought we would put the world tae rights. Just you get back home tae that pretty wife o' yours. We'll say no more about it.'

'I want you to know that I know you let Alison go on purpose the other night.'

'Like I said, son, for your own sake, get back home to your wife.'

'I also want you to know that I suspect you have something to do with the death of Ian Burns.'

The older man laughed. 'All this shite about me going round in your big stupid heid, when what you really should be thinking to yourself is who's shagging that tart o' a wife of mine?'

Before Speirs could move, Daley launched a fist into his stomach, making his colleague double up in pain.

'You stupid bastard, Daley! You can't leave anything alone,' Speirs gasped.

An uppercut caught him on the chin, sending him flying backwards into his hallway. Daley landed on top of him and caught him by the throat. 'What did you say?' he roared, squeezing Speirs's neck, making the other man's face turn crimson, the mocking look in his eyes now replaced by one of genuine fear.

'Can I have the police, please?' said Mrs Speirs into the phone in the lounge as quietly as she dared. Her hand holding the receiver was trembling. 'My husband – he's a police sergeant – is being attacked on our doorstep, and I don't know what to do.'

By the time the blue lights flashed behind him, Daley was on the main road back to his home in Renfrewshire. The police car overtook, signalling him to stop.

Calmly, Daley pulled up behind the marked car. He watched as two uniformed officers left the vehicle, adjusting their hats as they approached him.

'Can I help you, gents?'

'Acting DS Daley?' said the older of the two.

'Yup.'

'Please step out of the car, Sergeant. I'm afraid we're here to place you under arrest.'

In minutes, Acting Detective Sergeant James Daley of the Serious Crime Squad had been cautioned and charged and was on his way back to Glasgow, his crime: assaulting a fellow police officer.

The arresting officers, seeing him as an unlikely absconder, had dispensed with the obligatory handcuffs, and were chatting with their prisoner.

'Any chance I can give my wife a call? She's on a night out, but I know where she is. She'll worry if I'm not there when she gets home.'

The older cop turned round to face him from the front passenger seat. 'Aye, son, nae bother. But if I were you I'd be on the phone to Beltrami.'

The mention of Glasgow's most famous defence counsel saw Daley smile wryly. The cry of 'Get me Beltrami' was familiar to every police officer who'd made an arrest for serious crime in the city. He was well known for extricating serious criminals from what had been considered impossible legal predicaments.

Now that the fury had gone, Jim Daley knew he was in deep, deep trouble. Maybe he really would require the services of someone like Joseph Beltrami.

Kinloch, the present

The house had three bedrooms and stood beside some playing fields and a row of pensioners' cottages. On a rise about two hundred yards away, under a heather-clad hill, sprawled one of what had been Kinloch's two council schemes. Very few of these houses belonged to the council now, having been purchased by their occupants, or sold on, as was reflected by the wide assortment of colours adorning brickwork, doors and windows.

Ella Scott ran her finger across a worktop in the kitchen, examining the result with a shake of her head. 'It needs a bloody good clean.'

'Aye, well, obviously, dear. It's been lying empty for a good while now. A wee inspector called MacLeod lived here.'

'What happened tae him?'

'Oh, turned out he was a bad lot. It was him that Jimmy replaced,' replied Scott, vaguely. He had no wish to go into the sordid details regarding the wretched MacLeod.

'An inspector's house – pity you don't have the pips tae go wae it, Brian.'

'You know me, Ella. That's no' about tae happen.'

'I know fine – in fact I've known it for a long time. Fae the start, probably.'

'Did anyone tell you you're getting right cyclical in your auld age?'

Well used to her husband's tussles with the dictionary, she smiled. 'You mean cynical, Brian. Anyhow, I didnae marry you so I could tell my fancy friends you were the chief constable.'

'Just as well,' murmured Scott.

Suddenly there was a scream from the hall. The Scotts' footsteps echoed in the empty house as they ran to find out what was going on.

James Daley junior was yelling at the top of his voice,

pointing at a corner of the ceiling. Ella picked him up to reassure him. 'There, Jamie, son, it's just a spider. It'll no' do you any harm.'

'Unless it's one o' they tarantulas.' Scott made spider legs from his fingers, wriggling them in the air, making the toddler bawl even more vociferously.

'Spiders are bad,' he spluttered through his tears.

'There, son, just you ignore your Uncle Brian. He's no' got the brains he was born wae – aye, and that was precious few in the first place.' Ella glared at her husband. 'You'd think you'd never had weans o' your own – frightening the boy like that.'

'Och, he's spent too much time wae his mother. He needs toughening up. When I was his age I was acting as a lookout in case the tallyman came roond.'

'And a lot o' good that did you. I'm here tae bet this wee yin won't be spying on any tallyman. Though I'm no' sure where Jimmy's going tae get the time tae watch him. Aye, and if he'd know what to do wae him if he had.'

Mollified, James Daley indicated that he wished to be set back on his feet and began to run – somewhat unsteadily – up and down the hall, giggling to himself. All the same, he was careful to keep a leery eye on the spider's movements as he did so.

'Poor wee boy,' said Ella. 'We might no' have had much tae gie oor weans, but at least we were together. He doesnae know what growing up wae a mummy and daddy is a' aboot.'

'No' likely to, neither. If she's got a new man, they'll never get back together.'

'I just wish Jimmy could find a decent women. I'm telling you, I see a change in him. And not a change for the better, that's for sure.'

'We all get aulder, dear.'

'So we do. But he looks ill. At least she always kept him fed and curtailed his boozing. Do you know who he reminded me o' when I saw him last night?'

'Who?'

'You! No' eating properly, drinking far too much. He's at a bad age, tae. Men drop like flies at that time o' their lives. Especially wae the sort o' stress he's constantly under. Some of his own making, tae.'

'I'll keep an eye on him, Ella.'

'Oh well, that's fine – nothing tae worry about, then,' she said sarcastically.

'Enough aboot Jimmy. What aboot the hoose?'

She looked around. 'It's far too big, for a start. And like I said, it fair needs a good tidy up and a lick o' paint.'

'They'll dae that before we move in.'

'And we keep the hoose in Kirkie? I'm no' consigning myself tae the sticks for the duration.'

'Aye, of course. We can let it oot. Oor hoose is damn near paid for, and the rent on this is peppercorn. It's one o' the last auld-fashioned police hooses left, you know.'

'Well, it's going to the right man, for you're one o' the last auld-fashioned policemen.'

'So is that a yes?'

'Aye, I'll gie it a trial. I choose the colour scheme, mind.'

'That's good enough for me, Ella. It's a deal.'

Though Brian Scott had enjoyed the conviviality of the County Hotel, now he'd stopped drinking its appeal had waned. And like most men of his age, he needed his life-long companion with him. He missed his warm cosy house and bed when he was alone in a tatty hotel room.

And yes, he'd grown to like the beauty of Kinloch and the warmth and humour of the people, if not its wide variety of sailing craft.

He smiled benignly at his wife, now consoling James Daley junior a second time after a stumble in the hall.

He'd never really taken to Kirkintilloch, preferring his old haunts in Glasgow.

Life was good. Then his mobile rang.

Glasgow, 1994

Daley paced around the holding cell in Pitt Street, Strathclyde's force HQ. Though his mind was in a tumult, he felt he'd done the right thing. He knew how the police worked. Officers like Speirs disgusted him, yet worked with impunity, settling old scores, or covering for their mates – or, if what he suspected was true, murdering.

Now, though he'd done himself untold damage, there would be a proper hearing. He'd plead not guilty and bring his assault of Speirs to trial, that way drawing shining light into the darkest recesses of the world he was trying to expose. It could prove a massive sacrifice, though.

The old iron cell door swung open, and instead of the solicitor he was expecting, there stood DI John Donald, tanned face, expensive suit, slicked-back hair, the works. Any last vestige of his former uncouth demeanour appeared entirely banished – almost.

'I don't want to speak to you,' said Daley immediately. 'In any case, I've no legal representative, so you can't question me.' He sat on the cell's hard bed and folded his arms defensively.

'Come on, Jim. I'm not here to question you. They only

gave me access to you as a favour – you know, old friend and colleague, come to lend support in time of need, and all that jazz.'

'Old friend, my arse! Just do us both a favour and get out.'

'That's not very friendly,' said Donald, standing before him. Daley could smell his expensive aftershave in the dank cell. 'I'm here to see if you want anything. What about your wife – does she know yet?'

'Leave her out of this.'

'I know you've tried to call her. With no success, I hear.'

'I'll get her soon enough.'

'Och, no. Only fair that I help you out, my old friend. Make up for all those hours you and me spent on the beat up in the Townhead. The good old days, Jimmy boy. At least they must seem quite good now – in comparison with your current predicament, I mean.'

'Leave my wife out of it!'

'The bosses are anxious we contact her – put your mind at rest. You'll have a lot to think about in the next few weeks – years, even.'

'What?'

'Don't think you'll get bail, Jim. I'll see to that. No, you'll go to a hearing tomorrow and end up in custody in Barlinnie. They love wayward cops up there. You'll meet a few old friends, I don't doubt – bound to meet some of Brian's.'

'Fuck off!'

'Same old Jimmy Daley; never knows when it's time to shut up.' He smiled sickeningly. 'Make no mistake, there's no knight in shining armour like your old hero Ian Burns coming to your rescue this time. Basically, and I think this is the correct legal terminology, you're fucked, my boy.'

'Like I said, just go. I'm going to inform my brief about this little visit.'

'I'm trembling at the thought. I mean, your star is so bright at the moment. Who's going to believe me?'

'Believe what?'

Donald's grin grew even wider. 'This,' he said, and ran to the door and started hammering on it. 'Quick, let me out, Constable. This is assault, Daley!' he shouted, messing up his hair, as a key turned in the lock. Just before the door was flung open, Donald dashed his head against the cell's brick wall and sank to his knees, mewling in pain.

'What's happened?' asked the custody officer, a bewildered look on his face.

'Bugger went mad,' said Donald, reaching his hand out in order to be helped to his feet. A red lump was already appearing on his forehead, accompanied by a trickle of blood. 'I'm sorry, Jim, there's nothing I can do to help you now, son.'

As he was helped from the cell by the custody officer, behind his back he turned back to face the prisoner and mouthed *You're fucked*.

The heavy cell door slammed shut, loudly marking a full stop not just to Daley's career, but more than likely to his freedom.

40

Kinloch, the present

Daley was doing what had become a habit since his arrival in Kinloch – taking a walk.

As he wandered past the second pier and stepped on to the path that meandered round the south side of the loch, he took deep breaths of the invigorating sea air. The wind had died down and patches of blue could be seen between the clouds, reflected in the calm waters of the loch.

An old man stumbled towards him, clearly the worse for drink. 'How ye, big man,' he slurred, then carried on his rather unsteady way.

Who's worse off, Daley wondered. At first glance, here was the chief inspector of police, with a nice house, a good salary and a more than decent pension to look forward to, well met by one of the town's drunks, unkempt, addicted and probably with little more than two pennies to rub together. Yet, of the pair, who was more content?

A seal popped its head above the water with a plop, regarding Daley with apparent interest. It suddenly dawned on him that he should have contacted Hamish and arranged to take his son for a walk. He was at a loss as to what he was going to do with his only child while Liz was away. Hamish could barely cope, and he didn't want his offspring spending much of the next three weeks in the bar of the County Hotel.

He wondered about the man Liz had met. Was it someone new, or a mutual friend? Though her letter indicated the former, in his mind's eye the vision of his hated brother-in-law Mark Henderson appeared unbidden.

During these walks he always tried to get his mind back into gear; to refresh what was going on in both his life and the job. Sometimes this worked better than others. On this occasion, he was surprised to find that his thoughts kept drifting back to Liz.

He'd barely thought of her in the few months since the death of Mary Dunn, yet here he was, that old feeling of jealousy simmering in the pit of his stomach.

He looked across the loch to the hills beyond. Just out of sight, the graves of the last victims of the Midweek Murderer were pegged down under a thick tarpaulin sheet. Symington had placed herself at the head of the investigation, but he wondered how well she could be expected to do, given her scant knowledge of the case, or indeed the times in which it took place.

He supposed it was his job to fill the gaps in her knowledge, but how to do that? How could he convey the sense of failure and hatred that he felt, not just for the murderer, but also for some of his fellow officers who'd investigated the original inquiry? How could he make a modern police officer, someone who would find the job he'd been initiated into all those years ago utterly alien, understand the nuances and complexities of everything that had happened, and was happening?

The mobile phone in his pocket vibrated into life. Noting

the number of Kinloch Police Office, he sighed as he swiped the screen to answer.

'Sir, I have Helen McNeil at the front desk.' Sergeant Shaw's tone was buoyant.

Daley hurried back the way he'd come, passing the drunk man en route.

'Hey, whoot's the hurry, big chap? You damn near knocked me doon.'

Daley muttered an apology, striding on. Maybe his luck was changing? Fat chance, he thought.

With nothing to see, the seal disappeared beneath the waters of the loch in a flash of grey.

Scott was taking a note awkwardly, one hand holding the phone to his ear, while he tried to write and keep the pad from slipping on his desk with the other.

'So you reckon she'd got money – the lassie he married?'

'Aye, she'd money all right – or her family did,' came the reply, the voice sounding occasionally mechanical as the mobile signal wavered. 'They had a big house in Ayrshire somewhere.'

'Oh aye – any idea where? Ayrshire's no' exactly a village.'

'You know how it is, Brian. See, at our age, your memory's crap.' There was silence on the line while Scott's friend tried to remember the location of the property. 'North Ayrshire, I think. Kilbirnie, Dalry – one of these places.'

'Right, so they'd a big hoose there – doesnae mean they're that well off. I mean, the Garnock valley's hardly Beverly Hills. You can buy a mansion for two and six there, can you no'?'

'They'd a pad doon in the Borders, too. But they'd got coin, all right. If I mind right her faither had a chain of bookies' shops.'

Scott scribbled down this information as best he could. 'Any mair for me, Doug?'

'He'd a right eye for the ladies, our Dunky. But you'll remember that yourself. Mind he was shagging that inspector's wife fae Baird Street? They reckon that's why he took the plunge and swapped to Lothian and Borders.'

'It never did him any harm, anyway. Dunky Chisholm a DCI! Fuck me, if I'd joined the Edinburgh polis, I'd likely be chief constable by noo.'

'No you wouldn't, Brian. You're in the realms of fantasy there.'

'Thanks for that vote of confidence, Doug.'

'You know the likes of me an' you have never been cut out for that caper, Brian. I'm retiring in six months, and I tell you, I'm counting the seconds, never mind the weeks.'

'What are you going to do wae yoursel' – store detective, or barfly?'

'Now, in a way you're right on the last one. Me and the missus are selling up and buying a wee bar in the Costa del Sol.'

'Good luck wae that!' said Scott, remembering Ella's proposed change of career.

'Just come over any time and me and you can chew the fat about the old days over a bottle of whisky or three.'

'Aye, sure will. Listen, thanks for that, Doug. Good luck in Spain, mate. I might take you up on that offer,' said Scott, too weary to explain yet again why he no longer imbibed.

As he clicked off the phone and tidied up his notes, something nagged at his mind about North Ayrshire.

As he was thinking, in swept DCI Jim Daley, Nurse Helen McNeil at his heels.

Symington watched the car taking the Assistant Chief Constable back to the airport. Their meeting had been brief, but most certainly to the point. She was to take sole charge, with Daley in nominal command on the ground, while the Midweek Murder element of the investigation would be assisted wherever necessary by Bobby Speirs, who would shortly be on his way back to Kinloch.

With much shaking of head and raising of brow, the ACC had gone over the progress so far with his chief superintendent, declaring that there was a 'distinct lack of inspiration' dogging the whole process, and that if Daley couldn't deal with the past, or indeed his reduced personal circumstances, perhaps his deployment in Kinloch should be reassessed.

All of this left Symington standing at her window as the unmarked car disappeared, feeling utterly miserable.

Everyone had been so proud that she'd smashed the 'glass ceiling', and at an early stage in her career attained high rank. What those patting her on the back failed to realise was that it was hard – bloody hard at times – handing out orders to men who had, in some cases, been walking the beat when she was a toddler. The dynamic between Daley and Speirs added yet another degree of difficulty.

In the aftermath of her boss's visit, this was her immediate concern. She'd read the official files, and then heard more when the ACC had whispered a few undocumented truths about the events more than two decades before in her ear.

There was a sharp knock at her door.

'Helen McNeil's just arrived at the office, ma'am,' said Sergeant Shaw.

'What, just like that?'

'Yes, ma'am. She's with DCI Daley now.'

She thanked Shaw, and, once he'd gone, slumped in her big swivel chair and breathed a sigh of relief. At least that was one problem gone.

She turned her attention to her desktop computer, first consulting an email she'd received while talking to her superior, then initiating the Skype call that had been requested.

The man who appeared before her on the screen – in her opinion – looked surprisingly young to be the dean of an Oxford college, but that was what he was. Jonathan Stricklander looked straight into the camera with a confident smile, volumes of old books providing the backdrop. However, even via this medium, Symington could detect a certain wariness beneath the projected composure.

'Chief Superintendent Symington, I trust you are well?' Symington heard a hint of the north of England in his baritone voice.

The more she stared at his face, the more she felt that here was someone – replete with round, horn-rimmed glasses, bow tie, and a slicked-down side parting in his dark hair – trying to be something he wasn't.

'Hello, Professor Stricklander. As you know, I'm interested in finding out more about Anthea Francombe – the site manager of the archaeological team we have here.'

'Ah, yes, I did see your email.' He paused to cough. 'What can I do for you?'

'Huge parts of her records we received from you are redacted. The work she's carrying out here is hardly D-listed, so I just wondered why. As you know, we're in the process of investigating a long-standing murder inquiry, prompted by the find made by the team. You will understand that I need to know as much as I can about the individuals involved, no matter how tenuous their association with the case. It's just our procedure, Professor.'

Stricklander hesitated for a few moments, fingers intertwined in front of his mouth. Then he replied, 'Yes, I rather thought we could encounter this kind of problem.'

'What problem?'

'One of confidentiality, I'm sorry to say. As you must be aware, under data protection laws . . .'

'I'm well aware of these laws, Professor.'

'Yes, of course you are. But what I'm trying to say is that there are certain protocols I have to follow. I'm sure you understand.'

'What are we talking about here – is Francombe a rehabilitated murderer, or something?'

'Oh no, nothing like that; quite mundane stuff these days, in fact. But I must still consult with the wider university's HR and legal departments before I can throw any light on what you seek. Also, in this world of public/private cooperation, our faculty is blessed by a partnership with Coredig. They're an American company specialising in speculative archaeological projects across the world. Owned by one of these tech billionaires who has a passion for the subject . . .'

'Not to stop you, I'm sure this little financial project is very beneficial. However, in what way does this have a bearing on my request, Professor?'

'They are very keen on Anthea and her work – see her as rather a star, in fact. You know, telegenic, enthusiastic, all those things. More than likely the face of a potential streaming series on the subject – whatever streaming is.'

Symington, who'd already had a difficult day, was not inclined to beat about the bush with a reticent academic. 'Very well, Professor, by all means consult whomever you see fit, including this Coredig. But I'll tell you this: I'm seeking a court order allowing me access to Francombe's files, and if anything it contains has hindered this investigation I'll hold you personally responsible.'

Stricklander sat up in his chair, no doubt unused to being addressed in such a brusque manner. 'I assure you, Chief Superintendent, that I'll do my very best to provide you with the information you require. I just need time. You of all people must be aware how difficult it is to be governed by protocol, especially where a third party is concerned. Coredig have very deep pockets, and will, I believe, defend Professor Francombe's right to privacy with every resource at their disposal. Do you see my concern?'

'Be that as it may, I still want an unredacted file with me no later than tomorrow morning. I thank you for your time, Professor Stricklander. I'll let you get on with consulting the people you must consult. A very good day to you.' She smiled and leaned forward to end the video call.

'Oh, before you go, can I ask you a question?'

'Of course.'

'Would it be possible to get a message to her – Anthea, I mean? Please ask her to call me. I've tried her mobile on several occasions. I know the signal can come and go in places like Kintyre, but she hasn't replied to any of my messages, to her phone or hotel. To be honest, I'd much rather what there is to tell came from her rather than me, if you know what I mean.'

'I'll see what I can do, Professor.'

With that, the call ended, leaving Symington wondering just what it was that was best heard from the horse's mouth.

'So you just wanted some time alone, Helen?' said Daley, sitting in his glass box facing Nurse McNeil across his large desk.

'Yes. I was fed up with all the attention – looks from my colleagues, questions from your people, not to mention the press. I'd just had enough.'

'You must remember that I'm directly responsible for your safety, Helen. You've been abducted once; the last thing we want is for that to happen again.'

'Well, I want to get away properly. Have a holiday away from all this.'

'It's difficult at the moment . . .'

'So I'm effectively under arrest?'

'No, but we must take your wellbeing into account. You must understand, I'm thinking of you.' Daley searched her face, seeing a resolve hitherto absent in her manner.

'Well, I'm going home to think. Do what you want, put one of your officers at my door – whatever you feel is necessary. I'll think carefully about things, but I'll also consult my solicitor. If I decide to go away for a while, I'm sure there's nothing you can do to stop me.'

Before he could reply, she was on her feet. 'If you don't mind, I just want to get home, have a long bath and get to bed.'

As she swept from the room, Daley wondered what had happened to the timid, terrified woman he'd first encountered.

'Jimmy!' exclaimed Scott, bursting into his office without knocking, an uncharacteristic look of excitement on his face.

'Don't tell me – you've won the lottery.'

'No, way better than that. I think I've found something big.'

41

Grim-faced, Jim Daley drove through the slanting rain in his SUV, Scott at his side.

'Steady on, Jimmy, or you'll get both of us killed, the rate you're going,' said Scott. 'What the hell's got you in such a foul mood, and why dae we have tae rush back to Glasgow?'

'Here.' Daley reached into his pocket and threw his mobile across in Scott's general direction. 'Read the last text.'

After a brief struggle with the complexities of a strange phone, Scott managed to find what he was looking for.

Be back in Kinloch this evening. No sign of Burns's raincoat in forensics. Bobby.

'What raincoat?' asked Scott.

'Ian Burns's, surely you remember it.'

'Aye, thon auld beige job. Came oot the ark. I wonder how it didnae fall tae pieces. It must have been ancient.'

'He was wearing it when he died. I remember they retained it for future reference, even though they could get nothing from it at the time. If you remember, things were moving so fast with what they could do, it was standard procedure to retain productions that could possibly contain DNA or other evidence, just in case.'

'Aye, right enough,' replied Scott, now concerned that the

subject of Daley's obsession – finding Ian Burns's killer – was raising its head again.

'Well, don't you think it's a bit odd, Brian?'

'Aye, I suppose so. Though I'm no expert on forensics, mind. Leave that tae Dunky Chisholm.'

'And that's another reason why I want to get up the road. We'll take a trip to North Ayrshire while we're at it.'

'And they tell me Galt's been talking up in the hospital. He's in the RAH in Paisley.'

Daley gripped the wheel even tighter. 'So now you know why we have to get a move on, Brian.'

Scott looked on as they took a long sweep of road at the head of Loch Fyne, its sheltering hills almost invisible in the lowering rain clouds, the speedometer hitting ninety. Now the ghost of Ian Burns was back, anything was possible. He stared at the big man driving the car and could see the turmoil in his narrowed eyes.

Leaning forward, Scott flipped open the glove compartment where Daley kept some CDs. 'Here, a wee bit o' Bowie will help us on our way.'

As the first bars of 'Fashion' throbbed into life, the brakes screeched as Daley took a sharp corner at high speed and Scott looked out of the passenger window, humming along to take his mind off the rapidly rising road ahead.

Glasgow, 1994

ACC Taylor sat with Daley in the holding cell at Glasgow Sheriff Court. They'd run out of conversation, but he thought he'd give it one more try. 'Jim, if you plead not guilty like this, the case is cut and dried. Speirs has his wife as a witness – you did attack him. And, I must remind you, this was the second time in a few days. I've tried all I can. I'm afraid your career will be over. I think you'll go to bloody jail! Plead guilty and we can do a deal with the Fiscal – at least keep you from going behind bars.'

Daley was sitting head back, looking at the cell's grubby ceiling. 'But they'll have to give me a trial. If I plead not guilty, they've no choice.'

'Yes, sure. And the sentence will reflect the hassle. You'll be found guilty – you know that.'

Daley turned to look piercingly at him. 'But trials attract the press, sir. This one certainly will. Maybe we can throw light on what's been happening. Who knows, maybe one of them will break ranks, tell the truth. They must know there are people on their heels. Even Speirs isn't that stupid.'

'You think by sacrificing your freedom that Bobby Speirs and his mates will come clean and hold their hands up to possible corruption, even murder? You're a fool, Jim. That's something I didn't take you for.'

Despite his entreaties, Taylor could see the determination in the young detective's eyes. 'He wouldn't have wanted this, you know.'

'Who, Ian?'

'Yes, Ian. The last thing he'd have wanted to see would have been you losing your job, ruining your life and fuck knows what else – for this. You know how slippery they are, we both do. We have nothing on Speirs – or anyone, come to that. Come on, Jim, plead guilty; salvage something from this bloody mess.'

Daley remained silent, his jaw determinedly set.

ACC Taylor got to his feet. 'I need to go. If you won't listen to reason, there's nothing more I can do, apart from silence

DI John Donald. You realise you're on your own out there, Daley?'

'Yes, sir.' Daley's eyes were back on the ceiling.

'You're a brave lad, I'll give you that. What about your wife – how on earth does she feel about this? She must be worried out of her mind!'

Daley pursed his lips and said, 'Of course she's not jumping for joy, sir. But she respects that this is something I have to do.'

'Does she have any idea as to the potential consequences?'

Daley's silence spoke volumes.

Just as Taylor was finally about to take his leave, a key sounded in the cell door lock. A young man with blond hair and a dark suit, bearing a bulging briefcase, was ushered into the small room by a court officer. It was Daley's solicitor.

'Is it time, Braithwaite?' said Taylor resignedly.

'Well, yes, ACC Taylor. Time for us to pack up and go home, in fact.' The young lawyer smiled broadly.

'What?' Daley looked confused.

'Mr Speirs – Sergeant Bobby Speirs – has withdrawn his complaint. Apparently, he informed the Fiscal that it was just high jinks that got out of hand – rough and tumble after a few too many drinks. The Fiscal has agreed. He's not bloody happy, mind you.'

'And he's accepted this?' asked Taylor.

'Yes, sir. Detective Sergeant Daley has to wait to be processed – which will take a while, in my experience – but essentially, he's free to go.'

Taylor looked at his detective. 'Well, though it hasn't had the effect you were looking for, maybe there was some logic in what you tried to do here. Come on, don't look so bloody disappointed, man. You've just dodged a rather big bullet.'

Daley sighed, head in hands. 'You mean, they're still getting away with it, sir.'

Braithwaite angled his head to one side, looking from one to the other. 'Sorry, am I missing something?'

'Yes,' replied Taylor. 'In fact, I think we all are. Now let me speak to John Donald and end this sorry mess.'

Paisley, the present

A thousand memories flashed through Scott's mind as they drove through the streets he'd policed for so long; some good, more often than not bad. They played across his mind's eye in a bleak procession, a visceral display of police work and its unpleasant exigencies.

The large hospital loomed in front of them as they drove up a small rise.

'I bloody hate hospitals,' said Scott.

'If it wasn't for them you wouldn't be here, the number of close shaves you've had,' said Daley.

'Don't get me wrong, big man. The folk in there work miracles. Bloody brilliant, they are. But let's face it, it doesnae always have a happy ending.'

'No, no, it doesn't.'

Scott looked around the huge car park, wishing he hadn't hinted at the subject of death, guaranteed to have a negative impact on his colleague, so recently bereaved.

After almost five minutes' driving around, Daley managed to attract the attention of another driver and silently negotiated replacing his vehicle in the space the other was about to vacate by a process of complex semaphore through the windscreen.

They walked through the spacious vestibule of the Royal Alexandra Hospital, past newsagents, cafés and other outlets. Scott looked momentarily amazed. 'It's like a bloody shopping centre, Jimmy.'

'I suppose they have to make money somehow. The NHS has little enough funding as it is.'

After following the signs, and plodding along endless corridors, they arrived at intensive care, where Colin Galt was being treated.

At a busy nurses' station, Daley showed his ID and was taken to one side by a senior nurse, who talked quietly to him while Scott looked on.

'What?' Daley's raised voice was in marked contrast to the whispering nurse. 'The last I heard he was sitting up talking.'

'I'll find one of the doctors, DCI Daley. He'll be able to explain what happened much more clearly.'

Scott looked at his colleague. 'What's up, Jimmy?'

'Galt's dead, that's what's up, Brian.'

A harassed man in a shirt with rolled-up sleeves, a stethoscope draped around his neck, approached the police officers.

'I'm Dr Alan King,' he said. 'I gather you were here to speak to Colin Galt?'

'Yes,' said Daley.

'Unfortunately Mr Galt died about an hour and a half ago. He suffered a massive brain haemorrhage. It was unexpected. He was recovering well from his injuries.'

'How could you possibly miss that, especially in intensive care?'

'These things happen, DCI Daley. If I could save every patient who arrived here, trust me, I would. Every one of the people who staff this hospital feels the same. These things just

341

happen. Especially to middle-aged men who are overweight and over-stressed, as it happens.'

'But Galt was a fitness fanatic. If he wasn't out running, he was walking round a golf course.'

'I wasn't necessarily referring to him.' King eyed Daley up and down. 'I've seen far too many men die prematurely because they thought their work, their money worries, their relationships, their drinking or smoking or anything else was more important than staying alive. It's one of the great mysteries of existence, if you ask me.'

Ignoring the barb, Daley continued. 'So, you're saying this could have happened to him at any time?'

'Yes. Of course it's early days, and due to the circumstances he'll be examined thoroughly by a pathologist. Being shot won't have helped any underlying condition, but we can hardly legislate for that. Despite his being a fit man, I noted early on that his liver wasn't in the best shape possible. Heavy drinking over a number of years was by far the most likely cause. The body is like a machine: if one part struggles, or isn't maintained, the whole structure is under stress.'

'Your liver can repair itself, can it no'?' said Scott, suddenly looking anxious.

'Yes, indeed it can. But there's a limit. Anyway, I digress. As to the precise cause of death – we shall have to wait for the post-mortem for the complete picture. I'm very sorry. Now, gentlemen, I'm sure you appreciate that I have other pressing matters to deal with.'

Daley nodded, and he and Scott looked on as Dr King hurried back the way he had come.

'He was having a wee dig at you there, big man.'

'Eh?'

'About the health – stress an' that.' Scott shook his head sagely. 'You only get one chance at life.'

'Huh, listen to it. This coming from the man who still smokes, and whose liver's probably the size of a rugby ball.'

'Aye, but I'm getting better.'

'And the fags?'

Before Scott could think of a suitable riposte, Daley turned on his heel and hurried down the corridor. 'Next stop Beith, Brian.'

42

Carrie Symington pondered as she stared down at the rough tarpaulin covering the graves. The forensic team had just about finished their painstaking task, and soon the bricks weighing the protective cover down would be removed and the archaeology team could get back to work.

She climbed the hill, heading for the large tent that was being used by both archaeologists and police officers, when they were on site. She was surprised to find it empty, save for one young woman who was carefully brushing mud from something that looked to Symington like a rusty, twisted teaspoon.

'I'm Chief Superintendent Symington,' she said to the fresh-faced girl, whose long blonde hair was tied back in a ponytail. 'I'm looking for Professor Francombe. Do you know where she is?'

'Wish I did. I've been trying to have a word with her since yesterday. I haven't a clue where she is. I've had the dean of the college – our paymasters – on the phone nearly every hour asking the same thing.'

Symington smiled. 'So, no idea where she could be?'

'I've checked the hotel. She hasn't been spotted there either. I can only think she's on a mini field trip.'

'What?'

'Oh, she's famous for it. The prof gets bored easily, so she often goes and investigates nearby sites of possible interest while we do the legwork. I've been on a couple of digs with her. Off she goes with her one person tent and a rucksack. No mobile phone, of course – she hates them.'

'Why?'

'She thinks it's an intrusion. To be fair, when she does have it with her and it's on, the thing never stops. The old academics back at college may look crusty, but they've taken to mobiles and tablets like ducks to water. It's a control thing; and from what I know of the prof, she isn't one for being controlled.'

'So this absence isn't unusual – not being able to get in touch with her, I mean?'

'No, not at all. I told the dean so, too. I bet you my meagre salary that her mobile is lying about in her hotel room somewhere. She's just a free spirit, you know?'

Symington thought for a few moments. 'How do you get on with her?'

'Oh, she's great to work for. People can get funny about her – well, with the stories and all. But I've never had a problem.'

'Stories?'

She paused. 'Sorry, I've said too much. Anyway, it's just speculation – a story, as I say. There's nothing us archaeologists like better than a gossip.'

'Well, do tell. I love a good tale. You'll find police officers are just the same. Sorry, what's your name?'

'Caron, Caron Jennings. I'm sorry – I shouldn't have said anything, really. It's all just nonsense, probably. You've no idea how we go on – it's another hazard of the job. Too much time spent huddled in places like this waiting for the rain to go off.'

'Come on, you're not on trial. You've never come across real gossip until you've spent some time at a police station, let me assure you.'

'Okay.' Caron sighed and lowered her voice conspiratorially. 'The rumour is that Anthea has a past she's not keen on anyone finding out about.'

'Somehow that doesn't surprise me,' replied Symington, thinking about her own efforts to find out more about the mercurial professor.

'The rumour is that she's changed her name, or something. Has a dark secret she doesn't want anyone to know about.'

Momentarily, Symington was intrigued. She'd come across all manner of people who'd hidden or changed their identity for one reason or another. Not all felonious ones, either. Abused women regularly changed their names in order to avoid violent ex-partners and husbands. She was aware that rumours about her own past were now rife in police circles. The perils of being the boss, she thought. 'And how likely do you think this rumour is to be true, Caron?'

'Oh, very unlikely, I'd say. As I told you, she's good to work for, but doesn't suffer fools gladly. You can imagine she's ruffled a good few feathers in her time. It's all spite, probably. Lots of older colleagues – especially men – can't stand the idea that a young woman has beaten them to a good job and the respect the professor has within our small world.'

'Oh, trust me, I can imagine that quite easily.' Symington looked round the large tent.

'I couldn't care less. How people choose to lead their lives is none of my concern – why should it be? The younger lads – you know, graduate trainees and the like – are the worst. And older men, of course.' She thought for a moment. 'Mind you, there's not much about her online – up until a couple of years ago, at least. Strange, really.'

'Yes, that's another thing you don't need to tell me much about.'

Caron looked suddenly concerned. 'You won't tell her I told you? I mean, she's been very fair with me . . . I feel like a bit of a Judas, feeding you this.'

'Don't worry, your secret's safe with me. Anyhow, as you say, it's all probably worthless banter.'

Symington said goodbye to the archaeologist and left the tent. The day had improved. White clouds scudded across a pale blue sky on the light breeze, as seabirds swooped and soared on thermals. The tide lapped quietly on the white sand of the small bay far below. All the same, looking across the Kilbrannon Sound, she could see dark skies above the Ayrshire coast. The smells of gorse and sea mixed together, a hint of the summer about to arrive.

For a moment, she wondered how Daley was getting on, then thought about the heavily redacted file on Anthea Francombe. It would make sense that some personal details would be removed if the story that she'd just been told was true. But what could she be hiding? It was clear her employers knew about it, hence the file, so it couldn't be anything unlawful.

She leaned back through the flap of the marquee. 'Sorry, Caron. When you say that Professor Francombe could well be off on a little fact-finding expedition of her own, do you have any idea where?'

The young woman thought for a moment. 'Not really, apart from Machrie, or the oubliette where that poor woman was found. We've not got much else to work on. I couldn't sleep the other night thinking about her imprisoned down in that awful place. Your men are still examining it. Despite its recent use, it's a wonderful find. We can't wait to get our hands on it.'

Symington nodded thoughtfully. 'It was terrible – what happened to Nurse McNeil, I mean. Can you take me to it – if you have the time, that is? I've just driven here in a normal car, and I hear that the going is rather rough on the way to the castle.'

'Yeah, sure. I'm just about finished. We can take the old Land Rover. Hang on.'

As Caron packed away her equipment, Symington looked on. 'What are you working on?'

'It's a horseshoe. Whether it's a medieval one or one from the seventies is the question I'm trying to answer.'

'Your job sounds much like mine – well, the way it used to be, anyway.'

Soon they were bumping down the rough lane in the old Land Rover. Something about Anthea Francombe and Helen McNeil was nagging at Symington's.

They took the A737 from Paisley to Beith, a road Daley was very familiar with, having lived in Howwood, not too far from their destination. In fact, Liz still lived there, though their large detached house would be empty now she was off on holiday with – well, with whomever she had taken with her.

As the village approached, Daley kept his eyes on the road, looking neither left nor right. Scott, for once, stayed silent, guessing how his old friend must feel.

Though the traffic was heavy, the rain was now no more than a light drizzle. Daley had programmed the satnav, which burst into life from time to time giving him directions he already knew. The exact location of the house he was searching for was the only reason he was using it.

Daley thought about this. Here he was, only a handful of miles from what had been his home for years, but he barely knew the area at all, only the main road through it to somewhere else. After a short time in Kintyre, he could now envision great swathes of the peninsula and beyond, picturing even remote farmhouses or sandy beaches instantly if they ever came into conversation.

He realised that, despite being 'home', this place felt distant; alien, even. He thought of Kinloch as his home, loving both the place and its people, despite their occasionally unusual approach to life – and, indeed, justice.

He thought again about the big house in Howwood, in the new up-market estate. Each room had been themed by his wife, down to the smallest ornament and last lick of paint. He'd always felt like a stranger there; now it felt like another country, another time.

Turn left, then immediately right. The flat voice of the satnav dragged him from these miserable thoughts and on to a narrow B road. For a few moments he had to edge slowly forward, a recalcitrant sheep blocking the way. Realising it was outmatched by Daley's SUV, the animal quickly scrabbled over a ditch, through a gap in the fence, and back to the field whence it came.

'I've always wondered aboot sheep,' said Scott.

'You have?'

'Aye. The buggers seem that bloody stupid, but an auld farmer doon the road telt me that they're right clever beasts. They can recognise people better than dogs.'

'You know, your knowledge of the obscure and pointless never ceases to amaze me, Brian.'

'At least I've no' turned intae a fucking misery like you, Jimmy. You used tae be full o' fun – when you weren't chasing shadows, or obsessed wae some faceless killer. Now . . .'

'Now, what?'

'Ach, you've changed, man. You need tae find your auld self before it's lost altogether.'

'Listen to Freud over here.'

'That guy wae the dog food, how dae you work that oot?'

Take the second exit at the next roundabout.

'Never mind,' said Daley, less than inclined to take Scott on a trip through the great philosopher's family tree. 'In any case, you've had plenty of moments of being a grumpy bastard when you were on the bevvy.'

In three hundred yards, turn left.

'Och, you're just the same as Ella. The answer to every argument is *when you were on the bevvy.*'

'It's true, though. You could be a right pain in the arse when you were pished.'

Turn left now then follow the road for four hundred yards.

'Huh. At least I was enjoying myself.'

'You looked miserable half the time.'

At the end of the road turn right, then right again.

'Miserable? *You*'ve turned intae a right misery. Hamish telt me he sees you doon at the loch just staring at the water.'

'I'm enjoying the beauty of my surroundings – and thinking.' Daley was beginning to become irritated.

Bear right.

'You're just brooding.'

'If you think I'm worried about what Liz is getting up to, you're dead wrong, buddy.'

'Nah, you're still mourning that wee lassie Mary. Think I'm daft?'

Follow the road for two hundred yards and you've reached your destination.

'Shut up, Brian.'

'Just saying, big man. You've got tae get yourself back intae life. The past's the past.'

You've reached your destination.

Daley was still brooding as the pair drove down a short gravel drive and parked outside a sizeable Georgian mansion, ivy reaching up its old walls, a large oak tree, bristling with new life, to the side of the property, next to a modern double garage, designed to echo the architecture of the house, but failing.

They climbed the short set of steps and Scott pulled on an old-fashioned doorbell.

'I've no' seen one o' them for a long time. Is that a wee duck pond o'er there?'

'Hope they answer soon, or I'll be over staring at it,' said Daley sarcastically.

As Scott snorted derision a bright-faced young woman, somewhere in her late twenties, opened the door a crack, scrutinising the policemen with a puzzled look.

'DCI Daley and DS Scott, ma'am,' said Daley. They both showed their warrant cards – a minor miracle in itself as Scott had usually left his somewhere.

'Okay! Right, so not who I was expecting,' replied the young woman in clipped English tones. 'I rather feared that you were the boiler men, and you don't look at all apparelled for such a task. Do come in. I hope nothing terrible has happened.'

'No, not at all. We'd just like to ask a few questions about the house, or rather some of its occupants,' said Daley, as they were led through a long hallway, its polished floor covered with scattered Turkish carpets.

She showed the detectives into a wood-panelled lounge, where a log fire burned in an old iron hearth. The walls were adorned with red-and-cream striped wallpaper, paintings and framed photographs artfully placed here and there. The carpet was thick deep green pile, and the lady of the house sat the policemen on either end of a large Chesterfield couch, the patina of its leather adding to a feel of age, luxury and expense.

'I'm Milly Yorke,' she said, shaking each of them by the hand then taking a seat in a high-backed leather chair. 'My husband and I have been here for six months. We're gradually tearing the place out of the nineteenth century, but I rather like this little room the way it is. Nathan works for a whisky company in Glasgow – in an executive capacity. We didn't fancy holing up in the city, so we found this rather lovely little place.'

'I wouldnae exactly call it little,' said Scott.

'No, well, I dare say it depends on one's perspective. We still have a nice place in Buckinghamshire. We're here for three years at least, so we thought we'd better put down some kind of roots.'

Daley detected a slight note of regret in her voice and said, 'Who did you buy the property from, if you don't mind my asking?'

'Ah, now, that's where you'll have to contact Nathan. He's the man in the know when it comes to that sort of thing. I'm afraid I was rather more involved with the logistics of it all. You know, the move, finding new schools for the children, and so on. I left the buying side of things to him.'

'We're going into Glasgow next,' said Daley. 'Would it be okay to pay him a visit at the office? You can phone ahead and tell him it's nothing to worry about.'

'Can't do, I'm afraid. He's in Germany for the next few days – a sales trip. Some mega deal or other, you know the type of thing. I'm sorry, I feel rather useless.'

'It's okay. If we could have your husband's details, perhaps we can contact him when he gets back,' said Daley.

'Hold on.' She got up and rummaged in her over-sized handbag. 'Ah, here we are. His card, all the details you require are on there.'

'Thank you, and sorry to take up your time, Mrs Yorke.'

'Not at all,' she said, ushering them back through the large hallway. 'If you come across my boiler men on the road back, perhaps you could tell them to get a bloody move on!' She laughed.

As Daley and Scott went down the front steps back onto the drive she called them to a halt. 'I do remember one thing.'

'Oh, what's that?' Daley asked.

'The owner of the property died a couple of years before it was sold. Some relative of his was living here for a spell. I think I'm right in saying he was a police officer. I wonder if you know him?'

'Was his name Chisholm?' said Scott.

'As to that, I couldn't say. I just know he was a police officer, for some reason. Sorry, hopeless yet again.'

'Not at all,' said Daley. 'You've been a great help. I'll contact your husband when he returns.'

'Here,' said Scott. 'Thon's a lovely wee duck pond you've got.'

'Oh, we're draining the damned thing. Our youngest – Harry – is rather mesmerised by it. He stands staring at it for hours. We're rather afraid he'll fall in and drown. I'm sad to say he's a rather melancholy little boy. Anyhow, I hope you find what you're looking for.' She smiled again and waved them goodbye before shutting the big front door.

'Just you get back in the motor and keep away from that pond,' growled Scott.

43

Symington approached the white-suited men busy at work around the oubliette where Helen had been found. As always, this latest crime scene was cordoned off by striped police tape. Not being properly attired in a protective suit, she hailed the nearest officer, who loped through the long grass towards her.

For some reason this place made her shiver. Maybe screams from the tortured and imprisoned of the past, bottled up for hundreds of years, were now free to roam in the minds of those in the present. She shivered.

'Yes, ma'am, Constable Higgins, how can I help you?'

'I'd like a word with DCI Chisholm. I've a couple of things I need to clear up with him.'

'He's not here, ma'am. Left for Edinburgh, some kind of family crisis. I'm told he'll be back tomorrow. I thought you'd have been informed – perhaps DCI Daley . . .'

'Yes, perhaps. Anyhow, have you managed to glean anything from this awful place?'

'We've taken a few samples that might turn up something. I have to say, ma'am, more likely to point to Ms McNeil's presence here rather than her captor's. We're checking to see if we can find who fabricated the cage she was kept in during some of her time in here. But if you ask me, it's a DIY job, ma'am – an unusually thorough one, though.'

'Why do you say that?'

'I've been doing these types of investigations for more than twenty years now, ma'am. You get an instinct for it. Most places of unlawful imprisonment are hastily improvised: desperate measures for desperate situations. This locus feels different.'

'Go on, Constable.'

'Well, though in essence we're dealing with a structure that has been in place for hundreds of years, certain modifications have been carried out. For a start, there's a small hard standing near the entrance, and a modern cast iron plate to top it off. Whoever did this planned it carefully, and must have worked on it for some time. We'll also see if our colleagues can trace the iron closure, but the bets are on its being stolen, or appropriated in such a way as to ensure it's untraceable.'

'You mean, then, that whoever imprisoned Nurse McNeil intended to use the oubliette all along. It wasn't just an improvised lucky strike.'

'Yes, ma'am, that's right – in my opinion, at least. And, of course, nobody – well, hardly anybody – knew where it was. Ideal.'

Symington mulled this over; the need to find and speak to Francombe was becoming ever more vital. 'And what does DCI Chisholm say?'

Higgins paused.

'Well?'

'He hasn't really expressed an opinion, ma'am. I think he must have things on his mind.'

'He seems distracted, you mean?'

'Well, what with the burials over the way and so on, he's had a lot to think about.'

'Yes, I'm sure.' Symington turned on her heel. 'Let me know immediately if you manage to turn up something positive.'

'Yes, ma'am.'

'And tell DCI Chisholm I want a word the minute he returns.'

She made her way back to the track where the old Land Rover was parked. 'Any luck?' asked Caron.

'Luck? I never have much of that, my dear. But I'm fortunate enough to possess a few small talents.'

She made a mental note to ask certain questions of Jim Daley as soon as possible.

Glasgow, 1994

Daley stood to attention in front of ACC Taylor, staring at a spot on the wall above his superior's head.

'Sit down, Daley.' The order was sharp and to the point – very different from their first encounter in this room.

Daley did as he was bid, staring wordlessly back at the man who had given him the temporary rank of sergeant and placed him in the Serious Crime Squad.

'You know, Jim, in a way I wish you had been prosecuted today. You deserved to be.'

'Sir, I was only doing what I thought was right . . .'

'Thought was right! Instead of making your suspicions regarding Sergeant Speirs known to me, you decided to get tanked up on whisky, go to his house and assault a fellow officer.'

'I'd had a couple of drams. That doesn't constitute tanked up. These are Speirs's words.'

'That's the problem, Daley. Speirs now has the high ground. He's the bloody hero in all this. Let you off from a charge that could have led to your incarceration. Never mind saving an undercover female officer in a botched operation led by you. He's gained respect, while your reputation is in the dirt, son.'

'I'll hand in my resignation directly, sir.'

'So, on top of everything else you're a quitter, is that it?'

'No, sir, but I know when I've made an arse of things.'

'Ian Burns was right about your temper. It's something that will hold you back in this job, Daley. Assuming, that is, you still have the stomach for it?'

'Of course I have, sir.'

'I'll give it to you straight, Jim. You've fucked our little operation up. I've spoken to the chief constable – who wanted to dismiss you, by the way – and we've come up with a suitable punishment for your stupidity.'

'Which is?'

'You'll report back to Stewart Street tomorrow. It was the only option.'

'I don't want to be back under John Donald, sir.'

'Huh. Don't worry – John Donald's in the CID. You're going back on the beat.'

'Sir?'

'What did you expect, Daley, a pat on the back and a well done from the boss?' Taylor's face was reddening. 'I've done my best for you – will continue to do my best. I managed to placate DI Donald, whom you also attacked.'

'That's a lie, sir. He did that to himself – bounced his own head off the wall.'

'I can hardly believe all this. What on earth's going on?'

'He hates me, sir.'

Taylor shook his head. 'Anyway, with a bit of luck, I can get you back out of uniform in a few months, but it'll take some doing.'

'What about the Midweek Murderer, sir – about Ian's murder? I can't do anything in uniform!'

'No, you gave up any chance of that when you punched Bobby Speirs on his doorstep. Cool your heels, Daley; keep a low profile. Maybe, just maybe, we'll be able to resurrect your career. Until then, pull the padlocks, run your finger across the plate glass windows, stand at the alarms in the middle of the bloody night and arrest the drunks and shoplifters. Report to the Two Group sergeant for the early shift tomorrow morning.'

'Yes, sir.' Through his misery Daley thought for a moment. 'What about Brian, sir?'

'Our only consolation is that he can stay where he is – for the time being, at least. We haven't lost all of our clandestine scrutiny of the Crime Squad.'

'Good, sir.'

'I'm sorry, Jim. This must seem like a black day, and it is – but not just for you. It's a black day for all of us who want justice for Ian Burns, not to mention these poor women losing their lives to whatever monster we're facing.'

'Are you sure the monster's not just down the corridor, sir?' Daley's narrowed eyes flashed as he made his suspicions more than clear to the ACC.

Taylor sighed. 'You've brought this on yourself, Jim. Tomorrow morning at Stewart Street, Police Constable Daley.'

44

When Symington returned to the office the first thing she did was call DCI Chisholm's mobile number. She was about to hang up when he picked up.

'Hello, ma'am,' said Chisholm. 'What can I do for you?'

'You can tell me where you bloody well are, for a start.'

'Oh, sorry, ma'am. At my rank you don't suppose you have to check in with the line manager every two minutes.' The reply was brusque.

'All I ask is that you at least tell someone where you are – or answer your phone, which I note you haven't been doing.'

'I'm sorry, ma'am, some family problems. I'll be back in Kinloch tonight.' He paused. 'I'm prepared to tell you what it's all about, but I must admit I'd rather not.'

'We're all entitled to a private life, DCI Chisholm. I'll leave you to your difficulties. I hope you get whatever it is sorted soon. But I want to see you tomorrow morning in my office, the minute you get back.'

'Yes, ma'am.'

She ended the call and looked around the office, seeking inspiration from the white walls, bare save for a few police information posters about road safety and a photograph of the Queen. She knew that the two men who had occupied this space before her had met with unfortunate ends – in one way or another, at least.

She would find no inspiration here.

Her desktop burst into life, indicating a video call.

In front of the volumes of old books and dark wood-panelled walls sat Jonathan Stricklander, dean of Professor Francombe's college. Symington noticed something different about him, which at first she couldn't place, but then she realised that he'd removed his round horn-rimmed glasses and, in the process, a good ten years of age.

'Hello, Professor Stricklander. I'm delighted to hear from you so soon. I hope you have good news?'

'Well, yes and no would be the most fitting response to that, Chief Superintendent. Don't get me wrong, I've done my level best to help you, but the matter is now in the hands of our legal team, with whom you will liaise, should the need arise.'

'So, what does that mean? I fail to see much good news in it.'

'I can reveal one thing about Professor Francombe. Considering the seriousness of your investigations, in tandem with our responsibilities to our employees under the Data Protection Act, this is all I can offer freely.'

'Spit it out, man!'

Though his expression darkened at Symington's tone, Stricklander raised his chin, carrying on with his superior manner. 'I can confirm that Anthea Francombe changed her identity a while ago.'

'When?'

'A few years ago. I can find the exact date, though I don't have it in front of me at the moment.'

'Now the next obvious question: why?'

'Ah, as to that, you're now in the territory of our legal people. I'll give you their details. Best I can do, I'm afraid. By the way, have you traced her at all?'

'No, have you?'

'Obviously not.'

'Though I believe that these little absences aren't uncommon?'

Stricklander sighed. 'No, they're not. It would be helpful if she would carry her mobile as a matter of course. But as Anthea is one of the faculty's best archaeologists, she has possibly been afforded more leeway than is perhaps good for her.'

He gave Symington the details of the college's legal team, ending the call perfunctorily.

So, Caron was right. Perhaps Anthea Francombe had more to hide than even the gossips speculated upon.

She stared around her temporary office in Kinloch, and resolved to find something to liven up the depressing décor.

Glasgow, 1994

Daley sat in the muster room at Stewart Street Police Office, feeling uncomfortable and conspicuous in the uniform he thought he'd left behind for good.

He knew many of the cops who shuffled into the room, yawning, drinking coffee, eating bacon rolls, or sucking mints in order to mask their over-indulgence the night before. Though a few nodded hello, smiling at him, he knew he was the centre of gossip in just about every station in the city.

He wriggled in his chair. He'd filled out since he'd last worn this uniform, and had struggled to zip up the trousers and button his tunic. He resolved to put in a request for a new one.

Two sergeants made their way rather wearily into the room. One of them, the newly promoted Sergeant Dunside, stood at the lectern and went through the usual procedure of relating what had happened on the night shift, listing the registrations of stolen cars, and issuing descriptions of missing or wanted persons.

He was just about to allocate individual beats to each officer when the muster room door swung open, setting the badly oiled transom squealing.

There, resplendent in an expensively cut grey suit, immaculate white shirt, dark green tie and well-polished shoes, stood DI John Donald. He searched the room briefly with his dark eyes, until they landed upon Daley.

'Sergeant Dunside, I hope you can spare one today.'

'I suppose so, Inspector. Take your pick.'

'PC Daley, please. I have a job for him.' Donald grinned, no mirth behind his eyes. 'May I avail myself of your office for two minutes, Sergeant?'

'Yes, sir.'

'Good. Oh, and remove Daley from the shift list for the foreseeable future. Come with me, Daley.'

Their departure accompanied by a low murmur from the other officers, Daley followed Donald down the corridor and into the shift sergeants' office. Donald took his old desk – the one at the back of the room – and summoned his subordinate to stand in front of it.

'Jimmy, just like the old days, isn't it? How's your delectable wife taking this demotion, eh?'

'None of your business, sir.'

'Oh, just the fact you've been demoted – back into uniform as a lowly beat cop, must be a real dent in her confidence in you. But I suppose she's happy you're not currently residing at her majesty's pleasure. Though from what I hear, perhaps she'd enjoy the freedom, eh?'

Daley said nothing. He knew that his position was weak, and he was determined not to let Donald goad him.

'Anyway, best not go over the past – never a healthy pursuit, if you ask me. Now, I would like you to do me a favour.'

'Yes, sir.'

'Because of your intimate knowledge of the Townhead, I want you to spend some time up there. Lots going on, as usual. Drugs, nuisance kids, break-ins – well, you know the score, Jimmy.'

'Yes, sir.'

'Fine, then. Of course, these are mainly problems of the night, so I want you up there on night shift for a while.'

'How long's a while, sir?' Daley was already resigned to his fate.

'Oh, I'd say at least for the next three or four weeks. You will have your rest days in between, but who better to guard the good folk of the Toonheid in the dark of night than you, Jimmy. Fair takes me back, you know.'

'When, sir?'

'Report tonight at the usual time. The Four Shift sergeants have been informed. And look,' he said, reaching into his pocket. 'Something nostalgic for you.' He threw a small paper bag at Daley, who caught it deftly before it hit his face.

'Get them on. I'm sure you'll appreciate the gesture. Don't feel you need to thank me.'

Daley opened the bag. Within was a set of shoulder numerals, proudly displaying *A 213*.

'I'm sure you'll get used to having those back on your shoulders soon. In any case, I think you'll have plenty of time to reacquaint yourself with them. I don't see much future for you now in the job – apart from being the good old beat man, that is.' He grinned. 'Back to the old days, indeed, my friend. Oh, and Jimmy, get a request in for a new uniform; I do believe you're running to fat.'

45

Glasgow, the present

Daley and Scott had driven to the new Police Scotland Forensic Unit. All windows and aluminium – steel and glass, as one of Daley's favourite songs had it.

They had an appointment with the Cold Case Unit Forensic team, and after traversing a number of brightly illuminated corridors from which emanated a multitude of chemical smells and the whirr or deep hum of complex analytic equipment, passing a number of white-coated employees, they reached the door bearing the number 3.24U.

Daley knocked sharply and within seconds a young woman wearing safety goggles and a white lab coat opened the door, smiling at the detectives in turn. 'The famous DCI Daley and DS Brian Scott – my goodness, I feel quite honoured,' she said, removing her goggles to reveal bright green eyes.

'*Famous*? How?' asked Scott.

'Oh, you know. You're both so well known throughout the job,' she remarked quickly, as though regretting her opening gambit.

Famous because of my ruined love life, thought Daley ruefully. 'It's nice to be recognised,' he lied.

'I'm Adele McLintock,' she said, shaking each man firmly by the hand. 'I know the case you're enquiring about – the Ian Burns murder from ninety-four, yes?'

'Yes,' said Daley. Even now those words made his stomach churn.

'You'll be aware that I had the cold case officer in charge of this inquiry here just yesterday?'

'He's not in charge. I am,' Daley growled.

'Oh,' said Adele McLintock, clearly surprised. 'Well, whoever is in charge, the result is the same. I'm afraid we are missing the crucial production. It was a gaberdine raincoat, I believe.'

'Yes,' said Daley.

'How could it just disappear?' said Scott. 'Can't be a very tight ship aroond here, eh?'

She sighed. 'Yes, well, all I can say is that it's definitely much more secure now. Back in the day, when no one was sure if what we'd kept would be of any use, it was very easy for a production kept in anticipation of improving technology to be removed and not returned. A scandal, I know, but long before my time, I'm glad to say.'

'Do you at least have a record of who removed the item?' asked Daley.

'Ah, yes, in fact I do – well, sort of. Knowing you were on your way, I had a poke about. Found this in the old microfilm records. Thankfully, they've been digitised now.' McLintock walked to her desk and powered up her computer. 'Now, I filed it this morning . . . let me see.' The tip of her tongue poked out between her shiny lips as she concentrated on finding what she was looking for. 'Here we go, gents. Please, take a look for yourselves. Sad to say, it's difficult to decipher. I haven't a clue what's written there.'

Daley and Scott donned their reading glasses and squinted at the large monitor. The signature was in thick black ink, and to make matters more difficult, the magnification had distorted the lettering, so it appeared rough and ill defined.

'Can you take it down a bit – in terms of magnification, I mean?' said Daley.

'Sure. Maybe I need glasses, I couldn't make head or tail of it when it was at a lesser magnification.' She pressed a button and the signature blurred then resolved itself, smaller, but much more clearly.

Scott eyed Daley doubtfully. 'You know the laws of evidence, big man. A decent defence counsel will rip shreds off this.'

'Yes, but we know who that scrawl belongs to, Brian. And look at the date, that's definitely ninety-six, yeah?' Both Scott and McLintock nodded agreement.

'Gosh, you're good at this. I'm used to analysing DNA, not handwriting. Is that a C at the beginning of the surname?' she asked.

'Aye, lassie, it sure is,' replied Scott.

Daley stood back from the screen, his jaw muscles clearly working under the skin of his cheeks. 'I remember this case very well, Adele. In fact, I worked on it for a while back in the nineties. If I remember, they held one more item of Mr Burns's clothing over just in case it would bear fruit using more modern techniques.'

'Oh yes? What?'

'A scarf. A black woollen scarf.'

'Aye, I mind that,' said Scott. 'He never had the damn thing off – even in the summer. He was always cold, poor Ian. Mind you, there was nothing o' him. Thin as a rake, man.'

McLintock's attention was back on the screen. She scrolled

down a small list, clicking her tongue as she did so. 'No, nothing listed here. The raincoat is all we have – or had, I should say.'

Daley shook his head. 'No, I remember it clearly. The scarf was definitely retained.'

McLintock thought for a few moments. 'Because of the very basic nature of computer systems at the time, I've known productions logged on the same day be catalogued under other case references in error.'

'Aye, see they computers – just shite, if you pardon my French. I've said it since the bloody things came oot,' Scott declared.

'Not the fault of the systems – apart from perhaps some over-complicated input methods back then,' said McLintock, her eyes glued to the screen. 'But, like today, the system's only as good as the people who work with it. Much more user-friendly now, mind you.'

'You think? They're no' very friendly tae this user, I tell you that.'

'Wow!' exclaimed McLintock.

'I widnae say a middle-aged man no' being able tae use a computer well is that surprising, lassie.'

'No, here – take a look. This is the date of Mr Burns's murder, yes?'

'It is indeed,' replied Daley, staring at the screen.

'Look at the list of retained productions, sir.'

Daley looked, his tongue this time poking between his teeth. It was the case of a man found murdered in Ayrshire on the same day Ian Burns lost his life. There, as he searched down the list, was item six: production number CS 70025/94. One black woollen scarf. 'How can you be sure that's it, Adele?'

'Look, the rest of the productions have old Strathclyde reference numbers. CS is Central Scotland. I'm right in saying that Mr Burns was murdered in that force area, yes?'

'Yes, indeed.'

'So what you're saying is that some oaf wae bugger a' sense listed the scarf as a production in the wrong case?' said Scott.

'Well, I've seen it happen before,' said McLintock. 'With the older cases, I mean.'

'Aye, accidentally on purpose, Jimmy, eh?'

Daley nodded, grim-faced. 'Can we find this and have it analysed, Adele?'

'Certainly, sir. I'll get on to it now.' She hesitated. 'Word of caution, though, sir.'

'What?'

'Even if this is the scarf in question, it's still more than twenty years old. I'm just saying.' She shrugged apologetically.

'Dae your best, lassie. In any case, Jimmy, I think we've enough – between the hoose in Ayrshire and this – tae pull oor man in, no?'

'Oh, yes,' said Daley. 'I'll call Symington now.'

As he left the room to make the call on his mobile, Scott smiled. Despite the circumstances, it was good to see his old friend enlivened again.

As Scott watched Adele go about her business, the door swung open.

'Symington's spoken to Chisholm, Brian. Apparently, he's on his way back to Kinloch now. We'll follow suit. There's something else, too.'

'What?'

'Come on, I'll get you up to speed on our way down the road.'

'You'll have plenty o' time, right enough.'

They said their goodbyes to the forensic scientist, wishing her luck with the tests on the scarf.

Within minutes, the pair were heading towards signs for the Erskine Bridge and Kinloch.

Ella Scott arrived in the cosy bar of the County Hotel bearing carrier bags of various sizes, shapes and designs. The table closest to the bar was free – in fact, apart from one old man reading a newspaper by the fire nursing a half pint of beer, the place was empty. She set down her purchases and searched for her purse in her capacious handbag.

'Here, that's a lovely bag, Ella,' said Annie, her smile fixed.

'Och, it's a great lump o' a thing. My daughter gave it to me for my last birthday. You know yoursel', the bigger the bag, the mair room for rubbish. I've got half the hoose in here.'

'Don't worry, I'm jeest the same. When they big bags came intae fashion, I thought, whoot on earth dae folk find tae put in them. In a couple o' weeks, I didna know whoot I'd ever done without one. Is it a wee gin and tonic, by the way?'

'Less o' the wee, woman! Brian might be off the drink, but his wife's still boozing. You'll have one yourself, I hope?'

'You've twisted my arm, Ella. We're quiet jeest noo. Mind, there's a darts match on the night, so if I were you, I'd get that man o' yours tae take you oot for a bite tae eat. It can get quite rowdy.'

'I'm fae the Gorbals originally, hen. Rowdy is something I've been doing all my life.'

Annie laughed. Despite the pangs of jealousy she felt, she couldn't help liking Brian Scott's wife. 'I see you've been oot in the shops – such as they are.'

'Do you know, I really enjoyed it. I hate they great malls that have sprung up everywhere. It's great tae walk aboot in the sea air around some nice wee shops in the high street for a change. I got some wee presents for the weans.'

'Aw, that's nice.'

'Well, I'm saying weans, they're a' growed up and oot the door ages ago. I fair miss them. Have you kids yourself, Annie?'

'No,' Annie replied with a sigh, pouring a large measure of gin for Ella Scott and a similarly sized measure of vodka for herself. 'Och, I never found the right man.'

'Trust me, there's nae such thing.'

'But you and Brian – well, you're solid as the big island at the heid o' oor loch, right?' Annie tried to suppress the hope in her voice.

'Aye, I dare say we are now. It's no' always been the same, I'll tell you that.'

Annie handed Ella her drink. 'Here, have this one on the hoose since you're a valued guest.' She took a seat beside her. 'It must be a lonely business – being the wife o' a polisman, I mean?'

'And not just any polis, either: we're talking Brian Scott here. Honestly, he's been in mair scrapes than . . . than anyone else I know.'

'He's right popular doon here. The folk have fair taken tae him – and Jim Daley, tae.'

'He's another worry.'

'Aye, he's no' had his troubles tae seek, the poor man. How long have you known him for?'

'Damn near thirty years.' Ella stopped and took a gulp of her gin. 'Don't get me wrong, I love him tae bits. But he's a walking disaster when it comes tae women. A right brooder he is, tae – as deep as the Atlantic. It's no surprise tae me that he's ended up here beside it. Quite appropriate.'

'You don't like Liz, then?'

'Indeed not. She's the flyest, most manipulative woman that ever walked, if you ask me. How he never split up wae her years ago, I'll never know.'

'I liked her.'

'You didnae know her, Annie. She cheated on that poor man mair times than you can count. I've always been civil to her – for Brian's sake, you'll understand – but I could have fair clawed her eyes oot many a time.'

Before Annie could defend someone she'd come to think of as a friend, the door burst open. Hamish, two burly fishermen and young James Daley junior walked into the bar, all four laughing.

'Whoot's the joke, Hamish?' enquired Annie.

'Jeest an auld fisherman's yarn, that's all,' he replied, walking stick in one hand, the toddler's tiny paw in the other. 'We've had a great day, haven't we just, wee Jimmy?'

'You better no' let his mother hear you call him wee Jimmy,' said Ella. 'Oor Brian did it once and she near took his heid off. He's *James*.'

'Whootever,' said Hamish. 'Anyhow, whoot she canna see won't harm her. While he's wae me he's wee Jimmy, is that no' right, son?'

'Yes, Uncle Hameby,' said the young boy, struggling with Hamish's name.

'Uncle, tae – did you ever?' said Annie. 'Here, son, we'll get you a wee glass o' juice. Mair like Great-great-uncle *Hameby*!'

'I want a dram,' said James, clearly and determinedly.

'Noo, son, it's only auld men like me that can have drams.

Your daddy would arrest me if he came in here and you were getting knocked intae a whisky.'

'But I want one. I like the smell!'

'You jeest drink this, and if you're a good boy you'll get a packet o' crisps,' said Annie, placing his drink before him.

James Daley junior eyed the beverage, sniffed it, then sat back in his seat, arms folded in disgust. 'Bugger this rubbish,' he said flatly.

'See you,' said Annie, pointing her finger at Hamish. 'I knew you weren't fit tae be in charge o' a wean. He's swearing like an auld fishwife!'

'Noo, son, you've no' tae say they words or your Uncle Hamish will get in trouble.'

'But the boys on the boats say it all the time.'

'Aye, that's jeest because they have a limited vocabulary and their minds are fair pickled wae the drink. Is that no' right, lads?' said Hamish, addressing the younger fishermen with whom he'd arrived. They nodded heir heads obediently. 'You see, a man should be judged by his manners and gentlemanly behaviour.' He paused. 'Hey, where's that bloody drink, Annie? I've got a drooth like a smoked fuckin' kipper here.'

'I'd say your babysitting days are rapidly nearing their end, Hamish,' said Annie, glowering at the old man.

'Seconded!' agreed Ella enthusiastically.

46

Townhead, Glasgow, 1994

It was dark, cold and dank as Constable Jim Daley wound his way up to what was left of Parliamentary Road, cut across a patch of rough grass and descended a small hill towards the high flats that dominated the area of Glasgow known as the Townhead.

This was his old beat, and now his new one.

Depression weighed on him as he looked about, the tall street lamps picking out every drop of the heavy shower slanting past in their great orange pools of light.

He cowered in his thin uniform raincoat, which appeared to be leaking somewhere over his left shoulder. He could feel the rain soaking through his woollen tunic and on to his shirt.

Jim Daley had never had a particularly strong sense of entitlement, nor did he feel that life – or this job, come to that – owed him anything. But the sheer shock and disappointment of being back here in uniform, exactly where he'd begun, made him more dejected than he could ever express in words.

Liz had been decent enough about the whole situation surrounding his foolish assault on Bobby Speirs, but he could sense the resentment she now felt towards him. Only days before she'd been bragging to her friends that her husband was a sergeant in the Serious Crime Squad, and now here he was back pounding the beat, a lowly uniformed cop.

Distantly he could hear the squeal of tyres and the roar of an exhaust. About a hundred yards away, a car swung round a bend in the road far too fast, back end drifting out, loud music blaring from within.

Pulling the torch from his pocket, he flashed it at the approaching vehicle, which screeched to a stop level with him on the roadway.

The car was a customised Volkswagen, all blacked-out windows and go-fast stripes. It sported an over-long orange aerial, which swung in the wind like a whip.

Despite obeying his command to stop, the car continued to blare music with no sign of movement behind the darkened glass. Daley leaned forward and knocked loudly on the driver's window, mouthing the words *Turn down the music*, sure that no one in the car would be able to hear anything he said above the din.

He was surprised when the racket stopped immediately. The windows, though, remained tight shut.

'Right, wind down your window,' he said, moving to the front of the car to check the number plate and radio it in in order to find out whether the car was stolen and to whom it belonged, an automatic procedure.

He heard a click, then the front passenger door opened and out stepped a lean, wiry man, features hidden by the deep hood of his sweatshirt.

'I'd like to speak to the driver of the vehicle, not you,' said Daley.

'I don't give a flying fuck who you'd like to speak to,

Constable Daley.' The voice was familiar, the address riddled with disrespect and disdain.

'Like I said, I want to talk to the driver of the vehicle,' said Daley, the mic of his police radio now at his mouth.

'Put it down!' This command was sharp and emphatic. The man's hands moved from the pouch in his sweatshirt, slickly producing a handgun in the beat of a heart.

'I warn you,' said Daley, his hand moving to his trouser pocket for his baton. 'Put that away, now!' He could feel his heart pulse in his throat, which had constricted at the sight of the firearm.

With his other hand, the man removed the hood from his head, revealing sharp features, high cheekbones and piercing eyes, plainly visible despite the driving rain and poor light. His head was shaven, but his expression was unmistakable.

Notorious Glasgow gangster James Machie was pointing a gun straight at Daley's head.

Kinloch, the present

Daley was sitting in Symington's office as she read the short report he'd compiled on arrival back at Kinloch Police Office.

'And we've confirmed that the house near Beith belonged to DCI Chisholm's brother-in-law?' asked Symington.

'Yes, ma'am. I had a DC check it out with the land registry when we were on our way down the road.'

'And you say that one of Helen McNeil's father's last requests was that money be delivered to that address?'

'Yes. Not only that, we also know that DCI Chisholm was resident in the property at that time. He and his wife were house-sitting while the brother-in-law was in Singapore on a long business trip. Brian managed to trace his business, and the secretary was most forthcoming with his old diaries.'

'Don't you think they'll tip Chisholm off?'

'There's always that possibility, but Brian told her she'd be an accessory to a murder inquiry if she did – and in any case her boss is on holiday, so I hope not.'

Symington stared at Daley, deep in thought. 'But apart from this, how can we connect DCI Chisholm with Helen McNeil's father?' She perused the report again for a few moments. 'You've got to admit, Jim, this evidence is circumstantial. Even if the money was delivered to the house while Chisholm was there, it wasn't necessarily intended for him, was it?'

'No, Carrie, that's true. But it's a lead of some sort. I'd like permission to examine DCI Chisholm's personnel file. As you know, I knew him years ago when he worked with Strathclyde, but I have no knowledge of his time at the old Lothian and Borders force – nor how his career began.'

'Okay, Jim, I'll do the necessary. Leave it with me. He's due back here soon.'

'If he comes back, ma'am.'

'Do you think he has an inkling we're on to something?'

'Wouldn't be surprised, though it would have to be instinct, especially since we're not sure how this fits together ourselves yet.'

'We have another worry. Professor Francombe's still not turned up. I've requested information from her superiors, but it's scant. Apparently she often goes off by herself exploring other archaeological possibilities – a proper loner. They seem relaxed – I'm not.'

'No, me neither. If I can put the heavy hand on the shoulder of the university?'

'Be careful, Jim. We're in the realms of data protection and the lawyers are poised. But there's definitely something in her past she wants to remain secret.'

'Hard to do, these days, but it must be legal – if she has the backing of her employer, I mean.'

'It's a bloody mess, Jim.' She threw her head back and sighed. 'Oh, and worse still, Helen McNeil is determined to be off on holiday. What can we do?'

'She's been imprisoned for long enough, Carrie. Any attempt on our part to try to keep her here wouldn't look good.'

'My, Jim, you're finally getting all this PR stuff – well done!'

He smiled. 'You know what they say about old dogs and new tricks, ma'am – it's wrong. I suppose I'd better get up to the hospital and tell Marion Smythe-Brown about the loss of her lover.'

'Yes, we've informed Galt's family. I thought I'd leave this one to you.'

'It's Kinloch, ma'am; she probably knows already.'

'Yes, more than likely, but there's little we can do about that. Anyhow, I'll get going on Chisholm's files for you, Jim.'

47

Glasgow, 1994

'You've been a naughty boy, Jimmy Daley.' Machie's gun was still pointed unwaveringly at the big constable. 'No' the most popular man in Strathclyde Police right now, eh?'

'What would you know about it?'

'Well, you're standing here in a woolly suit and a crap raincoat, for a start. I think it's fair tae say you wouldnae need much up top to work out that your career's taken a wee bit o' a nosedive.'

'I'm calling this in, Machie. You don't have the balls to shoot me.' Daley pressed the button on the side of his radio mic, which squelched in response. 'Two One Three to Alpha, Code Twenty-One, Kennedy Path at Parliamentary Road, over!' His voice trembled as he said the words. Almost instantly, he heard the reassuring sound of the controller passing on the call for immediate assistance and his location to every officer in the division.

Machie smiled, lowering the gun. 'If I wanted you dead, you'd be dead already, Daley. They tell me polis are being murdered all the time, recently.' He turned to the car. 'Right, boys, better make it quick!'

As sirens wailed in the distance, three bulky men jumped out of the car, each brandishing a baseball bat.

'Take this as a warning, Daley. Keep your mouth shut. That's a message from some o' your colleagues, by the way.'

In seconds, Machie's thugs, their bats swinging in the rain, were beating Daley mercilessly. Just as he was about to lose consciousness, he heard Machie's voice.

'Right, that'll dae. Let's get tae fuck.'

As the first police car appeared at the scene, all that was to be found was the bloody, broken body of Constable James Daley, his world spinning out of sight.

Kinloch, the present

Daley and Scott trudged the short distance to Kinloch's hospital in the gathering gloaming. It had been a long day and both men would have been happier sinking off to sleep between the sheets rather than keeping on. However, this was a murder inquiry and every stop was being pulled out. In his bones, Daley could feel that the answer they were searching for was close at hand. It was an instinct that rarely let him down.

The lights at the hospital entrance shone bright in the gloom, like tree decorations on Christmas Eve. But there was little joy in what they had to do – so often the lot of a police officer: bringers of bad news, and worse times. Rarely did folk welcome a visit from the constabulary.

'If you don't mind, I'll sit this oot,' said Scott, looking particularly jaded. 'I've had tae tell mair folk about deid friends and relatives than I care tae remember. I'm desperately in need o' a coffee, big man.'

'Okay, Brian, you're off the hook. Have a poke about and see if there's any news on the intentions of Helen McNeil. She was at work today, apparently – someone might know something.'

'Aye, aye, man. I'll dae my bit, boss,' replied Scott with little enthusiasm.

Daley spoke to the duty nurse as Scott got ready to seek out the coffee machine.

'I'll not be long, Brian. Apparently she knows already.'

'Surprise, surprise – the gossips strike again. Nae need for the News Channel doon here.'

Daley cleared his throat and knocked on the door of the side room in which Marion Smyth-Browne was being treated.

'I know why you're here. Colin's gone.' She turned her head away on the pillow, but Daley could still hear her sobs.

'How long have you known Colin Galt, Marion?'

'A while,' she replied feebly.

'This is you and him way back, isn't it?' He showed her the photograph he'd got from his team's search of Galt's home.

At first she didn't look at the faded colour photograph of the two young people standing by the car, soaking up the sun from a summer many years before. Eventually, she nodded, fat tears spilling down her cheeks. 'We should have made a go of it, you know.'

'Why didn't you?'

'Bloody Kinloch – his business.' Suddenly there was fire in her voice. 'His father had been ill and Colin had to take up the reins.'

'Was this when you were students?'

'Yes, we met at university. I wasn't bright enough to stay at Oxford – didn't even get an interview. Clearing led me to

Glasgow. I hated it at first, and then – well, I kind of fell in love with Scotland.'

'And Colin Galt.'

'Yes, and Colin Galt. But I couldn't be trapped here, not even for love. It's still a grim little place; nosy, tight-knit people. I hated it from the start. I thought Colin loved me enough to leave it all behind, but he didn't.'

'You kept in touch, though.'

'Yes, we kept in touch. As you've no doubt worked out.'

'How long was he involved in helping you remove artefacts from the sites you worked on?'

'Nine, ten years or so. We always struggled to get small pieces out. They searched us archaeologists from time to time – you never knew quite when. But they weren't clever enough to search any of the haulage contractors' vehicles.'

'So, you found things and secreted them away until Colin could pick them up?'

'Something like that.' She stared at Daley. 'Oh, don't look at me like that. We get paid a pittance – well, not enough to support my lifestyle, at any rate. When my dad died all that was left was a mountain of debt. It feels as though I've spent a lifetime with men who hide too many secrets.'

'What about Colin – what was his excuse?'

'The business was struggling, I think. He wanted to re-invest, but his father's old partner would have nothing of it. Was happy with a couple of trucks and a bloody digger. Typical of this place – small minds, no ambition.' She stared at the ceiling and again the tears began to flow. 'But I loved him – always will.'

'I want to ask about one item.'

'What?'

'A modern necklace we found in Galt's little haul. I'm sure you realise, Marion, it's time to do some talking.'

'Yes, even I know when to admit defeat. To be honest, given Colin's death, I don't care any more.' She looked at Daley, her face swollen by tears. 'Funnily enough, I do remember the piece. Bernie took it from a Finds Bag at Kilmilken. It was obviously a modern piece. Probably picked up by some rookie, and Dumbo hadn't the sense to see that either.'

'So, definitely from the main site?'

'Yes, from the main site. I remember it because I joked with him about it.'

'How do you feel about Bernie, now?'

She stared at Daley, almost as though seeing him for the first time. 'Have you ever lost someone you loved – I mean really loved?'

'Yes, I'm rather sad to say that I have.'

'Well then, you'll know just exactly how I feel about Bernie.'

Daley nodded, and left Marion to her grief. The confident – bordering on arrogant – woman he'd first met was now a pale shadow of her former self. Daley knew too well how the loss of someone special could eat a person up from the inside.

Scott drained his coffee and frowned. The machine-vended brew had been bitter and unfulfilling. He realised that his coffee appreciation had risen rapidly on giving up alcohol. Sometimes he felt it a very poor substitute.

He was about to take a wander and ask about Helen McNeil when an older woman interrupted his thoughts by asking him to move his feet while she swept underneath them with a long, newfangled mop. Short and plump, she was dressed in a pale green uniform, her grey hair lightly tinted with blonde dye; clearly one of the hospital's domestic staff.

'Haud your horses,' said Scott, drawing his feet off the floor. 'Where's the fire?'

'They reckon we've got a surprise health and safety inspection tomorrow, so we've got tae be on oor toes. Those buggers are intae everything.'

'No' much o' a surprise if you know aboot it already.'

'They book rooms in the County every time they come doon. Annie always tips us the wink.'

'I would expect nothing less,' replied Scott with a smile.

'I hope Helen McNeil has a nice holiday. Whoot a time o' it she's had, the poor lassie.'

'No, she's no' had her troubles tae seek, that's for sure. I cannae imagine what she went through doon that hole.'

'I hope you find the bastard that did it.'

'So dae I. Mind you, it's kind o' hard tae get much oot o' her. She doesn't say a lot.'

'She's been the same since ever I knew her – way back tae when she was no' long oot of training.'

'Wait – I thought she'd only worked here for a few years?'

'Aye, but this is her second stint.'

'Second?'

'Och, she was here filling in for maternity leave years ago. I'm one o' the longest-serving members o' staff here. No' many will remember her fae then.'

'How long ago are we talking, Mrs Glendinning?' asked Scott, reading the name badge on her uniform.

'Noo, let me think. Oor Davie was still at the high school, and he's in his forties noo. Maybe twenty-five years, give or take.'

Along the corridor, Scott spotted Daley leaving Marion Smyth-Browne's room. 'Jimmy, over here. You'll want tae hear this.'

'What?' Daley made his way towards them.

'According to Mrs Glendinning here, Helen McNeil worked at this hospital before.'

'Enough o' the Mrs Glendinning, April's my name.'

'Were you born in April?'

'No, November, but my mother liked the name.'

'When did she work here before, April?' Daley asked.

'Your man's jeest asked me that. Och, I'd say early nineties, now I think aboot it. Ninety-three, ninety-four, something like that.'

The two detectives looked at each other.

'I cannae be sure, Jimmy, but when you think back . . .'

'She fits the bill,' said Daley.

'Aye – tall, thin. It cannae be, surely.'

'I jeest hope she has a nice holiday, cos she fair deserves it,' April put in.

'Do you know where she's headed?'

'Spain, I think. Aye, I'm sure she said something about Spain. Her flight's tonight. I know that because she telt me she'd never flown at night – wisna looking forward tae it, neithers.'

'Come on, Brian. We might still have time.'

Without taking their leave of April Glendinning, the detectives bolted down the corridor and out into the cool, dark night.

'Here, you!' shouted the cleaner. 'You've jeest left a great big streak o' muck on my clean floor.'

386

48

Daley, Symington and Scott were gathered in the AV suite at Kinloch Police Office, their collective attention focused firmly on the massive screen in front of them.

The concourse of Glasgow Airport was displayed, bustling with people – holidaymakers and businessmen and women – heading for the many scheduled flights. They thronged in all directions, despite the time of night. It was holiday season, and the place was still busy.

'Here, big Dunky won't be happy cooling his heels in your office, Jimmy.'

'I wouldn't worry, Brian. I'm sure he'll find something to do.' Daley smiled knowingly, leaving Scott confused.

The Kinloch officers listened intently to police radio traffic; the communication between plain-clothed officers invisible in the scrum of people.

Suddenly the pictured blurred then resolved.

'Tango One, target sighted, we have eyes on, over.'

Despite wearing a floppy hat and sporting a large pair of sunglasses, Helen McNeil was easily recognisable, standing tall, a blue, wheeled suitcase at her feet.

'That's her, right enough,' said Scott.

She was waiting in line at the check-in desk, passport and

boarding card in hand. With four people in front of her, the policemen in Kinloch almost held their breath as they waited for her to reach the head of the queue.

Suddenly she looked distracted. She opened the handbag hung over her shoulder and produced her mobile phone.

'Wait a minute,' said Symington, a worried look on her face.

On the screen, it was clear that Helen's body language had changed. She had a very brief conversation on her mobile then appeared instantly flustered. Hastily, she dropped the phone back into her bag and looked about. Angling her large hat down over her features, she grabbed the long handle of her case, turned and walked purposefully away from the check-in queue.

'She's been tipped off!' said Scott, barely able to contain himself.

'She sure has,' said Daley with a calmness at odds with his normal approach to such situations.

'Tango One to all stations, move in on subject, over.'

As Helen made for the exit doors leading out of the airport concourse, a number of figures jostled through the crowds towards her. In Kinloch, with a panoramic CCTV overview of the scene, this was obvious. But to those on the ground, the human net now closing in on Helen would be almost invisible.

She had almost reached the exit when a man and a woman, casually dressed, also with suitcases, approached her, the man grabbing her firmly by the wrist. The woman with him deftly produced a pair of rigid handcuffs, and in seconds Helen was securely under arrest.

In Kinloch they watched as other plain-clothes officers moved towards the arresting officers and their quarry. A few people had turned their heads to watch the tall woman being taken into custody. In the main, however, no one turned a hair at the proceedings; it wasn't their business. They were departing or arriving on very different journeys from that of Nurse Helen McNeil.

The operation had been a success – despite the mystery phone call.

In Daley's glass box sat DCI Duncan Chisholm. His face was ashen, and he was clearly unsettled when Daley and Symington entered the office.

Symington pulled down the blinds as Daley settled in his large leather chair.

'What's this, a party or a torture session?' said Chisholm, with forced humour.

'What were you up to in the last couple of days, Duncan?' asked Daley. He was direct, no preamble.

'What? I had family difficulties. I explained that to my officers. I know they passed it on to Chief Superintendent Symington.' He nodded at the senior officer, now seated beside him across from Daley at his large desk.

'I know what you were really doing, Duncan,' said Daley.

'What's this all about, ma'am?' Chisholm turned to Symington, a bewildered look on his face. She made no response.

'You visited a lockup in Airdrie, Duncan – on a number of occasions, in fact. Look, here are some pictures.' Daley threw some large photographs across the desk at Chisholm, who examined them, maintaining the same look of bewilderment on his face.

'It's personal – nothing to do with you or anyone else, Daley.' Suddenly Chisholm's tone was aggressive.

'Is this the same as in ninety-six when you signed out Ian Burns's coat from the old Productions Unit and conveniently forgot to put it back?'

'What are you talking about, man?'

'Here,' said Daley, turning his laptop to face Chisholm. A signature had been blown up on the screen – the same one Scott and he had seen earlier in Glasgow. 'We've had it checked by handwriting experts – it's yours, Duncan.'

'Bollocks! That's only an opinion.'

'Is this an opinion?' Daley handed two more photographs over the desk to Chisholm. Though they were monochrome, the image of a younger, slimmer Duncan Chisholm was clear. As was the bag he was carrying, leaving the then Strathclyde Police Productions Unit in Glasgow in 1996.

'I must admit, they're very thorough up here. Imagine keeping that footage for all this time,' observed Symington.

'Give me your mobile, Duncan,' Daley demanded.

'You've no right to do this – either of you. I want a Federation rep here, right now. This is a bloody set-up. I expected more of you, ma'am.'

'And this is a hot case, with suspects still at large – give me the phone, Duncan!' shouted Daley.

Shaking his head, Chisholm reluctantly handed the device across the desk to his colleague, who examined it quickly.

'What do you know. The last call was nine minutes ago – to Helen McNeil, in fact.'

'That doesn't prove anything, Jim, and you know it.' Chisholm smiled scornfully.

Daley reached under his desk, pulling up a small device. 'But this does.' He scrolled back time on the screen and pressed play.

Don't get on the plane, Helen. Keep calm, but get out of there and drive away as far away as possible. Use cash. I'll call you when I can. Just get out of the airport! And FFS, try and look calm.

Chisholm dropped his head.

'A forensic team – och, you likely know them – are going through what you had in the lockup in Airdrie, Duncan. Women's clothes, jewellery – a right little treasure trove, so I'm told,' said Daley.

'Or a rather ghoulish reminder of your past, DCI Chisholm,' said Symington.

'And you were first into each grave up on Kilmilken hill, Duncan. Your officers were certain, said you insisted on it.'

'Aye, so what? I was in charge of the scene.'

'You were looking for evidence – and little keepsakes for yourself, I dare say,' said Daley. 'You didn't legislate for some light-fingered archaeologist removing your treasures from plain sight where you thought it would be safe – safe for you to pick up later.'

'Hey, wait a minute. You can't think I'm the Midweek Murderer. Jimmy, come on, man!'

Daley looked him in the eye. 'You said it.'

Symington spoke sombrely. 'Duncan Chisholm, I'm arresting you . . .'

'Dunky Chisholm,' said Scott, alone with Daley now the arrest was over. 'I cannae believe it. I mean, I know he was fond o' the ladies, and that, but . . .'

'Not that fond of them, obviously,' said Daley.

'Aye, well, you know what I mean.'

'It's going to be a late one for you and me, Bri.'

'How come?'

'Time is of the essence. Helen will be brought here tomorrow for questioning, and I want to be prepared.' He hefted a large file, bursting at the seams with documents. 'I know how much you hate computers, my old pal. This has been sent by the MOD, and I want you to go through it.'

'What, all of it the night?'

'Yup.'

Scott sighed and shook his head. 'Well, I'll need coffee – aye, and something tae eat. I'll need to let oor Ella know. She'll no' be happy.'

'There's a Chinese carryout on the way. And give Ella a wee phone. You're not telling me she sits up and waits for you, not after all these years of nocturnal boozing.'

'Here we go again – the man who never takes a wee glass o' whisky. No' so wee these days, neither.'

'Right in my heart,' said Daley, feigning pain.

'It's good tae see you smile, Jimmy.'

Daley nodded. 'It's good to feel like smiling again, Brian.' He sat upright in his chair. 'Okay, I'll take you through what you're looking for, then it's time for me to wake up a few academics and some lawyers.'

'Whatever you say, big man, whatever you say.'

49

Glasgow, 1994

Jim Daley awoke with a start. His first instinct was to jump up in bed, but he found it too painful to move. He looked round at the machines he was attached to, bleeping and pulsing, then down at his body.

'You're awake, Mr Daley.' A nurse was standing by his bedside. 'Everyone's been very worried about you, but the doctors tell me you're doing just fine. One of them will be round to see you shortly. You took – well, you took some beating.'

'Yes, I can feel it,' said Daley weakly. 'Can I have a drink, please?'

'Of course.' She poured a glass of water from a jug and held it to his mouth. 'Just sips, take it slowly.'

'Thank you.' He laid his head heavily back on the pillow, the pain excruciating, there and just about everywhere else.

'There's someone here to see you. Do you feel up to it?'

'Is it Liz – my wife, I mean?'

'No, but she has phoned a couple of times. She says she'll be in as soon as you come round. I'll give her a call. I have an Assistant Chief Constable Taylor waiting to see you. He's been here most of the night.'

'Yes, I'll see him,' said Daley, rather disappointed that it wasn't his wife waiting anxiously in the corridor for news.

In a few moments ACC Taylor arrived in the room. He looked down at Daley with a mixture of relief, guilt and fading anxiety. 'How do you feel, Jim?'

'Not so hot, to be honest, sir.'

'I'm sure you've felt much better then this, son.' He paused. 'I'm afraid I've let you down.'

'Why, sir?'

'I should have realised that whatever scum we're harbouring in the force would take their revenge. We can't prove anything, of course.'

'Machie did say it was a message from my "colleagues".' Daley turned his head on the pillow.

'So it was Machie. I should have known that piece of shit would be behind something like this.'

'Even worse if one of our own hired him, sir.'

'Yes, it is.' Taylor sighed. 'We'll take a statement from you as soon as you feel well enough. You know the score, though – just your word against his, no CCTV up there, no witnesses. It'll be hard to pin anything on him. They left you bleeding in the road, Jim.'

'Yes, I know the score, sir. You won't find any witnesses. This is James Machie we're talking about.'

'We'll try, though, I promise you that.'

'Thank you, sir.'

'Also, when you've recovered, no more of this uniform work. You're too talented an officer to be out there pounding the beat. I made you vulnerable, and you've paid a heavy price for it, I'm ashamed to say.'

'Not your fault, sir. Just shows what we're facing – in the

job, I mean.'

'Indeed it does. Ian Burns was right. I dread to think what he'd be saying to me now if . . .'

'If he was here, sir.'

'Yes, if he was here, Jim.' Taylor lowered his head. 'One day we'll have them, Jim. We'll get justice for Ian – and for you. Also the countless others who have been ill-served by this bloody disease.'

'I hope so.'

'Meanwhile, you take your time to get better. As soon as you're fit, you'll take up duties as a DC in Paisley. I'll have you bumped up to sergeant as soon as I can.' He looked into Daley's bruised and battered face. 'That's if you've still got the stomach for it?'

Daley thought for a moment or two, feeling his broken bones, remembering the fear he'd felt in his heart when he was set upon; his hatred for the people who ordered his beating – worse still, the killing of Ian Burns. 'Don't worry, sir. I want to find out who killed Ian, and I will one day, I promise you.'

'I believe you, Jim. I really do. We'll all fight the good fight, as Ian would say.' He placed his braided cap back on his head. 'I'll send a car for your wife. I'm sure she'll be relieved to see you back with us.'

'Yes. Thank you, sir,' said Daley, thoughts of Liz caught up in the rest of his whirling emotions.

Kinloch, the present

As Daley emerged from his glass box every detective working late on the case stopped to look at him.

'Brian, and you two,' he said, pointing to DC Potts and DC Shona McQueen. 'I've had an idea. I think I know where Professor Francombe might be. Come on.'

'I've found a few interesting things, tae, boss,' said Scott.

They hurried out of Kinloch Police Office and took two unmarked cars, Daley and Scott in one, Potts and McQueen in the other.

They drove the short distance to the sandstone flats that overlooked the loch. There was a large moon, and the water was still. Faint echoes of the clear starry sky were reflected in the gently rippling water. Apart from a fishing boat chugging its way out of the harbour, all was quiet, save for the plaintive call of a sandpiper as it flew between the twin piers.

'This is where Helen McNeil lives, Jim.'

'And the award for stating the bloody obvious goes to Brian Scott – again!' said Daley with a grin.

As Potts and McQueen parked behind them, Daley hurried out of his SUV, opened the close door and took the steps to Helen's flat two at a time, the other detectives in his wake.

Daley tried the door, then looked under the mat, while Scott did the same with a plant pot, both items sitting on the neat landing beside the nurse's door.

'Worth a try, Jimmy.'

'Right, do the business, Brian.'

'What?'

'Kick in the door, man!'

'Och, here, I'm too old for that caper. Right, DC Potts, now's your big moment – kick in that door, son. It's called the chain o' command.'

'Should we not call the duty joiner – to access the property, I mean?' said DC McQueen, a look of surprise on her face.

'Have you just been up at the Police College, by any chance, lassie? Well, this is what you call practical policing. Boot that door open tout suite, son!'

After a couple of kicks the wood splintered. Daley and Potts put their shoulders to the door and it burst open with a sharp snap.

Across the landing, an old man's face appeared through a crack in his door. 'What's all this? I'm in my bed, you know.'

'No you're no,' said Scott. 'You're standing in the hall.'

'I mean I was in my bed, young man.'

'Aye, well, best get back intae it – there might be some right dangerous folk aboot.'

'You've never lost it, have you, Brian?' said Daley, stepping over the wrecked door and into the flat as Helen's old neighbour hurried back inside his, loudly bolting and locking the door.

'Lost what?'

'Your complete lack of tact.'

'That's a bit harsh, Jimmy,' Scott replied, following Daley into the property with Potts and McQueen.

'Oh, that's rancid!' said DC McQueen, wrinkling her nose.

'I hope we're not too late,' said Daley, stepping into the empty lounge.

'Sir, in here!' called DC Potts from a bedroom down the short hall.

When Daley entered the room the source of the stench was obvious. There, lying tied hand and foot to the bed, her mouth gagged, in a fetid pool of her own faeces and urine, lay Professor Anthea Francombe. Though her face was bloodless and drawn, her eyes flashed with anger.

Scott gently removed the gag from her mouth and set to work on her bonds with his ever-present penknife.

'You useless bastards!' she shouted as soon as she could draw breath. Her voice was weak, and she was gasping for air now she was free of the gag.

'Get her some water,' said Daley, and McQueen hurried to the kitchen.

'Some bloody detectives – I thought I was going to die here.'

As Potts radioed for an ambulance, Daley knelt down beside Francombe, whose arms were now unbound.

'I'm sorry, Anthea.'

'Sorry? Look at me, for fuck's sake. I held it as long as I could, but . . .'

'Don't worry. We'll have you cleaned up and in hospital to recover. You're safe now.'

'That McNeil woman is mad. Crazy.' Tears started to flow down her face. Daley thought they were more of anger than self-pity.

Scott was in the process of freeing her legs when DC McQueen came back with a mug of water. She tried to hold it to Francombe's mouth, but the stricken woman grabbed it, and in sheer fury propelled its contents over the unfortunate detective, hatred in her dark eyes.

Daley stood back. He'd pieced together enough about Anthea Francombe to raise his suspicions.

Now, though, he was sure.

50

The police helicopter landed on the town's green, just at the head of the loch. Inevitably, rumour having spread, a growing band of people had gathered nearby, anxious to be part of the unfolding drama.

'She used tae come and change my mother's dressings,' said one woman, a scowl on her face, as the aircraft's rotor blades slowed to a stop.

'Aye. When oor wee Gary was ill she was at oor hoose near every day for a fortnight,' said another.

'Lucky the bastard didna have you all murdered in your beds,' remarked a local fisherman. 'I always said there was something no' right aboot her.'

'You said nothing of the kind,' chided his wife. 'You telt me whoot a caring woman she was when you had that problem – doon below,' she added in a lowered voice, attracting the attention of many standing nearby, instantly curious as to what this 'problem' had been.

'Trust you, Jean. You never know when tae shut your . . .' He stopped in mid-sentence as the door to the aircraft opened. Then, walking carefully down the steps, handcuffed and guided by a police officer, Helen McNeil set foot back in Kinloch. The murmur from the crowd turned to boos and catcalls as she was walked across the grass to the small convoy of police vehicles parked at the head of the loch.

'I'm buggered if I know how the folk here find oot aboot stuff,' said Scott, sitting in Daley's SUV.

'The price of having local staff in the office, Bri.'

'It always astounds me. They're better detectives than we are.'

'Don't know how I missed all this for so long. It's been staring us in the face.'

'Wait, big man. I'm still a bit confused.'

With Helen safely stowed in a police van, the little convoy made its way back to Kinloch Police Office.

She sat straight-backed in the interview room, across from Symington and Daley. Despite looking rather flushed, it could have been Helen McNeil on any other day. Daley noted her self-possession.

'So,' began Symington. 'You know why you're here, and you have a lawyer. We'd like to ask you a few questions regarding the Midweek Murder case from the nineties, Ms McNeil.'

'Why?'

'Because we need to have answers, that's why. These were horrific crimes.'

She eyed the Chief Superintendent levelly and shrugged her shoulders. 'What do you want me to say?' She paused. 'As far as it goes, I suppose I'm guilty.'

'As far as it goes?' asked Daley.

She stared at him before replying. 'I adored my father. My mother abandoned us and he was all I had.'

'Go on.'

'There's not much to tell. Men have needs. I felt sorry for him – when I was older, I mean.'

'Why sorry?' asked Symington.

'He was too old to go to a club and pick up a woman. Don't get me wrong, women liked him – always did. But he preferred – well, younger women.'

'How young?' said Daley.

'Not what you're thinking. He wasn't a bloody pervert!' For the first time McNeil was animated.

'What do you mean he wasn't a pervert?' said Symington. 'He – you – both of you entrapped young women, who were then raped – dead or alive – brutally murdered, and dumped. How perverse do you want?'

'I'd nothing to do with all that.'

'What do you mean?' Daley looked into her emotionless face.

'I didn't kill anybody. All I've done for most of my life is help others.'

'Listen, Helen, whether you wielded the mallet that cracked their skulls, or tightened the rope on their necks, you befriended these women and took them to your father to rape and kill. You can't tell us you didn't know what he was doing.'

'Yes, I knew. But I didn't rape them – I didn't kill them. I felt sorry for them, in fact.'

Her flat statement was as eerie as her blank stare. Helen McNeil looked between the officers, unmoved by both what she was being asked and what she had to say by way of a reply.

'So this is how you've dealt with this for so long, Helen?' said Symington. 'Basically, you've wiped your hands clean of the blood of those murdered women just because you didn't take part in the horrors that were perpetrated upon them, is that right?'

'Yes. Why should I take the blame? I didn't do it.'

'You realise that you acted as his accomplice and therefore, under the law, you're as guilty as your father?'

'Then the law is stupid. I mean, you've never bothered with the bastard that made those calls and sent those texts to me, have you? What does the law say about that?'

'You cannot compare what happened to your father's victims to what happened to you, Helen. Don't you understand? He killed those women: mothers, daughters, wives, girlfriends – whatever they were. He took their lives!'

'But I didn't.'

As McNeil's lawyer whispered in her ear, Daley looked at Symington. It was clear Helen was mentally ill. It could have been an act, a sordid performance intended to save her skin; a cynical attempt to be consigned to a hospital, rather than a prison. But Daley had seen such attempts many times before. He was sure that was not what he was seeing. This woman – probably all along – had convinced herself that she was innocent. His mind rolled back to the night when PC Maggie Baird was befriended by the woman in the tatty nightclub. Despite the years, he knew he was looking at the same person. It was so obvious now; again he cursed himself for missing it.

'Why did you bury the last three victims here?' he asked.

McNeil took a drink of water. 'It was getting too dangerous – for my father, I mean. It was to save him from being caught.'

'So, while you were working in Kinloch for a brief time, years ago, you calmly drove the mutilated bodies of three dead women up a farm track and buried them in shallow graves on a hillside. Just what made you think of doing that, Helen?'

Without warning, fire blazed in her eyes. 'Because of him!'

'Who?'

'Duncan Chisholm.'

'He advised you and your father to bury the victims somewhere remote, rather than dump them around Glasgow, or throw them in the Clyde, did he?'

'Not before he'd had his way with them. He's the real pervert!'

'So he was involved with your father?'

'He found out – don't ask me how. He realised what my father was doing.'

'Caught him, you mean?'

'Yes, caught him.'

'But instead of arresting him, he joined in with the attacks on the victims, then advised you what to do with the bodies so none of this would be discovered?' asked Symington.

'Yes, he did. Liked to keep little mementos, too.'

'What?'

'Clothing, jewellery – bits and pieces. I hate him!'

'Yet he helped you and your father – why?' asked Symington.

'I don't know. All I know is that he took money from my father for years afterwards. Said he would have him arrested otherwise. He got thousands out of my father, the bastard! My father often referred to him as a friend. He was no friend. My father would still be alive if it wasn't for the grief Duncan caused him year after year.'

'Your father was in the army for a short time, wasn't he, Helen?' said Daley.

'Yes, national service. Why do you ask?'

Daley looked at Symington. 'We'll take a break.' He looked at his watch. 'Interview ends at fourteen thirty-two hours.'

'That's Dunky Chisholm buggered, anyhow,' said Scott, who'd been watching proceedings via a monitor. 'I've got tae say, I don't think anything in my career has shocked me like this.'

'More shocks in store for you, I think, Brian,' said Daley.

'You mean that stuff I found out about the army?'

'Yup. Time we had a chat with our other friend. I believe he's lunching at the County.'

'Here, what was that call you just had from Glasgow?'

'All will be revealed, Brian.'

'Fucking Ali Bongo, here.'

The pair left Kinloch Police Office and strolled down the hill towards the County Hotel in the warm sunshine. Just about every face in the street turned to look at the detectives as they made their progress.

'This must be how thon Wyatt Earp felt when he was heading for the Okay Corral,' said Scott.

'You're no Doc Holliday, Brian.'

'Aye, and you're too big roond the waist tae be Wyatt.'

They stepped through the big swing doors and into the hotel.

51

Annie looked up from her work at the reception desk as Daley and Scott arrived. Daley could see the curiosity on her face, but gave nothing away.

'Is Bobby still at his lunch, Annie?' asked Scott.

'Aye, through in the dining room, right noo. He's having the haddock on account o' the lasagne being too dry. He likes his grub, Bobby, eh?'

'He sure does,' said Daley. He and Scott looked through the glass doors into the large dining room. There indeed sat Bobby Speirs, napkin tucked into his collar, his face flushed and jowly, his attention firmly on a more than ample plate of fish and chips. The dome of his bald head was pale in comparison to his red face, his fringe of hair from ear to ear giving him his familiar monkish appearance.

'After you, Brian,' said Daley, holding the door open for his colleague.

Speirs looked up as the pair entered the room. 'Now, boys, you'll be out for a wee celebration, eh? Good result wae that nurse and big Dunky – the bastard,' he added as an afterthought.

'Oh, I'm about to have the biggest celebration of my life, Bobby.'

'Well deserved, I'm sure. Not every day you tie up a case

that's been on the go for mair than twenty years; and what a case, too, eh?'

'Still a lot of loose ends to be tied up, Bobby. You know how it is.'

Scott looked from one to the other. Daley had been acting strangely since his mysterious phone call from Glasgow. He'd been deflated by the arrest of Helen McNeil and Duncan Chisholm for their part in the Midweek Murders, which surprised Scott. Usually, having cracked such a case, he'd have been animated; euphoric, almost.

Now, for some reason, Scott saw the fire burning in his eyes.

'Take a seat, gentlemen,' said Speirs. 'Can I get you both a drink? Well, a ginger beer for you, Brian.'

'Your father was an army man, wasn't he, Bobby?' said Daley.

'Aye, then a cop. The reason I joined the job.'

'Did you know he was Duncan Chisholm's tutor cop – just before he retired, I mean?'

'Aye, I do believe it was mentioned. For what it's worth, he never took tae Dunky. Used tae call him "the Dandy" in they days. He was always dressed up for the women.'

'I remember a story Ian Burns told me. It was way back in the sixties, not long after he joined up.'

'Aw, let it go, Jimmy,' said Speirs. 'He's been deid for years and you're still banging on aboot him like he was still alive.'

'Please, humour me this one last time, Bobby.'

'If I must.'

'He told me that two crimes had been committed – nineteen sixty-three, I think it was. He was a young cop on the beat. Two young women, last seen out on the town in the middle of the week. The next thing, their bodies turned up, mutilated, just outside Airdrie. They'd been raped.'

'And?'

'Well, they never caught the perpetrator.'

'No' that unusual back then, Jim.'

'No, but for some reason, Ian thought somebody – somebody in the force – was covering for whoever did it. Ian actually thought it might be a cop who'd done it.'

'He'd some strange ideas, your hero.' Speirs laughed.

'Years passed, then we had the Midweek Murders. Ian saw that the MO was very similar right away.'

'Oh aye.'

'Always thought a cop was involved, that there was a cover-up on the go. He reckoned it was connected with the number of men who'd left the army and become police officers at the time – you know, old codes of loyalty, all that.'

'As I say, it sounds a bit fanciful tae me.'

'And yet, here we have a cop at the heart of the case – Duncan Chisholm, no less. The very man to whom your father taught the ropes.'

'If you don't mind my asking, Jimmy, just what the fuck are you driving at?'

'Hold on, Bobby. I've not finished yet.' Daley sat forward in his chair, his face close to Speirs. 'Did you know your father served in the army with one Stuart McNeil? Best of mates they were, apparently.'

'What are you trying to say, Daley?' Suddenly, Speirs's expression had darkened.

'Let's just imagine. An old pal of your dad's murders a woman. He panics – comes to your father for advice, which he gets.'

Speirs moved to get up, but Brian Scott placed his hand firmly on his shoulder, forcing him back into his chair.

'Years later, for whatever reason, this old pal does it again. He gets away with it a few times, then gets frightened. The net's closing in. Someone's tipped him off that the boys in blue have their suspicions. A young cop gets involved – in the beginning out of loyalty to his old tutor. But he soon finds he enjoys what's going on. He ends up as a more than willing accomplice. But someone gets wind of this – what's going on. Has a word with his father.'

'This is pish, Daley.'

'He sets out to bring the whole thing to a stop – yes, to make sure that the killing ends, but also that no one pays the price.'

'Bollocks. You've got some imagination, son. If you're no' careful you'll end up on the beat again!' shouted Speirs.

'Ian Burns, and a few old hands, some retired, some not, get together. Ian has a theory. It's passed on to people whose job it is to solve this kind of stuff. But, for his pains – his love of the police, its honour and integrity – he pays the ultimate price. Oh, he's known for some time that something's not right, so he decides to tell someone. Someone he can trust. He's had threatening letters, and he's worried. When the call comes from his trusted friend arranging to meet and discuss the matter, Ian jumps at the chance. It's his last mistake.'

'Fairy tales, Jimmy. You're no' right in the heid,' said Speirs, Scott still menacing at his side.

'Oh, I can prove it. You see, when the fuss about the Midweek Murderer dies down, Duncan is sent to remove any trace of Ian death from the Productions Unit. But some idiot's made a mistake. They've lodged one item of clothing with the wrong case. A scarf.'

'What?'

'Do you remember it, Bobby? I know you saw it.'

'Crazy stuff. You'll prove nothing, Daley.'

'Techniques improve through the years, and when the scarf is tested now there's blood on it. Granted, most belongs to poor Ian Burns. But he must have put up a fight, because there's another trace of blood – just tiny, but there. It belongs to you, Bobby.'

'Fuck this! I want a lawyer, right now. In fact, I want tae have words with the ACC!' roared Speirs.

'I hate you, Bobby – I hate you more than I've probably hated anyone. But I've kept my promise to a man who taught me what being a police officer was all about. Arrest Mr Speirs for the murder of Ian Burns, please, DS Scott.'

'With pleasure, sir. With pleasure.'

52

The gulls soared in the blue sky as the two women unpacked the picnic from large cool bags.

'Here, Ella, there's the mayonnaise,' said Annie. 'Aye, it's ginger beer only on this trip,' she continued, looking at Hamish lighting his pipe and sending clouds of smoke into the warm air.

'Aye, I know fine the wean likes it, don't you, son?' said Hamish, patting James Daley on the head, while feeling the heft of his hip flask of whisky in the bib of his dungarees.

Scott was lighting a small shop-bought barbecue; nothing more than a tin tray with some solid fuel. He swore under his breath as the flame of a third match was extinguished in the breeze.

Daley looked out across the Kilbrannon Sound. The sea was almost navy blue, contrasting with the white sand of the little bays dotted here and there. The air was rich with the scent of gorse and the tang of the sea, a hint of Hamish's pipe smoke as a backdrop.

A fishing boat, tiny at this distance, was heading past the Isle of Arran. Daley took in the sight of Goat Fell, then lowered his gaze to the field beneath them, where a small group of people were busy dismantling a large tent.

'Just you watch your language, Brian Scott,' chided Ella. 'Mind there's a young, impressionable pair of ears listening in.'

'Oor Jimmy's no' that young – fair pushing on, eh?'

'Like you're standing still,' replied Daley. 'Remember, I still have the pictures of you assaulting that seven-foot chicken.'

'He did what?' asked Ella, mouth agape.

'Yes, there's no end to your husband's cruelties, Ella.'

'Aye, fine I know it. I didnae think he'd be cruel tae animals, mind you.'

'Like it was a real chicken seven feet tall, Ella. Listen tae yourself, woman.'

'I'm going to take a wee walk down to say goodbye to the archaeologists,' said Daley. He left the Scotts discussing the merits of giant poultry and wandered through the long grass to the lane that led to the field below.

As he approached the site, three mounds of earth sat in a row, a testament to lives lost and thoughts of a past he might now just be able to consign to where it belonged.

'Hello, Professor,' he said, approaching Francombe. Though she still looked tired after her ordeal at the hands of Helen McNeil, she smiled a greeting.

'Congratulations are in order, I hear. Well done you. That woman is a monster; she deserves all she gets.'

'Indeed,' said Daley, searching her face for emotion. 'Is it okay if I have a quick word?'

'If it's about Bernie and Marion and their exploits, I've talked to your officers already. We need to get moving. We've another site to investigate next week down in Yorkshire, so time is of the essence.'

'No, I know all about that. Lucky in a way – for us, anyway.'

'Lucky? Why on earth do you say that?'

'If Duncan Chisholm hadn't removed that necklace and put it in among the recovered items to retrieve later as one of his gruesome mementos, I might not have cracked it.'

'Lucky for me that this isn't the only site she plied her grubby little trade from. There are a lot of very embarrassed site directors out there, I can tell you – me included.'

'Yes, I'm sure, Derek.'

She turned to face him, a furious look on her face. 'What did you call me?'

'Let's walk,' said Daley.

As they wandered slowly across the field, she looked up at him. 'How long have you known?'

'Not long. I remembered a young boy throwing a can of Coke over a WPC many years ago. It was on the pier at Greenock, where his murdered mother's body had just been washed up.'

'And I threw the water at your detective. Oh dear.'

'How long have *you* known, more to the point?' said Daley.

She stopped and drew in a deep breath of the sweet-scented spring air. 'I felt sorry for him at first. I'd just had my gender realignment operation at a private clinic. Things didn't go according to plan, so they sent me to an NHS hospital, better equipped to deal with my problems. Being in hospital was my choice; he had none. I knew he was dying.'

'Why Scotland?'

'The academic world is a small one. Surgeons are academics too, of a sort. I chose a Scottish clinic to be out of the way.'

'So, as you were recovering in hospital, you helped out. Talked to the older patients, ran little errands and the like until you were discharged.'

'Something like that,' she said flatly.

'And then you saw Helen McNeil.'

She gulped. 'I was almost sick on the spot. I recognised her straight away. That awful cheap perfume she wore. I can still smell it.'

'And then you made some plans.'

'Not hard to get information from an old, dying man wanting nothing more than to confess, is it? He was on morphine for the pain by this time. He rambled a lot. I learned enough to lead me here. I cloned his phone, recorded his voice. It wasn't hard.'

'If you don't mind my asking, why did you want to change so completely?'

'Simply, I hate men. Men killed my mother; men use women. I never felt male, and now I'm not.'

'So you worked away.'

'Yes. Soon I knew everything about them. Him and Helen, I mean. I knew where the bodies were buried – literally.'

'So you cloned his phone, and used a bogus theory to dig here.'

'In short, yes. I pottered here on the pretence of carrying out some survey work. Came across the oubliette by accident, really. The farmer who owned the land wasn't bothered what I was up to. I firmed it all up with a hard standing, a drain cover – an instant prison for my quarry.'

'What about the cage?'

'That was the hardest part. I made it myself in a small lockup I rent. I'm no welder – as you probably noticed.'

'Why the calls and texts? Why not just come clean and tell us?'

'It's hard to explain. I think I wanted her to suffer the way my mother had – the way I had. A child robbed of childhood and his mother; a pain that never goes away. Never!' She looked up at Daley, rage in her eyes. 'I was taken to England by an aunt, who brought me up. She was kind, did her best, but she wasn't my mum.'

'So, you made your plans – even down to a place of confinement. Quite a find – the oubliette.'

'Ironic, isn't it? My finest archaeological discovery, and I can't say anything about it. Can now, I suppose.' She stared at Daley. 'I can take the credit – now that I'm exposed, I mean.'

'Who said you were going to be exposed?'

'It's your job, isn't it?' She looked astonished.

'Yes. But someone told me, long ago, that police work has a lot to do with discretion.'

'So you're not here to arrest me?' Astonishment was quickly turning to relief.

Daley looked into her dark eyes. 'No. I think you've been through enough. You should never have done the things you did, but you know that. If Helen had been an innocent victim of a deranged, deviant father, things would be different. But she knew all along what was happening to those women. She was willing bait for his hook.'

'And what about Helen? She's bound to say something – about me, I mean.'

'I don't think anyone's about to take anything Helen says seriously. She's a very sick woman.' He paused. 'Listen, Anthea, I can't promise that some clever detective won't make the connection, but it's highly unlikely. Forensics have nothing, for a start.'

'I was very careful. I'm not stupid.'

'Indeed. And we don't have the resources to return again and again to cases that, ostensibly, have been solved.'

'What about your boss, Symington? She's no fool, I know that.'

'She's also knee-deep in accounts, human resources and the rest of the politics her job involves. This is a nice feather in her cap. After all, she was heading up the team who found the Midweek Murderer.'

'You sound very sure, Jim.'

'As sure as I can be.' It was his turn to draw a breath of the scented air. 'What's to be gained by another life ruined?'

'Maybe I should have felt more compassion for her – Helen McNeil, I mean.'

'I don't think so. Ill or not, she entrapped your mother and took her to her death. I couldn't feel compassion for Helen, if I was in your place.'

'So really, it's lose–lose for everyone, isn't it?'

'It always is,' said Daley, as a gull cried plaintively high up in the blue sky. Far below, the tide lapped relentlessly on a small cove of white sand.

Author's Notes and Acknowledgements

In 1977 three women – Anna Kenny, Agnes Cooney and Hilda McAuley – disappeared from Glasgow nightspots within months of each other. Anna's body was discovered in a shallow grave near Skipness in northeast Kintyre. The bodies of the two other women were found in separate locations in the Central Belt, all in the year of their tragic deaths. Though there were many theories as to the identity of their killer or killers, including the infamous 'Bible John', no one has ever been brought to justice for these dreadful crimes.

I remember vividly their faces staring from posters on the walls of police stations in which I worked in the following decade. At the time, the police interviewed many Kintyre folk who regularly travelled up and down the long and winding road to Glasgow, just in case they had noticed anything suspicious. This number included my own father, who was working at Faslane near Helensburgh for the Royal Navy at the time and who came back to Campbeltown every weekend to be with his family.

Sadly, no one could provide any clue as to the identity of the killer(s). The only slim lead came from Hilda McAuley's disappearance. She was last seen leaving the Plaza Ballroom in Glasgow with a 'well-dressed young man', again similar to the description of 'Bible John'.

My family were lucky; we lived in a virtually crime-free place. So I remember being struck by the horror of this as a child – I was only eleven years old when Anna Kenny's body was found – and the feeling stayed with me. Though this book is by no means an attempt to fictionalise these tragic crimes, I hope that the huge leaps forward in forensic and DNA technology used to catch criminals will, one day, bring justice for those women whose lives were so cruelly cut short, and closure – and at least a modicum of solace – for the members of their family and friends left behind.

Somerled, Lord of the Isles, was the formidable warlord who ran his west coast domain from his base in Kintyre. Long assumed to be of purely Gaelic descent, and even credited with driving the Vikings from the area, later research has unearthed that he was more likely a product of the union between the Norse and Gaels who populated the area at the time. Indeed DNA research has confirmed that chiefs from the MacDonald, MacDougall and MacAllister clans, who history tells us spring from Somerled, still possess the distinctive Y-chromosome redolent of Norse heritage.

It would appear that he was an ambitious man, and may have had his eyes on the Crown of Scotland. His attempted coup failed miserably, and he was killed at the battle of Renfrew in 1164 during a bid to gain a foothold in mainland Scotland. (Ironically, the present Lord of the Isles, Prince Charles, is descended from his killers.) Undoubtedly, though, he represents that connection between the Gaels and the men of the North popularly known as the Vikings, around whom such a glorious canon of myth, tales and legend passed down through the generations, and so strongly persists.

If you travel to Kintyre, take the opportunity to travel to Saddell Abbey, long associated with the great man, and a treasure trove for lovers of history. The name Saddell itself is a Norse one, as is nearby Carradale and many other places on the peninsula, further highlighting the strong connections between Kintyre and Scandinavia.

For further reading, I recommend *Somerled and the Emergence of Gaelic Scotland* by John Marsden, published by Birlinn in 2008.

Acknowledgements

As always I would like to thank my family – Fiona, Rachel and her new partner Lisa. Also to Sian, and her new brothers and sister Kieran, Morgan and Johnnie. Welcome to the clan, folks!

I would like to pass my warmest wishes to my GP Dr Cheema and his staff, as well as sincere and heartfelt thanks to the frontline staff of the Royal Alexandra Hospital, Paisley, and the Vale of Leven Hospital, Alexandria, all of whom treated me during my recent illness.

The NHS is precious, part of the glue that holds our nation together. It isn't perfect – no institution of its size is – but it is incumbent upon us all to strive to maintain and indeed improve the service it provides, as well as the pay and conditions of those who struggle at its sharp end. Here are the real heroes and heroines; forget footballers and movie stars, even writers – they won't save your life – these men and women will. God bless them.

To the memory of my late mother and father – you are always in my heart.

To my publisher at Birlinn/Polygon, Hugh Andrew; editors Alison Rae and Nancy Webber; and the rest of the team in Edinburgh who have done so much to bring Jim Daley, Brian Scott, Hamish, Annie et al to the page. I will always owe you a massive debt of gratitude. Good luck to Vikki in her new role.

To Anne Williams of KHLA, my formidable, dynamic agent, and her colleague Kate Hordern, who keep the wheels on the bus. I'm so grateful for your help and sage advice.

To my friends, who were there for me when things looked bleak, I cannot thank you enough. They are too many in number to mention here, but Mary Anderson, Ronnie Kelly, Douglas Skelton, Big Davie (who ceaselessly kept my spirits up) and Scott, the man who got me back on my feet with ruthless but caring efficiency – a tilt of my cap to you all. Also, to Malcolm, Campbell 'Rhinestone',

Patrick, Billy and Bert, and the rest of those forced to endure my company, my thanks you all.

As always, credit to the people of Kintyre, without whom none of this would have happened. Campbeltown was, is, and will for ever be home for me, regardless of where I find myself in the world.

And finally, and I make no apology for mentioning her again, my wife Fiona. You kept me going and never left my side. I love you.

D.A.M.
Gartocharn
August 2018

The DCI Daley thriller series

Whisky from Small Glasses
DCI Jim Daley is sent from the city to investigate a murder after the body of a woman is washed up on an idyllic beach on the west coast of Scotland. Far away from urban resources, he finds himself a stranger in a close-knit community.

The Last Witness
James Machie was a man with a genius for violence, his criminal empire spreading beyond Glasgow into the UK and mainland Europe. Fortunately, Machie is dead, assassinated in the back of a prison ambulance following his trial and conviction. But now, five years later, he is apparently back from the grave, set on avenging himself on those who brought him down.

Dark Suits and Sad Songs
When a senior Edinburgh civil servant spectacularly takes his own life in Kinloch harbour, DCI Jim Daley comes face to face with the murky world of politics. To add to his woes, two local drug dealers lie dead, ritually assassinated. It's clear that dark forces are at work in the town. With his boss under investigation, his marriage hanging by a thread, and his side-kick DS Scott wrestling with his own demons, Daley's world is in meltdown.

The Rat Stone Serenade
It's December, and the Shannon family are heading to their clifftop

mansion near Kinloch for their AGM. Shannon International, one of the world's biggest private companies, has brought untold wealth and privilege to the family. However, a century ago, Archibald Shannon stole the land upon which he built their home – and his descendants have been cursed ever since.

When heavy snow cuts off Kintyre, DCI Jim Daley and DS Brian Scott are assigned to protect their illustrious visitors. But ghosts of the past are coming to haunt the Shannons.

The Well of the Winds
As World War Two nears its end, a man is stabbed to death on the Kinloch shoreline, in the shadow of the great warships in the harbour.

Many years later, the postman on Gairsay, a tiny island off the coast of Kintyre, discovers that the Bremner family are missing from their farm.

When DCI Daley comes into possession of a journal written by his wartime predecessor in Kinloch, he soon realises that he must solve a murder from the past to uncover the shocking events of the present.

One Last Dram Before Midnight: The Complete Collected D.C.I. Daley Short Stories
Published together for the first time in one not-to-be-missed volume are all Denzil Meyrick's short stories and novellas.

Discover how DCI Daley and DS Scott first met on the mean streets of Glasgow in two prequels that shed light on their earlier lives. Join Hamish and his old mentor, skipper Sandy Hoynes, as they become embroiled with some Russian fishermen and an illicit whisky plot. And in present-day Kinloch Daley and Scott investigate ghosts from the past, search for a silent missing man, and follow the trail of an elusive historical necklace that still has power over the people of Kinloch.

All of the DCI Daley thrillers are available as eBook editions, along with an eBook-only novella and the two short stories below.

Dalintober Moon: A DCI Daley Story
When a body is found in a whisky barrel buried on Dalintober beach, it appears that a notorious local crime, committed over a century ago, has finally been solved. However, the legacy of murder still resonates within the community, and the tortured screams of a man who died long ago still echo across Kinloch.

Two One Three: A Constable Jim Daley Short Story (Prequel)
Glasgow, 1986. Only a few months into his new job, Constable Jim Daley is walking the beat. When he is seconded to the CID to help catch a possible serial killer, he makes a new friend, DC Brian Scott. Jim Daley tackles his first serious crime on the mean streets of Glasgow, in an investigation that will change his life for ever.

Empty Nets and Promises: A Kinloch Novella
It's July 1968, and fishing-boat skipper Sandy Hoynes has his daughter's wedding to pay for – but where are all the fish? He and the crew of the *Girl Maggie* come to the conclusion that a new-fangled supersonic jet which is being tested in the skies over Kinloch is scaring off the herring.

First mate Hamish comes up with a cunning plan to bring the laws of nature back into balance. But little do they know that they face the forces of law and order in the shape of a vindictive fishery officer, an exciseman who suspects Hoynes of smuggling illicit whisky, and the local police sergeant who is about to become Hoynes' son-in-law – not to mention a ghostly piper and some Russians.

Single End: A DC Daley Short Story
It's 1989, and Jim Daley is now a fully fledged detective constable. When ruthless gangster James Machie's accountant is found stabbed

to death in a multi-storey car park, it's clear all is not well within Machie's organisation.

Meanwhile Daley's friend and colleague DC Brian Scott has been having some problems of his own. To save his job, he must revisit his past in an attempt to uncover the identity of a corrupt police officer.